Roberta Kray was born i
Reggie Kray and they ma
together until his death i
Reggie, Roberta has a uni ... world of the
London gangland.

Also by Roberta Kray

The Debt
The Pact
The Lost

Non-fiction

Reg Kray: A Man Apart

STRONG WOMEN

ROBERTA KRAY

sphere

SPHERE

First published in Great Britain in 2009 by Sphere
This paperback edition published in 2009 by Sphere
Reprinted 2009 (three times)

All characters and events in this publication, other than those clearly in the public domain, are fictitious and any resemblance to real persons, living or dead, is purely coincidental.

A CIP catalogue record for this book is available from the British Library.

Typeset in Garamond by M Rules
Printed and bound in Great Britain by
Clays Ltd, St Ives plc

Papers used by Sphere are natural, renewable and recyclable products sourced from well-managed forests and certified in accordance with the rules of the Forest Stewardship Council.

Mixed Sources
Product group from well-managed forests and other controlled sources
FSC www.fsc.org Cert no. SGS-COC-004081
© 1996 Forest Stewardship Council

Sphere
An imprint of
Little, Brown Book Group
100 Victoria Embankment
London EC4Y 0DY

An Hachette UK Company
www.hachette.co.uk

www.littlebrown.co.uk

STRONG WOMEN

Chapter One

Jo Strong gazed down at the sheet of paper. There was nothing new typed on it, nothing she hadn't read before, but the words still made her stomach turn over. It was almost two years now and the notes kept on arriving with unnerving regularity.

'You know what I think?' Carla said.

Jo's sister-in-law had her back to her and was standing by the sink, her plump hips gently swaying to a song on the radio. As such, Jo felt safe in raising her eyes to the ceiling. It was a gesture born of resignation rather than anything more hostile. She knew what was coming next.

'It's pure nastiness, that's all. Rip it up and chuck it in the bin.' Carla looked over her shoulder. 'Put it where it belongs. You have to move on. It's what Peter would have wanted.'

Would he? Jo frowned. Surely, if what the writer claimed was true, that might not be the case. But then again, how could it be true? It was a question she often asked herself but which she no longer repeated out loud.

Two mugs were placed on the table. It was her kitchen but whenever Carla came round she always made the coffee.

This had started shortly after Peter had died and had somehow grown into a habit. Pulling out a chair, Carla sat down and nodded towards the note.

'You shouldn't even open them. What's the point? It's just some sad old cow who gets her kicks out of tormenting people. How many has it been now?'

'A few.'

'More than that. And you know what the cops said.'

Jo shrugged. She wound a strand of pale blonde hair behind her ear. She remembered exactly what the police had said, even though it was eighteen months since she'd last talked to them. They'd been keen at first, taking the letters away for analysis, but when they'd found no fingerprints, no clues, their interest had soon waned. 'A crank,' one of them had suggested. And then, four weeks later, when she'd taken the latest communication down to the station, a pasty-faced sergeant had looked her up and down. 'Do *you* have a computer, Mrs Strong?'

It had taken a moment for the implication to sink in.

'They thought it was me,' Jo said, still astounded after all this time. 'They thought I was writing them myself, that I was some kind of neurotic, grief-stricken, attention-seeking widow who couldn't accept the findings of the inquest.'

Carla shook her head. 'I'm sure they didn't, love, not really. No one who knows you could ever . . . I mean, it's just ridiculous.'

'Try telling that to Sergeant Hannon.' Jo could still recall her initial burst of indignation at the policeman, followed by the anger and humiliation. A light flush rose to her cheeks. Even now the memory had the power to upset her.

She had turned on her heel and walked out. She hadn't been back since.

'You have to stop reading them,' Carla said briskly. 'It isn't good for you. Whoever she is, she'll get sick of it eventually.'

'What makes you so sure it's a woman?'

'It usually is. They're more spiteful than men, more persistent.'

'Maybe.' Jo lifted the mug to her lips, blew on the surface and took a sip of her coffee. 'Unless it's a double bluff, someone who wants me to think that.'

Carla raised her brows.

As soon as Jo had said it, she wished that she hadn't. She didn't want her to know just how much she dwelled on it all. 'You're right. I should get rid.' Standing up, she grabbed the note and its envelope, walked across the kitchen and dropped them in the bin. She would retrieve them later after her sister-in-law had gone. She would put them in the drawer with the other twenty-two. Eventually she would find out who was doing this and when she did, she intended to have the evidence to confront them with.

'Best place for it,' Carla said approvingly.

Jo sat down again and swiftly changed the subject. 'So how are the kids?'

As Carla embarked on what was likely to be a long and detailed account of the achievements of twelve-year-old Mitch and his younger sister Lily, Jo smiled absently. She was fond of them both but today her thoughts were elsewhere. Her gaze drifted towards the window.

The flat was a first-floor conversion in an old Victorian house on Barley Road. The front rooms, well-proportioned and bright, overlooked Kellston Green. The Green was not as grand as it sounded; about twice the size of a football pitch, it was really no more than a basic expanse of grass with a central concreted path, several wooden benches and a few spindly trees and bushes dotted around the perimeter. At the moment it was almost empty. Only three boys, dressed identically in grey hooded tops, jeans and pricey trainers, leaned idly against their bikes but in a few hours, when the trains and buses discharged their cargo of commuters, it would be heaving. How many times had she watched Peter walk across? If she half closed her eyes, she could almost imagine him striding towards her now . . .

Jo quickly blinked the image away. On the far side of the Green was the High Street, with its organic food stalls, its fancy designer outlets and overpriced coffee shops. Kellston was one of those East London boroughs, nestled between Bethnal Green and Shoreditch, which had recently been 'discovered' by the middle classes. The old and the new, the dilapidated high-rises and the smart executive homes, the well-off and the struggling co-existed, although not always in a state of harmony. Relations between the residents gently simmered and occasionally threatened to boil over.

Her gaze shifted to the red pillar box along the road. All the letters had been posted locally, maybe even there, right under her nose. Could her unwanted correspondent be one of her neighbours? Could it be someone she saw every day, maybe even someone she spoke to? Her mouth began to dry. She had considered moving away but couldn't quite find the will to do it. To sell the flat would mean leaving a part of Peter behind and she wasn't ready for that yet.

'. . . not that he's the slightest bit interested in anything *I* have to say.'

Jo caught the end of the sentence and guiltily refocused her attention. Despite missing the start of the complaint, she had no doubt as to whom Carla was referring. Her husband Tony was, to put it mildly, a philandering drunk, and it had all got much worse recently. She reached out a hand and touched her lightly on the wrist. 'Are you okay?'

Carla forced a weak smile before she subtly withdrew her arm. She was a giver of sympathy, not a receiver. 'I'm fine. Don't worry about me.' Expelling one of her familiar sighs, she slowly rose to her feet. 'I'd better make a move. I'll see you on Sunday unless the old witch has croaked by then. Not that we'd ever be so lucky. You are coming, aren't you?'

Jo pulled a face. 'Er . . .' She looked forward to these monthly lunches with the same level of enthusiasm she reserved for the mail dropping through the door. Ruby Strong was a sly, bitter old woman and a bully to boot. Unfortunately, she was also Peter's mother.

'Please say you'll be there. I can't cope on my own.'

She had been thinking about making an excuse, any excuse, to get out of it, but seeing Carla's growing look of horror, she didn't have the heart to abandon her. She knew what it was like to be at the receiving end of Ruby's relentless snipes and criticisms. 'Of course I will.'

'Thank God for that.'

After they had said their goodbyes, Jo stood by the window and watched as she walked along the street and climbed into the brand new, gleaming red Toyota. Carla, she noted, had her own pricey way of making her husband pay for his infidelities.

When the car was out of sight she turned, flipped open the bin and plucked out the letter and its envelope. She took them over to the table and straightened out the creases. The note was soggy, stained brown by lying on wet tea bags. She was not entirely convinced that the letters were intended to be hurtful. Yes, they were anonymous. Yes, they were disturbing. But were they actually malicious?

Jo stared down at the limp sheet of paper. The typed words, read so many times before, were already seared into her heart: *Your husband's death was not an accident.*

Chapter Two

The Speckled Hen was at the end of a short cobbled alley running off the High Street. They had managed to find a table in the busy courtyard garden and the evening air, retaining the heat from a glorious June afternoon, smelled of hot dust, exhaust fumes and spicy cooking.

Laura had called in the afternoon. 'Are you free tonight? Please say you are. Something's happened. I have to talk to you.'

So here they were – and if Jo thought *she* had problems, they were rapidly paling into insignificance.

'This is him,' Laura said.

Jo put down her glass and picked up the small black and white photograph. The man who returned her gaze was on the wrong side of forty, with the frown lines to prove it. It wasn't a handsome face but one that in a dim light might just pass for interesting.

'How did you ever get involved with him?'

'Don't ask,' Laura said. 'It was a big mistake and one I haven't stopped regretting since.' She sank her head into her hands. 'It was a moment of madness. I mean, what was I thinking? I should have had more sense than to get entangled with the likes of Gabe Miller. I'm such a bloody fool.'

Jo shook her head. 'Don't beat yourself up about it. It's like you said, you just made a mistake.'

'Not the kind of mistake that the senior partners are ever going to forgive me for. I'm supposed to be a lawyer, for God's sake! Number one rule – never get personally involved with the clients . . . and especially not with the lowlife like Miller. If I want to save my job, my career, I've got to get that laptop back. It's got all my files on it, all the information about my cases. Apart from the fact that I need the damn thing, how am I going to explain how it's gone missing? The bastard even took my memory stick.'

'You could just tell them it had been stolen.'

Laura gave a low frustrated groan. 'Yes, I could if it hadn't been gone two days already. It's too late now. If I suddenly report it as stolen, it's going to look suspicious. I'm either going to have to explain exactly how, where and when it was taken – and my sleeping with Gabe Miller is hardly going to go down too well with the bosses – or lie about it. And if I lie about it and the cops start asking difficult questions then . . .'

'It could be a bluff. Are you sure he's serious?'

Laura's fingers tightened around her glass. 'Oh, he's that all right. When it comes to payback, no one's more serious than Gabe Miller. He knew I was on the brink of finishing with him and he doesn't take kindly to being dumped. He wants two grand or he's going to stroll into the office with my laptop and make sure the whole firm knows about our little liaison.'

'Blackmail,' Jo said softly.

'It's not that he even needs the money. It's just revenge or control or whatever it is that drives that twisted brain of his. So what choice do I have? I've already agreed to pay.'

Jo frowned. 'But even if you do, that won't stop him from coming back for more.'

'I know. And he could still tell the world but I don't think he will. Once I've got the laptop, he won't have any solid evidence – it's all password-protected.'

'So when are you seeing him?'

'I'm not. At least I won't be if it all goes according to plan.'

'But I thought—'

The corners of Laura's mouth curled up. 'I said that I'd agreed to pay. I didn't say that I meant it. As it happens, I've had a much better idea. He's staying at that new hotel near Euston, the Lumière. I've arranged to meet him in the bar tomorrow night at seven.'

'And then?' Jo said tentatively. She had the feeling that she wasn't going to like what was coming next. Laura James had what could only be described as an impulsive nature, an interesting trait in some respects – she could never be described as boring – but one that was almost guaranteed to get her into trouble.

'And then, while he's waiting for me, I'm going to go to his room and snatch the laptop back!'

'What?' Jo's response was so loud that a couple at a nearby table turned their heads to look. She quickly lowered her voice. 'You must be kidding. You're going to do *what*?'

'It's the only way. He won't have it on him, I know he

won't. He likes to play games; he'll want to try and screw with my head for as long as he can. Nothing's ever simple or straightforward with him.'

'But you can't break in,' Jo insisted. 'I mean, apart from anything else, what if you get caught? In fact you will get caught. That kind of hotel's bound to have cameras, CCTV.'

'Who said anything about breaking in?'

Jo stared back at her.

'I've thought it through,' Laura explained, 'and I'm sure it'll work. Once Miller's safely in the bar, I can turn up at reception with some fancy luggage and claim that I'm his wife. So long as I look the part, so long as I'm suitably dressed and utterly charming, why shouldn't they let me into his room?'

Jo opened her mouth to object but then smartly closed it again. It was true that Laura could be extremely persuasive when she put her mind to it. With her long auburn hair and hazel eyes she was also stunningly attractive, a bonus when it came to fooling any unsuspecting person on a hotel desk, especially if they were male.

'He'll have a double room,' Laura continued. 'He always does, just in case he gets lucky. I'll say that there must have been some misunderstanding over the booking, that it should have been for Mr *and* Mrs Miller. I'll be disgustingly polite and sweetly patient. I'll even ask them to ring up and check with him if necessary. But of course he won't be there. He'll be in the bar waiting for me.'

'And if they still say no?'

'They won't.'

'They might,' Jo said. 'You can't take it for granted. Security can be tight in these places. What if they ask for identification?'

Laura shrugged. 'You know me. I'll think of something.'

Jo finished her wine, reached for the bottle and quickly refilled their glasses. This wasn't a plan they should even be discussing. The whole idea was crazy. Or was it? Perhaps not completely crazy but it was hardly foolproof. 'There must be a better way of dealing with this.'

'Any suggestions?'

Jo hadn't. Coming clean clearly wasn't an option. From what she'd gathered about Laura's bosses, they were hardly the forgiving sort. 'But it's so risky. Even if you do manage to get into his room, how can you be sure he won't catch you in the act? What if he gets tired of waiting, realises you're not going to turn up and comes back and finds you there?'

'Quite,' Laura said. 'That's why I could do with some help.' She dropped her gaze to the table and slowly looked up again. Her eyes were pleading. 'It's a big favour, a huge one, but I was wondering . . . well, I was wondering if you could keep him occupied while I'm getting into the room. We're only talking fifteen minutes, twenty max. I wouldn't ask, I really wouldn't, unless I was desperate.'

Jo had no doubt as to the state of her desperation. What she did have doubts about, however, was her ability to keep Miller occupied for five minutes, never mind twenty. Since Peter had died, she hadn't even glanced at another man. Her seduction skills, such as they were, had been placed firmly on ice. 'I don't think I can.'

'All you'll have to do is chat to him.'

'Chat him up you mean.'

Laura gave a small brittle laugh. 'Oh, believe me *he'll* be the one doing the chatting up. All you'll have to do is pretend to be interested. If you're sitting alone at the bar, it won't take him long to notice you. He'll make a move.'

'And if he doesn't?'

'Of course he will. God, Jo, don't you ever look in the mirror? You're young, slim and blonde; you have the face of an angel and there's nothing Miller likes more than corrupting the innocent. He won't be able to resist. He'll be all over you.'

Jo wasn't quite so confident. At twenty-eight she no longer felt especially innocent and her resistibility factor, on a sliding scale of one to ten, could well be into double figures. 'But if he's expecting you at any minute . . .'

'That won't stop him. Anyway, I'll give him a call, tell him that I'm going to be late. That way he'll think he has some time to kill – and Gabe always likes to use his time usefully.'

Jo hesitated, twisting the glass between her fingers. She wanted to help, she really wanted to say yes, but a voice of caution was still whispering in her ear. *What if it all goes wrong?*

'Forget it,' Laura said. 'I shouldn't have asked. You've got your own problems; you don't need me adding to them.'

But if there was one thing Jo valued, it was loyalty. They might only have known each other a few months but it was long enough for the friendship to become firmly established. After all the darkness, all the grieving over Peter,

Laura had finally brought some fun and laughter back into her life; to say there was never a dull moment was a complete understatement. Her friend had shown that there was more to this world than pain and misery – or stressing over Ruby Strong's unfavourable opinion of her. So maybe it was time to give something back in return. And, if she was being honest, the idea of preventing a seedy, blackmailing Romeo from profiting from his sins had a certain appeal. Laura's plan might be slightly dishonest, even marginally illegal, but it couldn't be said to be immoral.

Taking a large gulp of wine, Jo swallowed it down. She breathed in deeply and slowly exhaled. 'Okay,' she said. 'Count me in. I'll do it.'

Chapter Three

The cab turned off Euston Road and twenty seconds later drew up beside the entrance to the Lumière. It was five past seven. Jo got out first, stumbling in her haste. She quickly stood up straight and then waited as Laura calmly picked up her Louis Vuitton overnight bag, glided on to the pavement and leaned over to pay the driver.

They stood in silence as the taxi pulled away.

Laura smiled at her. 'Are you okay?'

Jo's nerves were on edge, her stomach turning somersaults, but it was too late to back out now, even if she wanted to. 'Just about.'

Laura smoothed down the skirt of her cream designer suit. 'You'll be fine,' she said. 'Are you sure I look the part?'

'Every inch. You're positively oozing sophistication.'

'Fingers crossed that our friends inside are of the same opinion.' She got out her phone. 'You go on in. He should be there by now. I'll make the call.'

Jo nodded. 'Good luck,' she said. Then, before her courage could fail her, she turned, walked up the steps and quickly pushed through the revolving doors.

She had never been inside before and the foyer was as

bright and spacious as the hotel's name suggested. It was also, she was pleased to discover, exceedingly busy. Laura's plan had a better chance of succeeding if the front desk was under pressure.

Her heels clicked along the smooth marble floor. She followed the signs to the bar, pausing just before she reached it to check her reflection in one of the fancy gilt-edged mirrors. All things considered she hadn't scrubbed up too badly. The simple navy dress was short but not too revealing. The single string of pearls was classy but not ostentatious. Her make-up was intact. It was only as she touched the nape of her neck that her face abruptly fell. The skin felt too bare, too naked; it was over three months since she'd decided to cut off her long hair and she still hadn't got used to it.

Jo attempted a smile but her mouth had begun to tremble. She imagined a big arrow pointed towards her head with *liar* written in bold black print at its end. What if he saw straight through her? What if he realised what she was up to?

To try and bolster her confidence, she ran through the plan again. It was simple enough. All she had to do was go to the bar, find Miller and take a seat close by. She was just a nice girl waiting for a friend . . . a friend who was late. If Laura was right about his predatory nature, then he would do the rest. As soon as Laura had got the laptop, as soon as she had left the hotel and hailed a cab, she'd call on the mobile. *Twenty minutes max.* Then it was merely a case of making her excuses. Simple. Wasn't it?

She walked slowly round the corner. Her legs had begun to feel leaden. She stopped by the door to the bar. It was crowded inside, humming with pre-dinner activity. The lighting was subdued, the music an upbeat rhythmic jazz. For a second, assailed by another wave of anxiety, she stood by the entrance absorbing the mingling smells of perfume, aftershave and early evening cocktails. She felt frozen. She couldn't do it. *But she had to.*

Rapidly, she scanned the room. What if he wasn't here? She almost hoped he wouldn't be but then, as her gaze jumped from table to table, she suddenly saw him – the man in the photograph made flesh, the despicable Gabe Miller. He wasn't at a table but was sitting at the far end of the bar where it curved into shadow, nursing what appeared to be a glass of whisky.

Come on, she urged. *Move!* By now Laura could already be in the lift, ascending towards his floor. Before she could become completely paralysed, Jo forced herself forward. At the bar she was careful to keep a discreet but not too generous a distance between them. After clambering up on to one of the chrome high-backed stools – an ungainly struggle that rather questioned her credentials as a woman of elegance – she smiled at the barman. He had a name tag on his chest that identified him as Georgio.

'Good evening, madam.'

'A dry white wine, please.'

While she waited, she allowed her gaze to drift casually towards Miller. He was dressed in a good-quality grey suit, white shirt and tie. His shoulders were broad and she guessed, from the length of his legs, that he must be over six feet tall. His dark brown hair was cut short and brushed back from his forehead. The best that could be said of his face was that it had been lived in. He was in need of a shave, a bluish tinge shadowing the high sharp cheekbones, and his nose had been broken more than once. His mouth was thin and faintly cruel.

Jo tried not to stare. Had he noticed her? No, not even a glimmer of interest. He was more beguiled by the contents of his glass than by her feminine charms. *So much for her sex appeal.* But then, just when she had given up, he raised his eyes and gave her a cool assessing look.

Success! She almost jumped off her seat. It was a kick; she couldn't deny it. A brief rush of adrenaline pumped through her body. Her instinct was to look away but that wasn't what she was here for. Instead she held his gaze for those few requisite seconds, enough to establish an interest without appearing too keen, enough to suggest that – should the circumstances be right – she might just be approachable.

Her drink arrived and she rummaged in her bag, giving him plenty of time to intervene, to offer to pay – except he didn't. Disappointed, she took a fiver from her purse and passed it across the bar. 'Thank you.'

So what now? Jo returned her attention to the room. It had that distinctive Friday night feeling. The atmosphere was imbued with a heady almost reckless air as if the working week was a dragon temporarily slain, its resurrection still two clear and hopeful days away. In the meantime anything could happen.

Except it didn't appear to be happening to her.

Almost ten minutes had passed since she'd first entered the hotel. Only another ten to go. She was drinking too fast, too nervously. She was halfway through the glass of wine and he still hadn't made an approach. On a personal level it wasn't doing much for her ego; on a more practical one she was growing increasingly anxious that he might get up and leave.

It was only when he looked at his watch for the third time that Jo decided she had to do something. Leaning across she said: 'Excuse me, but is there another bar in this hotel?'

He raised his head slowly. 'I don't believe so.'

His voice was deep and husky. She wondered if it was naturally seductive or simply the product of a bad chain-smoking habit.

'Oh, right,' she said. 'Thank you.'

'Are you waiting for someone?'

'Well, I thought I was but . . .'

Miller nodded. His eyes, which she had presumed from the photo were brown, were actually a dark, almost charcoal, shade of grey. Their scrutiny seemed more pitying than predatory. 'Sorry.'

Jo stared at him. *Sorry*? What kind of a response was that? She waited but he made no further comment. He'd already returned his attention to his glass and there was only a mouthful left. She fought off a frown. Sympathy was bad enough but utter indifference was a hundred times worse. Was she really that undesirable? She felt like giving up, like walking away, but knew that she mustn't.

'I could be in the wrong place.'

Miller looked up again, his dark brows lifting a fraction. 'Well, we've all been there at one time or another. I wouldn't worry about it.'

Jo realised that he thought she had been stood up, that

she was here on a date rather than waiting for a girlfriend. Still, so long as he was talking to her it didn't really matter what he thought. She may as well play along. 'Easy for you to say, Mr . . .?'

He leaned across and put out his hand. 'Gabe. Gabe Miller.'

It was only as his fingers squeezed hers that she realised she hadn't thought of a suitable pseudonym. Bearing in mind the circumstances, it would hardly be smart to provide him with her real identity. Her brain scrabbled for an alternative. 'Helen Seymour,' she finally blurted out, the name of a girl she'd been at school with.

'Nice to meet you, Helen.' His hand held on to hers for a little longer than was strictly necessary. 'And yes, although I hate to admit it, it's happened to me more often than I care to dwell on.'

Jo smiled. 'I hope you're not trying to make me feel sorry for you. Isn't this supposed to be my moment of supreme humiliation?'

'No need to be selfish. And I don't suppose you have much to worry about. He probably just got overexcited and stepped out in front of a car.'

She laughed. 'There's a thought worth holding on to.'

He lifted his empty glass. 'Would you care to join me?'

Unwilling to appear too enthusiastic, she took a few seconds to pretend to think about it.

'All right then. Why not?'

Miller ordered the drinks. When they arrived, he stood up, paid for them and then sat down a little closer to her. He chinked his glass against hers. 'To absent friends.'

'I'm not sure I should toast to that. A girl has her dignity to consider.'

'An overrated virtue,' he said. 'Along with modesty, purity and—'

'Honesty?' she suggested, thinking about the laptop, about how he was blackmailing Laura.

Miller shrugged. 'I don't object to honesty – in its place.'

She tried to keep the contempt from her voice. 'And what place would that be exactly?'

His gaze slid down to the wedding ring on her finger.

God, she had forgotten all about it! Jo suddenly realised what was going through his mind. A rosy flush suffused her cheeks. He didn't just think she was on a date but that she was cheating on her husband too. 'I-I'm not . . .' she began but then stopped abruptly. She didn't have to explain herself to this lousy scumbag. She glanced at the clock behind the bar. Time was almost up.

'I wasn't passing judgement,' he said.

She nodded and quickly changed the subject. 'I've never been to this bar before. Are you staying in the hotel?'

'Just for the night.'

His accent was hard to pin down. She tried to figure it out but there was nothing distinctive about it; a hint of London perhaps, but a more neutral, smoothed out version. 'Business or pleasure?'

'Business,' he said, 'although I've never been averse to combining the two.' As if to add unnecessary emphasis to the statement, his eyes made a fast lecherous sweep from her face to her breasts, down the length of her legs, and back up again.

Jo felt herself stiffen under his gaze. The guy had about as much subtlety as a randy teenager. 'And here was me believing it was only women who could multitask.'

He grinned. 'You'd be surprised.'

And so would he, she thought smugly, if he had any idea of what she was really doing here. 'So, what brings you to London? What line of work are you in?'

'This and that,' he said evasively. 'And you?'

'Oh, much the same,' she replied, playing him at his own game.

'There's a coincidence.'

Jo sipped her wine. What was Laura doing? She should have called by now. The twenty minutes had come and gone. How long did it take to search a room? Something must have gone wrong. Perhaps Miller had the laptop with him. She looked down at the floor, scanning the space around his feet, but it wasn't there. She began to have visions of Laura being arrested, of being led away by the police in handcuffs.

'Are you all right?' he said.

She looked up brightly. 'Fine,' she said. 'Why shouldn't I be?'

'I don't know. You just seem a little—'

Suddenly she heard the series of beeps that heralded an incoming message. Reaching into her bag, she pulled out the phone. 'Excuse me,' she said. Keeping the screen shielded from him, she eagerly read the text. It was from Laura. *GOT IT! TIME TO GO.* She read it again, relief streaming through her.

'Good news?' he said.

'Er . . . Yes, I guess so. I'm afraid I have to go.'

Miller pulled a face. 'Good news for you, maybe.'

Jo smiled as she got to her feet. 'Sorry, but thanks for the drink.'

'A pleasure,' he said. 'Give me a call if you ever find yourself at a loose end.' He took out his wallet and produced a small white card. It had only his name and mobile number printed in it – no address and no occupation.

She dropped it into her bag with the phone. 'I will,' she lied. It took every inch of her willpower to walk from the room without breaking into a run.

Chapter Four

Jo hurried across the foyer, pushed through the door and clattered down the steps. She was awash with a stream of nervous elation, the kind of rush that made her want to jump up and down and laugh out loud. All they had to do now was to make their getaway before Miller discovered the laptop was missing!

She ground to a halt on the pavement, her high spirits giving way to a confused surprise. The black cab should be idling by the entrance but it wasn't. Frowning, she scoured the street. No sign. The plan had been to meet again outside the hotel – she was sure of it. She walked a few yards and then retraced her steps. She unzipped her bag and got out her phone. Almost immediately it began to ring. It was Laura.

'Hey,' Jo said, smiling again. 'Where are you?'

'I'm really sorry but something's come up, an urgent call from work. I've had to take off.'

'Work?' Jo repeated. Her face fell. 'What?'

'It's a client, some idiot who's got himself in trouble. Thanks for everything – you're a real darling. I don't know what I'd have done without you.'

'You've gone?' Jo said. She gazed stupidly up and down the street again.

'I'm sorry. I didn't mean to leave you stranded. I feel like a real bitch but you know what it's like – I couldn't say no. Just grab a cab and I'll pay you back when I see you.'

'You haven't even told me how it went.'

Laura's voice sounded impatient. 'Great, perfect. It went like a dream. You're a real mate. Look, I'm almost there. I've got to go. I'll give you a buzz tomorrow and fill you in on all the details.'

'But I thought we were supposed to be—'

Jo didn't get to the end of the sentence. The line was already dead. She put the phone back in her bag. Her disappointment at the lack of any victory celebration was coupled with a deeper sense of irritation. Why couldn't Laura have waited for a few minutes? It wasn't much to ask after what she'd just done for her. And somehow the whole work thing didn't quite ring true; Laura wouldn't have been on call tonight – not when she'd planned all this.

But there was no time to dwell on that now. It wasn't smart to hang around; she might bump into Miller again and that wasn't a prospect that appealed.

Jo set off at a brisk pace, keeping her eyes peeled for an empty cab. The evening air had a chill in it and she wished she'd brought a coat. Her high-heeled shoes, more suitable for posing than walking, were beginning to pinch her feet. She cut down on to Euston Road and was almost at the station when she heard the shout behind her.

'Hey!'

Jo didn't react. This was London and people were always

raising their voices. It was only as she became aware of footsteps pounding the pavement that she glanced over her shoulder. Oh no! Gabe Miller was racing towards her.

Her stomach barely had time to sink before he had grabbed hold of her elbows and shoved her roughly back against the wall. 'Very smart. Very cute,' he snarled. 'You want to tell me where she is?'

She stared back at him, her eyes widening with alarm. 'What?'

'Skip the innocent act, Helen.' He squeezed his hands tighter around her arms and pushed his face into hers. 'Where is she?'

'I – I don't know who you're talking about.'

'Don't give me that crap!'

His eyes were blazing and the pressure from his fingers was painful. 'You're hurting me,' she said, trying to pull away. But his grip only tightened.

'Tell me,' he demanded again.

Jo was growing seriously afraid. He looked like he wanted to kill her. People were passing by, a few of them giving curious glances, but nobody – as was so often the case in the city – seemed willing to intervene. If she wanted help she was probably going to have to scream for it.

She opened her mouth, intending to do just that, when he suddenly let go. He took a step back and groaned. 'Jesus,' he said. Still softly swearing, he tore his fingers through his hair and began to pace in front of her, three steps to the left, three steps to the right. 'Have you any idea of what you've done?'

Jo rubbed at her arms. Coming from a blackmailer that

seemed kind of rich but it was hardly a point to start debating at this particular moment. She had more important things to worry about. Gabe Miller was clearly a bad loser, a man who didn't like his victims turning the tables. Twisted – wasn't that how Laura had described him? She was beginning to understand what she meant.

'I really have no—'

'Don't even go there,' he said. 'I don't want to hear it.' He stopped pacing and glared at her. 'I've just been robbed. Doesn't that bother you at all?'

She stared silently back at him.

'Please don't do this,' he said. His voice had turned curiously pleading. He raised his hands and dropped them again. 'Look, whatever you've been paid, I'll double it. It'll be just between you and me, no one else. I promise. Just tell me where she is.'

'Nobody paid me,' Jo croaked.

Miller stood in front of her, his wild eyes staring into hers. 'Don't you see what this makes you? A bloody accessory!'

'So call the cops,' she snapped back, her indignation abruptly reviving what little was left of her courage. As soon as she'd spoken, she wished she hadn't. His expression grew even blacker. She wanted to believe that nothing truly bad could happen to her in a public place but that was a hope that was gradually diminishing.

'You'll regret it,' he said.

'This has got nothing to do with me.'

'The fuck it hasn't!'

As she tried to walk away, Miller grabbed hold of her arm again. Jo struggled to free herself. 'Leave me alone!'

He jerked her closer, his hot whisky breath in her face. 'As soon as you tell me who paid you to play Mata Hari.'

'For God's sake,' she protested. 'It's only a laptop!'

'What?'

'You had no right to take it in the first place and I'm sure it won't take you long to find someone else to blackmail.'

Miller instantly released her arm, stood back and laughed. It was a bleak, empty kind of sound. 'Blackmail?' He rolled his eyes towards the heavens. 'Get real. Shit. You can't really be that stupid!'

Jo didn't know what he meant. And she wasn't prepared to stay and find out. The sooner she got away from him the better. Finally freed from his grasp, she started walking down the street.

'Fine,' he called out after her. 'You do that. You take off. But don't think he won't find you and when he does he's going to blame you just as much as me.'

The words stopped her dead in her tracks. 'He?' Jo said, turning to look at him. 'Who are you talking about?'

Miller shook his head. 'You go on home, sweetheart, and pour yourself a stiff drink. You'll need it.' He paused. 'Only make sure you lock all the doors and don't say I didn't warn you.'

Jo swallowed hard. He was just winding her up. He had to be. Laura had got her laptop back and he couldn't deal with it. Except . . . there was something worryingly real about the fear in his eyes. The skin around his cheekbones had tightened and his face was gaunt and grey.

'What's that supposed to mean?'

He took a step closer. 'That you're in as much damn trouble as I am.'

'I don't think so.'

'Oh, yes. Your partner in crime is long gone. They're probably miles away by now. And they've left you to pick up the pieces. They've landed you well and truly in the shit.'

Jo's mouth fell open. Surely Laura couldn't have . . . 'It's only a laptop. Why should anyone—'

'There is no laptop,' he said, his voice rising again. 'This has nothing to do with any bloody laptop. Can't you get that simple fact though your thick skull?'

Jo glared back at him. 'So what *has* been stolen?'

Miller hesitated and then shook his head. 'That's none of your business.'

'Make your mind up. A moment ago it was very much my business. You can't just—'

Miller glanced sideways, his attention caught by something. A thin hiss escaped from his lips. 'Christ,' he murmured. Then, dashing straight out into the road, he stopped a passing cab and yanked the door open. 'Come on!'

Jo remained where she was. She looked at him, then back along the street. Two very large men were approaching from the direction of the Lumière, both of them dressed in smart dark suits. If it hadn't been for the excessive amount of gold bling they were exhibiting, she might have mistaken them for hotel security but these were clearly professionals of a different sort. Friendly wasn't the first word that jumped into her head. Like a pair of oversized grim reapers, there was an air of vicious determination about them. When they noticed Miller they began to run.

'Helen!' he yelled.

Jo froze. What was worse, getting into a cab with a man who was possibly deranged or taking her chances with . . . Perhaps it was some kind of better the devil you know instinct that finally kicked in. However mad Gabe Miller was, she didn't fancy facing those two thugs alone.

Chapter Five

She slammed the door behind her and perched on the edge of the seat. Her heart was pumping, slamming against her ribs.

'Straight on,' Miller quickly instructed the driver.

As the taxi pulled away, Jo gazed back at their pursuers. They were lumbering to a halt as they realised the chase was over. One of them took a phone from his pocket, flipped it open and jabbed at the numbers.

'Who are they?'

'Nobody you'd like to meet,' he said. 'Believe me.'

Jo did. But she wasn't too keen on the company she'd chosen either. Moving as far from him as she could, she hugged her arms to her chest and hunched into the corner. Everything felt unreal, like a bad dream she was struggling to wake up from. 'Are you going to tell me what's going on?'

'I was hoping you'd be able to do that.'

The cabbie leaned back in his seat. 'Where to, guv?'

'Well?' Miller said to her. 'I presume you live in London. Where are we going?'

Jo shook her head. '*We* are not going anywhere. Just tell him where you want to be dropped off and I'll take the cab on from there.'

'I don't think so, love. We've some serious talking to do.'

'I've already told you. I don't—'

'Spare me,' he said. 'I haven't got the time. Either you choose somewhere or I will.'

Jo thought about it. She didn't want to end up miles from the flat and even if she stopped the cab right now, Miller could get out too. She was safer in the taxi than alone with him on the street. As her overriding desire was to get home as fast as she could, she shifted forward and addressed the driver: 'Kellston, please. The station.'

Miller nodded and closed the sliding window so the cabbie couldn't hear any more of the conversation. 'Let's skip the games. We're both up to our necks and we have to figure out what we're going to do next. Our friends back there will already be searching for us.'

'For *you*,' she insisted. 'Not me.'

He barked out a laugh. 'You may not have signed up to any contract, darling, but you're in this as deep as I am. You're involved whether you like it or not. I sincerely hope that whoever you're trying to protect is worth it.'

Jo shuddered and stared down at her bag. She wanted to ring Laura but couldn't while he was sitting right beside her.

'It's not me you need to be afraid of,' Miller said softly. 'It really isn't. I apologise for earlier; I didn't mean to scare you.'

'Yes you did,' she retorted. She might have been wiser to keep silent but she couldn't. This had all become too nasty.

He lifted his shoulders in a slight dismissive shrug. 'You have to understand that what's been taken . . . Well, it doesn't belong to me. I was only looking after it.'

'And that's a good enough reason to shove someone up against a wall, to threaten them?'

'Maybe not, under normal circumstances. But these are far from that. And please don't even try to deny that you deliberately set me up.'

'I didn't. You bought me a drink, that's all. I didn't force you into—'

Miller snorted. 'Are you kidding? You virtually threw yourself at me.'

'I did not!'

'As near as damn it.' He slapped a hand against his thigh. 'For God's sake, Helen, stop messing about and give me some answers. This has nothing to do with any blackmail plot, with any laptop, with any of that shit.'

'Then tell me what it is to do with.'

He glared down at the floor. A few seconds passed before he looked up again. 'What if I said "silver" to you? Would that mean anything?'

Jo instantly thought of Ruby's, of the jewellery shop on the High Street. 'Silver what?'

His dark eyes gazed unblinkingly into hers. Then, satisfied that she might be as ignorant as she appeared to be, he said: 'You ever hear of a man called Vic Delaney?'

'No.'

'He's a businessman, of sorts. A few weeks ago he employed me to retrieve . . . let's just call it an item, something that had gone missing that he wanted back. It took some time and a fair amount of grief but I managed it in the end. We had a meet arranged for tonight at nine o'clock. The hotel was a good place, mutual ground for the exchange. You know how it works – I hand over the goods and he hands over the cash.'

Jo wasn't sure how anything worked in Gabe Miller's world but the concept wasn't too hard to grasp. 'So he was one of those guys back there?'

'Hell no, I can't remember when Delaney last broke sweat. They were just the hired muscle.'

She instinctively jumped. 'Muscle' suggested henchmen which in turn suggested crime, violence, gangsters and all those other dubious things she'd read about in the tabloids. 'So why . . . why did they get there so early?'

'Good question,' he said. 'Presumably because some kind soul tipped him off that I wasn't going to be able to deliver – the same kind soul, no doubt, who got you involved in all this in the first place.'

'Laura wouldn't do that,' she retorted.

'Laura?'

Jo turned away and stared out through the window. They were on the outskirts of the East End, winding through the backstreets, and what she saw was as grey and as bleak as the thoughts that were running through her head. She knew exactly how and when she'd been drawn into this nightmare but still couldn't understand why. None of it made any sense. She and Laura were friends. Or at least she thought they were.

'You need to start talking,' Miller said.

'Why should I tell you anything? Why should I trust you?'

'Because I just saved you from a highly unpleasant encounter with two very nasty goons – an encounter, I might add, that might have left you with a rather less pretty face than you have at the moment.' He paused. 'I could have left you standing on the pavement but I didn't. Give me credit for that. And to be honest, you don't have many options: either you go on home and hope they don't catch up with you or you do the sensible thing and tell me what you know.'

Jo leaned even closer into the side of the cab. She felt sick to the stomach.

'Okay,' he said. 'You don't feel too happy about all this. I get it. I'm not exactly overjoyed myself. We've both been turned over for one reason or another. What we have to sort out now is what we do next.'

'Do?' she repeated glumly.

'Tell me about this Laura.'

'You tell me. She's *your* ex. You were supposed to be meeting her in the bar tonight.'

Miller shook his head. 'No. No on both counts. I take it she's a friend of yours. How long have you known her?'

'A while,' she said evasively.

'How long is a while?'

Jo frowned. The truth was they'd only met several months ago. Laura had come into Ruby's and they'd got chatting. She hadn't bought anything but a few days later they'd bumped into each other on the High Street and gone for a coffee. Whose idea had that been? She suspected it was Laura's, although she couldn't be sure. Since then they'd been meeting up regularly, at least once and sometimes twice a week. 'A few months.'

Miller made a choking sound in the back of his throat.

'Jesus,' he said. 'Do you always go round planning robberies with people you barely know?'

'I didn't plan any . . .' Her objection fizzled out almost as soon as it had begun. There was no arguing with the fact that she had agreed to help Laura retrieve the laptop. She cleared her throat and carried on. 'I mean, I didn't see it as a robbery, more of a . . . a repossession. She was only taking back what was hers.'

'Except it wasn't hers, was it?'

'I wasn't aware of that.'

'Maybe not,' he said. His voice had a bitter edge to it. 'But now that you do, it's time to start sharing what you are aware of.'

Jo wasn't sure how to respond. She didn't like Miller, didn't trust him, but her loyalty towards Laura was beginning to feel rather misplaced too. It was dawning on her just how little she actually knew about her so-called friend. Laura had never spoken much about her life and Jo, wrapped up in her own ongoing problems, hadn't thought to ask. After losing Peter she'd become distanced from so many of her old friends, their awkward sympathy and embarrassment – matched by her chronic inability to overcome it – creating a barrier between them. With Laura it had all been so much easier, a friendship based entirely on the present.

'We could start with a surname,' he said.

She sighed. 'James.'

'And?'

'And what?'

'I've never heard of a Laura James,' he said. 'Describe her. How old is she? What does she do? Where does she live?'

Jo hesitated.

'Oh for God's sake,' Miller said. 'You don't owe her any favours. She's involved you in a robbery, done a runner and left you to face the music. She's stitched us both up. If I can't track her down, if I can't get Delaney's property back, then we're—' He stopped, sighed and closed his eyes for a second. When he opened them, they had that pleading look in them again.

Jo stared at him. She had the impression that he wasn't a man who was easily scared – which made his current expression even more disturbing. 'If this silver thing has been stolen, why don't you call the police?'

As if her level of stupidity had just gone off the Richter scale, Miller glared back at her.

'Haven't I made it clear? Delaney isn't the type of guy who likes the cops involved in his business. But fine, you call them if you want. You've got a phone – go ahead and use it. Dial 999. I won't stop you. You can explain all this to them – about how you tried to set me up, how you planned to steal from me. I'm sure they'll be very understanding. Of course, I can't guarantee how Delaney will react. It'll be entirely up to them to protect you from his less than pleasant temper. Let's hope they have the necessary resources.'

Jo didn't even look at her bag, never mind take out her phone. Delaney aside – and it was a big aside – she had a dreadful image of walking into Kellston Police Station and coming face to face with the vile Sergeant Hannon again. After the business with the letters, she could imagine how he'd react. He'd already got her classified as some kind of nutter.

'We're running out of time,' Miller urged. 'And, yes, I understand you don't know me from Adam but it strikes me you don't know this Laura too well either. If nothing else you could give me a description. That's not too much to ask, is it?'

'Okay,' she snapped back. 'She's a bit taller than me, about five foot six or seven, in her late twenties, attractive, slim, long brown hair, hazel eyes.'

'Great,' he said. 'Very helpful.'

Jo shrugged. 'I don't know what else to tell you.'

'Anything,' he said, 'any minor difference that might distinguish her from all the other lovely brown-haired girls out there.'

Jo tried to conjure up a picture of Laura in her head. 'No, there isn't . . .' She stopped suddenly, recalling one small detail. 'Hang on. There is something: she's got a tiny chip in the corner of one of her front teeth.'

There was a second's delay before Miller went rigid, his whole body tensing. 'This one,' he said, raising a finger to his mouth and tapping at his right incisor.

Jo nodded. 'So you do know her.'

Miller didn't reply. She had the impression he was holding his breath. Then the frown lines on his brow dissolved, his shoulders loosened and he slumped back in the seat. 'Susan,' he whispered. 'My God, I should have guessed.'

Chapter Six

There was a moment as they got out of the cab and he was passing over the fare when Jo thought about asking for the driver's help. She could jump back inside and tell him to lock the doors. She could get him to drive her away from here. There was no way Miller could track her down.

She was not sure what prevented her. Perhaps it was simply the fear of the unknown. If she was going to run, she wanted to know exactly what she was running from. And Miller was the only person who could tell her that. It seemed unlikely that Laura (or should that be Susan?) would be doing much explaining in the near future.

'We can go to Connolly's,' she said, nodding towards the café.

'We need somewhere private. What's wrong with your place?'

But she didn't intend to be alone with him again. 'That's not possible.'

Miller glanced at her left hand, at the finger with the gold band. 'Oh right,' he said. 'I don't suppose the old man would be too pleased if you showed up with company . . . or if he knew what you'd been doing tonight.'

Jo frowned, unwilling to disabuse him of the notion that she had a husband waiting for her at home, a husband who would undoubtedly raise the alarm if she failed to turn up. She wished with all her heart that Peter was there. She wished she could just rush into his arms and . . . but it was pointless to dwell on empty longings and shattered dreams. She was on her own. There was no one to fall back on.

'Connolly's will be fine,' she said firmly. 'It won't be busy.'

Miller didn't make any further objections. They walked side by side to the café and passed through the heavy glass doors together. Inside, as Jo had predicted, there were only a few other customers. They chose a table at the very rear of the room. He took a seat from where he had a clear view of the entrance.

A young bottle blonde with a red slash for a mouth sashayed over to them. She was wearing a black T-shirt and a very mini miniskirt. 'What can I get you?'

'Two coffees,' Miller said.

'Espresso, cappuccino, latte—'

'Just plain old coffee, sweetheart,' he said, before she could recite the entire list. 'If the damn stuff still exists.'

The waitress looked him up and down. Clearly approving of what she saw, she smiled, moved forward and put a hand on her skinny hip. 'Two plain old coffees,' she repeated before dropping her voice into a huskier, more provocative tone. 'And is there anything else you'd like?'

Jo raised her brows. The girl's leg was almost touching Miller's. If she got any closer, she might accidentally fall into his lap.

'Not right now,' he said. 'But if anything comes to mind, I'll be sure to let you know.'

Her red lips formed a sultry pout before she turned on her heel and strutted off.

Miller made a brazen study of her long legs as she headed towards the counter, then transferred his gaze back to Jo. 'Well, there you go,' he said. 'Perhaps this might not turn out to be the worst night of my life after all.'

She scowled, wondering at his ability to be thinking about sex at a time like this. The man had all the restraint of a dog on heat. 'What happened to urgent? A while ago you couldn't wait to talk.'

As if her antagonism might be down to a latent form of jealousy, Miller grinned. 'Oh, don't worry, love. You have my full and undivided attention.'

'So tell me what's going on.'

'Now I know who we're dealing with . . .' He placed his elbows on the table, half closed his eyes and then, as if he was rolling through the thought in his head, slowly nodded. 'Yeah, it's not as bad as it could have been.'

'Care to enlighten me?'

'Care to tell me what your real name is?'

Jo flushed. 'What makes you—'

'No offence, *Helen*, but you're hardly the best liar I've ever met. And you weren't too well prepared either. Back in the bar, it took you over five seconds to even come up with the name.'

'Fine,' she huffed defensively. 'I suppose being a good liar is considered a bonus in certain social circles but some of us have different values.'

Miller's gaze fixed on her. 'As you barely know me, and have no real idea of what I value and what I don't, I'll put that particular insult down to stress.'

Jo's cheeks turned a deeper shade of pink. Hearing the affront in his voice she almost regretted what she'd said. She was tempted to apologise but then, recalling what he'd done, remembering the way he'd shoved her back against the wall, had second thoughts. 'Whatever.'

He continued to stare before his mouth gradually slid into a smile again. 'Do you take everything so seriously?'

She glared back at him. 'What's not to be serious about?'

'You're not going to start blubbing, are you?'

It was only as he said it that Jo realised how close to tears she actually was. She could feel her eyes beginning to water. A lump was expanding in her throat.

'Why should I do that? I mean, it's been the ideal Friday night. First I get to spend some quality time with you, then I get abandoned by a so-called friend. Later, I learn that I'm on the run from a crazy gangster over something I don't have a clue about, and now I'm sitting in a café listening to you telling me that it's not so bad after all. Who could ask for a more perfect evening?'

'I guess that's one way of putting it.'

'Have you got a better one?'

'You're not entirely innocent in all this,' he said.

'Did I say I was?'

The waitress arrived with their coffee. Before she was

forced to witness another of their over-familiar exchanges, Jo stood up and headed for the Ladies. 'Excuse me.'

'There isn't a window in there, is there?' Miller called out after her.

She didn't bother answering.

Chapter Seven

Jo splashed her face with cold water, patted it dry and stared into the mirror. The blue eyes that returned her gaze were filled with dismay. How had this happened? Why? As the truth sank in, her frustration was gradually being replaced by anger and resentment. Yet a part of her was still unwilling to accept what Miller was telling her.

She took out her mobile. *One last chance.* She pressed in Laura's number, raised the phone to her ear and waited. Anticipating the beep, she readied herself to leave a message but instead she just got a continuous tone. The line had been disconnected.

Then she had another idea. Digging out a pen and a scrap of paper, she called a directory enquiry service, gave them the details for Hopkins, Ridley & Co. and asked to be put straight through. It only took a moment. She listened to a recorded message telling her that the office was closed but that a solicitor could be reached on the following number. She quickly scribbled it down.

It was a man who answered the phone, his tone brisk and efficient. 'Anthony Morris.'

'Oh, hello,' Jo said. 'Er . . . I'm trying to contact Laura James.'

'I'm sorry?'

'Laura James,' she repeated. 'It's urgent. I really need to talk to her. I understand she's a solicitor with Hopkins, Ridley.'

'I don't believe so.'

Jo knew it was pointless but she persisted anyway. 'Are you sure? You don't know anyone by that name?'

A sigh drifted down the line. 'Yes, I'm absolutely sure. But if you're in need of representation—'

'No,' she said. 'It's okay. I'm sorry to have bothered you. I must have made a mistake.'

Jo hung up and put the phone back in her bag. She looked in the mirror again. The truth was staring her in the face. She was a fool. She'd been duped, taken for a ride and she hadn't seen it coming. Just how gullible did that make her? For a moment, she leaned forward, her hands gripping the edge of the cool white sink. She felt the coldness running through her, turning her blood to ice. But Laura was her friend, wasn't she? No, she wasn't. She couldn't be. But how could that be true? How could all those months of chats, of shared confidences, have meant so little? In a gesture of anger and frustration, Jo picked up her bag and hurled it across the lavatory. Breaking open, it spilled its contents across the floor. She stared at the mess before bursting into tears.

Back at the table, Jo sat down and carefully raised the mug of coffee to her lips. She could have done with something stronger but caffeine was better than nothing.

Miller gave her a sly look. 'I take it there was no reply.'

'What makes you think that?'

'Just call it a hunch.'

Jo wasn't in the mood for his hunches. Laura's betrayal had cut her to the quick. 'Why don't you just say I told you so and get it over with?'

'Perhaps I'm not the type who likes to gloat.'

'Somehow I doubt that.'

He sat back, looking almost too disgustingly relaxed and casual. 'My, I have made a good impression. You know what I think? Seeing as fate has seen fit to throw us together, we should make the effort to be nice. Let's start again. I'm Gabe Miller. Pleased to meet you.'

She ignored him.

'Now you're supposed to give me your name. I believe that's how it works in polite society.'

Jo shrugged. She was unwilling to reveal any more than she already had.

Miller suddenly leaned forward, grabbed her bag and started to root through it.

'Hey!' she said, trying to snatch it back. 'What are you doing?'

But it was too late. He'd already got her purse out and was staring at her driver's licence. 'Mrs Josephine Strong,' he said, reading off the details. 'Twelve Barley Road. That's quite close to here, isn't it?'

She glared at him. 'You had no right to do that.'

He dropped the purse back into her bag and pushed it across the table. 'You know my name,' he said. 'Why shouldn't I know yours? What do they call you – Josie?'

'None of your business.'

'Don't be like that. Okay, I'll just call you Josephine.'

She gave him another black look. She loathed the full version of her name. 'Jo,' she admitted reluctantly.

He grinned. 'Well, Jo, now that we're on real first-name terms, we need to get on with the problem of finding Susan Clark. I don't suppose you've got anything as useful as an address?'

She didn't answer. 'Look, the quicker you tell me what you know, the sooner you'll be rid of me. That is what you want, isn't it?'

Jo couldn't argue with that. 'She told me she lived in Docklands.'

Miller waited. 'And?'

'I don't have a street name. I never actually went there. We always met up in Kellston. She said she was a lawyer, that she worked for one of the local firms.'

He gave a soft laugh. 'I bet she was pretty convincing too. I wouldn't be too upset at being taken in by her. She's very good at what she does.'

'Conning people?'

'It's more complicated than that. *She's* more complicated.'

'You say that as if she means something to you.'

'She does, did . . . once upon a time. We were an item for a while so she wasn't lying when she described me as her ex. If it helps, I don't think she intended to cause you any grief; she couldn't have known that I'd catch up with you.'

'Is that supposed to make me feel better?'

'Better than I feel knowing that she tipped Delaney off.

His guys don't mess about. If I hadn't legged it as fast as I did, I wouldn't be the perfect physical specimen you see before you now.'

Jo curled her lip. 'You obviously made a good impression on her too.'

'Yeah, I'm beginning to realise that.'

'So are you going to tell me about this thing she's stolen?'

Miller reached into his pocket and took out a slip of paper. He pushed it across the table. 'This was left in the room at the hotel.'

Jo looked down. The note was short and to the point. *The price for safe return is £500,000.* Her eyes widened. 'That's a lot of money for a piece of silver.'

'Delaney thinks it's worth it.'

'You've talked to him?'

'Only briefly. But obviously he'll pay whatever it costs to get—' As if about to say something he shouldn't, he stopped abruptly and looked away.

She wondered what he was holding back. 'I take it there's something dodgy about this silver article?'

'You're better off not knowing.'

'Oh, come on! You're the one who keeps harping on about telling the truth. You can't keep me in the dark. I'm already involved, you said so yourself.'

Miller was still watching the room. 'All right,' he said, eventually meeting her eyes again. 'I'll tell you if you promise not to overreact.'

Her heart did one of those nervous flips. 'Why should I?'

His gaze held hers but he didn't immediately reply.

'All right,' she said. 'Fine. I promise.'

He hesitated for a second. 'What you need to understand is that silver isn't exactly an *article*.'

'What do you mean?'

'Are you sure about this?'

'Yes,' she said impatiently. 'Just get on with it.'

Miller took an audible breath, made another quick survey of the surrounding tables, and then leaned in so close there were only inches between them. His voice was barely a whisper. 'Silver's a girl, a fourteen-year-old girl. She's Vic Delaney's daughter.'

Jo's mouth dropped open.

Chapter Eight

Her mouth was still open fifteen seconds later, her brain desperately trying to absorb the information. Assailed by an ongoing battering of shock, confusion, fear and disgust, *No* was the single word that kept revolving in her head.

'A girl? Laura's taken a *girl*?'

'Keep your voice down,' Miller said. 'You want the whole caff to hear?'

Jo covered her face with her hands. 'She can't have. She couldn't.'

'She has.'

'But why?'

'Why do you think?' Picking up the slip of paper, he flapped it in front of her. 'This is what's commonly referred to as a ransom note.'

She peered between her fingers and groaned. 'Oh God.'

'I thought you were going to stay calm about this.'

Jo dropped her hands and stared up at him, his callousness having the useful effect of jolting her thoughts back into some kind of order. 'Jesus,' she said. 'You told me you'd been robbed. You referred to that girl as an item, a thing, a piece of property.'

'It was just a turn of phrase. It wasn't meant . . . I had to be careful. I wasn't sure how much you knew.'

'You talked about "retrieving" her, about a meeting with Delaney. He was supposed to pay you. Cash on delivery, right?' She stared at him. 'What the hell did that mean?'

'It's a long story.'

'I'm sure it is.' What she was equally sure of was that having a fourteen-year-old girl in your hotel room, a girl you were being paid to return, went way beyond the dubious.

'It's not what you think,' he said.

'You don't know what I think.'

'I can take a pretty good guess. It's written all over your face. You've already decided that I'm some kind of pervert. But you shouldn't go jumping to any conclusions. If you'll just give me a chance to explain, to—'

'What for?' She shook her head. 'I don't even understand what we're doing here. This is a young girl's life we're talking about. We have to go to the police.'

Miller raised his eyes to the ceiling. 'We've already been through all that.'

'Hardly,' she protested, astounded by his attitude. 'You weren't exactly straight with me. This changes everything. Surely even you can see that.'

'Susan isn't going to harm her. I know what she's like, what she's capable of and what she isn't.'

'And if you're wrong?'

'I'm not,' he said firmly. 'Silver's perfectly safe. I'd put my life on it. And if I can find Susan, if I can track her down quickly, then there's a chance I'll be able to sort this before anyone gets hurt. But if you insist on involving the cops, it's going to make my job ten times as hard – maybe even impossible.'

Jo wasn't convinced. 'You mean the police are going to want to know what you were doing with a fourteen-year-old girl in the first place.'

'What I mean is that the cops will screw it up. Despite what you may think, I don't have anything to hide. But they'll be all over Delaney – about which he won't be best pleased – and I'll be spending hours in some lousy police cell.'

'So this is all about saving your own skin?'

'Yeah, that's it.' He gave an exaggerated sigh. 'That's why I jumped in that cab and left you standing in the street. That's why I'm sitting here now, telling you all this and trying to figure out a way of sorting the problem. Let's face it, love, I could be miles away if I wanted to be, somewhere Delaney and the cops would never think of looking.'

'Fine,' she retorted, 'but that poor man's still missing his daughter. He has the right to know who's taken her. He must be worried sick and we're just—'

He brought his hand down on the table. 'Will you just open your ears and listen? Maybe in your narrow, righteous universe the truth is everything but Delaney's world is a different one altogether. I wouldn't waste too much sympathy on him – he's not so generous with his own compassion. Silver isn't the issue here, she's not the one who's in danger. Susan is. What you need to understand is that she won't be able to pull this off. At some point she'll make a mistake, a big one, and then he won't think twice about meting out his own brand of justice. Would you like me to spell out what that means or can you take an educated guess?'

Jo's head was beginning to swim again. She had never met anyone like Gabe Miller before, someone who could turn almost any argument around and make their own twisted logic sound perfectly reasonable. And it wasn't just his mental agility that bothered her; she was suddenly aware of how physically strong he was too. He was the type of man, she imagined, who wasn't used to being contradicted.

'I have to find Susan before it gets that far,' he continued. 'You can help me or not. And if you can't – or you won't – you can at least do me the favour of keeping your mouth shut for the next few days.'

Jo couldn't contain her scepticism. 'You seem more concerned about Susan than the actual victim in all this.'

'Perhaps that's because we have differing opinions as to who the actual victim is. I realise that you're probably not feeling too sympathetic towards her at the present but do you really want her dead?'

'That's not fair!' Jo couldn't deny that she was angry at what Laura had done, how she'd used her, but that was a far cry from what Miller was suggesting. She knew she was being manipulated, forced into a corner, but she was still determined to get some answers before making a decision. 'Perhaps it would help if you explained what Silver was doing in your hotel room.'

'If that's what it takes.'

'I'm listening.'

Miller folded his arms on the table. He leaned forward again. 'Okay,' he said. 'What you need to understand about

Silver is that on top of being your normal troubled teenager, she lost her mother when she was a kid and has a bimbo stepmother young enough to be her sister. Add into the mix a father who rarely takes much notice of her and you're probably beginning to see the picture. Delaney gives her all the material possessions she wants and enough cash to get her into the kind of trouble that he then resents her for, but that's as far as it goes. When it comes to any kind of relationship, he doesn't have a clue.'

'But you do?'

He raised a hand and dropped it back down. 'Is there any point to this? You've already made up your mind.'

'And who's the one making presumptions now?'

Miller shrugged, thought about it and carried on. 'What Silver has got in the habit of doing when she wants some attention is running away. This was her third great escape of the year. She doesn't usually go far or make it that difficult for Delaney to find her but this time was different. About a month ago she nicked a couple of grand from Daddy's safe and took off with a no-mark called Ritchie Naylor. He's nineteen and a user in every sense of the word. Delaney didn't hear from her and started to worry. That's when he called me in.'

'And you tracked her down.'

'Eventually,' he said. 'She was holed up in a B&B in Blackpool, a nasty backstreet dive with nothing to recommend it other than the price. Ritchie, unsurprisingly, had bailed as soon as the cash ran out and with his habit that hadn't taken long. As you can imagine, she was feeling pretty sorry for herself.'

'So you dragged her back to London and kept her in your hotel room.'

Miller's eyes flashed. 'I didn't *drag* her anywhere. And I didn't force her into doing anything she didn't want to do. Let's just say that we talked it through and I managed to persuade her that coming back, although it might involve a small loss of face and a few apologies, was still a better option than staying where she was.'

'Mr Diplomacy,' she said.

'Whatever.' He shrugged again. 'I've been called worse.'

'So why not take her straight home? What's with the whole hotel business?'

'We weren't sharing a bed if that's what you think.'

Jo's cheeks flushed pink again. 'I didn't suggest you were.'

'Sorry. I just got the impression that you were thinking the worst. Forgive me if I was wrong. Anyway, we only drove down from Blackpool today. It was Delaney who booked the room. He's been in Spain, doing a spot of business, and his flight wasn't due in until this evening. It made sense to meet up at the hotel. It suited us both; I prefer to get paid on neutral territory and he didn't want Silver returning to the house without him. Nina – that's the wicked stepmother – isn't exactly the welcoming sort.'

'He's been in Spain while his daughter was missing?'

'Yeah, he's a real sweetheart.'

Jo finished her coffee and stared down into the empty mug. Her own father wasn't the most attentive parent in the world but even he wouldn't have been so heartless. She slowly lifted her gaze as another thought occurred to her. 'I still don't understand how Laura . . . how *Susan* . . . knew where you'd be. She told me last night that you were staying at the Lumière.'

'That's been bothering me too. The exchange was only arranged yesterday. Someone must have tipped her off, someone close to Delaney. There's no other way she could have found out.'

'So she's not working on her own.'

'I doubt it,' he said. 'You can always find some hard-nosed, greedy bastard prepared to sacrifice his loyalty on the altar of hard cash.'

'And do you have any idea as to who that might be?'

'Not yet. Delaney's surrounded by creeps. It could be any one of them.'

Jo looked down into her empty mug again.

'Do you want another?'

'What?'

'Another coffee,' he said.

At that moment the door to the café opened. Jo wouldn't have noticed if it hadn't been for the way Miller looked over her shoulder. She saw his body tense and quickly turned around. Two tall men were heading towards them. Her heart began to pound. She had a few seconds of blind sweaty panic – *were they the guys who had been at Euston?* – before her vision eventually made contact with her brain. These two weren't the same at all. They were younger, milder, dressed in T-shirts and jeans. Sliding down on to the seats at a nearby table, they laughed and gestured the waitress over.

Jo swallowed hard and pressed her hand against her mouth. It took a while for the fear to subside.

'This is ridiculous,' Miller said softly. 'Isn't there anywhere else we can go?'

'No,' she said.

'I need to call Delaney again.'

'So do it. No one's stopping you.'

He sighed. 'It's hardly the type of call I can make in public.'

'So use the Gents.'

'Oh yeah,' he said, 'like that's really bloody private.' He glanced towards the toilets. 'Unless you'd like to stand guard outside the door and make sure nobody comes in for the next five minutes?'

Jo didn't like.

'I didn't think so,' Miller said. 'Christ, we shouldn't even be sitting here. We're asking for trouble. This caff is like a goldfish bowl. Anyone could walk past and see us.'

Jo knew he was trying to scare her. Unfortunately, she also knew that he was right.

'You owe me,' he persisted. 'I'm in the shit and you helped to put me here. I need to keep my head down. We both do. Just for a few hours.'

'No,' she said again. She wasn't going to take him to the flat. There might be a risk in sitting here but at least there would be witnesses if anything happened. And that was preferable to being alone with him.

'Okay,' he said. 'It's your decision. I can't force you. But let's just get one thing clear: if I'm out on the street and Delaney's men pick me up – and they're going to be swarming all over the place – I'll have to tell them exactly what happened tonight. And as that involves you—'

Jo felt a cold chill run the length of her spine. 'You wouldn't,' she whispered.

His dark eyes gazed coldly back at her. 'It's your choice, sweetheart.'

Chapter Nine

Marty Gull peered through the narrow slats of the grille. There was only a dim light inside, a single low-wattage bulb hanging from the ceiling. The girl was lying on the mattress, her body limp, her long fair hair spread out across the pillow. He watched, wanting to be sure that she was still breathing. The last thing he needed was a corpse on his hands.

He glanced over his shoulder. 'How much has she had?'

'I've no idea. You gave Ritchie the stuff.'

He looked back into the room. Ritchie Naylor was a cretin; there was no knowing what he'd mixed it with. It was only as she moved, as her fingers trembled against the blanket, that he finally allowed himself to relax. Poor little Silver. She wouldn't be too happy when she came to in the morning – that Rohypnol crap gave you one hell of a headache. Her days of silk sheets and fancy living were well and truly over. No more parties. No more fun. From now on, the only tune she'd be dancing to was his.

The woman whispered behind him. 'Are you sure Delaney will pay?'

Marty slid the grille shut. 'Course he will. She might be a pain in the ass but she's still his little girl.'

'You'd better be right.'

He smiled. The stupidity of women never ceased to amaze him. It had long been his belief that if you wanted something risky doing, you should get someone else to do it. That way, when the shit hit the fan, you were always in the clear. And Susan Clark, with all her rage and bitterness, fitted the bill perfectly.

'I have to get off,' he said. 'Make sure you keep an eye on her.'

Her voice, edged with anxiety, rose a little. 'Where are you going?'

'Where do you think? Vic's doing his nut. If I'm not back in the next half-hour, he'll want to know why.' He jogged smartly up the stone steps and passed through the kitchen into the living room. 'And don't call unless you have to. The less contact we have, the better.' He put his leather jacket on. 'I'll try and get over tomorrow.'

'What do you mean, you'll try? You can't just leave me to—'

'I'm not,' he said. 'We're in this together, babe, but we have to be careful. You've got your job and I've got mine. I have to stay close to Delaney, find out what's he's thinking. Just keep things ticking over. So long as she's got food and water, she'll be fine. Keep watch but don't get too close. Don't go into the room unless you have to and, whatever happens, don't let her see your face.'

'She might panic when she wakes up.'

Marty looked in the mirror and smoothed down his short black hair. He took a moment to admire his reflection, his smooth olive skin and dark brown eyes. Not bad for forty, even if he did say so himself. 'She'll be okay. I'll be back as soon as I can.'

'How soon?'

He shifted his gaze to focus on her. 'Don't stress. I've already told you – tomorrow or the day after. It depends on what's happening.'

'Are you sure Naylor's going to keep his mouth shut?'

He turned, struggling to keep his tone patient. 'What's with all the questions? I told you I'd sort it and I have.'

'You didn't sort Miller.'

'Yeah, well, that was just bad luck. The boys were a bit slow on their feet. But it's not a problem. He'll be well gone by now.'

'I wouldn't be so sure.'

Marty frowned. He was less than pleased about earlier events and he didn't like to be reminded of his failures. He headed towards the hall. 'Look, Suzy—'

'It's Susan,' she said sharply.

'Okay, okay,' he said, holding up his hands. 'No need to bite my head off.' God, she could be a stroppy bitch. Women like her deserved a good slap, a reminder of who was really in charge, but for now he had to keep her sweet. 'All I was trying to say was that he won't start sniffing round. Why should he? Vic's gonna kill him if he comes within a hundred yards.'

'Gabe's been stitched up and he's not going to like it.'

'Who does?' He laughed and opened the door. 'See you later, *Susan*.'

As he walked along the path, he was aware of her still standing there. Without turning, he raised his hand and gave her a wave. Immediately, he heard a firm click as the door closed behind him. It was followed by the sound of a bolt being shot across. He smiled. He thought of his girl, his precious spoiled Silver, all safe and secure inside. It gave him a nice warm feeling.

Chapter Ten

It was almost dark outside, the lowering sky striped with deep cobalt blue and slashes of pink. Jo looked left and right before quickly crossing the road and passing through the gateway to the Green. She could smell the sweet scent of the grass, freshly mown that afternoon. For a while Miller kept silent, his steps keeping steady pace with hers. They were ten yards in before he spoke again.

'What about your husband? What are you going to tell him?'

'I don't need to tell him anything. He's not there.'

Miller nodded. 'You don't make a habit of this, do you?'

'What?' she said, still angry at being forced to make a decision she hadn't wanted to make. 'Taking strangers back to my flat? No, it doesn't rate as one of my favourite pastimes.'

'I meant walking across here on your own. It's kind of quiet.'

'It's a bit late to be worrying about my welfare. The age of chivalry, as you so perfectly made clear, is long dead.'

Miller shoved his hands in his pockets and laughed. 'I can see why Susan liked you.'

'Oh yes?'

'You've got a lot in common. You're almost as irritating as she is.'

Jo stared up at him, her eyes bright with indignation. 'I'm nothing like Susan. I don't use my friends and I don't steal other people's children.'

'I'd call it more borrowing than stealing. She does intend to give her back.'

'You think it's funny?' Jo snapped.

'Just trying to look on the bright side.'

'Well, there isn't one. There's just some poor kid out there who's scared to death and wondering if she'll ever see tomorrow.'

'I've told you,' he said. 'Susan won't let any harm come to her.'

'You don't even know who she's working with.'

Miller's only reply was a shrug.

It occurred to her that he was more concerned than he was letting on. She tried to read his face but without success. She was still in two minds as to whether she was doing the right thing. Before long they'd be at the flat and then . . . To try and calm herself, she began talking again.

'Susan told me that the two of you were supposed to be meeting tonight. So, if it wasn't her, who was your appointment with?'

'I got a call about another job. Nobody I know but that's not unusual. Most of my work is through word of mouth. A guy calling himself Billy Hare rang late this afternoon and said he had to talk. He said it was urgent.'

'And you thought it was okay to meet him?'

'Why shouldn't I?'

Jo wrinkled her nose, amazed as ever by his attitude. 'Because you were supposed to be taking care of Silver?'

'She's fourteen not four; she doesn't need babysitting. Silver was perfectly content slouched on the sofa, swigging Diet Coke and watching TV. As it happens, she had it tuned to an endless stream of music videos. Have you ever had to listen to that stuff, to watch it? I was glad of the chance to escape for a while. Delaney wasn't due for a couple of hours, the door to the room was locked and there was no reason to think that she was—'

'No, I don't suppose there was.'

His steps slowed for a second and he drew in his breath. 'Okay, I made a mistake. I admit it. I screwed up! Is that what you want to hear? Gabe Miller is not infallible and he occasionally gets it wrong. Does that make you feel better?'

She turned her face away, unable to resist a smile. 'Marginally.'

'Well, good. So long as you're happy.'

'I'd hardly call it that.'

'I don't suppose you would. That's something else you have in common with Susan – you're both impossible to please.'

Jo's smile instantly vanished. She had no desire to be compared to Laura again. And why did she keep thinking of her as Laura? She was *Susan Clark*, a virtual stranger. Their friendship had been based entirely on lies.

As they reached the far side of the Green, Jo turned left along Barley Road, crossed over, and walked up the path to number twelve. She had just put the key in the lock when there was a slight scuffling sound from the side of the house. The noise had barely registered with her before Miller took off. He flew across the narrow strip of lawn, swerved around the car and disappeared around the corner. The next thing she heard was a crash of metal, a stream of curses and a muffled squeal of pain.

Rushing after him, Jo almost tripped over a bike lying on the gravel. She quickly side-stepped the spinning wheels and peered through the gloom. There was just enough light for her to recognise their would-be assailant. She let out a groan. 'Oh no.'

This was no oversized goon, no vicious henchman lying in wait. It was poor Leo Kearns from downstairs. Miller had the boy pressed against the wall, his nose against the brick-work and his arm twisted up behind his back.

Dashing forward, she grabbed hold of Miller's sleeve and tried to pull him off. 'What are you doing? Stop it! Leave him alone. He isn't . . . he *lives* here.'

It took a moment for her words to penetrate. Miller's grip eventually relaxed and he slowly released his captive.

Leo turned and leaned forward, panting hard and rub-bing at his arm. He was fourteen but tall for his age, a wiry kid with a thin solemn face. When he finally looked up, his eyes were bright and scared.

'It's me,' she said softly. 'It's Jo. I'm so sorry. Are you okay?'

'Jesus,' Miller said. 'Sorry, mate. I thought—'

'We thought you were a burglar,' Jo interrupted before he came out with anything more damaging.

Leo's eyes swiftly darted from one to the other before

settling on Miller. His gaze took in the older man's superior size and strength. As if fearing another unprovoked attack, he sidled closer to Jo. His Adam's apple was dancing in his throat. 'I was just . . . just . . .'

'I know,' she said. 'It's not your fault. I'm really sorry. We heard a noise and thought it was someone trying to break in.' She reached out. 'Is your arm all right?'

Leo, realising that he was still holding on to it, quickly let go. The shock was gradually receding. Knowing that he was safe, he stood up straight and threw Miller a defiant glare. 'It's cool. He just took me by surprise. He didn't hurt me.'

She smiled. There was something touching about his male teenage pride. 'Good. So long as you're okay.'

Leo lived in the ground floor flat with his mother, Constance. Originally from Thailand, she was a small attractive woman who worked at the local hospital but otherwise kept herself pretty much to herself. She was not inclined towards conversation and had spurned all of Jo's perhaps rather clumsy attempts at getting to know her better. Now the only words they ever exchanged were polite hellos when their paths crossed. Leo, however, had always been friendly, always happy to stop and chat.

Mortified, Jo bent to pick up the bicycle. 'I hope it's not broken.'

'Let me take a look,' Miller said.

'Leave it,' Leo said, grabbing the handlebars and positioning the bike like a barrier between them.

'Okay,' Miller said, raising his hands and stepping back. 'Only trying to help.'

Leo glared at him. 'I can manage.'

Jo apologised again. 'We're really sorry.'

Leo's voice softened a little. His mouth quivered into a smile. 'I'm fine. Really. It wasn't your fault.'

'No, it was mine,' Miller said. 'I didn't mean to . . . I guess I'm just a bit jumpy.'

'Whatever,' Leo mumbled.

'We'll pay for any damage, any repairs that need doing,' Jo said. 'Just let me know. Are you sure that you're okay, that—'

'Yeah,' Leo said. 'No worries.' He nodded, gazed at her for a moment, then started to wheel his bike along the gravel towards the shed at the back.

Jo watched until he passed around the corner. She sighed into the night. She turned to stare at Miller. 'What were you thinking? You could have broken his arm.'

'You know what I was thinking.'

'But didn't you realise he was a kid? Didn't you even *look*?'

Miller rolled his eyes towards the heavens. 'Sure, that's what I always do when I think someone's about to try and take me out – stop and take a good hard look. I usually ask for a character reference too.'

Jo turned away from him and walked towards the front of the house.

'How was I to know he lived here?' Miller said. 'He shouldn't have been skulking.'

'It's hardly skulking when you're standing outside your own home.'

'He wasn't just standing.'

She turned the key that was still in the lock, pushed open

the door and switched on the light. 'He could call the cops, do you for assault.'

'He won't.'

'How can you be sure? The last thing we need with—'

'Because he wouldn't want you to think he's a loser. And he wouldn't want to cause you any bother either.' Miller stepped into the hall behind her. 'As I'm sure you're more than aware, that kid's got the hots for you.'

Jo snorted. 'Don't be ridiculous! Leo's just a boy.'

He grinned. 'A teenage boy with raging hormones. Didn't you notice the way he was looking at you? Even a blind man could have seen it. Oh yes, your little Leo's got a mighty crush.'

'Rubbish,' she said, pushing him aside to close the door and pull the bolts across. But at the very same moment as she was dismissing the idea, she was also recalling all the occasions, especially over the last few months, she had bumped into him on her way in or out of the house – too many times, perhaps, for it to count as pure coincidence. Her heart sank as she wondered if she had inadvertently encouraged him.

'You know I'm right,' Miller said.

'I don't know anything of the sort.' She flapped a hand towards the stairs.

Miller, still smiling, started to climb. 'You know what you are? You're the woman of his dreams!'

Chapter Eleven

Jo headed straight for the kitchen and turned on the kettle. She was still fretting over Leo and whether his interest went beyond the purely neighbourly. It was hardly the most urgent of her worries but it served as a useful distraction. While she was thinking about Leo, she couldn't be stressing about Silver and Laura and all the other madness that had gone on tonight.

Miller leaned against the door as she cleaned out the percolator. He watched as she dumped the dregs in the bin, poured fresh grounds into the machine, picked two clean mugs off the draining board and got a pint of milk from the fridge.

'You got anything to drink?'

'I'm making coffee.'

'I meant something stronger.'

Jo glanced at him. 'Shouldn't you be keeping a clear head?'

'What for?' he said. 'It's not going to change anything. There's not much I can do tonight other than call Delaney again – and I'd rather do that half-cut than sober.'

Jo hesitated. She had an unopened bottle of Bushmills

and could do with a drink herself. She just wasn't sure if a half-cut Miller would be a better or worse prospect than the one she was currently faced with. She dithered, messing about with the coffee, while she tried to decide. In the end it was her own need, her desire to take the edge off things, which finally made up her mind.

'In the cupboard,' she said, pointing up towards his left. 'There are glasses in there too. Take them through to the living room.'

By the time she joined him, ten minutes later, Miller was standing to the side of the window with a drink in his hand. He had switched off the main light and turned on the two lamps. The room was filled with a soft golden glow.

'Nice place,' he said.

She laid the two mugs down on the coffee table next to the bottle. 'Thank you.'

'It's very . . . tasteful.'

'Tasteful?' Jo repeated, inferring from his pause that the comment contained an underlying element of criticism. She glanced around the room, trying to see it as a stranger might: the bare polished boards, the cream walls, the long wheat-coloured drapes. There was a dark brown leather sofa and two matching easy chairs. The place was tidy, uncluttered. There was a mirror over the mantelpiece and a single print – a panoramic landscape – hung on the wall opposite.

'Simple,' he said.

'Right.' She supposed that what he meant by that was masculine and it was true that there was nothing girly about the room, no fluffiness, no ornaments, not even any of those more subtle feminine touches that a woman in residence might be tempted to introduce. Peter had lived here for five years. On moving in with him, she hadn't attempted to make any immediate changes and after his death, only eight months later, she hadn't wanted to.

'I poured you a drink,' he said.

Jo nodded and picked up the glass. She took a gulp, the smooth whiskey flowing warmly down her throat. She moved from one foot to another, feeling uneasy in her own home. He was staring out of the window. 'Is there . . . can you see anyone?'

'No,' he said. 'They don't know where we are.'

She crossed the room to stand by him. She looked out across the Green. 'They could have followed us.'

'Let's hope not.'

'So what now?'

Miller took a pack of cigarettes from his pocket. 'Do you mind?'

She shook her head.

He lit one, inhaled deeply and exhaled the smoke. He opened the window and leaned out. His grey eyes scanned the horizon. 'We play it smart,' he said. 'We find Susan before Delaney does.'

'And how are we going to do that?'

'She might not be that far away. If you've known her for a few months, that's because she's been hanging around and if that's the case, it has to be for a reason. She could have been looking for somewhere to rent, somewhere she could safely keep Silver.'

'You're kidding. You can't really think she's in Kellston.'

'Where else?' he said.

'She could be miles away. She could be anywhere.'

'I don't think so. She knows this area; it's familiar territory, somewhere she'd feel comfortable. How often have you seen her recently?'

Jo thought about it. 'I don't know. Once, twice a week.'

'Exactly,' he said. 'No offence, but I doubt she's been spending that much time in the area just to see you. Bearing in mind that she isn't actually a hot-shot lawyer, that she doesn't actually work in Kellston, then she's clearly had another motive for being here.'

'And there was me thinking it was just my charming company.'

Miller turned his head and grinned. 'If it's any consolation, I'd have hung around to see you.'

'It isn't,' Jo said, shifting away. She turned her back, took a few steps across the room and sat down on the sofa.

Miller stubbed out his fag on the window sill and threw the butt into the front garden. 'I could be wrong.' He closed the window and pulled the curtains across. He started to roam restlessly around, pacing from one side of the room to the other. As he passed the mantelpiece for the third time, he stopped and picked up the framed photograph of Peter. He stared at it. 'Is this the old man?'

'Put it down,' she said.

His brows shifted into a cynical arch. 'What's the big deal? He hasn't run out on you, has he?'

'None of your business,' she retorted. 'Just leave it alone.'

'Please don't tell me he's due back tonight. That could be awkward. I'm not really in the mood for another spat with one of your admirers.'

'Haven't you got a call to make?'

Miller replaced the picture. 'Thanks for reminding me.' As he turned, his gaze moved swiftly from her face to her crossed legs, where it stayed deliberately focused on the exposed bare stretch of thigh. His mouth slid into that familiar lecherous grin.

Jo glanced down. Suddenly her dress seemed obscenely short. She tugged self-consciously at the hem, achieving nothing more useful than drawing even more attention to the flesh she was trying to hide. Abruptly, she stood up. 'Excuse me. I won't be a minute.'

'Don't rush on my account,' he said. 'I'm not going anywhere.'

Jo went into the bedroom, closing the door firmly behind her. For a second she squeezed her eyes shut and leaned back against the oak. God, the man was intolerable. Why had she brought him here? It had been an error of judgement, a mistake. But then the whole damn evening had been a mistake. *Bloody Laura!* If she ever came across that bitch again . . .

But now wasn't the time for futile rage or recriminations. She had to stay calm, to decide what to do next. Her main priority had to be getting rid of Gabe Miller. Once that was achieved, she'd be free to make her own decisions. She could think again about going to the police. Would that be the right or the wrong thing to do? It would certainly be the easiest but not necessarily the best. She thought about the kidnapped girl and frowned.

Quickly, Jo kicked off her shoes and put on a pair of jeans. Keeping an eye on the door, she stripped off her dress and flung it on the bed. From the drawer she grabbed a plain long-sleeved white T-shirt and pulled it over her head. It was only as she glanced in the mirror, as she unclasped the pearls from her neck, that she saw how pale she looked. She stared at her reflection and groaned.

'Oh, you fool, Jo. You complete and utter fool!'

Chapter Twelve

As Jo opened the door she could hear Miller's voice. She stopped and listened. Having pulled back a curtain he was at the window again, his phone in one hand and a fresh cigarette in the other. Although she couldn't see his face, she could tell from his stiff, rigid pose that the conversation wasn't going well.

'Look, I may have screwed up, I'm not disputing that, but it doesn't mean—'

There was a short pause.

'Yeah, I see that, of course I do. Why do you think I'm calling again? If I could put back the clock I would. Jesus, Vic, I'm not involved in this. How long have you known me? If I'd even suspected that someone was planning to . . . but I didn't. How could I? I want to find her as much as you do. And we can either work together or—'

He held the phone away from his ear.

Even from where she was standing, Jo could grasp the tone if not the actual words. A fast, thin angry sound spurted out across the room. It made the hairs on the back of her neck stand on end.

'Okay,' Miller said. 'There's no need to yell. I get the

message. Can you calm down for a moment?' He put his hand out of the window and impatiently flicked the ash off his fag. 'All I'm asking for is some time.'

There was another longer pause.

'Yeah, I'm listening,' he said. 'What else would I be doing?'

The reply was obviously a long and aggressive one. While it was floating down the line, Miller's head drooped and he slumped against the side of the window. 'I'm going to find her,' he said insistently. 'You have my word. I'm going to find her and then—' He stopped. 'Vic? Hello? Vic, are you still there?'

But the line had gone dead.

'Shit,' Miller said. He flipped the mobile shut and put it in his pocket.

Jo walked into the living room. 'You really think you should be making those sorts of promises?'

He started, surprised to see her. 'Did you hear all that?'

'Some of it. I take it he's not overly impressed.'

'The bastard wants to chop me up and feed me to the pigs.'

'Oh,' she said.

'Oh indeed.' He drew hard on his cigarette, expelling the smoke in a fast narrow stream. Then he angrily stubbed it out and threw the butt out of the window again.

'Do you have to do that?' she said.

'Well, pardon me for not adhering to the strict etiquette of the glorious borough of Kellston.' He picked up his glass and poured its contents down his throat. He walked over to the sofa, sat down, poured himself another drink and swallowed half of it in one. He stared down at the carpet, gave a small groan and looked up at her. 'Sorry,' he said. 'I shouldn't have . . . You must be wishing you'd never set eyes on me.'

'Not just you,' Jo said.

He almost smiled.

Jo, steering clear of the sofa, sat down on one of the chairs instead. She curled her legs and feet beneath her. 'So tell me about Susan.'

'Like what?'

'Like why she's doing this. And please don't say it's just for the money because if that's what it was about, if it was *all* it was about, I don't think you'd be here now.'

'I've told you,' he said. 'She's got problems. She's not . . . she's not behaving rationally.'

Jo waited but he didn't elaborate. If she wanted to get to the truth, she was going to have to work for it. 'But why did Susan choose this particular girl? There are lots of rich kids out there. Why the daughter of some mad crazy gangster?'

Miller buried his face in his glass.

Jo persisted. 'Does she know him? Does she know *her?* Is it something personal?'

'No. So far as I'm aware she's never met either of them.'

'So why would Silver have left with her?'

'She wouldn't . . . at least not voluntarily.'

Jo sighed. This was like getting blood out of a stone. 'But I don't see how Susan could have forced her. She's not that strong and you can't drag a fourteen-year-old girl kicking and screaming through a hotel foyer without anyone noticing.'

'Quite,' he said. 'Which makes me think that Susan

didn't go to the room at all. Someone else did.' He paused, screwing up his eyes. 'It could have been Ritchie Naylor.'

Jo frowned. 'What, the guy who dumped her? Why on earth would Silver leave with him?'

'Why do girls do half the things they do? She thinks she's in love. She thinks he's in love with her too. Silver's not the sharpest knife in the drawer. All he had to do was provide some lousy excuse for why he'd deserted her, turn on the charm and job done. If it came to a choice between leaving with him or going home with Daddy . . .'

'She can't be that naïve.'

'People have a tendency to believe what they want to believe.'

'Really?' she said sarcastically. By people Jo suspected he meant women. She had the feeling, especially when it came to matters of the heart, that he didn't rate the female sex too highly. But then again, why should he? Men like Miller thrived on emotional manipulation. He was one of a type and, like the delightful Naylor, wouldn't think twice about lying through his teeth to get what he wanted.

'Yeah, really. Haven't you noticed?' He gave her one of his thin smiles. 'Still, you can't blame the poor kid. It's not as though she's been overwhelmed by love and attention. Ritchie may be a shit – and deep down she knows it – but he's the only person who's shown an interest in the past ten years.'

'Okay,' Jo said. 'So what you're thinking is that he's the inside man, the one Susan's been working with and—'

'No!' he interrupted, his face twisting with frustration. He slapped his palm down on his thigh and looked at her like she was an imbecile. 'Ritchie isn't employed by Delaney. He doesn't work for anyone. No one in their right mind would employ a fucked-up junkie like that.' He took another drink and stared down into his glass.

Jo was starting to despair. 'For God's sake, all I'm trying to do is make some sense of all this. I don't know Delaney or Naylor or Silver . . . or even Susan come to that. I'm working in the dark and you're not doing much to enlighten me.'

A few seconds passed before he slowly looked up again. 'You're right. I'm sorry.' He raked his fingers through his hair, shook his head and groaned. 'I just can't believe this has happened.'

'Join the club,' she said.

There was a short silence.

Miller was the first to speak again. He sounded tired, exhausted, as if everything was finally catching up with him. 'Susan might have paid him for a one-off, used him to get Silver out of the hotel, but that's all. He's not the connection to Delaney. Ritchie couldn't have known where she was.'

'Unless Silver called him. She's got a phone, hasn't she?'

'Not one with any credit,' he said. 'That ran out weeks ago.'

'She could have called from the hotel room, when you were down in the bar.'

'Yeah,' he said, 'she could but I don't think she did. Anyway, this wasn't a spur-of-the-moment thing. It was planned. Susan was talking to you last night, persuading you to help her out. Why would she have been doing that if she didn't already know that I'd found Silver? She must have heard that we were heading back and that we were booked into the Lumière – and the only other person who knew that was Delaney.'

'So who did he tell?'

'If I had the answer to that,' Miller said, 'we wouldn't be having this conversation.'

Chapter Thirteen

Marty Gull waited impatiently by the entrance. He peered out at the camera and beeped his horn. There was another delay before the gates slowly swept aside. He swore under his breath, put his foot down and sped along the drive.

Pulling the Saab into the space beside Delaney's Jag, he cut the engine and gazed through the windscreen. The house was one of those large Tudor-type constructions, all black and white stripes and mullioned windows. To his left, beyond a low brick wall, were a landscaped garden, a tennis court and an outdoor heated pool. Not much change from three million he reckoned. Chigwell wouldn't have been his first choice when choosing a home – he was more of a city centre man himself – but he supposed, when the time came, that he'd get used to it.

Marty got out of the car. The house was lit up like a Christmas tree, every window ablaze, two thousand watts spilling out across the gravel. So much for saving the environment. Delaney's only contribution to a greener world came with the switching off of other people's lights.

He walked to the glossy black door and glared at it. It still pissed him off that he was obliged to knock before he was allowed in, that he had to use that ridiculous brass lion's head. It made him feel like a delivery boy. This was the first time in years that he hadn't been given a key. Nina had seen to that.

He rapped twice and stepped back.

The skinny foreign woman who answered stared at him like she always did – as if she'd never seen him before. 'Yes?' she enquired solemnly. She was an ugly bint in her late thirties. Her face was narrow, as pointed as a fox's, and she had bad skin. She was dressed in a ridiculous uniform, a black dress with a white apron and a little white cap on her head. No doubt another of Nina's brilliant ideas.

'I'm expected,' Marty said, pushing past her into the hall. He strode through to the living room, took off his jacket and threw it across the back of a chair.

'Excuse,' the maid said, trotting in behind. 'I have not told . . . you cannot . . . I must—'

'It's all right, Louisa,' Nina said.

She was stretched out on a plush gold sofa, her upper half propped up by two matching velvet cushions. At first sight, with her pale oval face, dark hair and wide brown eyes she reminded Marty of a fragile but beautiful invalid, like a woman he had seen in a picture long ago. It was an impression that rapidly faded. She was actually in the process of painting her nails.

Louisa stood her ground. 'But Mr Delaney, he say I should always—'

'Yes, don't worry about that now. You can go. Just be a dear and pop upstairs. Tell him that Mr Gull has arrived.'

Louisa hesitated, her hands dancing in mid-air, her thin body shifting anxiously from one foot to another.

'Upstairs,' Nina urged, pointing towards the ceiling with a scarlet talon. She raised her voice as if an extra few decibels might help overcome the language barrier. 'Go upstairs and tell Mr Delaney that—'

Finally getting the gist, Louisa nodded her head and retreated. She closed the door behind her.

'Jesus,' Nina sighed. 'Where does he get them? A goddamn monkey would be more useful.'

Marty grinned. 'A monkey wouldn't wash your filthy sheets or make your breakfast in the morning.' Walking past her, he went over to the drinks cabinet and poured himself a brandy. Delaney always liked the help to speak minimal English, enough to understand basic domestic orders but not enough to comprehend any of his more iffy conversations. 'You want one?' he said, lifting the bottle.

'You haven't even asked how I am.'

'Sorry, babe,' he said, returning to lean over her. He kissed her mouth while his hands slid down around her breasts. She had a good pair of tits although their size was more down to the skill of the surgeon than to anything nature had provided. 'How is the sweetest bitch in Chigwell?'

'Don't,' she said, twisting her face and slapping him away. 'What the fuck are you doing? Vic could be down any minute.'

'Vic doesn't get anywhere in a minute. He's too bloody fat.'

She giggled. 'Get me that drink,' she said. 'I need it. You have no idea of the grief he's put me through tonight. That demented daughter of his has a lot to answer for.'

'How's he doing?'

'How do you think,' she said, glancing up again at the ceiling.

He looked up too. 'Has Miller rung?'

'A while ago.'

'I don't suppose he mentioned where he was.'

Nina made a soft sarcastic noise in the back of her throat. 'Oh sure. He sent through a map. You want me to get it for you?'

'Have I ever told you what a cow you are?'

She smirked. 'Love you too, sweetheart. I'll have a Baileys if it isn't too much trouble. Two cubes of ice.'

Marty straightened up and walked back to the cabinet. Nina Delaney thought she was someone but she wasn't. She was just a tart, a pea-brained greedy bimbo who had managed to get lucky. She thought she was in charge, in control, but he knew better. The only game that was being played out here was *his*. He made the drink, took it over and gave it to her.

'Ta,' she said.

He sat down with his brandy and gazed around. Never had so much been spent on so little. Some of the furnishings were old, some new, but none of them blended together. The room was a shocking combination of conflicting styles and colours. It was a prime example of why women with no taste should always be refused credit.

'What's eating you?' Nina said. 'You're not really taking this ransom thing seriously are you?'

'Aren't you?'

'Of course not,' she said, examining her nails. 'It's just

another of Silver's sick games. She'll do anything to get Daddy running round in circles. Vic's such a sucker. What's the betting that she's shacked up with that creep of a boyfriend. She'll be hiding out in some dingy flat, smoking dope and laughing her stupid socks off.'

'Your tender responses never fail to amaze me.'

Nina stretched her arms above her head, opened her mouth and yawned. 'You try living with her and see how tender you feel by the end of a week.'

He was about to reply when Delaney burst through the door. 'Where the fuck have you been?'

Marty got to his feet. It was more through habit than respect, a knee-jerk reaction. 'Sorry, Vic. The traffic's bad. I got here as fast as I could.'

'I don't care about the fuckin' traffic. My daughter's missing. You want to explain why Miller is still out there?'

'He did a runner, gave Parry and Devlin the slip. He must have realised we were on to him. I've been working on it; I'm trying to track him down.'

Delaney's small mean eyes glared out from between the folds of flesh. 'Yeah,' he snarled, 'and that's been exactly how successful?'

'I've put the word out. I've got the boys watching his flat and checking out his regular haunts. I've got all the bases covered. He can't go to ground for ever. He'll surface soon and then we'll have him.'

'You should never have lost the bastard in the first place.'

Marty nodded, looking suitably chastised. He had long since learned to take the path of least resistance. Once it had been down to necessity, to self-preservation, but now it was more to do with expedience. A little grovelling, a little patience, was a small price to pay for keeping the peace. It was nineteen years since they'd first met, when they were both doing a stretch inside. Delaney had been a vicious bastard with an appealing streak of sadism. They had hit it off instantly.

Delaney was drunk and unsteady on his feet. 'Don't just stand there,' he said. 'What are you staring at? You screwed up. You all screwed up. You make me fuckin' sick.'

Marty felt sick too. It disgusted him to even look at Vic now. The man had always been solid, thickset, but the years of good living had taken their toll: the muscle had turned to fat and he was grossly overweight. A pendulous belly drooped down over his belt, his chin had multiplied and a welter of tiny red veins mapped a path across his sallow cheeks. His nose was puce, bulbous, and a few greasy strands of grey were all that remained of his once pale brown hair.

Delaney pushed his fat face into Marty's and breathed out his stale whisky breath. 'Miller swears he had nothing to do with it.'

'Yeah? Well he would, wouldn't he? He's taking the piss. Who else could have known where Silver was tonight?'

'Perhaps Miller's telling the truth,' Nina piped up.

They both turned to look at her.

She shrugged and rolled her eyes. 'Jeez, I'm only making a suggestion. You know what she's like. She could have planned all this herself.'

'Haven't you got something to do?' Delaney said. 'I'm trying to have a conversation here.'

'Well, pardon me for speaking,' she said, getting up. She slipped her bare feet into her high heels. 'I'll leave you two to chat in private.'

She smiled at Marty as she passed. He watched her backside as it wriggled out of the room. She had her charms, he couldn't deny it, but they were of the purely superficial variety. She was good but not that good. Delaney's wives came and went and this one, he reckoned, would be history by Christmas.

Vic slumped down on the sofa. 'Devlin said Miller got in a cab, that he had a girl with him.'

'Yeah, just a tart that he picked up in the bar. She's not important. He probably dumped her down the road.'

'What if she calls the filth, if they start sniffing around? If anything happens to Silver—'

'It won't,' Marty said, sitting down beside him.

Vic placed his white clammy palm on his thigh. His voice was full of menace. 'You'd better be right.'

Marty narrowed his eyes. 'Miller's not stupid. He won't have told her anything. Why should he?' In truth, the girl was rapidly becoming a priority. She was the only lead he had to Miller, to where he may be hiding now. He couldn't afford to have him on the loose, poking his nose into things that didn't concern him, maybe even trying to track down Naylor. It was Susan who'd arranged the set-up with the blonde. He had tried to get a name, an address out of her but she'd refused to spill. *Leave her alone, she's got nothing to do with this.*

'I want my girl found.' Delaney's fingers moved up towards Marty's groin, tightened, and dug into his flesh.

Marty flinched, a gasp escaping from his lips. 'Your little girl's all I'm thinking about, Vic.' He took a breath. 'I'll find her. I'll bring her home. I swear I will.'

Delaney prolonged his agonising grasp for a few more seconds before his hold gradually relaxed. His eyes turned faintly tearful and his voice softened into some semblance of affection. 'Yeah, you're a good boy, Marty. I know you won't let me down.'

Marty, still feeling the pain, forced a smile. Nineteen years he'd been at his master's beck and call. It was time for a change. He was due a reward, some payback for all that loyalty and dedication. And just as Delaney had once possessed him, had made him so utterly and completely his own, he would shortly do the same with Silver.

Chapter Fourteen

It was well past midnight and Susan was looking through the grille again. She couldn't help herself. Every time she went upstairs, she turned right around and came back down. She worried that the girl might wake up, might get sick. That stuff Naylor had given her could wear off at any moment.

Silver, however, was still unconscious. Susan watched as the girl's small chest slowly rose and fell. Was she warm enough? She was only wearing a T-shirt and jeans. She was partially covered by a blanket but the air in the cellar felt damp and cool. In the dim light she looked even younger than she actually was, closer to twelve than fourteen. Her eyelids flickered as she slept her dreamless sleep.

Susan's gaze slid along the blanket towards the motionless hand. Silver's wrist was manacled, cuffed securely and attached by a long steel chain to a ring set into the wall beside the mattress. The chain was long enough for her to move around, to walk across the room and reach the toilet and the old wash basin with its rusted taps. Susan had left out loo paper, soap, towels, a toothbrush, toothpaste and a bottle of drinking water; it wasn't quite the luxury a princess was used to but it would have to do.

She wondered what it was like to be Silver Delaney, to grow up with everything you wanted, to never have to go without. She imagined the clothes she must possess, the fancy shoes and the flashy jewellery. Susan had been raised on a council estate, a crumbling filthy slum full of dealers, pimps and spaced-out junkies. It was a place she never intended to go back to.

She gazed at Silver and sighed. Some people didn't know how lucky they were. The kid had no mother, of course, but Susan didn't lay much store by mothers; they were, in her opinion, completely overrated. Her own excuse for a parent, a gutless, disappointed, downtrodden woman, was an utter waste of space.

She stood back, glanced at the steps and squatted down on the cold concrete floor. This way she would hear if Silver moved or called out. Her vigil had more to do with protecting her investment than with anything more solicitous. If she felt any emotion for the girl it was only a faint curiosity. Under normal circumstances she wouldn't have much cared if she lived or died but this was altogether different. The kid was a cash cow, true enough, but she mattered for another reason too.

It was a reason Susan didn't want to think about right now.

She shifted into a more comfortable position and frowned. Bastards like Delaney didn't deserve to have kids. And half a million, all things considered, wasn't much to get a beloved daughter back. With his bulging bank account, he'd barely notice the withdrawal. It was just a shame she'd had to link up with Marty Gull in order to get what she wanted. He was a liability, a twisted arrogant fuck-up of a man. And he'd messed up big time over Miller. Had Marty been doing his job properly, he'd never have allowed him to get away. And if he hadn't got away Jo wouldn't have ended up in the cab with him. She hoped that wasn't going to be a major complication.

'No,' she murmured, shaking her head. She smiled and leaned back against the wall.

There were no real worries on that score. She had done all the groundwork, portraying Gabe Miller as a first-rate liar, a blackmailer, the lowest of the low. Even if Jo was forced into listening to him, she wouldn't believe a word he said. And she certainly wouldn't have taken him back to where she lived. That flat of hers was sacrosanct, an altar to the memory of her dead husband. The only men who ever crossed the threshold were the ones who came to read the meter.

Susan stretched out her legs and kicked off her shoes. It had amused her, making friends with Jo Strong. She had never done the whole girly thing before, spending long evenings in another woman's company, drinking wine and sharing 'confidences'. It had been an interesting experience. She had felt almost normal for a while. But a while, she reflected, was more than enough. Normal was ordinary, commonplace and she could never be that.

Her thoughts returned to Gabe. If it had all gone to plan he'd be out of the way by now. But it hadn't and he wasn't. He was still out there somewhere, a threat to everything she had planned.

Susan got to her feet and looked through the grille again.

She had to stop stressing. Whatever else might have gone wrong, no matter how badly the cards had fallen, she still had the ace lying right in front of her.

'Don't worry, baby,' she whispered. 'I'm going to take good care of you.'

Chapter Fifteen

It was twenty past eight when Jo's eyes flickered open. Squinting at the alarm clock, she was aware that her head was throbbing. It took a few blurry seconds before she remembered what had happened the night before. She sat bolt upright and listened.

There was no sound from the living room.

He must still be asleep. It had been after two before she'd got to bed, before he'd drained her brain of everything and anything Susan Clark had ever said to her. Jo rubbed at her temples. She had drunk too much whiskey and her mouth felt stale and dry. She shouldn't have let him stay but then again, what choice had she had? Kicking him out in the early hours had hardly been an option. He wouldn't have left, she thought, even if she'd asked him to. Gabe Miller was a law unto himself. Scrunching the duvet around her, she sank her face into its folds and groaned.

The minutes ticked by. She needed a shower. If she didn't move soon she'd be late for work and Saturday was their busiest day. Reluctantly, she got up, put on her dressing gown and carefully opened the door. She peered into the living room. The sofa was empty, the blankets she had provided him with neatly folded on the nearest chair. She looked towards the kitchen – no sign –then softly padded to the bathroom. That was empty too.

She let out a sigh of relief. He was gone! Thank God for that.

It was five minutes to nine when Jo started walking across the Green and five minutes past when she arrived at the shop. Despite the morning sun and the briskness of her pace she felt cold and shivery. Perhaps that mug of strong black coffee, especially on an empty stomach, hadn't been the most brilliant of ideas.

She didn't go in straight away but stopped and stared at the new window display. How did it look? With her head tilted to one side, Jo let her gaze roam over the latest collections. Sapphires were the theme for the month and the pieces were alight with a pure glowing blue. She tried to examine the display critically, objectively, as if she were just a casual passer-by, but couldn't concentrate. Her thoughts kept slipping back to the kidnapped girl. Was she right to do nothing, to let Miller try to sort it out his own way? What if he was wrong about Susan? What if the girl *was* in danger? What if—

Before her fears could overwhelm her, she quickly pushed through the door. She was usually in by eight-thirty, before they opened, and a few eager customers were already browsing through the store. She took off her coat and scurried behind the counter. 'Sorry I'm late. I got . . . I was just—'

Lifting a hand, Jacob swept her apology aside. 'How many times have I told you? You don't need to explain. You're the boss.'

Jo still found it surprising, even slightly alarming, that this place actually belonged to her. Situated slap-bang in the middle of the High Street, Ruby's was flanked on one side by a designer clothes store and on the other by a well-reviewed restaurant. This fortunate positioning allowed for a perfect shopping experience for the more well-heeled customer – the opportunity to buy a new outfit, choose the jewellery to go with it, then indulge in an excellent lunch, all without putting too much wear and tear on the feet.

She smiled and nodded. If it wasn't for Jacob Mandel, she wouldn't be here now. He was a small hunched man in his early seventies, his lined face topped by a thatch of bright white hair. She remembered when Peter had first made the introductions. Those sharp black eyes had cut straight through her, dismissing her, she was certain, as some dumb blonde who wouldn't be on the scene for long. A lot had changed since then.

After Peter had died, his brother Tony had offered to buy the shop, to 'take the place off your hands' as he had so condescendingly put it. And Ruby, her sly mouth pursed for a fight, had been right behind him. 'It's for the best, dear. What do you know about running a business?' Only Carla had remained silent although that was probably down to an unwillingness to side with the two people she despised most in the world than anything more actively supportive.

Still in shock, almost paralysed by grief, the last thing Jo had needed was to be at war with the family. How could she refuse? But Jacob had given her a reason. Determined to prevent the sale, he had cajoled, insisted and eventually talked her round. 'You must keep the shop. Do it for him! It's what Peter would have wanted. I'm quite sure of it.'

As Peter hadn't made a will, there was no knowing what he'd specifically wanted. She had still had Ruby's words echoing in her ears. 'But I don't know anything about the jewellery business.'

'Then you *learn*, Mrs Strong, you put the effort in. I'll help. We can do this together. Your husband put his heart and soul into building up this business. If he'd wanted that waster to have it, he'd have said so.'

She had been aware that Jacob had his own agenda – he must have feared for his own job, his own future – but she was glad now that he'd persisted. She still had plenty to learn but her knowledge was increasing by the day. What had begun as a way to fill the empty hours had, over the past two years, become a pleasure and the business was thriving. This was all down to Peter's initial hard work, Jacob's expertise and the flair of Deborah Hayes.

She shoved her bag under the counter and positioned herself behind the till. On the far side of the store, Deborah was artfully rearranging one of the displays. She was a tall, elegant redhead in her late thirties. Jo, if she was being honest, had never really liked her but was smart enough to recognise her value. Along with experience and efficiency, Deborah brought a vibrant energy to the store. She was full of ideas, everything from showcasing up-and-coming designers, through searching out talent in the local art colleges, to making the place more customer-friendly. She was even good at schmoozing the press; they'd had three flattering articles published about them in the last few months and that was the kind of publicity money couldn't buy. The reputation of Ruby's was steadily growing.

A young woman approached and passed over a pair of earrings. Jo wrapped them carefully. The earrings weren't expensive but they were well-made, bold and original. She was pleased that there was still plenty of good, affordable jewellery on sale. It had never been Peter's intention to make the place too exclusive; fashionable, yes, but not beyond the pockets of the less wealthy locals.

As the customer left, Jo glanced at Deborah again. How Peter had ever persuaded her to leave the hallowed ground of Asprey's was a mystery – or perhaps it wasn't. He had been a quiet, private man but he had been a charming one too. She suspected, although she had no solid evidence, that there had once been something between them. It was just a feeling. Although Deborah had never been unpleasant to her – indeed she was often overly-polite – there was no mistaking an underlying coolness. Had there been a fling, some kind of affair before she'd met and married Peter? Her empty stomach shifted a little. At least she hoped it had been before they—'

'Passion and fire,' Jacob said.

Jo's cheeks flushed pink. She spun round, her heart beginning to race. 'What do you mean?'

Startled by her sharpness, Jacob took a step back. His thick white brows shot up and he hesitated for a moment before stretching out his hand. She looked down. Nestled in his wrinkled palm was a small but brilliant gem. 'The ruby,' he said. 'I thought . . .'

'Oh,' she murmured, wincing as the true meaning

behind his words gradually sank in. After giving up so many of his evenings to try and teach her about precious stones, Jacob had formed the disconcerting habit of testing her when she least expected it. She should have realised. Instead, for one awful second she had thought he was referring to . . . Quickly, she pushed the thought aside. Dismayed to have snapped at him, she raised her face and sighed. 'I'm sorry. I was miles away.'

'Ah,' he said, his smile reappearing. 'I understand. It was a good night, yes? I'm the one who should apologise. You have a fragile head and I shouldn't be talking so much.'

'I'm not hung over.' Jo swept a damp strand of hair behind her ear; she hadn't had time to dry it properly before leaving the flat. 'Well, maybe a bit. Is it that obvious?'

'You think I don't remember what it means to go out on the town? You think I'm too old and decrepit?'

'No, of course not.'

'You young people – you imagine you invented the art of sex and debauchery.'

'Jacob!' she exclaimed, beginning to laugh. 'It was hardly that. It was only . . .' But, thinking back to the night before, what it had only been was perhaps best left unspoken.

'So?' he said.

Jo reached out and took the ruby from his hand. She held it between her fingers. It was a pretty thing, glowing even under the bright fluorescent light. Drawing on their lessons, she recited what she'd learned. 'From the latin, *ruber*,' she said, 'meaning red. The best are usually from Burma but they're also mined in Thailand, Vietnam and Sri Lanka. The finest examples have high colour saturation.'

She looked at it more closely. 'Like this one. The colour should be intense, not too pale or too dark. The most desirable, and the most valuable, are a pure and vivid shade of red.'

She continued to stare down at the stone. Peter had had a dislike of rubies – a loathing that bordered on revulsion. It was perhaps not entirely disconnected to an association with his mother. She thought of the lunch she had promised to attend tomorrow and felt her stomach shift again. After everything that had happened, the prospect of an afternoon with Ruby Strong was like the icing on a poisoned cake.

'And?' Jacob said.

Jo racked her brains. She knew this stuff – or she ought to. She'd spent enough nights trawling through the books. 'Rubies tend to have more inclusions than sapphires,' she said, 'but these can enhance the beauty of a stone.'

'What's an inclusion?' Jacob asked.

'A foreign body enclosed in a mass.'

'Meaning?'

Jo's head was starting to bang again. If she remembered correctly it was something to do with mineral threads, with needles, with the way they were spread through the stone. Unable to recall the exact scientific jargon, she resorted to a less specific description she had read: 'Meaning that where there might have been darkness, there is actually light.'

'Okay,' Jacob said. 'Forget the rubies. Is he smart? Is he rich?' His black eyes looked at her inquisitively. 'Is he handsome?'

Jo stared back at him, confounded. 'Who?'

He tapped the side of his nose. 'Mr Mandel always knows when there's a man on the scene.'

She shook her head. How wrong could he be? The only male she'd met in the past twenty-four hours was one she never wanted to see again. The mere thought of Gabe Miller made her feel queasy. 'There isn't,' she insisted. 'Absolutely not.'

'You women,' he said, raising his eyes to the ceiling. 'You say one thing and always mean another.'

Jo passed the ruby back to him and smiled. It was better perhaps that he thought her in love, mooning over some romantic notion of a man, than stressing over past affairs or kidnapped girls.

Chapter Sixteen

Leo Kearns rolled back the sleeve of his shirt and studied the bruises. There were two on his upper arm and two more on his wrist, all a shade of dull mustard yellow. He thought of the big man's fingers digging into his flesh and instinctively flinched. If it hadn't been for Jo . . .

The memory of her intervention provoked two deep and conflicting emotions: pain that she had witnessed his humiliation and pleasure at her obvious concern. That he had been so easily overwhelmed caused him nothing but anguish. He hated being fourteen, skinny and weak. And yet there was a plus side to his shame: it was his very vulnerability, perhaps, that had finally proved her affection. She had rushed to save him! She had shown him that she cared! That had been clear from everything she'd said and done.

So what was she doing with a brute like that?

What made it even worse was that he'd stayed the night. Leo's guts twisted at the thought of his strong vile hands touching her, undressing her. It made him want to puke. But at the same time he couldn't stop thinking about it. He could imagine them kissing, their mouths meeting, the thin straps of her black dress slowly slipping from her slender shoulders, revealing first the soft skin beneath her neck, then her breasts and then . . .

He rapidly blinked his eyes, trying to expunge the image. She wasn't like the cheap girls in the glossy magazines. He couldn't think of her that way. Real love went beyond sex, beyond the merely physical.

Turning towards the computer, he opened one of the files and flicked through the old pictures. Most were of Peter and Jo, taken on his mobile phone as they had come into the house or left it, along with a few he'd managed to snap along the High Street. He nodded as the images swept past. They had been the perfect couple but, at this moment, it was Jo he was concentrating on most. Back then her hair had been long, a pale blonde curtain reaching almost to her waist. He wondered why she had cut it all off. He sensed that it was connected to sadness and grief and change, although he didn't completely understand it.

Reaching out, he gently touched the image on the screen. Even though she had seemed more glamorous when her hair was long, he liked it short too. It made her seem younger somehow, more approachable. Her face, with its high cheekbones, was heart-shaped and delicate and her eyes were a soft shade of blue. Leo's gaze automatically slid down to her breasts, her slim waist and legs. There was no denying that she had a great figure . . .

Quickly, he concentrated on her face again. Real love, he thought, should be sacred and lasting. Leo knew that if he was married to her and she died, he would always be faithful to her memory. *Just as she should have always been faithful to Peter's.*

He banged his fist down on the table. And yet he wasn't really angry. Not at her at least. She had made a mistake but he couldn't condemn her for it. She was vulnerable, still in mourning. Jo was too beautiful for this world, too soft and delicate – the bastard had plainly taken advantage. His fingers gradually uncurled. No, last night had been an aberration, a moment of weakness and for Peter's sake, as well as hers, he would make sure it never happened again.

Leo treasured his memories of Peter Strong. He had a lot to thank him for. It was Peter who had come to their rescue five years ago. He could still vividly recall the two cramped rooms he'd been living in with his mother, the peeling wallpaper and the pervasive odour of damp and decay. There had been the noises too, the sounds from the hallway that went on through the night, the screams and the shouts. He couldn't forget the fear that she had always tried to hide.

It had been like one of those crazy stories, a miracle, when they'd been transported to this clean and roomy flat in Kellston. And it wasn't just their surroundings that had altered, there had been more money too, a complete change in their circumstances. Not that they were rich or anything but life was certainly more comfortable.

Why Peter had done it was a mystery. He had often asked his mother and always got the same reply.

'He wanted to help. He was a friend of your dad's.'

'But why should he—'

'Because good friends take care of each other.'

And that, no matter how often he asked, was all she would say. He sensed it was not the whole story but he'd given up trying to pursue it. She was a generous mother, loving and kind, but obstinate too. On certain subjects she refused to be moved. It was, perhaps, too hard for her to talk about the past. His father, Leonard, had died when he was two. He had been named after him although she always called him Leo. He wished he could remember something, anything, about him but he couldn't.

He clicked on a picture, the only photo he had of his dad. The original was in the prayer book beside his mother's bed. He had taken it out and scanned it into the computer. It was actually of both his parents, taken shortly after they were married. They seemed strangely young and unfamiliar. He didn't directly resemble either of them, although some of their features were evident when he looked in the mirror. He had inherited *her* straight black hair and pale brown skin, *his* grey eyes, skinny build and height. And yet none of these were exact reproductions. It was as if their DNA had been put in a blender, given a whir and poured out to create the thin blurry soup that was Leo Kearns.

He often thought about his dad. Mum said he'd been a salesman but that was too bland and boring. The very fact that he had died abroad imbued him with a kind of glamour that Leo longed to know more about. But how could he find out? How could he ask? Questions like that only disturbed and upset her.

And Leo didn't like to see her unhappy.

The last time she'd been really stressed was after Peter's death. And it hadn't just been at the loss of a friend. She'd become anxious, pacing the flat, talking about having to move again. But the weeks had passed, then the months and now, almost two years later, they were still here.

His thoughts returned to the man Jo had brought home. Leo's bedroom was at the front of the house and he'd heard the door click at dawn as the bastard crept out. Except, of course, he hadn't crept – he'd swaggered down the path as though he owned the place. From behind the shelter of the curtains, Leo had watched him cross the road and cut across the Green. He'd felt a surge of anger. If he'd had a gun he could have opened the window, taken aim and fired. In his mind's eye he saw the rose blossoming on his assailant's back and could imagine his surprise as he crumpled to his knees and slowly fell forward.

Leo rubbed at his arm and smiled. Perhaps he *should* buy a gun. There were lads from the Mansfield Estate, guys who hung around the Green, who could get anything you wanted – for a price. He had no idea what a weapon like that would cost, hundreds perhaps, but it would be worth it. London was full of dangerous people and it was his duty to protect the ones he loved.

His mother called to him from the kitchen. 'Leo? Do you want a drink?'

'Thanks.'

'What are you doing?'

'Homework,' he said, quickly closing the file on his computer.

She didn't approve of violence but then women rarely did. They didn't understand the true order of the world. Approving or disapproving was beside the point; life, no matter how you viewed it, was ultimately to do with the survival of the fittest. And if you weren't the fittest – and fourteen-year-old boys rarely were – then you had to be the smartest.

Chapter Seventeen

It was almost twenty-four hours since Silver had been taken from the hotel. On Monday morning Delaney would receive the next note, giving him three days to get the ransom together. But even then, they wouldn't return her straight away. This wasn't just about the cash – it was about making him suffer too.

Why exactly Marty loathed him so much Susan had yet to discover. Perhaps she never would. He knew her reason but she didn't know his. That Delaney was a violent bully was probably reason enough but she sensed it went deeper than that. Sometimes hate was like a slow-growing cancer, gradually eating away at the soul until all that was left was an urgent need for retribution.

She looked out of the kitchen window. From here she could see the tips of the three tall towers of the Mansfield Estate, a looming reminder – should she ever need it – of her harsh, unhappy childhood. Was that why she was doing this? No, her motives lay beyond the arbitrary circumstances of her birth. On the whole she felt only contempt for people who blamed poverty and deprivation for their problems. Those disadvantages could be overcome, not forgotten perhaps, but left firmly in their place. Her resentment ran deeper than that.

'Have you fed her?' Marty said.

She turned to him. He talked about Silver like she was an exhibit in a private zoo. When he'd been down in the cellar he'd looked at her that way too, as if she wasn't human but a creature imprisoned solely for his own entertainment.

'Of course I have. I don't intend to starve her to death.'

Susan watched as Marty's eyes narrowed into slits. He didn't like it when she snapped or answered back. She smiled, pretending she'd been joking. She had to be more careful. Marty Gull had a temper and now wasn't the time to start testing its limits. At the moment he needed her, the girl had to be cared for by someone, but later she could easily become disposable.

He nodded. 'Any trouble when she woke up?'

'Only what you'd expect. A few tears but nothing I couldn't deal with.'

In truth, it hadn't been the easiest of days. Hardened as her heart was, it had been impossible to deny a small pang of pity as the kid came to terms with her predicament. She had thought Silver might raise hell, scream and shout, even do herself some harm but instead, after a short frantic struggle with the chain, she had lain down on the mattress and started to whimper. It had been one of those plaintive sounds, like the mewling of an abandoned kitten.

Susan had opened the grille and talked to her softly. 'Shush now, be quiet. No one's going to hear you. And no one's going to hurt you either – so long as you behave. Be a good girl and you'll be fine. You'll be home before you know it.'

'Where's Ritchie?' she'd sobbed. 'I want Ritchie.'

'He's not here.'

'He said . . . he promised . . . he told me . . .'

'Just be quiet, love, and you'll be fine.'

But the crying hadn't subsided and in the end, unable to bear the noise any more, Susan had climbed up the steps, slammed the door shut and left her to it.

'You didn't go in, did you?' Marty said.

'I just pushed some food through. She wasn't too grateful but I'm sure she'll eat when she gets hungry enough.'

It was Marty who had been responsible for inserting both the grille near the top of the door and the small 'cat flap' opening at its base, a somewhat basic exercise in carpentry that had taken him an entire morning and a vast amount of cursing. He was hardly a natural when it came to woodwork.

'Does she understand what's going on?'

Susan shrugged. 'I don't know. She's still confused. She keeps asking after Ritchie.'

Marty sat down in one of the flimsy armchairs and spread his legs apart. 'She should have figured it out by now. She can't be *that* stupid.' Leaning back, he put his hands behind his head and laughed. 'Oh, please don't tell me that all that expensive education has gone to waste! All that bloody money! Surely even a product of Delaney's feeble loins should be able to put two and two together.'

Susan stared at him. 'There's a difference between working it out and believing in it. The kid's still in shock.'

'You're not feeling sorry for her, are you?'

She heard the challenge in his voice and instantly rose to

it. 'What about Gabe Miller?' she retorted. 'Have you found him yet?'

'It would help if you gave me the address of your friend.'

'No,' she said, 'it wouldn't help at all. Gabe isn't with her. I'd only be wasting your time.'

'Let me be the judge of that.'

'I don't think so.' Susan laid about as much weight on his judgement as she did on his morality. If he was prepared to betray Delaney after all these years, he couldn't be trusted with Jo either. Providing him with her address would be tantamount to giving him permission to do exactly as he liked – and what Marty Gull liked was rarely conducive to any woman's well-being.

'He isn't there,' she said. 'I'm sure of it.'

Standing up, he combed through his hair in front of the mirror. 'Not to worry. I'm sure he'll turn up soon enough.'

Marty Gull whistled as he strolled down the path. Once Miller was off the scene he could get on with the more essential business of tormenting Delaney. He would need to take the photographs soon, a few poignant stills to prove that his slut of a daughter was still alive. He didn't want him dragging his feet over the ransom.

He got in the car, leaned back and smiled. Just seeing Silver again, shackled and defenceless, had been enough to fuel his fantasies. As soon as he'd peered through the grille, she had sat up and stared.

'Who is it? W-what do you want?'

It was the fear that had really turned him on, the panic in her shaky voice. She couldn't see him clearly, the light was too poor and the slats obscured most of his face. But, as if sensing his intentions, she'd instinctively shrunk back. He hadn't said a word, although it didn't really matter if she recognised him or not. Her time was running out. Her days were numbered. Poor little Silver, however much she begged, would not be leaving here alive.

Chapter Eighteen

Had Jo been asked to compile a list of the ten most hideous ways to spend a Sunday afternoon, lunch with Ruby Strong would have featured right at the top. But there was no getting out of it now – she'd given Carla her word and a promise was a promise.

As the cab approached Canonbury, Jo glanced down at her simple cream shirt and light brown linen trousers. She wrinkled her nose. Why did she always try and dress so neutrally when she came here? It was a desire, perhaps, to blend into the background. But whatever she wore, Ruby would still find fault; it would be too smart or too casual, too stylish or too bland. There was no pleasing her. She was not the kind of woman who liked to be pleased.

Her fingers tightened around the carrier bag. Inside was a chilled bottle of Chablis. Alcohol was part of her survival kit for these dreaded afternoons, a few large glasses of wine having the useful effect of dulling the senses and taking the edge off the worst of the experience.

She gazed out of the window. It was always at this time, just before she arrived, that she could almost sympathise with her brother-in-law. Tony had little to recommend him but his burden was a heavy one. Having a mother like Ruby was enough to test the toughest of men.

Jo leaned forward and told the cabbie to stop. 'Just here,' she said. She wanted to walk the rest of the distance. She needed a few minutes to get her head together.

As the taxi moved off, she was reminded of Friday evening, of another cab slowly pulling away. Was Silver still out there or had Miller managed to find her? But how could he? Susan could have taken her anywhere; they might not even be in London. She had been listening to the news since Saturday morning, even tuning in to the radio at work, but there had been nothing about a missing girl.

Jo wondered if her reasons for not reporting the crime were justifiable. Gabe Miller had made a good argument but her acceptance of it was possibly more to do with the humiliating way she'd been treated by the police in the past. She could only hope that she wouldn't regret the decision.

Turning the corner, Jo started to drag her heels. From here she could see the house and she didn't want to get there any quicker than she had to. It was a tall four-storey building, a large and externally attractive terrace in the De Beauvoir conservation area. Mitchell Strong had bought it over thirty years ago and since then it had vastly appreciated in value. Why Ruby chose to stay there, rattling around in so many empty rooms, was anybody's guess. Had she been a different sort of woman, Jo might have put it down to sentiment but, knowing her as she did, suspected it was more to do with power and control. Sitting on such a prime piece of real estate, along with the rest of the money, kept her one remaining son entirely dependent on her. If he wanted to inherit, he would have to toe the line.

She stopped in front of the house and took a moment. Before ringing the bell, she lifted her face to the sun. It was a pleasant June day, the sky clear and blue with the sun shining brightly. It was the kind of afternoon that should be spent outside in a park or a garden. Instead she was about to enter the dismal mausoleum that Ruby Strong called home.

The door was opened by Mrs Dark, the latest in a long line of personal assistants-cum-companions. They had all been slightly weird but this one was bordering on the sinister. Claiming to be a medium, she was an insect-thin woman with small piercing eyes. Her hair, screwed up in a tight bun, was dyed a severe and unflattering midnight black. Her face was heavily powdered and her wide narrow mouth was a startling shade of red. The name, Jo decided, had to be made up – it was too much of a cliché to be real.

'Come in, dear,' Mrs Dark said softly. 'We've been expecting you.'

There was something in her tone, a suggestion perhaps that this expectation could have been down to her psychic powers rather than any actual invitation, which gave Jo a nervous urge to giggle. She bit her lip and followed her along the hall. The chill in the house never ceased to amaze. Even when it was blistering outside, the heat didn't penetrate. She could understand why Peter had loathed the place so much.

They entered the smaller of the two receptions, a cheerless north-facing room filled with old, ugly furniture. The walls were a dark muddy green. Their drabness could've been relieved by a few bright or interesting paintings but instead they were decorated – if such a word could be used – with a series of oils depicting the grim and bloody battle scenes of Waterloo. To add to the gloom, two pairs of heavy velvet drapes were pulled part way across the windows. Everything smelled stuffy, faintly musty, as if the windows were never opened.

Carla was sitting on one sofa and Tony was lounging on the other. He had a glass in his hand and already looked less than sober. Ruby, centre stage as always, was enthroned on a high-backed plum-coloured armchair. She was a wide, solid woman, several stone overweight, and was dressed head to foot in black. It was a mode of attire she had adopted after Mitchell's death and had not seen fit to abandon since. Her mourning, like every other part of her life, had to be more important, more dramatic and more lasting than anyone else's.

'Ah,' Ruby said, deliberately looking down at her watch before slowly raising her head again. 'Josephine. How nice. We were beginning to think you weren't coming.'

Jo knew exactly what the time was: three minutes to one. 'I'm not late, am I?'

'No,' Carla said, promptly patting the empty space beside her. 'Not at all. We've only just got here. Come and sit down.'

Jo was halfway across the room when she remembered the carrier bag she was holding. 'Oh, I brought some wine. Should I—?'

Mrs Dark instantly swooped on her. 'I'll take that,' she

said firmly. Like a firearms officer removing a potentially lethal weapon, she plucked the bag from her fingers and retreated back into the hall.

'How are things?' Carla said.

'Good, thanks. And you?'

Before she had the chance to reply, Ruby leaned forward and peered at her. 'You're looking very . . . pale.'

'Am I?'

'You could be anaemic. Have you thought about iron tablets?'

Jo suspected that a mild dose of anaemia came way down the scale in her mother-in-law's hopes for her future. Nothing less serious than a terminal illness would suffice. She sat down and neatly crossed her legs. 'Do you know, I've never felt better.'

Ruby's mouth tightened and her pale eyes grew dark. 'Perhaps it's the hair then. You looked so much prettier when it was long.'

There was one of those silences. In other company it might have been awkward but of the four people present in the room, three of them had long since come to terms with Ruby's acid tongue. Interestingly, she had never been quite so rude when Peter was alive.

'I like it,' Carla said. 'I think it suits you.'

Ruby grunted. 'As if anyone cares what you think!'

Carla opened her mouth but smartly closed it again. She was hardly a shrinking violet but knew better than to provoke an unnecessary argument.

Tony peered over the rim of his glass. 'Do you have to?' he said. It was a question spoken more in resignation than outrage, a token protest made not so much to defend his wife as to appease her.

Ruby had the gall to look affronted. 'Well, it's a sorry state of affairs when I can't even show concern for my poor son's widow without being criticised for it.'

'I wasn't—'

'Really,' Jo said. 'There's nothing wrong with me. I'm absolutely fine.'

But Ruby swept her response aside. 'I mean, *someone* has to take an interest.' As if the weight of this troublesome responsibility had fallen somewhat unfairly to her, she sighed and rolled her heavy shoulders. 'How are your parents, dear?'

'Very well, thank you.' Even as she answered, Jo felt herself flinch. It was over ten years since her parents had left Britain and they hadn't returned since, not even for Peter's funeral. She had once made a joke that they had gone to Sydney to get away from her. It had been one of those careless, slightly defensive quips that Ruby had instinctively picked up on and had been exploiting ever since. Ruby Strong's great skill lay in ferreting out the weaknesses of others; she would dig and dig until she hit pay dirt.

'No sign of a visit yet? I suppose it is a long way to travel.'

Jo stared at her. She saw a plump round face that in another woman might have been considered jolly but there was only malevolence and spite in these particular features.

'They're very busy.'

'They must be,' Ruby said. 'People do tend to lead such hectic lives these days. And jobs can be so demanding – all that stress and pressure. Remind me again of what your father does.'

Jo knew what was coming next and gritted her teeth. 'He's retired but—'

'Oh yes,' Ruby said, her sly mouth shifting into smugness. 'I'm sorry. Of course he is. How silly of me to forget. Still, I suppose there must be lots to do out there. Australia's such a big country, isn't it?' She paused. 'I'm sure they'll recall they have a daughter eventually.'

'Mother!' Tony objected, sitting forward. 'Do you have to be so—'

Ruby turned her head.

He slowly sank back into his seat.

How farcical, Jo thought, that she had once welcomed the idea of being part of this family. Peter had warned her but she hadn't listened. With no brothers or sisters of her own, her childhood had been a lonely affair, her parents so wrapped up in each other that they'd barely noticed she was there. She had been a late, unplanned and thoroughly unwanted addition to the loving but insular partnership that was Anne and Andrew Grey.

Jo turned to Carla. For all her disappointments, there were still some things she couldn't regret. Even if it was only by marriage, she was still an aunt. 'Where are the kids? Are they playing outside?'

Carla's eyes wouldn't quite meet hers. 'Er . . . they've got the sniffles, one of those summer colds. Lily's got a bit of a temperature so they're spending the day at my mum's.'

Jo's heart took a dive. Apart from the fact she'd been looking forward to seeing them, it was only the presence of Mitch and Lily that curbed the worst of Ruby's excesses. In their absence she wouldn't hold back.

'You mollycoddle them too much,' Ruby said. 'Children need to get out and about. It doesn't do to wrap them up in cotton wool.'

'I don't.'

'So why aren't they here?'

Tony leapt to his feet. So abrupt was the movement, so sudden, that an expectant hush fell over the room. Everyone stared up at him. Jo held her breath. There was something in his face, a tightness that she hadn't seen before. Perhaps, finally, he was going to challenge the tyranny of his mother's dictatorship.

But then his eyes glazed over. As if surprised to find himself the centre of attention, he frowned and raised his empty glass. 'I don't know about anyone else,' he said, 'but I need a drink.'

Chapter Nineteen

It was ten past two when they sat down to eat in the light and spacious dining room. These were nicer surroundings; even Ruby couldn't do anything to spoil the lovely view across the garden. However, she had other ways of inflicting misery on her hapless guests.

Jo gazed down at her lunch. The food was virtually inedible: the beef resembled leather, the potatoes were undercooked, the carrots and broccoli boiled to oblivion. But if she wished to avoid insulting her hostess's culinary skills she would have to try to clear her plate. Reaching for her glass, she took another gulp of wine.

She was seated to the right of Tony and opposite Mrs Dark. The latter was holding forth on the state of the government, a relentless monologue that required only the minimum of attention. While she gave the occasional nod, Jo was also able to listen in on another conversation. Ruby was busy lecturing her son on the basics of good business.

'How many times have I told you – profit and loss, profit and loss; it's not that hard to grasp.'

'No,' he muttered.

'So I don't understand why we need to have this discussion every month. Are you completely incapable of balancing the books?'

It was, of course, a rhetorical question. Tony lived beyond his means. Although the Hatton Garden shop provided him with a generous income, enough to keep his family in comfort, it was not enough to subsidise his less savoury habits: gambling, drinking and womanising were expensive pastimes.

Ruby shook her head and sighed. 'When I think of how hard your father worked . . .'

'I know,' Tony said.

'I sometimes wonder if you do.'

Strong's was an exclusive jewellery chain. It was once renowned for its originality and style but now catered almost entirely to the kind of mindless celebrities who had more money than taste. Its profits were vast but then so were Tony's outgoings. Mitchell, although he had bequeathed the flagship of his mini-empire to his younger son, had left all the other outlets to Ruby. She had immediately sold them on and stashed the money in the bank. If Tony wished to get the regular handouts he so desperately needed, he had no choice but to stay on the right side of her. She was more than capable of cutting him off and leaving her millions to the dog's home.

Jo glanced along the table. Ruby was wearing her familiar gloating expression. Her hair, a distinctive silver grey, was cut in a neat bob and the long lobes of her ears were adorned with a pair of bright sparkling diamonds. There was another much larger rock on her left hand. She might always dress in black but she never skimped on the accessories.

'Are you even listening to me?'

'Yes,' Tony said. 'I'm listening.'

'And so . . .'

'And so I'll be more careful in future.'

'How many times have I heard that before?'

Had she been a more responsible or even slightly nicer person, Ruby may have tried harder to curb her son's excesses. Instead she went through this regular charade of first berating him and then writing out a hefty cheque.

Jo wondered why she was still invited to these gatherings. It certainly wasn't out of affection; Ruby didn't even pretend to like her. More to the point, why did she continue to accept? It was partly, perhaps, out of a sense of duty – the woman was Peter's mother, after all – but also because of Carla and the kids.

'Even Josephine can manage to turn a profit,' Ruby said, as if this was proof-positive of just how incompetent he actually was.

Tony turned his head, grinned at Jo and winked. 'She's a very smart woman.'

Jo quickly looked away. 'Well, it's a much smaller place. We don't have the same overheads or—'

'Yes,' Ruby sighed. 'I don't think we need a lengthy speech on the subject. We're all aware of the details.'

That Jo had refused to sell the business still stuck in her craw. Ruby's had been Mitchell Strong's first shop but not an especially successful one. Back then, Kellston had been a rough, down-at-heel East End borough without any of the potential it now possessed; the locals just hadn't had the money to spend. How Mitchell had managed to up his game and move to Hatton Garden was a mystery but from that moment his fortunes had changed. Although Ruby's had continued to trade, it had never been a part of the highly acclaimed Strong's chain of stores. Like a poor and faintly embarrassing relative, it had been kept on purely because no one knew what else to do with it.

Tony, still smiling, refilled his glass. 'Oh, credit where credit's due, Mother. You can't deny that she's doing a great job. I'm sure Peter would be proud of her – carrying on the good work and all.'

Ruby put down her knife and fork and glared at him.

Jo's heart sank. Any discussion of this nature was bound to end badly. She didn't know what had caused the rift between her husband and his father, only that it hadn't been resolved before Mitchell's death. By then they hadn't been in contact for years. Peter had been living abroad and hadn't returned until after his father had been buried. His inheritance, he had told her, was his dad's idea of a final slap in the face – he had left him the only business that was firmly in the red. It was also, perhaps, why Peter had worked so hard to turn Ruby's around and to make it a success. Proving points seemed to run in the Strong genes.

'That shop,' Ruby said, 'has sentimental value. It should have stayed in the family.'

'Oh, come on, Mother. No one took the slightest bit of interest in it for years. And anyway, Jo is family.'

Ruby gave the kind of derogatory snort that suggested otherwise. 'Peter didn't expect her to run it. He would have wanted us to step in and relieve her of all that unnecessary worry.'

'And we offered to do just that, as I'm sure you remember.'

Jo could feel the heat burning in her cheeks. There was nothing worse than being talked about as though you weren't even in the room. 'It's not a worry,' she blurted out. 'I enjoy it. I like working there.' She could see the hateful look in Ruby's eyes but continued regardless. There was a limit to how much anyone could be pushed around and with everything that had happened over the past forty-eight hours, she'd just about reached her limit. 'And it has sentimental value for me too. Peter was my husband, after all. I think I know exactly what he would or wouldn't have wanted me to do with it.'

The shock of her speaking out stunned the table into momentary silence.

'Well,' Ruby said. 'I'm sure no one meant to cause offence.'

Jo felt like snorting herself but wisely resisted. Someone had to behave like an adult.

She'd said her piece and hopefully that would be enough to put an end to the matter.

Tony refilled his glass from the decanter. He took a drink, sat back and smiled. 'How delightful, all of us being together like this. I do so love these family occasions.'

The next twenty minutes seemed to drag on for ever. A few faltering attempts at conversation petered into nothing. There was only the thin scraping of plates interspersed with Ruby's plaintive sighs. Jo knew that she was waiting for an apology, waiting for her to back down, but it wasn't going to happen. For once, Jo Strong was going to hold her ground.

It was a relief when the meal came to an end. Ruby dabbed at her mouth with a napkin and looked at her son. 'I believe we have some business to attend to.' Then, slowly lumbering to her feet, she addressed the rest of them. 'I'm sure you can manage to entertain yourselves for a while.'

Tony pushed back his chair and stood up too. He still had a glass in his hand.

Ruby took it from him and put it back on the table. 'And Carla,' she said, 'if it isn't too much trouble, you could make some coffee and bring it through to the study.'

Jo was surprised by the request – wasn't that usually Mrs Dark's job? – but Carla, aware that a much-needed cheque was about to be signed, nodded obediently and followed them out.

No sooner had the door closed than Mrs Dark moved around the table and sat down beside her.

'How are you, dear?' she said softly, reaching out to place her warm hand over Jo's. 'Not too upset, I hope?'

Instinctively, she wanted to pull away but the long slender fingers were placed quite firmly over her own. To remove them would require the kind of effort that would appear both rude and ungainly. 'Not upset at all. Why should I be?'

'I sense . . .' Mrs Dark hesitated. 'Your aura . . . you're troubled. You have a lot on your mind.'

'Haven't we all,' Jo said lightly.

'Indeed,' she agreed. 'But so many responsibilities for

you, so many pressures – I see storm clouds gathering. There's been a change. Yes, I definitely sense a change. There's confusion about who to trust. You have difficult choices to make but you mustn't let your heart rule your head. The past flows into the future and—' She suddenly stopped and tilted up her face as if she was listening to someone. She nodded and looked back at Jo. 'It may be time to let go, to move on and make a fresh start.'

Jo stared at her, incredulous.

Mrs Dark's eyes flickered and half closed. 'The spirits are with us. Would you like me to—'

'No!' Jo said sharply. 'Please don't.' She had already heard more than enough. It was patently clear that Ruby had set up this whole charade. Even now she wasn't giving up. The old witch would try anything to get her to sell the shop. 'Please don't bother them. I'm sure they have better things to do with their Sunday afternoons.'

Mrs Dark's eyes opened fully again and her scarlet lips widened into a smile. 'There's no need to be afraid, dear. I frequently do readings for Mrs Strong. She finds them very comforting. We often receive messages from her husband.'

'Even so,' Jo said. She thought it more likely that Ruby was sending messages rather than receiving them. Even in death Mitchell would have no escape from her constant interference and demands.

'I can feel them pressing in around us. They wish to talk.'

With her free hand Jo reached for her glass and took a swig of wine. She wasn't drunk yet but she was working on it.

'It's something to do with gold.'

Jo tried not to groan. Next she'd be spouting some nonsense about journeys across the sea and tall, dark, handsome strangers. Although Jo couldn't entirely dismiss the possibility of psychic powers – she wanted to believe in an afterlife – she was naturally suspicious of any medium who chose to spend a disproportionate amount of time in the company of rich old ladies. Not that Ruby Strong could ever be described as vulnerable; she was more than capable of taking care of herself. Anyone trying to fleece her would have their work cut out.

'No, it's not gold, it's silver. Why do they keep saying silver?'

That caught Jo's attention. She turned her head. 'What?'

'There's fear there. I can feel it. The spirits are warning me of danger.' There was a long pause. 'He has no pity. He brings only death and destruction.'

Although Jo wanted to laugh, she couldn't. The hairs on the back of her neck were standing on end. 'Who are you talking about?'

'He's watching, watching all the time.'

'Who?' Jo urged.

'He's never far away.'

She waited, her heart starting to race. But there was nothing more. 'Mrs Dark?'

For a moment her fingers tightened around Jo's before she gave a faint shudder, let go of her hand and slumped back in her chair.

Chapter Twenty

It hadn't taken Marty long to track him down; junkies were creatures of habit and dogs always returned to their own vomit. Quietly, he crossed the room. Lying prostrate on an old worn sofa, Ritchie was fast asleep with one arm raised above his head. He was snoring softly. Marty reached out a foot and gently nudged his ribs with the toe of his shoe. The kid twitched and shifted a little. The snoring stopped but he didn't wake up.

Marty had keys to all the rooms. The dilapidated house in Clapton, one of Delaney's many properties, was split into eight small bedsits. He looked around, trying not to breathe too deeply. How anyone could live like this was beyond him. It was almost dark but even through the gloom he could see it was a pit. Strewn with dirty clothes, empty bottles and takeaway pizza cartons, it clearly hadn't been cleaned for months. On the coffee table were three chipped mugs, all with a greeny-blue mould floating in their liquid dregs. An ashtray had tumbled on to the carpet. The stink rose up to invade his nostrils.

Leaning over, he ran the back of his hand across the sleeping boy's face. The contrast between Ritchie and his surroundings was extreme. Tall, slim and blond, he was almost disgracefully beautiful. Marty smiled. He had the kind of youthful good looks that had they been allied with any semblance of intelligence could have been lethal. Fortunately, the gods – perhaps momentarily distracted by the vision they'd created – had forgotten to insert a brain.

He sighed. It was almost a crime to destroy something so perfect.

He continued to stare until he noticed the time. It was nine-thirty in the evening. He'd better get a move on before Vic started hassling him again. Grabbing Naylor by the shoulder, he shook him hard. 'Ritchie!'

'Ugh?'

'Wake up!'

'What?' As his blue eyes opened and he saw a face looming over him, he had a moment of panic. Fear distorted his pretty features. His jaw dropped and his mouth twisted in alarm. A small choked noise escaped from his throat. His arms flailed and he jumped away, but in doing so found himself trapped against the back of the sofa.

'It's only me,' Marty said soothingly.

An unexpected visit from Marty Gull would have increased the terror in a smarter person but Ritchie instantly relaxed and rubbed his bloodshot eyes. He let out a long breath. 'Shit, man. What are you doing? What are you doing here?'

'Got a job for you.'

'Huh? What time is it?'

Marty figured that he'd probably been wasted since getting paid on Friday. 'Too early to be asleep.'

Slowly Ritchie swung his legs over the side of the sofa, stretched out his arms and yawned. He was wearing tight black jeans and a crumpled white T-shirt. 'It's Sunday,' he protested.

'What are you,' Marty laughed, 'some fucking God-botherer? Come on, shift your ass. I'll make it worth your while.'

'What sort of job?'

'Just a little breaking and entering. Nothing too strenuous. We'll be in and out in ten minutes.'

'I dunno. I'm knackered, man. I'm not in the mood.'

Marty took a step back and glowered at him.

Ritchie, for all his stupidity, quickly got the message. He nodded. 'Okay, okay, but I need to take a shower.'

'Yeah, you do. You smell like a pig. But it'll have to wait. We have to make a move – and now!'

Ritchie was still looking dazed as they drove into Stack Street. His blond head lolled against the window. 'I'm hungry,' he whined. 'Can't we get something to eat?'

'Sure,' Marty said. 'Once we're done. We'll grab a takeaway, anything you like.'

'Chinese. I fancy a Chinese.'

'Whatever.' Marty peered to the left and right. There were plenty of parked cars but no sign of Parry or Devlin. That was good. It was their job to be here, watching the flat, but it was over twenty minutes now since Vic had got the call. Marty had persuaded a lowlife he knew, another junkie in need of a fix, to give Delaney a bell and tip him off that Miller had been spotted at King's Cross.

He'd been counting on the fact that Vic would send the

two big guys. The station wasn't far and there wasn't much purpose to them being here if Miller wasn't coming back.

Marty found a space, pulled in and killed the engine. He looked over at the house. It was a small semi-detached conversion and all the lights were out. The house next door was in darkness too. Bloody perfect! Not that he'd expected anything less. He'd had that feeling in his guts all day, the knowledge that nothing could go wrong. The incredible Marty Gull was on a roll.

'Stay put. I'll only be a minute.'

Marty climbed out of the van and walked around to the side. Sliding open the door, he jumped inside, took off his jacket and folded it neatly. This was likely to get messy and he wasn't going to take the chance of ruining over three hundred quid's worth of Italian soft black leather. He pulled on a pair of grubby off-white overalls and shoved a cap on his head. Then he picked up the holdall, carefully closed the door and strolled back round to the passenger seat. 'Ready?'

Ritchie nodded but didn't move. He was so out of it that he didn't even notice that Marty had changed his clothes. 'So what's the deal, man?'

'I just need someone to watch my back. You can do that, can't you?'

'Whose place did you say it was?'

'I didn't – and it's none of your business. Just get out of the frigging van.'

'Okay,' he said sulkily. 'I was only asking.'

Marty pulled the cap down over his eyes as they walked across the road. It was dark enough now for his features to be hidden – there was only the thin orangey glow from the streetlamps – but better to be safe than sorry. A short path led up to the house. Miller's flat was on the ground floor. It had its own entrance and there was even a convenient brick porch to hide them from any prying eyes. He smiled as he stepped inside. The guy really should take more care over his security.

Ritchie shuffled in behind him.

Marty put down the holdall and listened. What he was about to do would create some noise but hopefully not enough to alert anyone to a break-in. He crouched down and unzipped the bag. He took out two pairs of gloves and shoved a pair at Ritchie.

'Put these on. We don't want any prints.'

Marty slipped on his own gloves before feeling for the torch. He switched it on. 'Here, shine this on the door.' He took out the crowbar and stood up. If there'd been more time he'd have got Ritchie to do it; he didn't want the job to appear too professional, but that could take for ever. Instead he deliberately made a few false attempts, badly splintering the wood, before finally forcing it open.

Inside, there was a short hallway. Marty used the torch to negotiate his way to the living room. He pulled the curtains across the wide bay window and turned on a lamp. He squinted for a second until his eyes adjusted to the light. He quickly looked around. The place was clean and tidy. It had the kind of furnishings that came with a particular type of rented property – not too cheap, not too fancy. The carpets and curtains were beige. There was a tan sofa and a matching chair. Everything was neutral, bland and durable.

'What are we after?' Ritchie whispered.

'Shut it! *You're* not after anything. Just stay by the door and keep your fucking eyes and ears open.'

Ritchie pulled a face but retreated back into the hall.

Marty went into the kitchen. A slim pine table was set against the wall. On it was a well-thumbed London A-Z, a pepper mill and an electricity bill made out to Mr G. Miller. He picked up the book and flicked through it. There was nothing useful, no notes or markers, not even a clue to suggest where Miller might be hiding out. He threw it back on the table.

In a cupboard above the sink was tea and coffee, an unopened pack of pasta and a few assorted tins. Marty opened the fridge. Apart from a tub of margarine, it was empty. In a drawer he found the usual supply of cutlery along with a couple of decent-sized chopping knives. He lifted the larger one out and examined the blade. It was the kind of weapon a man might pick up if he was taken by surprise – a few frantic stabs to defend himself from a violent intruder? He thought about it before slowly putting it down again. It was never a good idea to change your plans at the last minute.

He went back into the living room, checked that Ritchie was still awake and walked through to the bedroom. The double bed was neatly covered with a grey striped duvet. There was no sign that anyone had slept in it recently. In the wardrobe there were two smart suits and half a dozen shirts. In the drawer beneath he found underwear and socks, a pair of jeans and a few T-shirts.

Above the wardrobe was a single suitcase. Miller was plainly a man who travelled light. He pulled it down and opened it. There was nothing inside. He threw it across the floor. Next, he searched the bedside cabinet. There was nothing there either: no papers, no cheque book, no passport. He must have the important stuff stashed somewhere else. Never mind. Although those things could have been useful, it wasn't what he was here for.

Marty sat down on the bed and looked at his watch. It was a pity he was so short on time. What he had to do next should be savoured, not rushed. He thought back to Friday. It had gone like clockwork. Susan had sent in the tart to keep Miller occupied and he'd dropped off Ritchie. In less than fifteen minutes, after a heavily spiked drink, Ritchie had dragged Silver out of the hotel and passed her into the loving care of yours truly. By then she had barely been able to stand.

For all that, perhaps, Ritchie should be congratulated – he'd done what he'd been paid for – but the bastard hadn't even asked about her since. And that wasn't right, was it? Marty frowned. Silver, for all her sluttish aspirations, still deserved *some* respect.

He went to the door and hissed. 'Ritchie!'

'Yeah?'

'Shift the TV into the hall.'

Ritchie's mouth broke into a grin. He was always up for a spot of thieving. 'Nice bit of kit, this,' he said, bending to pull the plug out. 'Should be worth a few quid.'

Marty stood by the sofa, watching as he disconnected the aerial. This had to look right – as if Miller had come back unexpectedly and caught him in the act. And any man, at least any man with an inch of pride, would have had a go.

As Ritchie stood up with the flat screen in his arms, Marty swiftly moved forward, jabbed with his fist and caught him hard on the jaw. The boy was still grinning as his chin snapped back; he gave a grunt, dropped the TV and crumpled to the ground.

Marty pounced, pinning him down with his knees. Surprised by what had happened, and still too groggy to realise what it meant, Ritchie's blue eyes widened. He didn't struggle. He barely moved. He seemed more confused than anything else. Marty punched him again, this time breaking his nose. A stream of blood flowed out and slid between his lips. Marty stared at him. There was something touching about his bruised and battered face, something curiously beautiful. He took a picture in his head, a snapshot he would be able to conjure up later. There was still time to change his mind but he wouldn't. He couldn't.

In a series of fast, practised movements, Marty grabbed his shoulders, flipped him over, and with his left hand on the back of his neck, pressed his face into the carpet. He took one last glance at his pretty blond head before leaning back to pick up the crowbar. He brought it down with speed and accuracy. There was a satisfying crunch as the iron hit the skull, splitting it open as easily as an egg. A dramatic explosion of blood, tissue, skin and brains flew up into the air and spilled across the carpet.

It was all over in a couple of seconds. Finished. Done with. A dark red stain began to spread and then . . .

And then there was only silence.

It always got to him. Marty placed his left palm on the boy's back. He felt the warmth still emanating from the flesh. He gave a soft groan and ran his hand along his spine. He stroked the sharp shoulder blades and coiled the wet scarlet hair between his fingers. Should he turn him over? He decided not.

Laying the bloodied crowbar down, he leaned back and listened. It was not the neighbours he was listening for, not any indication that someone might have overheard, but that other sound – that thin whisper as the soul departed. It could take a minute, maybe two. He had heard it first when his father had died . . . and so many times since.

Marty had respect for death. No life should be taken easily. He held his breath. Slowly his lips widened into a smile. There it was!

He got up, turned off the light, pulled aside the curtains and opened the window. The soul needed an exit, an escape route. There was, of course, the broken front door but if Ritchie's poor soul was as stupid as the rest of him, it might take a wrong turning in the hall and be trapped in the flat for ever.

Marty stood for a while, breathing in the evening air. Eventually he felt a cool breeze brush his cheek. When he turned again, he saw only a corpse. There was no emotion, no lingering sentiment attached to it. Ritchie was gone. All that remained was a useless lump of skin and bone.

As soon as he was in the car, he would get one of the tarts he knew to call the filth and report a disturbance. There'd be a nice surprise waiting for them when they arrived. Marty smiled. He was well pleased with himself. Not only had he got rid of Naylor but he'd also landed Miller in the shit – with a murdered boy in his flat, he'd have more important things to worry about than the whereabouts of Delaney's wayward daughter.

But he couldn't afford to dwell on his brilliance. He had a job to finish. Leaning over the body, he removed a wallet from the back pocket. There was ninety quid inside. He took the whole lot. It wasn't as if Ritchie would need it and the break-in had to look authentic – there weren't many junkies roaming the streets with this kind of cash on them. He slid the wallet back and gave Ritchie a friendly pat on the butt.

'Thanks, mate.'

Next, he wiped his prints off the handles of the holdall. He shoved a few items into the bag: the DVD player, a small pile of DVDs and CDs, and a half-full bottle of whisky. In the bedroom he overturned the mattress, pulled out the drawers and scattered Miller's clothes. He emptied out the drawers in the kitchen too, kicking the cutlery across the floor.

In the bathroom cupboard he found a bottle of aspirin, a razor and some shaving gel. He opened the bottle and dropped the contents in the basin. On his way out, he paused to look in the mirror. He ran his fingers through his hair and examined his face. Did he look any different? He thought there was a faint glow to his cheeks, a heightening of colour. His eyes seemed a little brighter too.

Did he feel bad about what he'd done? Not bad exactly but slightly regretful. Ritchie, for all his faults, hadn't been entirely devoid of charm. He would miss him . . . for a while. Still, if it hadn't been this it would have been jail; losers like Ritchie always ended up behind bars eventually.

And a boy with his looks wouldn't last five minutes. There would always be a Delaney ready to take advantage. At least he had spared him that.

Marty stared into the mirror and nodded. Yeah, all things considered, he had done Ritchie Naylor one almighty favour.

Chapter Twenty-one

It was early, only a few minutes past seven, but after another restless night Jo had decided there were more useful things she could be doing than lying in bed and gazing at the ceiling. She opened the door of Ruby's and carefully locked it again behind her – Kellston, for all its gentrification, still had its fair share of crime – and went through to the kitchen.

She heard the noise, the sound of running water, only a fraction of a second before she stepped into the room. By then it was too late to retreat. Her eyes widened as she became aware of someone standing by the sink. As the figure turned, her hand leapt to her chest and she stifled a scream. 'God, Jacob, what are you doing here?'

He looked almost as surprised as she was.

Jo took a moment to regain her breath. 'Sorry, I didn't mean . . . I just didn't think you'd be in yet.'

'I usually have my breakfast here.' He paused, frowning. 'You don't mind, do you? I like to make an early start.'

Jo shook her head. 'Of course not.'

'I didn't mean to startle you.'

'You didn't.' And then, realising that she still had her hand raised to her chest, she laughed. 'Well, only a bit.'

'Would you care for a coffee? I've just made a pot.'

'Thanks.'

She pulled out a chair and watched as he moved spryly around the kitchen. Despite working alongside him for the past two years, it occurred to her how little she actually knew of Jacob's life. She was aware that he lived in a flat nearby and that he was widowed. Beyond that, her knowledge was decidedly sketchy. And that, she realised, was yet another item to add to her list of guilty worries.

'I couldn't sleep,' she said.

'You wait until you're my age; sleep becomes a distant memory. I count myself lucky if I manage a few hours.' He looked over his shoulder and smiled. 'But you do look tired. Has something happened?'

'No,' she lied. She still had Mrs Dark's words revolving in her head, that weird disturbing stuff about Silver. And she'd heard nothing from Miller since he'd left on Saturday morning. All that 'no news is good news' guff was so utterly misleading – all silence did was stress you out even more.

'I may be getting on, Jo, but I am a good listener. If you have troubles, if there's something on your mind . . .'

She hadn't intended to mention it to anyone but his kindness and her fatigue combined to lower her usual reserve. The words jumped out before she could prevent them. 'Do you believe in psychics?'

'Absolutely not,' he said without a second's hesitation.

'Why not?'

His dark eyes glinted with humour. 'You think people can see into the future?'

'I don't know. Are *you* sure they can't?'

'No,' he said. He brought over two mugs, placed them on the table, and sat down beside her. His expression grew more serious. 'The older I get, the less sure I am of anything. But, if you believe in all that, you also have to believe that life is predestined, laid out, a path we have no choice but to follow. And if that is the truth, then—' He raised his shoulders in a small dismissive shrug. 'What's the point of it? We'd just be puppets going through the motions.'

Jo nodded. 'I suppose.'

'Is this about Peter?'

'No,' she said. And then, realising that she had to provide a rational explanation for the original query, quickly added: 'Not exactly. I had lunch at Ruby's yesterday.'

'Ah,' he sighed, as if that explained everything.

Jo sipped her coffee. It was good, freshly ground, and it smelled like heaven. She sank her face into the steam. Now that he had mentioned Peter, she was reminded of another niggling question that had never been adequately answered. 'Do you know why they fell out, Peter and his father?'

'Didn't he tell you?'

'Some of it,' she said. 'I know that Mitchell wasn't happy when Peter decided to leave the business but I got the impression that wasn't the whole story. I mean, Peter was abroad for years and in all that time they didn't talk, never mind see each other. He didn't even come back for the funeral.'

Jacob shrugged his shoulders again. 'Fathers and sons – it can be complicated. The two of them never got on, even when Peter was a child. Mitchell always pushed too hard; he was proud of his son but he didn't understand him.'

Jo instantly recalled Gabe Miller claiming exactly the same thing about Delaney and his daughter. 'But was that it?' she said. 'Was it just a disagreement that got out of hand?'

He peered at her over the rim of his mug. 'What did that lunatic psychic say to you?'

She smiled, alert at the same time to the deliberate evasion. She suspected he knew more than he was letting on. 'Oh, nothing really. It wasn't specifically to do with Peter. She was talking about all kinds of things. I just got to thinking and—'

'What's in the past can't be changed. Sometimes, no matter how hard it may seem, we just have to let go.'

Jo nodded. She might have pursued it if she hadn't been so tired. A small dull throb was beating in her temples. It was Monday, the start of a new week and she needed to get herself together. Suddenly, remembering a call she'd taken late on Saturday from an art student eager to show off her designs, she said: 'Remind me to talk to Deborah.'

'Deborah?' he repeated sharply. 'What would she know about it?'

Jo stared at him. Until now she'd thought exactly nothing, but his response told her otherwise. Did she dare to ask? Her heart was sinking as she took a quick breath. 'Well, they were close, weren't they?'

His cheeks burned bright red before he smartly looked away.

'Jacob?'

He didn't reply. He didn't need to. He'd already confirmed her worst fears.

Chapter Twenty-two

Susan stared at the phone and put it down. Calling Jo was risky, although no more risky perhaps than letting things lie. What if Marty Gull was right and Gabe *was* with her? It was unlikely but not impossible. They had got into the cab together. That was a worry. What had he told her? And, more to the point, what had she told him? If the two of them had got talking, it wouldn't have taken him long to have realised who 'Laura James' was, and once he'd done that . . .

Susan shook her head. She'd hardly slept for the last three nights and it was all too easy to get paranoid, to start inventing problems where none existed. Chances were that he had simply dropped her off and was miles away by now; no sensible man would hang around when Delaney was after his blood.

'No *sensible* man,' she repeated aloud.

Whether that could ever be applied to Gabe Miller was debatable. He was impossible to predict. She felt that small but familiar stab in her chest. They could have made a good team, the perfect partnership, if only . . . but pondering on *if onlys* was a pointless exercise, a waste of time and energy. What was past was past. She had to focus on the future.

Susan crossed the room and gazed out through the window. It was a warm but slightly hazy morning as if the sun was shining through a filter. She checked her watch. It was just after nine. Delaney should have got the letter by now, the letter that had been sent by special delivery. She had typed it herself. It was a demand as harsh and brutal as he was: half a million quid in exchange for his daughter being returned in one piece, three days to get the cash together or the only way Silver would be coming home was in a series of small and bloody parcels.

Susan didn't care about the nastiness of it. Why should she? He deserved nothing less. Marty, if he was doing his job, should already be there with him, ready to fuel his anxieties and to stamp on any inconvenient notions of getting the Law involved. Not that Delaney was ever likely to go down that path – with the kind of business he was in, he couldn't afford to have the cops sniffing round – but there was no accounting for those instinctive knee-jerk reactions.

Feeling restless, she turned and began to pace up and down the room. She was starting to feel stir-crazy. She hated being trapped in the house, almost as much a prisoner as Silver was, but it was too risky to go out. It would be just her luck to bump straight into Jo. Still, it wasn't for long, a week at the most. Just long enough to cause Vic Delaney the maximum of pain and worry before they finally relieved him of his cash.

With nothing else to do, she walked into the kitchen, opened the door to the cellar and went down to check on her unhappy little friend.

The girl was sitting on the mattress, reading a magazine.

As well as the dim overhead bulb, which always stayed on, there was a lamp she could turn on and off herself. On hearing the grille being opened, Silver quickly raised her face. 'Is that you?'

'Sure, it's me.'

Immediately, Silver relaxed and began her plaintive whining. 'Why are you doing this? Why can't you let me go? Why can't—'

'How often do you need telling?' Susan wasn't in the mood. If she'd answered the question once, she'd answered it a hundred times. 'It's a simple business transaction. Once your daddy pays up you'll be out of here.'

'But what if he doesn't?'

'What do you think?'

'You . . . you're going to . . .' Silver hesitated. Her eyes widened as she stared towards the grille. 'You're going to kill me?'

Susan groaned. 'I'll kill you right now if you don't stop whining.'

Silver's upper lip quivered and she shifted back against the wall.

Susan felt a pang of remorse. It hadn't been her intention to terrify her. None of this was the kid's fault; she was only a means to an end. 'Look, I've already told you – just keep quiet, behave, and you'll have nothing to worry about. No one's going to hurt you. I give you my word.'

'Is he coming back?'

'Who?'

'*Him.* The other one. You know who I mean.'

Susan stared at her, wondering what Marty had said or

done when he'd been down here on Saturday night. She should never have left him alone with her.

'He's scary,' Silver said. 'I don't like him.'

Well, that was something they had in common. 'It's just me,' she said softly. 'There's no one else here. Do you need anything? Are you hungry?'

'No.'

'Okay.' Susan put her hand up to close the grille.

'Don't go!'

'I have to. I've got things to do.'

'Just five minutes. *Please.* Stay and talk to me.'

'About what?'

'Anything,' Silver said. She wrapped her arms around her knees and looked up pleadingly. 'I'm scared. I don't like being alone.'

Susan thought about all the times *she* hadn't liked being alone. She should have felt some sympathy but instead all she experienced was a surge of irritation: a few days locked in a cellar was nothing compared to the years of hell she'd had to endure. The princess had a lot to learn. *You'll get used to it,* she almost retorted but didn't. Keeping Silver calm, no matter what the provocation, had to be her main priority. 'You'll be fine.'

'Are you going to stay?'

'I've got things to do.'

'Please,' Silver begged again. 'Don't go, please don't go.'

Susan raised her eyes to the ceiling. She had no desire to talk to her but if she went back upstairs she'd just be pacing the rooms again, looking at her watch and counting off the hours. Of course there was that phone call she'd thought about making, but it could wait. Jo would be at work by now, not the best time to catch her.

'Just a few minutes,' Silver pleaded.

'All right, okay.' Susan leaned her head against the bars. Perhaps it wouldn't do any harm to chat for a while. Marty wouldn't like it – he'd given her express instructions not to speak any more than she had to – but what he didn't know he wouldn't grieve over.

Chapter Twenty-three

Jo was scrutinising Deborah Hayes from behind the counter. She'd been watching her, on and off, for most of the day. Now, once again, she was going through that typically female process of weighing up her looks and trying to decide where she rated in the attractiveness stakes. Being ten years younger, Jo had the advantage of age, but Deborah won hands down when it came to sophistication: tall, slim and impeccably dressed, she was the epitome of elegance.

Aware that she was staring, Jo quickly looked away. Even if Deborah had slept with him, did it matter? Not so long as it had stopped before they'd got married. But after Jacob's reaction, she wasn't sure that it had. And she was starting to remember those all-too frequent evenings when Peter had been late home, when he'd claimed he had meetings, when . . .

Of course the simple solution would be to take her aside and ask her directly but she couldn't. She had the British disease, a congenital fear of embarrassment. Once said, it couldn't be unsaid, and Deborah was hardly likely to confess to anything. And if she was wrong or, even worse, if she was right, then how could they ever work together again?

Jo's gaze swivelled back to Deborah. She looked her up and down again. Love, as she knew, wasn't rooted in appearance; that was just the superficial stuff, the lust, the initial attraction. It was the deeper connection that mattered.

Deborah was married and had a couple of kids. Her husband, Tom, came into the shop from time to time, a smart grey-haired man with a pleasant easy manner. Jo had made him a coffee only last week and they had stood and chatted in the kitchen. Was it possible that they had both been cheated on?

Jo turned, suddenly aware that she was being watched too.

'Why don't you go home?' Jacob said.

'It's only two o'clock.'

'Go home,' he said again, this time more insistently. 'We're not busy. I'll lock up. Get some rest, catch up on some sleep.'

What he was really saying, she thought, was *Don't do anything you may regret later.*

If she'd been braver, she might have taken him aside and pushed him for an answer. But then this wasn't just to do with courage, it was about common decency too. She had no right to put him in such an awkward position.

The afternoon was hot and sunny but Jo was barely aware of it. Walking slowly across the Green, she was thinking back to when Peter had died. It had been during the first week in July, a close, humid day when the air was heavy and thunder rumbled softly in the distance. He had told her in the morning that he was going to be late, that he had some work to catch up on, and she hadn't bothered to enquire further. Why should she? She'd had no reason to distrust him.

It had been around seven-thirty when the speeding car had knocked him down. He had been across the other side of Kellston, a twenty-minute walk from Ruby's, in a quiet residential street called Fairlea Avenue. The car hadn't stopped. There were no witnesses, no descriptions of the vehicle, but a few of the residents had heard the impact. One of them had called an ambulance but it was too late: Peter was already dead.

Jo had never found out what he was doing there. Perhaps he had just fancied a stroll, an opportunity to stretch his legs after a long day in the shop. Or perhaps he had gone to meet someone. She tried to block out her misgivings – she didn't want her memories sullied with any ugly suspicions – but her brain refused to co-operate.

She had believed the police when they'd put it down to a hit-and-run. A stolen car, they assumed, which was why the driver hadn't stopped. An unfortunate case of being in the wrong place at the wrong time. It was only later, when the first anonymous letter arrived, that she'd begun to have her doubts.

But why should anyone want to kill him? It didn't make sense. Unless it had been a crime of passion. Maybe he had finished his affair with Deborah or threatened to tell her husband and in a moment of madness, of rage, she had . . . Jo took a deep breath and instantly dismissed the theory. It was ridiculous! She might not like Deborah Hayes but she was an unlikely murderess.

So could it have been someone else, another woman? She'd thought they were good together but Peter hadn't been the easiest man to read. He had told her he was happy but that wasn't necessarily the same thing as *being* happy. And they had married so quickly, only six months after meeting. Perhaps he had been repenting in a less than leisurely fashion.

Jo's hands clenched in her pockets and guilty tears rose to her eyes. What was she thinking? Peter had never given her a reason to doubt him and now, two years after his death, she was busily accusing him of adultery without a single shred of evidence. It was wrong, shameful. He deserved better.

Jo passed through the gate and crossed over Barley Road. She was almost home when she saw Constance Kearns coming towards her. As they grew closer, she tried to decide whether she should mention Leo, apologise for what had happened on Friday night, but then wondered if she even knew about the incident and if she didn't . . . By the time she had considered all the options, Constance had already passed by with her usual nod and small tight smile.

Relieved, Jo dug her keys out of her bag and walked up the drive. She had enough on her mind without having to explain why Miller had launched an attack on her son. She had just opened the door when she heard the approaching footsteps. Glancing over her shoulder, she gasped. Gabe Miller was standing right behind her. As if just by thinking about him she had managed to conjure him up, Jo blinked her eyes twice and frowned.

'What are you doing here?'

'It's good to see you too.'

He looked rough, as if he hadn't washed or shaved since she had last seen him. She grasped her keys tightly, feeling the hard edges dig into the soft flesh of her palms. 'You haven't answered my question.'

'I thought you might have heard.'

Jo knew it was bad news. Her immediate thought was of the girl. 'Please don't tell me she's—'

'It's not Silver,' he said.

She relaxed a little. 'Then—'

'It's Ritchie Naylor, the boy she was seeing. He's . . . he's been . . . look, can we go inside? I really don't want to have this conversation here.'

Jo didn't want to have it at all. And she didn't want him in the flat. But in this matter, as in so many others, what she did or didn't want was apparently irrelevant. Without waiting for a reply, he had already moved past her and was climbing up the stairs.

Chapter Twenty-four

As Jo reluctantly followed him up, she noticed he was dressed in the same clothes he'd been wearing on Friday. His jacket was creased and the hems of his trousers were lined with a fine, grey film of dust. He stank of stale cigarette smoke and sweat.

'What's happened?'

'I thought you might have heard,' he said again.

'If I had, I wouldn't be asking.'

Miller walked into the living room and sat down on the sofa. Hunching forward, he put his head in his hands. 'He's dead. Ritchie's dead.'

Even though she'd been expecting it – she had known from his expression that it was going to be serious – she still felt a jolt of shock. Jo swallowed hard. 'So what was it, some kind of overdose? It was drugs, right? You said he was a junkie. You said—'

'No.'

Still hoping, against all the odds, that the death might have been accidental, she opened her mouth to ask but the question wouldn't come. Her throat was tight and dry.

'Yeah,' he said, looking up. 'He was murdered – battered to death with a crowbar.'

'Jesus,' she said. It emerged as no more than a whisper. Feeling her legs start to shake, she stumbled over to a chair.

'And there's worse.'

She curled up, wrapping her arms around her knees. She wasn't sure how much worse it could get.

No sooner had she sat down than Miller jumped up and walked over to the window. He placed his hands against the glass and gazed out over the Green. She heard him take a few deep breaths. When he turned, his face was grey and twisted. 'I'm in trouble, Jo. They found him at my flat.'

'What?'

'Ritchie was killed in my flat.'

'But how could he—' As the logical conclusion sank in, she shrank back against the chair. Her eyes widened with alarm.

Miller gave a low groan. 'Oh, *please*! I wouldn't. I couldn't. I haven't been near the place. Why would I with Delaney's goons still searching for me? A mate of mine heard it on the news and—' He paused, his dark eyes boring into her. 'Please don't say you think it was me.'

'I don't,' she said quickly.

'You believe me?'

She nodded. 'Of course I do.' In truth, she wasn't sure what to believe. And until she'd made up her mind, the wisest course of action was to go along with him.

'Good. Only I need somewhere to stay for a few days.'

Her stomach lurched. Reserving judgement was one thing, harbouring a possible killer quite another. 'No, you can't. I'm sorry but . . .' Unable to meet his eyes, she looked desperately around the room. Her gaze alighted on the picture of Peter. 'My husband will be back soon and—'

'And what?' he said.

'How am I supposed to explain what you're doing here?'

'You could tell him you picked me up in a bar.'

Jo stared at him. 'Don't be ridiculous.'

He crossed the room and stood in front of her. 'Come on,' he said. 'We both know there's no one coming back. There's no one living here but you.'

'That's not . . .' she began, but didn't have the heart to continue. He must have figured it out. One sneaky look in the bathroom cabinet last time he was here would have been enough to reveal her solitary status.

'I need your help. All I'm asking for is a few days. You must see what's going on. I've been framed, Jo. I've been set up. Someone wants me out of the way.'

'Then go to the police.'

'I can't.'

'You *can*,' she urged. 'You have to. There's forensics and stuff. There's DNA. They can do tests. They'll prove it wasn't you.'

'And how long do you reckon that's going to take?' He turned and strode back to the window. 'Anyway, I can't take the chance. Not right now. The forensics could be inconclusive and the circumstantial evidence all points to me – it was my damn flat he was murdered in.'

'But if you tell them about Silver, about Delaney—'

'No, I need to be out here looking for Susan, not stuck down the cop shop trying to prove my innocence.'

'Well, what about an alibi?' Her voice grew more cautious. 'You do have an alibi for when he was killed, don't you?'

'Yes,' he said. He hesitated. 'No, not really. I've spent the last couple of nights kipping in a car I borrowed. I couldn't risk going back to the Lumière and picking up my own. Delaney's men would be crawling all over the place.' He put his head in his hands and groaned. 'Shit, the hotel's probably had it towed by now.'

Jo gave a sigh. 'I think you've got more important things to be worrying about than that.'

'Yeah,' he agreed, looking up again. 'You're right. Anyway, after I left here, I went over to Dalston, picked up a pal's Mondeo, and then spent the rest of the weekend driving around Kellston looking for anything that might give me a clue as to where Susan might be. It doesn't help much, does it? To be honest, I don't even know exactly when Ritchie was killed.'

Jo shook her head. As far as alibis went, it wasn't the most convincing she'd ever heard, but it was its lack of substance that somehow gave it the ring of truth. Perversely, she'd have been less inclined to trust him if he'd come up with a cast-iron alibi. But that didn't mean that she was sure of his innocence. She racked her brains, trying to think of other reasons why he should be at the police station rather than holed up in Barley Road. Then something occurred to her. 'What about your clothes?' she said excitedly. 'You're wearing the same things you were on Friday. If you'd killed him, there'd be evidence, blood stains, wouldn't there? You can't bludgeon someone to death without . . .'

'Good theory,' he said, 'but how am I supposed to prove they're the same clothes?'

He had a point. Still, at least the idea had the useful effect of making *her* feel a little better. His suit was crumpled and his shirt wasn't quite as white as when she'd last seen him but there wasn't a blood spot in sight. She felt her body relax. Perhaps he was being straight with her.

'So what are you thinking?' she said.

'If I'm right, whoever's working with Susan was responsible for Ritchie's death. The kid must have been involved in some way and was killed to shut him up. Doing it at my flat had the advantage of taking me out of the picture too.'

Jo's heart flipped over. 'But you swore Silver was safe, that no one would hurt her. If this guy, this *maniac*, has her, then God knows what he's going to do next. You can't let this carry on. You have to go to the police.'

He shook his head. 'I don't think so. If you're really worried about the girl, help me find her.'

'I can't. I mean, I want to but I don't see how I can.'

'She's round here, somewhere,' he said. 'I'm sure of it.'

'Kellston's a big place. We could be searching for ever.'

'I've got a few ideas but . . .' He bent his head and sniffed at his clothes. 'Look, would you mind if I took a shower first and got cleaned up? I must smell like a skunk.'

Jo shrugged. It was hardly polite to agree but she couldn't deny it either. And if he was locked in the bathroom, he wouldn't be out here. That was a definite plus. It would also give her the opportunity to think about what to do next. She could still call the police if she chose to.

'Help yourself,' she said. 'There are clean towels in the

cupboard.' Then she had another thought. 'Oh, and leave out your clothes; I can put them through the machine.'

'Thanks,' he said. 'I appreciate it.' He went to the bathroom, opened the door, looked back at her and grinned. 'And don't worry, I won't be offended if you check them for evidence. If I was you, I'd do the same. Better to be safe than sorry, huh?'

Jo blushed. 'That wasn't why . . .'

But he'd already closed the door.

She got up and retraced his steps to the window. The kids were out of school, milling around on the grass. It was mainly boys but there were a few teenage girls too. She immediately thought of Silver. Jo wanted to do what was best for her but still wasn't sure what that was.

The bathroom door opened again and Miller deposited his clothes in a pile.

She approached them with caution. First she picked up his jacket and trousers – they would need to be dry cleaned – and, after a brief examination, laid them over the back of a chair. His black shoes were dusty but had no suspicious marks. She took longer to study his shirt, slowly turning it over, but found nothing more offensive than a couple of grease stains. Finally, with the tips of her fingers, she gingerly lifted up his socks and underwear, dropped them on to the shirt and took the bundle through to the kitchen.

Throwing it into the machine, she felt reassured by the absence of any obvious blood stains. Although that didn't mean he hadn't done it. He could have changed out of his suit, committed the gruesome act and then . . . She quickly dismissed the thought. She had to try and stay calm and she couldn't do that if she thought a psycho was showering in the bathroom.

Jo could hear the water running. If she was going to make a decision, she had to make it fast. Would calling 999 be likely to help or hinder Silver's release? Surely, with all their resources, they stood a better chance of tracking her down. On the other hand, Susan and whoever she was working with might panic if they realised the police were involved. And she could imagine just how cynically the Law would react to Miller's story. Perhaps she *should* give him a few days, a chance – slim as it was – to find Susan.

She weighed up the pros and cons but couldn't decide. Whatever path she chose could have terrible consequences. In the end, doing nothing seemed the most attractive option. At least that gave her time to think things through. Forty-eight hours, she decided, and nothing more. If he hadn't made any progress by then, she would definitely call the police.

Having made up her mind, she went to the study and dug out an old pair of tracksuit bottoms and a T-shirt. The thought of him in Peter's clothes was abhorrent but she had to find something for him to wear. He would hardly fit into anything that belonged to her.

Fifteen minutes later Miller emerged with a towel around his waist. He was a man who, despite his smoking habit, obviously took some care over his body. There were clearly defined muscles in his arms and stomach. She tried not to look too hard. A line of dark silky hair snaked its way around his chest and down towards his groin. She tried not to let her eyes stray too far from his face.

'Thanks,' he said. 'That's better.'

Frowning, Jo wondered how on earth this had happened. Not so long ago she'd been an ordinary widow, just trying to get on with her life, and now she had a half-naked fugitive standing in the middle of her flat.

Chapter Twenty-five

Nina didn't seem quite her usual chirpy self this evening. She wasn't saying much and what little she did say was tinged with bitterness. Marty sat back and eyed her over the rim of his glass. There was a purple swelling on her left cheek, no doubt the legacy of one of Delaney's more violent outbursts. It wouldn't be the only bruise she had.

Marty didn't feel much sympathy. Nina had a big mouth and if she hadn't learned when to keep it shut, she deserved all she got. He'd had his fair share of beatings through the years and still had the scars to prove it. However, no one would ever catch him whining about it; you either put up or shut up. Those were the rules and they couldn't be broken.

The news of Ritchie Naylor's murder had started to filter through in the morning. First it had just been a report of a body found in north London. Later, by lunchtime, a name had been provided and by the six o'clock bulletin Gabriel Miller had been mentioned by the cops as someone who was wanted 'in connection with inquiries'.

Marty had no idea of when the pigs had finally arrived at the flat. It amused him to think of them walking casually through that broken door, expecting nothing more than a routine break-in, then finding Ritchie laid out on the floor. His mouth curled up at the corners but he quickly fought to suppress the smile. It was the last thing Delaney needed to see.

'I'm tired,' Nina said, getting to her feet. 'I'm going to bed.'

'You're not going anywhere unless I tell you to.' Delaney held out his empty glass. 'Make yourself useful and get me a drink.'

She hesitated. Her lips parted in protest before she sensibly thought better of it, walked across the room and obediently retrieved the glass.

'And you can get Marty another one too.'

As she came towards his chair, obscuring Delaney's view of him, Marty frowned and silently mouthed: 'You okay?' He didn't really give a toss but he had to keep her sweet. She could still be useful to him; he had to know what Vic was doing when he wasn't around. He made sure his fingers touched hers as she reached out for his glass.

She gave a nod and a small smile.

Vic's women, as he had learned to his advantage, were usually grateful for a little TLC. Some well-timed sympathy always went down a treat.

'How long does it take to get a bloody drink?' Delaney snarled.

Nina jumped, grabbed Marty's glass and went over to the cabinet.

Delaney was still holding the ransom letter in his hand. He looked down and bared his yellow teeth. 'Where is she? Where the hell is she?'

'What did I tell you?' Marty said. 'I knew it was Miller behind all this. It had to be. He and Ritchie Naylor were in it together. They must have fallen out – or maybe he planned it this way all along. Use Naylor and then get rid of him. Yeah, that would make sense. He wouldn't want to share the cash, would he?'

Nina returned with Delaney's drink and he snatched it off her. 'I want him dead,' he said. 'Fuckin' dead.'

Marty nodded. 'Don't we all. And it's going to happen, course it is. But we need to be smart, Vic. We need to be organised. You have to get the notes together.'

'You what?' Delaney half-rose out of his seat, raised his fists and then, too drunk to follow through, smartly slumped down again. 'You think I'm going to pay half a million quid to that piece of shit? You think—'

'No,' Marty said calmly. 'That's not what I'm suggesting. We just need to be prepared, right? We need to make it look as though we're agreeing to his demands. I mean, this is Silver we're talking about. We can't afford to take any risks. We have to go along with it, pretend we're co-operating and then we can sort it, we can sort *him*, when it comes to the exchange.'

Delaney's small dull eyes gradually grew brighter. He was probably too pissed to think about anything very clearly but the gist of the argument was beginning to sink in. 'Yeah,' he said, 'you could be right.' He looked up at Nina. 'What are you still doing here?'

'You said—'

'Don't tell me what I said. You're not my bleedin' echo. Just piss off and leave us alone.'

Nina was more relieved than insulted. Before he could change his mind, she was out of the door and up the stairs.

If she had any sense, Marty thought, she'd find a room with a lock on it. There was no accounting for what Vic might do when he was in a mood like this.

'Stupid bitch,' Delaney muttered.

'C'mon, we've got more important things to worry about,' Marty said. 'We need to concentrate, work out what we're going to do next. How soon can you get the cash together?'

Delaney twisted the letter between his fingers. 'If he hurts one hair on her head . . .'

'He won't. And he'll get what's coming to him. We'll make sure of that.'

Chapter Twenty-six

It was getting on for eleven by the time Marty arrived in Kellston. He parked the car outside the house, took a moment to look around, then got out and strode briskly up the drive. He could tell Susan had a strop on from the moment she answered the door. She looked like a wasp had crawled into her mouth.

'What's going on?' she spluttered, before he'd even crossed the threshold. 'Don't you ever check your phone? I've left messages. I've been trying to call you all day.'

'Have you?'

'You must have seen the news.'

She was, of course, referring to the murder of Ritchie Naylor. Marty stepped inside, rearranged his smug expression, and turned to present a more sympathetic face. 'So you've heard. Sorry, babe, I didn't find out myself until a few hours ago. I've been with Vic. You know I can't answer that phone in front of him; I have to keep it switched off.'

Susan shut the door, her lips still pursed and angry. 'I don't understand what Ritchie was doing at Gabe Miller's place.'

'Yeah, well it's not me you should be asking, love – it's that bloody boyfriend of yours.'

'He's not my—' She stopped and glared at him. 'Why would he have killed Ritchie? Why would he have done that?'

'I don't suppose he was best pleased to find some toe-rag had broken into his home.'

'But that's no reason to . . . I don't understand what Ritchie was even doing there.'

'What do you think?' Marty said. 'Trying to rob the place. He must have overheard me talking, knew that Miller's flat was empty and decided to go and help himself. He's a junkie, *was* a junkie. He never could resist the opportunity of some easy cash.'

'You said he wasn't going to be a problem.'

Marty gave a low, mean laugh. 'Well, he certainly isn't now. Mr Miller, it seems, has done us a favour. At least that's one less thing to worry about.'

Susan followed him into the kitchen. 'And you swear you didn't have anything to do with it?'

'What are you talking about?' He pulled a face and sat down at the table. He'd been expecting a cross-examination and had prepared himself accordingly. 'Jesus, I haven't had the time, never mind the inclination, to go chasing around after that piece of shit.'

'But Ritchie knew about Silver,' she said, her eyes still wary.

'All Ritchie knew was what I told him. He was paid to take her to Blackpool and paid again to persuade her to leave the hotel in London. That was it. He had no idea about our other plans. And he didn't ask any questions. Ritchie didn't give a toss about the reasons – so long as he got his money he was happy.'

Susan, standing by the sink, crossed her arms and thought about it. 'I suppose.'

Marty nodded. Susan was smarter than most of the tarts he knew but she was still just a woman and it was a simple biological fact that women were inferior to men; not only were their bodies weaker but their brains were smaller too. Driven by emotion, needy and pathetic, they were strangers to the concept of rational behaviour. 'So can we move on or is there anything else you'd like to accuse me of?' He smiled as if to prove how ridiculous her suspicions were. 'You haven't even asked how it went with Delaney.'

'So how did it go?'

He sat back triumphantly. 'Without a hitch – we've got him right where we want him. Now all we need are the visuals to keep him on track. Three days is tight to get all that cash together. We don't want him dragging his feet.' Reaching into his pocket, he took out a small digital camera and stared down at the lens. 'Two or three good shots should do the trick.'

'You'll need the flash,' she said, 'and we'll have to open the door. You won't get a clear view through that grille.'

Marty stood up, went to one of the kitchen drawers and took out a black balaclava. He pulled it over his face. 'Right. Let's go and wake the sleeping beauty.'

Susan stared at him. 'You're going to scare the hell out of her looking like that.'

Beneath the wool of his ominous black mask, Marty grinned. 'Let's hope so. We wouldn't want Daddy to think we're not being serious.'

Chapter Twenty-seven

Jo brought in the duvet and put it on the chair. Miller was helping to reorganise the study, shifting the desk and piling up the boxes so that the futon could be extended.

'You don't need to do this,' he said. 'I'll be fine on the sofa.'

But Jo didn't want him on the sofa. The only way to the bathroom was through the living room and she'd prefer to make the journey without his lecherous eyes on her.

'You'll be more comfortable in here,' she said.

The afternoon had been a busy one. She had dropped off his suit at the dry cleaners and then, with the money he had given her, bought a pair of jeans, shirts, socks and underwear. It had felt odd, wrong, buying clothes for a man she was barely acquainted with. In the supermarket she had added a pack of disposable razors, shaving foam and a toothbrush to her basket, all the time looking around in case she bumped into anyone she knew.

'I wasn't sure you'd come back,' he said. 'This afternoon, when you went out, I thought that might be the last I'd see of you.'

'I said you could stay, didn't I?'

'Yeah, but I figured you might have second thoughts once you didn't have me breathing down your neck.'

As if the idea had never occurred to her, Jo raised her brows. 'Very trusting, I'm sure.' In fact, she'd had second, third and fourth thoughts. She had even walked along Cowan Road, right past the police station, just to see if she was tempted to go in. Stopping, she had peered inside and rehearsed what she might say: *I have someone in my flat, someone who you're looking for.* But her feet had remained firmly rooted to the spot. Once she passed through that door, once she opened her mouth, it would set off a chain reaction over which she would have no control.

'I appreciate it,' he said.

Jo reached down and unrolled the mattress. Flapping open a sheet, she spread it across and tucked down the corners. She neither wanted nor needed his gratitude. 'I'm not doing it for you. And I'm not doing it for Susan either. All I'm interested in is getting that girl home safely.'

'Talking of which,' he said, 'how about we take another look at the map?'

She glanced at her watch. It was only ten-thirty, too early for bed, and she didn't need to get up in the morning. When she had called, telling Jacob she was going to take a few days off, he had sounded relieved: 'Good. You're doing the right thing. You need some rest. Put your feet up and take it easy. And don't worry about anything here; I'll get one of the students in to cover.'

Had it been relief she'd heard in his voice? Or was it simply concern? Maybe it was a combination of the two. Things hadn't been exactly normal recently, not with her worries about the missing girl and her suspicions over Deborah. She had been on edge, unable to think straight. And just because Jacob was encouraging her to stay away, to take some time out, didn't mean that he had anything to hide. She could easily be imagining things, creating crises where—

'Jo?'

She looked up. 'Huh?'

'If you're too tired, we can leave it until the morning.'

'No, it's fine. I'm fine. Let's get on with it.'

They went through to the living room and sat down on the sofa. The map of Kellston was still laid out on the coffee table, its four corners anchored by a quartet of paperbacks. Two small black crosses had been marked, one indicating where they were in Barley Road and the other, half a mile away, showing the position of the Mansfield Estate. It was only a few hours since Jo had learned that Susan's mother was living in one of the high-rise blocks.

'Are you sure she couldn't have taken Silver there?' she said.

'No, there's no chance.'

'So why the cross?'

'Because the location matters; it's important to her. It's where Susan grew up.'

He leaned forward and traced a finger along the surrounding streets. 'She never got on with her mother but she always kept in touch. I'll go and see her tomorrow. Pat Clark and sobriety rarely touch base but if I get there early enough I might learn something useful.'

'Are you kidding?' Jo said, staring at him. 'You're not

going anywhere. You can't step foot outside this flat. What if someone recognises you?'

Miller grinned. 'I didn't know you cared.'

'I don't,' she said smartly, averting her eyes and shifting away from him. She was aware, even as she spoke, that the denial had risen a little too quickly to her lips.

'But you're a wanted man and if the police find out that you've been staying here . . .'

'I won't tell them if you don't.'

'Your name has been all over the news. How do you think Pat Clark is going to react when you go knocking on her door?'

'I doubt she even watches the news.'

'And you're happy to take that chance?'

'Not happy, exactly, but what choice do I have? I can't hide out here for ever. She's the only person I can think of who might have a clue as to where Susan is.'

Jo hesitated. There was another option but she wasn't sure if she wanted to suggest it. She took a quick breath. 'I could go.'

Miller shook his head. 'No way.'

'Why not? It's safer for me than for you. I could say I was an old friend passing through, that I'd lost touch with Susan and—'

'It's not a good idea.'

'It's better than yours.'

'No,' he said. 'End of conversation.'

But his refusal to even discuss it made her more determined. 'I'm involved in this too,' she said, 'as you weren't slow in pointing out on Friday night. You can't just make a unilateral decision. This is to do with what's best for Silver and I don't see how that includes you taking unnecessary risks. Your being locked up in a police cell isn't going to help her.'

Miller jumped to his feet and started his familiar pacing across the room.

'Let me give it a try,' Jo urged. There was sense to her argument but he was just too obstinate to admit it. 'What have we got to lose?'

'Pat's not an easy woman to deal with.'

She gave a small laugh. 'You've never met my mother-in-law.'

Miller stopped and looked at the photograph of Peter. 'And where is your husband, if you don't mind me asking?'

Jo glanced down at the floor. There was no reason to lie about it but it was always the sympathy that got to her, the awkward expressions of sorrow and regret. She could just say that he had left her – in a sense that was true – but she couldn't quite bring herself to do it. It would feel like a betrayal and she'd been doing too much of that in the last twenty-four hours. She raised her face and looked him squarely in the eye.

'Peter's dead,' she said. 'He was killed in a hit-and-run two years ago.'

Miller was silent.

She waited for the inevitable response, the reply that was bound to come, the *Oh, I'm so sorry* or *That must have been terrible for you.*

Instead he merely shrugged and said, 'So, you're a merry widow?'

'That's it!' she retorted, staggered by his insensitivity. Although why she should be even faintly amazed was a mystery to her. What else should she have expected? 'Yeah, you've got it in one. I haven't stopped dancing since it happened.'

'Sorry,' he said. 'That wasn't very tactful, was it? Still, I imagine you've had enough tea and sympathy to last you a lifetime.'

Jo couldn't disagree with that. But she still resented his indifference. The man had a heart of stone.

'He was older than you,' Miller said, his gaze drifting back to the photo. 'What did he do? I mean, what line was he in?'

She didn't answer. She was still annoyed by the merry widow quip and couldn't see how Peter's age or his occupation was any of his business.

'Ah, something dodgy was it?'

Provoked into making a response, she said: 'No, it wasn't. He was a jeweller, a perfectly *legitimate* jeweller.'

Miller grinned. 'Good choice. A girl can never have too many diamonds.'

She knew what he was insinuating and glared at him.

He promptly raised his hands. 'Sorry,' he said again. 'I should just keep my mouth shut, right?'

'You said it.'

Miller turned and resumed his pacing, walking from one side of the room to the other. A couple of minutes passed.

'For God's sake,' Jo said. 'Will you stop doing that? It's driving me mad.'

'I'm thinking.'

'So do it standing still. Or sitting down.'

Miller drew to a halt facing the print on the wall. Forced into immobility, he stood staring at it with his head to one side. 'Where is this? Somewhere in Asia?'

'Burma,' she said. As she looked at the picture, her voice softened. 'Peter travelled a lot when he was younger. He loved the place, despite all its troubles. It was special to him. He used to go there with his father before they . . .' She stopped, aware that her tongue was running away with her. The Strong family history, fascinating as it was, didn't need broadcasting.

'Of course,' Miller said.

Jo frowned at him. 'What do you mean, *of course*?'

'Rubies and jade,' he said. 'Burma's famous for them. What jeweller wouldn't love a country like that?'

'That wasn't why—' She shook her head. 'Oh, forget it.' It was pointless trying to explain anything to a man as cynical as Miller.

As if he couldn't help himself, he started pacing again.

Jo continued to stare at the picture. A memory was beginning to stir. It was to do with a night when Peter had got drunk. That had been unusual; he had enjoyed the occasional pint, a few glasses of wine, but had never drunk to excess. But then this hadn't been just any night. It had been Ruby's birthday and they had spent the evening in Canonbury along with Tony and Carla. Over dinner, a comment had been made about Burma and everyone had instantly shut up. She could still hear the brittle silence, still feel the wave of unease that had swept around the table. When they had got home, Peter had been sullen and quiet. He had opened a bottle of brandy and carried on drinking.

Jo shifted on the sofa. She half closed her eyes. It had been about three in the morning when she'd been woken by the sound of shattering glass. Peter had picked up the bottle and hurled it against the wall. At least she had thought it had been aimed at the wall. That it had smashed against the picture was just a mistake – or was it?

Miller, having reached the window for the fifth time, pulled back a corner of the curtain and looked out across the Green.

'So what's the deal with you and Susan?' Jo said. She wanted to fill the silence, to stop her thoughts from dwelling on that night.

Miller dropped the curtain. 'No big deal,' he said. 'We met a few years back. We got on. We stopped getting on. End of story. I haven't seen her since.'

'And?'

'That's not enough?'

'No,' she said. 'It isn't. You wouldn't be here if that was all it was. And you wouldn't be so determined to find her.'

Miller looked almost embarrassed. 'Okay,' he said. 'We were together for almost a year. I thought there might be something . . . something more . . . but there wasn't. Happy now?'

'Something?' she repeated. Sensing a chink in his armour, she continued to probe. 'Are you trying to say love?'

Miller gave a mock shudder. 'Do you mind? Anyway, I was wrong, way off the mark. She didn't . . . let's just say I got it wrong.'

Jo might have left it if she hadn't so distinctly recalled the first time they'd met and the way he had looked across the bar and mocked her. She could recall exactly what he'd said and repeated it almost verbatim: 'Well, we've all been *there* at one time or another.'

It took him a moment to get the reference and then he laughed. 'I guess I had that coming.'

Jo smiled too before quickly clamping her lips together. She didn't want that kind of connection with him. She didn't want any connection at all. 'So can we make a decision about tomorrow?'

'Do we have to?'

'I *can* do it,' Jo insisted. 'Let me go and see Pat. Let me give it a try.'

Chapter Twenty-eight

As Jo approached the Mansfield Estate, her steps began to falter. Perhaps Miller had been right; this wasn't such a great idea. She shielded her eyes from the sun as she looked up. High above her loomed the peaks of the three crumbling towers. Each of the buildings, identical in design and ugliness, presented the same bleak exterior with endless rows of windows, flaking paintwork and rusting balconies. The overall impression was of grey. Even the graffiti was depressingly uniform, the dull monotonous tags appearing over and over again.

What was more disturbing, however, was the pervading sense of menace. It was like a pall that hung over the place, a heavy and intimidating cloud. Despite the warmth of the morning, Jo shivered. Suddenly she felt vulnerable. It was not smart, she thought, to stand around gawping. But then it was hardly smart to be here at all. There was still time to change her mind, to scuttle back to where the car was parked, but her pride wouldn't permit it.

Jo quickly walked on. She turned right and headed along the path towards Carlton House. She was twenty feet from the door when a couple of lads, both with their hoods pulled partly over their faces, emerged from the building and leaned against the wall. They were sharing a joint, passing it from one to the other, and she could feel their eyes on her.

She felt her stomach flutter but it was too late to turn back. She had read somewhere that if you acted like a victim, you were more likely to become one. The trick was to behave confidently, to walk with your head held high and your shoulders back. But that was easier said than done when your imagination was working overtime.

Preparing herself for the worst, her body stiffened as she grew closer. She was ten feet away, then six and then two. The boys were still watching her. She drew adjacent, deliberately avoiding any eye contact, and was almost at the door when one of them called out 'Morning, love.'

Jo flinched. Should she simply ignore him or would that make matters worse? With only a moment to decide, she turned and smiled. 'Hi.'

'You looking for someone?'

She couldn't see what business it was of his but then again she had no desire to provoke him either. 'Just visiting a friend.'

'You from the Social?'

'No,' she said.

The boy cocked his head to one side and stared at her. He was a lanky kid, about fifteen or sixteen, with small brown eyes and a cold sore on his lower lip. 'What floor you after?'

Again she was tempted to ask what concern it was of his but again she refrained. The sooner this was over with, the better. 'The twelfth.'

As if he had asked a series of particularly complex questions and was still processing her answers, the boy frowned. There was a short delay before he nodded. 'Don't use the first lift on your left. It's shit.'

Jo smiled at him. 'Thanks.' She heard a snigger as she walked through the door but couldn't say from which of the boys it had come.

The foyer, cool and characterless, was strewn with litter. It was empty but this made her feel more nervous, rather than less. She had a quick look round. Originally there had been patterned tiles on the walls, as if the architect had made one late effort to redeem himself, but the few that had survived were chipped and covered in graffiti. The pungent stench of urine, faintly overlain with the smell of dope, rose up to invade her nostrils.

There were four lifts, three of them with their doors open. As she had been advised, Jo ignored the first on the left and examined the other two. They were equally vile inside, both old and filthy, containing not just tin cans and fag ends but pools of suspicious-looking liquid too. She noticed a stone stairwell and considered walking instead. But twelve floors? She wasn't sure if she would make it . . . or whether she'd be able to talk if she did.

Before she could change her mind, Jo chose the lift without the used condom nestled in the corner, stepped inside and smartly pressed the button. It was only as the doors were closing that she wondered if the boy had deliberately misled her. Had that been why one of them had laughed? Perhaps, just for fun, they had removed an out-of-order sign.

It was too late to do anything about it now. There was a short pause before the lift gave a judder and began its lumbering ascent. She watched the light make slow progress from one number to the next. She held her breath, partly through fear that she would be trapped inside but mainly because of the smell. In the close confines of the metal box, the stink of urine was nauseating.

Jo tried to concentrate on something else. The first thought that came into her head was what the boy had said. Did she really look like a social worker? She glanced down at her clothes – jeans and a light cotton sweater – and made a mental note to review her wardrobe.

After what felt like an eternity, the twelfth floor was finally conquered. She gave a sigh of relief and waited for the doors to open . . . but they didn't. 'Come on!' she urged impatiently. Her voice grew more pleading. 'Please.' She jabbed at a button on the panel but still nothing happened. A few more seconds passed. Her legs began to tremble. Just as panic was starting to set in, visions of being suspended here for hours or of the lift suddenly plummeting to earth, the doors gave a soft weary creak and reluctantly drew apart.

Jo jumped out, her heart thumping. She stumbled to the landing, gripped the top of the concrete wall and gulped in the fresh air. For a while she stood there, giving her legs time to recover. Beneath her lay an amazing view over the borough of Kellston and beyond. It was a view she might have appreciated if she hadn't felt so sick.

It was a few minutes before she had recovered enough to start looking for Pat Clark's flat. First she backtracked to the lifts and checked out the numbers painted on the wall.

These places were like rabbit warrens; if you set off in the wrong direction, you could be wandering for ever.

Jo had walked the length of a landing, made a right-angle turn and walked halfway along another before she finally reached number eighty-eight. Here she stopped and took a few deep breaths. Was she prepared? About as much as she'd ever be. Before pressing on the bell, she quickly ran through the story she'd prepared with Miller. She stood back and waited. There was no response. She tried it again, this time leaning in closer. Was the bell working? Jo raised her hand and rapped twice.

This time she heard a definite movement from inside. There was the sound of a bolt being released, of a key being turned. A tall, thin woman pulled open the door. She was somewhere in her fifties although it was hard to tell exactly where. Her eyes were like Susan's, a pretty shade of hazel, but her skin was dull and tired. There was a fading bruise on her left cheek and her hair, a drab shade of blonde, had an inch of dark brown showing through at the roots.

Jo put on her best smile. 'Hi.'

'Oh,' the woman responded, her face instantly dropping as if she'd been expecting someone else.

'It's Mrs Clark, isn't it? It's nice to see you again.'

Pat Clark gave a half nod.

'We've met before,' Jo said, 'but it was a long time ago. Helen? Helen Seymour? I'm a friend of Susan's. We used to work together.' She paused as if waiting for a sign of recognition.

Pat smiled tentatively back. Like most people she was unwilling to admit to not recognising someone she ought to but this was allied with a caution probably endemic to the more law-abiding residents of the Mansfield Estate. 'Susan doesn't live here.'

'I know,' Jo said. 'I was just hoping you might have a number for her or an address. We kind of lost touch and . . . It's my fault. I've been away for a while, working up north. I just got back and tried to ring but her line's been disconnected.'

Pat's small pink tongue crept out to lick her lips. As if still struggling to place her, she narrowed her eyes. 'Helen?'

'That's right,' Jo said. 'And I was really looking forward to seeing her again. I'm only here for a few days. I was hoping we could go out, catch up on all the news.'

Jo waited as Pat Clark thought about it. Had she been a beauty once like Susan? It was hard to tell. She was wearing a pair of fawn trousers and a cream short-sleeved blouse. There was a distinctive whiff of alcohol although it was still early, only ten-fifteen.

'The thing is,' Pat said eventually, 'Susan usually rings *me*. She's always so busy, you know, with work and everything.'

'Of course,' Jo said, as if this arrangement was perfectly natural. She wondered what imaginary career Susan had invented for her mother. 'Well, maybe I could just pop round and put a note through the door. Do you have an address?'

'I'm not sure if . . . I don't think . . .' Pat hesitated, her hands fluttering to her chest.

Jo wasn't sure if she didn't have an address or simply wasn't willing to reveal it. Either way, this wasn't going well.

Was she really going to return with nothing? Miller would not be pleased. She made a final attempt to salvage something from the visit.

'Okay, how about if I leave you my number and then if Susan calls you can pass it on to her? Would that be all right?'

Pat seemed to relax a little, her hands returning to her sides. 'I suppose.'

'That's great,' Jo said. 'Thanks. Only I'd really love to see her again. It's such a shame when you lose touch, isn't it?'

'Hold on a moment.' Pat went inside, carefully closing the door behind her.

A minute passed. Jo presumed she'd gone for paper and a pen but maybe she had read it all wrong. Perhaps Mrs Clark had smelled a rat and decided to withdraw. She stood on the landing, shifting uneasily from one foot to another whilst examining the peeling paint on the door. She wasn't having much luck with doors today. A few more minutes went by. Jo was beginning to lose hope when Pat suddenly appeared again.

'Sorry, I couldn't find it. I knew I'd put it somewhere safe but . . .' She held out a piece of paper with a number scribbled on it. 'I'm only supposed to use it for emergencies but, seeing as it's you, I'm sure she won't mind.'

Jo's face lit up. 'No,' she said, 'thank you. I'm sure she won't mind at all.'

Chapter Twenty-nine

Unwilling to risk the lift again, Jo took the longer route back to terra firma. She trotted briskly down the winding stone steps, only slowing as she reached the lower floors and her breath began to run out. Her fingers curled around the piece of paper in her pocket. She was pleased with herself. It might not be as useful as an address but at least she was not going back empty-handed.

Her heart was pumping by the time she reached the ground. She could feel the pinkness in her face and a prickling of sweat on her temples. She would have liked to stop, to rest for a while, but the foyer was not a pleasant place to linger. She hurried through the door, eager to escape.

Outside, there was no sign of the two boys. Since her ascent into the heavens, the estate had grown busier and now a steady flow of residents, many of them women laden with supermarket bags, criss-crossed the intersecting paths. Feeling less threatened, Jo slowed down. She made her way to the main thoroughfare and out through the gates.

The sun was shining brightly and the sky was blue and cloudless. She gulped in the fresh air as she walked. It was only when she reached the car that she realised she wasn't intending to go straight home. Why should she? It was a beautiful day and the thought of being in the flat, the flat so thoroughly occupied by Miller, filled her with a sense of dread. She needed to be outside, to be alone for a while. She needed time to think.

Jo got in the car, took the piece of paper from her pocket and laid it on her knee. She rooted in her bag until she found the card Miller had given her at the hotel. He answered on the second ring.

'I've got a number,' she said. 'No address, I'm afraid. You want to write it down?'

'That's great. Well done.'

'There's no saying she'll pick up.'

'Maybe not,' Miller said. 'But she will check her messages. Hold on, I'll grab a pen.' There was a short pause before he came back on the line again. 'Okay.'

Jo read the number out to him and then repeated it.

'Got it,' he said.

'Right, I'll see you in an hour or so.'

She heard the wariness in his voice. 'You're not coming straight back?'

'No. Is that a problem?'

'Depends what you're doing,' he said only half-jokingly. 'Should I be expecting a knock on the door any time soon?'

'If I was going to call the cops, I'd have done it by now. You should learn to be more trusting.' Then, because she felt faintly guilty about adding to his already overburdened stress levels, she added: 'Look, I'm just going to take a walk, that's all.'

'Okay,' he said. 'I didn't mean—'

'I'll see you later.'

Jo hung up and threw her phone on to the passenger seat. She leaned forward and turned the key in the ignition. Where to? She felt suddenly light, free, as if she'd received a temporary pass from jail. If she wanted, she could just drive and drive . . . and never come back. Of course this wasn't true – there was work, responsibilities, Gabe Miller – but the idea was enough to lift her spirits.

Jo set off with no clear destination in mind. She wound through the backstreets for a while and had an idea about going to Victoria Park. She could have that walk, even buy a magazine and lie on the grass. For a while, if she was lucky, she could forget about everything.

As she approached the junction of Cambridge Heath Road and Roman Road, she glanced to her right and saw Bethnal Green tube station. She could never pass the building without a small shudder. It was here, in 1943, that over 170 people had died trying to reach shelter from the German bombs. She thought of the panic as they surged down the dark wet steps, of that dreadful moment when the woman carrying a small child slipped and fell . . . and then the horror as the others tumbled over her. Those behind, not knowing what was happening, had continued to relentlessly push their way forward.

Jo felt a lump rise to her throat as she thought about the tragedy. The awful irony, of course, was that there hadn't been a bombing raid at all. Suddenly, recalling all those poor lost souls, she wasn't in the mood for a walk any more. Instead she took the next turning and headed for home.

There was no point in trying to escape from her problems; they would still be waiting for her when she got back.

As she entered Kellston again, Jo realised she wasn't that far from Fairlea Avenue. She resolved to drive straight past. For months after Peter had been killed, she had returned to the street every day, hopeless and desperate, seeking . . . seeking what? Perhaps some answers as to what he had been doing there, why he had died there. She would sit for hours, watching the people come and go, seeing everything and nothing. It hadn't been a healthy thing to do and having long since weaned herself off the habit, she had no desire to return to it.

Yet, despite her best intentions, she slowed as the avenue came into view. She flipped on the indicator. It was as if a magnetic force was pulling her, forcing her to take one more look. She turned left and drew into the first available parking space.

'What are you doing?' she murmured. 'You shouldn't be here.'

But still she switched off the engine, knowing that she wouldn't be leaving in a hurry. She opened the window, leaned back and gazed through the windscreen. Fairlea Avenue was a short quiet street, consisting mainly of identical two-up, two-down terraced houses but with a small block of modern flats on the far corner. That was where he had been standing when the car had shot up the road, mounted the pavement and . . .

Jo briefly shut her eyes. Why was she doing this? It was her suspicions about Deborah, she thought, that had stirred up these old horrors. Not to mention all the other madness that had been going on recently. It was hardly surprising that her head was in a spin.

She peered into the dazzling sun and sighed. She began to wonder again just how well she had really known Peter. How much of his life, and especially his past, had he kept hidden from her? There was the estrangement from his father, never fully explained. There was all the time he had lived abroad. And then there were the dreams, the dreadful nightmares that haunted his sleep, the cold sweats and the cries. When he woke, pale and trembling, he would cling to her, the tears running down his face. But he wouldn't speak of what he had experienced. They were nothing, he would say, just phantoms.

For the next twenty minutes, Jo sat in the car and waited. All thoughts of visiting the park had left her. She was not sure what she was waiting for – a revelation, some sign from above? She sighed again. She had been Peter's wife but not his confidante and wasn't sure if it was a failure on her part. Perhaps, in time, things might have changed between them but that time was lost to them for ever.

Before she could start to slide down into the old abyss, Jo decided to head back to the flat. Suddenly even Miller's company felt preferable to her own. With Silver to worry about, and the problem of Susan, there wouldn't be room for these gloomy contemplations. She had to 'pull herself together' as her mother had so often insisted during those long-distance calls after Peter's death, she had to 'move on'.

Thoughts of her parents kept Jo occupied as she drove through Kellston. Andrew and Anne Grey, as she had learned to her cost, were experts in the practicalities of moving on. She couldn't even remember the last time she had talked to them. It must have been months ago. And she was always the one who had to pick up the phone.

The traffic was jammed along the High Street. Bumper to bumper, the cars edged slowly forward, the hot metal shimmering in the sun, the exhausts belching out their filthy smoke. She should have gone round, taken the longer but ultimately quicker route, but it was too late to backtrack now.

It was when she was almost adjacent to Ruby's that she saw them. The traffic had come to a standstill again. It was Jacob she noticed first, standing outside the door, deep in conversation with a small dark-haired woman. There was nothing particularly odd about it and Jo wouldn't have thought twice if the woman hadn't shifted slightly, stood aside to let someone pass and in doing so revealed her face. It was Leo's mother and her neighbour, Constance Kearns.

Jo wasn't sure why she was so surprised. There was no reason why they shouldn't know each other and yet she hadn't been aware of it. In the two years since she had taken over Ruby's, she had never seen Constance in the shop. Still, their paths could have crossed in any number of ways. Perhaps they belonged to the same bridge club. Perhaps they shopped in the same supermarket. Perhaps Peter had introduced them.

The lights had changed and the cars were moving forward again. She kept her eyes fixed on the road, hoping they wouldn't look over in her direction. For a reason she couldn't logically explain, she didn't want them to see her. Or, to be more precise, she didn't want Jacob and Constance to know that she had seen *them*.

Chapter Thirty

It was early afternoon when Susan heard the phone ring. She was down in the cellar, trying to tempt Silver with pizza and chips. The girl hadn't eaten much since she'd arrived; if she got any skinnier she'd fade away. At least she was drinking the bottled water. That was something. You could survive on just water for weeks.

Susan didn't rush to answer it. It would only be Marty giving her a time to expect him. She never answered the door to anyone else; the fewer people who saw her face, the better. He'd guess where she was and either call back or leave a message.

'Just try a bit,' she urged.

'I'm not hungry.'

Susan guessed that last night's episode hadn't done much to enhance her appetite. Marty, in his balaclava, had scared the poor kid witless. Susan didn't take any pleasure in it, but some evils were necessary ones. And the photos, she had to admit, were pretty good.

'Please yourself,' Susan said. 'I'll leave it with you.'

By the time she had climbed the steps and put down the untouched breakfast tray – still laden with cereal, a carton of milk, two slices of toast, a boiled egg, butter and marmalade – the mobile had long since stopped ringing. She pressed the button to retrieve her voicemail.

Expecting to hear Marty's rough tones, she almost dropped the phone. It was another voice that came floating down the line.

'Hello, Susan. It's Gabe. You can probably guess why I'm calling. I know who you're working with so unless you want me to tip off Delaney you'd better call me back. The time is twelve-twenty. You have exactly one hour.'

Susan could feel the blood draining from her face. Coldness swept over her. She gripped the phone tighter, her pulse beginning to race. A liquid, as acrid as bile, rose in her throat and leaked into her mouth. She swallowed hard and played the message again. The threatening words remained the same.

'You bastard,' she whispered.

She threw the phone down on the table and in a moment of anger and frustration, upended the tray and sent everything flying. The cereal box disgorged its cornflakes. The marmalade jar shattered. The milk carton split open, spilling its contents over the floor. She raised her hands and covered her eyes. 'Bastard!' she said again.

It was a while before she could even begin to think straight. She paced the kitchen, the broken glass and cornflakes crunching under her feet. What she mustn't do is panic. She had to try to keep a cool head. Her first impulse was to call Marty Gull, to tell him what had happened, but then she had second thoughts. His solution to most problems was one of zero tolerance.

Susan sat down and took a few deep breaths. It wasn't the end of the world. She had an hour. There could still be a way for her to sort this. Could Gabe really know about Marty Gull or was he just calling her bluff? And how had he got hold of this number? Only two people had it, Marty and . . . She gave a soft groan. It had to be her stupid bloody mother!

Susan grabbed the phone. She punched in a number. There were seven rings before it was finally answered. Then there was another delay, a fumbling, before the receiver finally made contact with her mother's loose mouth.

'Erm . . . yes? Hello?'

From her many years of experience, Susan could tell that she was on at least her third bottle of wine. Accordingly, she skipped the formalities. 'How many times have I told you about handing out my phone number?'

'What?'

'You heard me,' Susan said abruptly. 'Don't come over all innocent. I know it was you.' It wouldn't have taken Gabe long to worm his way in. He could turn on the charm when he had to. A few niceties, a few easy compliments and she'd have been putty in his hands. The stupid cow had probably put the kettle on and made him a cup of tea.

'I didn't think you'd mind.'

'Exes are called exes for a reason.'

'What?'

'For God's sake,' Susan said. 'Didn't it even occur to you that I might not want to hear from him?'

'I didn't—'

'Yes you *did*,' Susan interrupted. 'I know you did. What's

the point in denying it? He just called me. I thought we had an agreement. I ring you every week, every single week. I make sure you're okay, that you haven't walked into your latest boyfriend's careless fist, fallen over the cat or got too far behind with the bloody rent – and all I demand in return is that you never *ever* give out my number. That's not too much to ask, is it?'

Her mother, always close to tears when the booze was swirling through her veins, produced a small pathetic sniffle. 'I only gave it to that nice girl.'

Susan started. 'What?'

'Your friend,' she whined, 'the one you used to work with.'

'I've no idea who you're talking about.'

There was a pause, a small gulping sound as her mother sought solace from her glass. 'A pretty girl, short blonde hair. Helen, er . . . Smith or something? I can't remember. She came round this morning. She said you used to work together. She was very nice.'

'Shit,' Susan murmured. It had to be Jo.

'I thought, you know, as you were friends, you wouldn't mind.'

'Right,' Susan said. 'And you didn't think to ask first? No, of course you didn't. Do you ever listen to a word I say?'

'I'm sorry, love. I didn't mean to—'

'It doesn't matter.' Now she knew who'd been poking around, Susan had heard enough. What was done was done and the quicker she ended this call the better. 'Forget it. Just promise not to do it again, okay? They don't like me taking private calls at work.'

'Okay.'

'I'll give you a bell at the weekend.' Susan said goodbye, put the phone down and glared at the table. So Jo had been doing Gabe's dirty work, creeping around behind her back. It was the last thing she'd expected. Still, he could be very persuasive. She wondered how much he'd told her – and where. Gabe, as she clearly recalled, did most of his talking in bed.

Frowning, Susan looked at her watch. There were fifty minutes left. She had three choices: do nothing, call Marty Gull or do as Gabe requested. She quickly eliminated the first; doing nothing barely counted as a choice – it left her out of the loop and out of control. The second, calling Marty, wasn't much of an improvement either. Ritchie Naylor's murder was still preying on her mind. She was not convinced by Marty's accusations – Gabe could have easily floored Naylor without resorting to a crowbar – or his protestations of innocence. The boy's death had been just a little too convenient.

Susan had no real feelings for Ritchie Naylor. He'd been lowlife, a piece of scum. She didn't even care that he was dead. What she did care about was that Marty might have done it. They were in this together and whatever he did could eventually rebound on her. Kidnap was one thing, murder quite another.

Which left only one choice: much as it pained her she would have to contact Gabe. But if she was going to do that, she would need to find a way to turn it to her advantage.

Susan made a strong black coffee, sat down and began to work through a plan. It was another twenty minutes before she had it clear in her head. It wasn't foolproof but she was prepared to take a gamble. She glanced towards the steps to the cellar. She had come too far and was too close to her dream to let it all slip away from her now.

She took a deep breath and picked up the phone.

Gabe answered straight away. 'Susan?'

'So what's the deal?' she said abruptly. 'What do you want?'

'You know what I want. This is crazy. You have to let Silver go.'

'I can't do that.' She paused. 'Not yet.'

'You *can* and you have to.'

'It isn't just down to me.'

'No, I'd kind of gathered that. But Delaney has his own way of sorting things and once he finds out who your partner is—'

'Are you going to tell him?'

'Why shouldn't I?' He groaned down the line. 'Jesus, do you really think you can get away with this? It's pure madness. It isn't going to happen, you know it isn't.'

'Do you want the girl dead?' she said. 'Because that's going to be the outcome if you talk to Delaney. I won't be able to prevent it. I'll have to warn him you see – my partner – and he's not going to be happy. He won't be happy at all.'

'Like he wasn't happy with Ritchie.'

It was a statement rather than a question, a confirmation of her worst fears. But she refused to rise to the bait. 'Why can't you just leave it alone? Go away, keep your head down for a while. This is none of your business.'

'Of course it's my fucking business,' he said. 'Silver was in my care and Delaney thinks I'm responsible for snatching her. Oh, and as if that isn't enough, I'm also well and truly in the frame for killing Naylor.'

'All the more reason to make yourself scarce. As soon as Daddy pays up, we'll release her. She'll tell him you had nothing to do with it. You'll be in the clear.'

'And the other little matter?'

'I'm sure, given time, you can find yourself a decent alibi.'

'Forget it,' Gabe said. 'I'm not going anywhere.'

'Well then, I don't think we have anything else to say to each other.'

'No, wait!' he insisted before she could hang up. 'Meet me. Just for ten, fifteen minutes. I've got an idea. There may be another way round this.'

She gave a cynical laugh. 'What, so you can turn up with Delaney or the cops? I don't think so.'

'I wouldn't do that. You know I wouldn't. I'm trying to help you, Susan, not stitch you up.'

'You're trying to help yourself.'

'Okay,' he said. 'That too. But I'm not asking for much. I swear, I won't tell anyone else about it. It'll just be you and me.'

'Why should I trust you?'

'What have you got to lose?'

'What have I got to gain?'

'Peace of mind,' he said. 'This has all got out of control, you know it has. And you don't want Silver's death on your conscience any more than I do.'

'I . . .' Susan hesitated as though she was thinking about it. She left a long enough pause to make it sound convincing. 'All right,' she eventually agreed. 'But let's get one thing clear: if you double-cross me, you'll be sorry.'

'I won't. I'll come alone – I swear.'

'And I can choose where we meet?'

'Anywhere,' he said.

'There's a pub on the corner of Clover Street in Kellston. It's called The George. I'll see you there at seven.'

'Why not now?'

'Because I can't get away right now. That's the deal, take it or leave it. If you can't make it then—'

'Okay,' he said. 'The George at seven. I'll be there.'

Susan fired a parting shot. 'And keep this in mind: if you screw me over it's not just Silver you'll have to worry about – there's the lovely Jo too.'

'This has nothing to with—'

She quickly put down the phone and smiled. What a sucker! Standing up, she opened the cupboard over the sink, took out a bottle of brandy and poured herself a shot. She never drank much – she had no intention of ending up like her mother – but she needed something to keep her nerves steady. The next call would be even harder to make.

Fortunately, Gabe had already told her everything she needed to know. He had made an educated guess that she was working with someone close to Delaney but didn't have a clue as to their actual identity. If he'd had a name, he would have mentioned it. She didn't need to worry. He was just whistling in the wind.

With the glass in her hand, she dialled the 0800 number

for Crimestoppers. Guaranteed anonymity. She cleared her throat as the phone was answered. 'I have some information,' she said in her best Dublin accent. 'The London police are looking for a man, Gabriel Miller. He's wanted for murder. Let them know that they can find him in Kellston at seven o'clock tonight. He'll be in a pub called The George.'

Chapter Thirty-one

Leo had already been waiting for over twenty minutes, leaning on his bike and watching as the other lads made their surreptitious purchases and scuttled off across the Green. He had witnessed these transactions a hundred times and was careful not to stare too hard, to not draw attention to himself.

Stevie Hills was the kind of boy Leo's mother would have described as 'trouble'. He dealt in dope and stolen goods, nicked cars, and already had a couple of ASBOs under his belt. At sixteen he was two years older than Leo but a few inches shorter. What he lacked in height, however, he made up for in sheer intimidation. His arms and knuckles were decorated with crude tattoos and his eyes were a cold icy blue. His hair, invisible now beneath the hood, was shaved close to his skull.

Leo took a few deep breaths. There was still time for him to change his mind, to walk on past, to just go on home. But he couldn't. He had heard the footsteps again last night, the heavy creak across the floorboards. He knew the man was back – the man who had taken advantage of Jo. This morning Leo had even picked up his discarded cigarette butts on the tiny square of lawn in front of the house.

With the last of his clients having been served, Stevie was preparing to leave. Leo wheeled his bike over and stood in front of him. 'I need something,' he muttered.

'You name it, I've got it.' Stevie grinned. 'So long as you've got the cash.'

'I've got it.'

'Come on then, spit it out. I ain't got all day. Bit of skunk, is it, a few Es?'

'No, it's . . .' Leo said. His voice had gone hoarse. He stopped, cleared his throat and tried again. 'I need a gun.'

Stevie pushed his hands deep into his pockets and looked him up and down. 'Fuck off!'

Leo had to muster all his courage. Stevie scared the hell out of him but he couldn't allow him to see it. Bullies could smell fear, could sniff it out at a hundred paces. He straightened his shoulders and puffed out his chest. 'What's the matter? Too big for you?'

'No.'

'So?'

Stevie glared at him. He didn't like his reputation being called into question, especially by some scrawny loser in a school uniform. He shrugged. 'You're just a kid. You can't afford it.'

Leo took the money he had, the two twenties and the six tens he'd withdrawn from his savings account earlier that afternoon, and showed it to him. 'A hundred,' he said.

Stevie stared at the cash, his cold eyes gleaming. That put a different slant on things. Eventually, he nodded. 'Okay, put it away. You want everyone to see? I may be able to help. What kind of gun?'

'Small,' Leo said, thinking about how he would have to hide it from his mother. 'And I'll need some ammo too.'

'What do you want it for?'

Leo knew better than to answer that. 'Can you get it or not?'

Stevie gave him another long hard look. 'Maybe,' he said. 'But it'll take a few days.'

Leo's fingers grasped the handlebars. A few days were a few days too long. He thought of the brute upstairs and of what he might do to Jo. 'No, that's no good. I need it quicker than that. Can't you—'

'I'm not a fuckin' miracle worker. Have some patience. These things can't be rushed. There are people to call, arrangements to make. Shooters are serious stuff, man. You can't just walk into Tesco and pick one off the bleedin' shelf.'

'I know,' Leo said. He was about to say sorry but quickly bit down on his tongue. Apologising to the likes of Stevie Hills was tantamount to lying down and asking to be kicked. 'I just need it soon, right? The sooner the better.'

'I'll see what I can do. You got a number?'

But Leo didn't want him ringing him. He'd watched the crime programmes on TV, seen how the police could trace calls. If Stevie got arrested, Leo didn't want to be the last person he had rung. Come to that, he didn't even want to be in his address book. He could imagine his mother's face, the shock and the shame, if the cops turned up on their doorstep. He shook his head. 'I had it nicked a couple of days ago. I haven't got a new one yet.'

Stevie narrowed his eyes and stared at him. He didn't seem convinced. 'So how do I get in touch?'

'I'll see you here. You're around most days, aren't you?'

'Yeah, but it's the first time I've seen *you*. What if I sort things out, go to all that trouble and then you change your mind? I'm left with some piece I might not be able to get rid of. That's not good, man. It's not good at all.'

Leo quickly shook his head. 'That won't happen.'

'Not good enough.'

'What do you mean?'

Stevie folded his thick arms across his chest. He made a show of looking around the Green, of acting out some big screen drama. He leaned in close and lowered his voice. 'I need security, mate. I need a deposit. Fifty ought to do it.'

Leo hesitated. 'And how do I know that *you* won't just disappear?'

'Chance you'll have to take,' he sneered.

Leo weighed up the odds. Stevie Hills, for all his talk, for all his bravado, was purely small-time. Fifty quid might be useful but it was not enough for him to abandon his pitch. He was a local boy with local connections. The money he got from dealing might not be a fortune but it was regular, reliable and enough to keep him coming back. However, knowing that he was coming back didn't necessarily mean he would deliver. What if Stevie took the cash but didn't bother getting him the gun? He could hardly go to the cops. The world of negotiation, as Leo was rapidly discovering, was a minefield.

'I'll give you twenty,' Leo said.

'No.'

Leo took a gamble. 'Forget it. I'll try someone else.'

'You don't know anyone else.'

'I might.'

'You don't.' Stevie quickly reached out his hand, palm up. 'Make it forty and I'll have the piece for you by Friday.'

'Make it thirty and you've got a deal.'

'Go on then, but if you let me down—'

Leo peeled off the notes and passed them over. 'I won't. I'll see you here, same time on Friday.'

Stevie shoved the notes in his pocket and stared at him. 'Well? What are you waiting for, a bleedin' conversation?'

Leo flushed, put his head down and wheeled his bike towards the gates. Aware that Stevie was still watching him, he decided to cycle around for a while until he was gone. He didn't want him seeing where he lived.

Chapter Thirty-two

The sun was casting its evening rays across the Green, bisecting it into two clear halves of light and shadow. The windows to the flat were open and a light summer breeze drifted gently through the kitchen. They were sitting at the table. Jo picked at the ham salad, too nervous to eat properly. She didn't like Gabe Miller's plan for meeting up with Susan.

'I spent hours slaving over that dressing,' he said. 'Come on, it's hardly the Last Supper.'

She lifted her head, glancing across at the counter where a bottle of Tesco's finest French dressing was standing by the kettle. 'Yeah, right.' She paused. 'Look, I don't trust her. Anyone could be waiting for you there.'

'You don't need to worry.'

Jo stared at him. The whole day had been decidedly odd and it wasn't getting any better. 'It's Silver I'm worried about,' she insisted, in case he got any ideas about her being overly concerned for *his* welfare. 'What's going to happen to the girl if you're not around?'

'What's going to happen to her if I'm just sitting in this flat doing zilch? This could be my one and only chance of talking to Susan face-to-face, of finding out who she's working with, of maybe even convincing her that she has to let the kid go.'

'And how likely is that?'

Gabe shrugged. 'It's possible. She couldn't have known that Ritchie Naylor was going to be knocked off and I'm damn sure she's not happy about it. She's in too deep. I think she's looking for a way out.'

'And if she isn't?'

'Then I'll have to persuade her.'

Jo speared a slice of cucumber and put it in her mouth. She chewed, tasting nothing, swallowed and put down her fork. She had one of those cold dread feelings spreading through her gut. This all felt wrong, terribly wrong. 'It could be a set-up.'

'It's not,' he said.

'Why not? She wasn't too worried about having you beaten up on Friday.'

'This is different. Things have changed since then. Now she thinks I know who she's working with she can't take the risk of me telling Delaney.'

'You won't be able to tell him if you're not breathing any more.'

'True,' he said, 'but is she really going to take the chance that I haven't already passed the information on to someone else? Or at least made contingency plans so that if anything *does* happen to me . . .'

'You could be overestimating her intelligence,' Jo said. Then, realising that the comment sounded rather more catty than she'd intended, quickly added: 'I mean, you don't really know what she's thinking or the risks she might be prepared to take. It's hours since you talked to her. She could have been straight on the phone to her partner. By now they could have made all kinds of arrangements. They could have completely changed their plans so that it doesn't matter if Delaney knows the guy's identity or not.'

'That's a chance I'll have to take.'

'No,' she said, 'you don't have to take it.' Jo suspected that his feelings for Susan were clouding his judgement. That was the trouble with men like Gabe Miller, they had a tendency – no matter what the evidence to the contrary – to overestimate their appeal to the women they had slept with. 'Is it a chance you're taking or an unnecessary risk?'

'It's hardly unnecessary. You got any better ideas?'

'Yes. Call her back. Tell her you've changed your mind. Tell her you've decided to leave, to go away.'

Gabe shook his head and laughed. 'What? And that's your idea of a plan?'

'Why not?' she said. She was suddenly determined to change his mind. 'I never thought I'd be saying this but perhaps it's safer for Silver if you just back off and let the whole thing go ahead. That way they won't panic, won't do anything too rash. Delaney pays the ransom and they release her. By interfering you could be putting her in more danger rather than less.'

'And you really think, once the ransom has been paid, they're just going to hand her over?'

'Why not?'

'Because I think there's more to this than just money.'

Jo felt a shiver run down her spine. 'You think,' she said, 'or you *know*?'

Gabe didn't answer immediately. He picked up his wine, took a drink and looked at her over the rim of the glass. For a moment she thought he was about to confide in her, to tell what he really knew, but he glanced away. 'I don't know anything for certain – how could I?'

'But?' she said. She was certain there was more

'But nothing. I have to go there tonight. I have to see her.' He looked at his watch. 'I've made an arrangement and I'm going to stick to it.'

'Even if it means—'

'It doesn't,' he said. He raised his eyes to the ceiling. 'Look, you don't have to worry. It's all under control. Can we talk about something else?'

Jo pushed her plate aside. She couldn't see what was more important than this. 'Like what, for instance?'

'Well, how about those letters you've got stashed away? Do you really think your husband was murdered?'

Jo's heart almost stopped. She looked towards the drawer and back at him. 'What?'

'Hey, I wasn't snooping. I just spilled some water while you were out. I was searching for a cloth and—'

'And just happened to come across some private letters that you couldn't resist reading?'

Gabe's dark eyes gazed back at her. 'I wouldn't call them letters exactly – more a series of notes and very repetitive ones at that.'

She was so angry she could barely speak. 'You . . . you had no right to read them.'

He gave another of his casual shrugs. 'No, I didn't. But I'm naturally curious and if you wanted to keep them private the kitchen drawer might not have been the ideal place to hide them in.'

'I wasn't trying to hide anything.'

'So what's the problem?'

'The problem is that you had no right to go poking around in my things.'

There was a short silence before he spoke again. 'Have you shown them to the cops?'

'They're not interested,' she said. 'They don't care. They just think it's some crank.'

'But you don't.'

Jo buried her face in her hands. 'I don't know what to think. Can we just drop the subject, please?'

'Sure,' he said, 'but we're rapidly running out of things to talk about.'

She raised her head and gave him a look. 'That's probably because we have so little in common.'

Gabe grinned. 'Yeah, that's often the way, isn't it? You think everything's just hunky dory, you move in together and next thing you know it's all awkward silences or petty rows over who left the top off the toothpaste.'

Jo felt a warm flush rise to her cheeks. She told herself it was sheer horror at the idea of their having any kind of relationship. 'I'm glad you find it so amusing.'

'Well, you know me, sweetheart, always looking for the bright side.' He stood up and pulled on his jacket. 'Anyway, never let it be said that I can't take a hint. I'll leave you in peace.'

She glanced at the clock. 'What are you doing? It's only half past six. It won't take you more than ten minutes to walk there.'

'Best to get there early and have a recce, make sure there aren't any undesirables hanging around.'

Now that the moment had come, she felt a sudden rush of panic. What if he didn't come back? What if something dreadful happened? He had, for all his faults, a few good points too. On top of which, he was the only person who currently made her feel safe. The idea of losing him created a confusing tangle of fear and anxiety within her. 'You don't have to do this. There's still time to change your mind.'

'I think we've already had that conversation.'

'Yes, but—' Jo stopped and nodded. She could see there was no way to persuade him. Gabe Miller was as stubborn as a mule. She couldn't let him go, however, without uttering some words of moral support. 'Okay. But . . . but you will be careful, won't you?'

'No need to ask,' he said. 'I'll be back before you know it.' He paused and grinned again. 'Although that's probably the last thing you want to hear.'

Jo thought of uttering something suitably caustic in return. A few choice words rose to her lips but she swallowed them back down again. Not only was he entirely mistaken – she did want to see him safely back – but this wasn't the most appropriate time for point scoring. 'Later, then.'

'Yeah, see you later.'

She heard him jog down the stairs and open the front

door but, instead of the expected click of the latch, she heard voices. Jo froze for a moment before she leapt out of her chair and ran out on to the landing. Her heart took a dive as she looked down. Carla was standing on the doorstep.

Chapter Thirty-three

'Hi,' Carla said, grinning like a Cheshire cat. 'Is it all right for me to come in?'

Gabe had already gone and Jo had no idea of what had been said in the few seconds it had taken her to get to the top of the stairs. Lord, of all the bad timing . . .

She forced a smile, trying to think of any acceptable reason to refuse the request. There wasn't one or at least not one that wouldn't make things worse. 'Of course. Can you close the door behind you?'

Carla looked over her shoulder. She could probably still see Gabe from where she was standing. 'I'm not interrupting anything, am I? I mean, if he's coming back or—'

'He's not,' Jo said, perhaps a little too sharply. 'It's fine. Just come on up.' She retreated to the kitchen, softly cursing. Damn! She knew exactly what Carla was thinking and the kind of cross-examination that was about to ensue. She flicked on the kettle and waited.

Carla was still grinning as she walked into the room. Her gaze instantly alighted on the table, still strewn with the remains of the meal and with the place settings for two.

'Sorry to turn up unannounced. I was just passing and . . . Are you sure it's okay?'

'Why shouldn't it be?' Jo said, trying to appear calm and relaxed. Her response might have been more convincing if she hadn't had her arms crossed defensively over her chest.

She quickly dropped them to her sides.

Carla lifted her brows. 'Your friend seems very nice, rather fit in fact. Tall, dark and sexy.' She laughed. 'Come on, spill the beans. Don't keep me in suspense. What's his name? Where did you meet him?'

'It's not what you think.' Jo said, rapidly trying to construct a cover story. 'He's just an old friend. He called me yesterday and—'

'God, Jo, you don't have to make excuses to me.' Carla pulled out a chair and sat down. 'You're perfectly entitled to see any man you choose. It's been two years since Peter died. No one expects you to live like a nun.'

'It's not like that.'

Carla stared at her. She pulled a face. 'Sorry, I was only—'

'It's okay,' Jo said, sitting down too. She knew that Carla's heart was in the right place, that she only wanted the best for her but she couldn't even begin to pretend that Peter had been replaced by someone like Gabe Miller. 'It's just that he isn't . . . I'm not . . . it really isn't like that. He's very nice but we're just friends. He's just a friend.'

'That's a shame,' Carla said. 'I only caught a glimpse but I certainly wouldn't throw him out of *my* bed!'

'Tony might have something to say about that.'

'I doubt he'd even notice.' She dipped her finger and

thumb into the salad bowl and picked out a piece of red pepper. She popped it into her mouth. 'So what's his name?'

Jo didn't like lying to her but she didn't have much choice. 'Mike,' she said. 'Mike Seymour.' Her history of making up names hadn't had much success to date but she could hardly tell her the truth. Gabe was a wanted man but not in the sense that Carla was imagining. 'He's only in London for a few days. He's just passing through.'

'That's a shame. What does he do?'

Jo racked her brains. *This and that*, Gabe's own reply to the question, would only arouse more curiosity. She tried to think of something suitably vague. 'He's er . . . in the building trade.'

'What, some kind of property developer?'

'Yes,' Jo said.

'Well, there's money in that. Perhaps you shouldn't be too quick to dismiss him.'

Jo shrugged. If Carla had her way, she'd have her down the aisle by the weekend. 'So what brings you round on a Tuesday evening?'

'Oh, I had to drop off some groceries for Ruby. She claims she's got the flu and can't even manage to stagger down the road to the local shop. Actually, she hasn't got as much as a sniffle. She's just doing what she always does – pulling the strings and making us all dance to her tune.'

'What about Mrs Dark? I thought that was her job.'

'The sensitive Mrs Dark has one of her headaches. All that communing with the spirits tends to drain her energy.'

Jo remembered what she'd said about silver. 'You think she's a fake?'

'Is the Pope Catholic? You don't believe any of that psychic shit, do you?'

'No, but I'm surprised that Ruby does.'

'That cow believes whatever it's convenient for her to believe.'

The kettle had boiled and Carla automatically stood up to make the coffee. Jo waved her back down. 'It's okay. I'll do it.' While she was on her feet she had a quick look round, hoping that Gabe hadn't left anything behind. Now she'd finally got her sister-in-law off the subject she didn't want her returning to it again. She glanced at the clock. How long was he likely to be? She had to get rid of Carla before he came back.

'Is Tony taking care of the kids?' Jo asked, subtly reminding her of her maternal duties.

'If you can call lounging in front of the TV with a drink in his hand "taking care" of them. That's why I thought I'd call in – a spot of sanity between the horrors of Ruby and the chaos that's likely to be waiting for me by the time I get home.'

Jo laughed, put the two mugs of coffee on the table and sat down again.

'Ta,' Carla said. 'So how are things? Everything okay at the shop?'

'Yes, fine.' She didn't tell her that she'd taken a couple of days off. Carla was only too likely to make a link between that and Gabe being here. But the mention of the shop suddenly reminded her of what she'd witnessed that morning. 'Actually, I meant to ask you – you've known Jacob Mandel for years, haven't you?'

Carla wrinkled her nose. 'We've met a few times but only in passing. Tony knows him better than I do. Why? Are you having problems with him?'

'No, not at all,' she said quickly. 'It's nothing like that. It's just . . .' Jo paused. Now she was trying to put it into words, her earlier uneasiness felt rather ridiculous. 'It's just that I saw him in the street talking to Constance Kearns, the woman who lives downstairs, and I didn't realise they even knew each other.' She took a sip of her coffee. 'It doesn't really matter. I was just curious. Jacob's never mentioned her, you see.'

'Is there any reason why he should?'

'No,' Jo said. 'I don't suppose there is. Only you'd think with her being my neighbour and all . . .'

'If it's bothering you so much, why don't you ask him?'

Jo frowned. 'It's not bothering me, exactly. It's just one of those things that . . . and I wouldn't want it to look like I've been spying on him. I mean, it's none of my business really, is it?'

'Well, Kellston isn't that big a place. Perhaps she went into Ruby's one day and they got chatting.'

'Yeah,' Jo said, 'that's probably it.' She bent her face over the mug. Something was still bugging her but until her thoughts were clearer it was best to move on, to leave it alone.

There was another question she wanted to ask – the crucial one about Peter and Deborah – but couldn't quite bring herself to do it. Anyway, this wasn't the time. If they went down that road, Carla might never leave. It was best, she decided, to stick to more neutral topics. 'So how's Tony?' she said.

But for Carla this clearly wasn't neutral. She narrowed her eyes and growled. 'I think the bastard's seeing someone else.'

'Someone else?'

'Some tart.'

'Are you sure?' Jo said.

'Oh, believe me, I know all the signs: his pathetic excuses, turning his phone off for hours on end, disappearing at the weekends.' She shook her head. 'Christ, he even bought me flowers yesterday. He never buys me flowers unless he's got a guilty conscience! What more proof do I need?'

Jo was beginning to understand why she had called round so unexpectedly. It wasn't just to do with Ruby, with some inconvenient shopping trip. Tony was up to his old tricks and Carla wasn't happy.

'So what are you going to do?'

'The same as always,' Carla said. 'Sit tight and wait for the silly bitch to grow tired of him. And she will . . . eventually. Tony's charms have a tendency to wear thin.'

Jo often wondered why they stayed together. There was certainly no love lost between them. Perhaps it was for the kids, although she wasn't convinced that being in the middle of a battlefield was a particularly healthy place to grow up. Still, what did she know? She'd been raised with a set of parents who worshipped each other and that hadn't been a bed of roses either.

It was another fifteen minutes before Jo manoeuvred her wrist and looked discreetly at her watch. It was almost seven. Had Susan turned up? Was Gabe talking to her now?

She was getting that sinking feeling in her stomach again. Something wasn't right. Half an hour ago she'd been concerned that Gabe might come back while Carla was still here. Now she was starting to worry that he might not come back at all.

Chapter Thirty-four

From the upstairs bedroom window Susan had a clear view of the pub on the corner. It was ten past seven when the coppers dragged Gabe Miller out and it took two of them to do it. He was still struggling, even though his hands were cuffed behind his back. She stood back a little and smiled. She might have known he wouldn't go quietly and now they'd be able to add resisting arrest to the charge sheet.

Susan didn't intend to tell Marty about any of this. If he found out that Jo had been snooping around or that Gabe had been in touch, he'd have a bleeding fit. Marty didn't know anything about her mother and she meant to keep it that way.

Telling the cops about Gabe had been a calculated risk. She was counting on the fact that he wouldn't grass her up. There was too much at stake. If he spilled his guts, telling them everything he knew or thought he knew, he'd be aware that he was putting Silver's life on the line. She was sure he wouldn't do that . . . or at least not straight away. In order to establish that the girl was actually missing, the law would have to go to Vic Delaney and the moment they did that,

Marty would hear about it. And the moment he heard about it . . .

No, Gabe wouldn't talk.

She watched as they pushed down his head and bundled him into the waiting car. If only he hadn't interfered. Why hadn't he just kept out of it? But she knew why. The sad thing, the truly pathetic thing, was that he had been trying to protect her. He really thought he could save Susan Clark from herself. Damsels in distress, even if they did have hearts of stone, had always been a weakness of his.

She sighed. Perhaps the stupid sod deserved some help in return. She would ring his lawyer, Paul Emerson, and let him know what had happened. With a murder charge hanging over him, Gabe would need all the advice he could get – and the sooner the better. It would take a while before the cops got him back to whatever station they were going to, got him processed and finally allowed him to make a call to his solicitor. He would then have to sweat in a cell until Emerson arrived. This way, she could cut the waiting time in half.

Of course, contacting Emerson wasn't a completely selfless act. Susan knew herself well enough to accept that she was thoroughly incapable of any real altruism. She never did anything unless there was something in it for her. Calling him would provide her with the opportunity to pass on a message to Gabe, a message that would emphasise the importance of keeping his mouth firmly shut about Silver Delaney.

As the cop car pulled away, Susan left the window and went back downstairs. She sat for a while at the kitchen table. This was all getting more and more complicated. For a moment she wondered if it was actually worth the grief but quickly stamped on the thought. Just for starters, there was the money to consider: half a million quid wasn't to be sneered at. Her share of the ransom would give her the new life she craved, a chance to escape, not just from this godforsaken country, but from all of the horrors of the past. Reminding herself of why she was *really* doing this, she grabbed her bag and took out the little plastic wallet with the photographs inside.

She slowly flicked through the pictures. It was the third one that pulled her up short. She stopped and gazed at it. There was something in the expression that always brought a lump to her throat. She closed her eyes and opened them again. She stroked her thumb across the thin plastic film. 'It's okay,' she murmured. 'I haven't forgotten. I won't let you down.'

Immediately, she picked up the phone and rang Emerson. It was a short call lasting only a few minutes. She recited the facts and he listened carefully to what she had to tell him. Then she gave him the message for Gabe. After asking him to repeat it, she was sure he would relay it accurately: *Be very careful or the silverware could get melted down.* He hadn't asked her to explain. The experienced Mr Emerson knew better than to enquire too closely.

After finishing the conversation, Susan sat back with the phone in her hand. There was another call she had to make but there was no immediate rush. Jo wouldn't expect to hear any news for an hour or so. That gave her time to work out exactly what she was going to say. She had to scare her enough to guarantee her silence but not so much that she would go running to the cops.

Susan slid the wallet back into her bag. She stood up, opened the fridge and took some ice-cream out of the freezer. She scooped it into a bowl and placed it on a tray. What else could she tempt Silver with? She added a hunk of French bread, butter, cheese, two bags of crisps, a bar of chocolate and a glass of milk. It was not, perhaps, the most healthy meal in the world but it might encourage her to start eating a bit more. The previous offerings, the chips and pizza, had been barely touched. The kid's stomach must be rumbling by now.

Susan took the tray down to the cellar. She opened the grille and looked into the room. Silver was curled up in a corner of the mattress with her arms wrapped around her knees and her long fair hair obscuring her face.

'Hey, I've got some food.'

Silver mumbled into her hair. 'Not hungry.'

'Yes, you are,' Susan said. 'You think your dad's going to be happy if you starve to death?'

'Where's Gabe?' she said.

Susan started. It was the first time Silver had mentioned him. Coincidence or what? She was usually droning on about Ritchie. 'Who cares? He wasn't there when you needed him. Men never are, sweetheart. You can't rely on them.'

'He's okay,' Silver said. 'It's not his fault.'

And Susan couldn't disagree with that. She had a sudden image in her head, the way Gabe had looked as they had dragged him out of the pub. She didn't want to think about it. Quickly, she knelt down and pushed the tray through the flap at the base of the door. 'Here,' she said. 'Do you want coffee or anything? I could make you a flask.'

'No,' Silver said.

Susan stood up and peered through the grille again. 'Well, don't just leave it sitting there.'

Silver obediently got up and padded barefoot across the cellar. The chain clattered on the cold stone floor. She picked up the tray and put it on the little table by the mattress. 'I need a shower.'

'It's not a hotel. You'll have to use the basin.'

Silver's only response was to lie down and turn her back.

'Not feeling talkative today?' Susan said.

There was no reply.

'Suit yourself.' She shut the grille and leaned back against the wall. She didn't feel any guilt about Gabe. Why should she? She had done him a small favour in calling Emerson but a much bigger one in not telling Marty Gull about the fact he had contacted her. Marty wouldn't have thought twice about taking him out, and Gabe was better off in jail than six feet under.

Chapter Thirty-five

Jo had cleared the table, done the washing-up and was now looking for something else to do. She had to keep occupied, to keep moving. It was a quarter to eight and Carla had left over twenty minutes ago.

She went into the living room and gazed out across the Green. There was still no sign of him. But that was good, wasn't it? It meant that Susan was there, that they were talking, that some kind of resolution could be within reach. She frowned. Or that they *couldn't* reach an agreement. Or that she hadn't turned up and he was still waiting for her. Would Susan really be prepared to throw away the chance of half a million? Maybe, if she had one small shred of decency inside her. But that was debatable.

Jo tidied away the newspapers, plumped up the cushions and watered a drooping geranium on the window ledge. What would she do if Gabe didn't come back? No, she couldn't start thinking like that. It was still early. There was plenty of time. She looked out across the Green again; it was all in shadow now and the air had grown cool.

From around the corner, Leo came cycling down the road, his dark hair flying out behind him. He jumped off his bike at the gate, looked up and gave her a wave. Jo smiled and waved back. She hadn't seen him since Friday night, since Gabe Miller had thrown him so unceremoniously up against the wall. She watched as he wheeled his bike along the drive. He didn't seem any the worse for the experience but who knew what went on in a teenage boy's head. And then there was that other small matter. Did he really have a crush on her? Maybe Gabe had just been winding her up, trying to make her feel uncomfortable. He was good at that.

Her thoughts were interrupted by the ringing of the phone. It had to be him! She ran across the room and snatched it up.

'Gabe?'

'Hello, Jo.'

She caught her breath. It was Susan.

There was a short pause and then a laugh. 'Well, aren't you going to ask me how I am?'

'Why should I?' Jo snapped, all her fear and anger instantly rising to the surface. 'It's not you I've been worried about. What the hell are you doing? Are you completely mad? Is the girl all right? Where is she? Is—'

'Just shut up!' Susan's voice sounded hard and cruel. 'Jesus, I didn't call you to get the third degree. In fact I didn't have to call you at all. I could have just left you to find out for yourself.'

'Find out?' Jo repeated. Her heart began to race. 'What do you mean?'

'I'm afraid I've got a bit of bad news. Gabe's been arrested. I don't think you'll be seeing him in the very near future.'

'What?'

'You heard. Sadly, he's about to embark on a rather long and unpleasant interview about the presence of a young man's body in his flat. And then after that . . .'

'You tipped them off,' Jo said accusingly. 'You told them he'd be at The George.'

Susan didn't deny it. 'I warned him. I gave him every chance. I told him not to interfere but he just couldn't help himself. That's the trouble with Gabe, he's never learned when to back off, when to leave things alone.'

Jo felt her knees begin to shake. She sat down on the floor and gasped. She had known it was the wrong thing to do. She had told him not to go. Why hadn't he listened to her? 'What have you done? How could you? You know he didn't kill Ritchie Naylor.'

'Well he's got nothing to worry about then, has he? Oh, and before you even think about going to the cops and making a statement of your own, a word to the wise – you so much as step into a police station and we'll hear about it. Keep your mouth shut about Silver or you'll have to live with the consequences. Could you really bear to have that on your conscience?'

'You wouldn't,' Jo murmured.

'It's not me you need to worry about. It's out of my hands. Let's just say that the involvement of the law might panic my friend into doing something desperate. He's rather highly strung, you see. Do you understand what I mean?'

Jo, stunned into silence, nodded down the phone.

'Jo?'

'Yes,' she said quickly. 'I understand.'

'Good. So long as we've got that clear.' Susan's tone softened a little. 'Look, I never meant for you to get involved in all this. It was just . . . unfortunate. In a few days it will all be over. You can forget it ever happened. We'll have our cash and Delaney will have his daughter back. No one gets hurt and everyone's happy.'

'Apart from Ritchie Naylor,' Jo said. 'And Gabe.'

'Gabe can take care of himself. And anyway, by the time it comes to trial – if it even gets that far – I'm sure that expensive lawyer of his will have come up with a suitably convincing defence.'

'Don't you care about anyone but yourself?'

Susan gave a thin laugh. 'I think you already know the answer to that. Just do as you're told, okay, and sweet little Silver gets to go home. That's what you want, isn't it?'

'Of course it is. But . . .' Jo, worried that Susan might hang up and that she might never get the chance to speak to her again, tried to think of something to keep her on the line. 'Come on, you know you won't get away with it. Vic Delaney isn't the type of man to just let it go. He isn't going to rest until he tracks you down. Even if you do manage to get the money, you'll be looking over your shoulder for the rest of your life. Do you really want that?'

'God,' Susan said mockingly, 'you're beginning to sound just like Gabe. You two must have been spending a lot of time together. I'm surprised, I really am. I wouldn't have thought he was your type. Still, it never did take him long to sweet-talk any woman into bed.'

'He—' Jo began angrily but then abruptly stopped. There had been an edge of bitterness, she thought, to the last comment. Perhaps Susan cared more about Gabe Miller than she liked to admit. 'That's really no concern of yours, is it?'

There was a brief telling silence before Susan snorted. 'My,' she said, 'is the little kitten turning into a cat? You'll be telling that bitch of a mother-in-law to mind her own business next.'

'Perhaps I will.'

'Well, good luck with that – and with the prison visits. They can be a bit trying at first but I'm sure you'll get used to them.'

'You'd really let an innocent man go to jail?'

'I'd hardly describe Gabe as innocent. Perhaps you don't know as much about him as you imagine.'

Jo's fingers tightened around the phone. 'So why don't you tell me?'

'I don't think so,' Susan said. 'I'll leave that up to him – if he ever gets around to it. He tends to grow a touch shy when he's talking about his past. But hey, close as you are, I'm sure he's already told you about the more colourful aspects of his history.' She deliberately paused. 'Or maybe not. Personally, I've found it's never a good idea to interfere in other people's relationships. In fact, it's never a good idea to interfere, full stop. I was kind of hoping that you'd gathered that by now.'

Jo stared down at the floor, saying nothing.

'So we understand each other?'

'Yes,' Jo said.

'Fine. We'll leave it at that. But just remember this one last thing – I didn't need to call you. I didn't need to tell you anything. Please don't make me sorry that I did.'

'I won't.'

'This is a young girl's life we're talking about.'

'I realise that. Yes, I promise. I swear I won't—'

But the line had already gone dead.

Jo slowly put the phone down. Her palms were sweating, her heart beating ten times faster than it should have been. She stood up, her legs still shaking, and went over to the open window. She leaned out, breathing deeply. The faint and lingering scent of cut grass reminded her of Friday evening. She had thought things were bad then, but they had just grown a whole lot worse.

It was after ten before the phone rang again. Jo had spent the last two hours pacing around the flat, trying to decide what to do. She wished she had the nerve to go to the police, to tell them what she knew, but she didn't. Susan's threats were still revolving in her head.

The phone rang and rang. She wanted to ignore it – how much more bad news could she take? – but eventually she picked up. 'Yes?'

A smooth male voice said: 'Is that Mrs Strong?'

'Yes.'

'I hope I'm not disturbing you. I'm sorry to call so late. My name's Paul Emerson: I'm Gabe Miller's solicitor.'

Before he had the opportunity to say anything else, Jo asked: 'How is he? Is he okay? Has he been charged?'

He didn't answer directly. 'It might be better, if it's not too inconvenient, for us to talk in person. I'm not that far away. Would it be all right if I called round?'

'That's fine. The address is—'

'I already have the address,' he said. 'Barley Road, number twelve?'

'Yes,' she said again.

'I'll be ten minutes.'

It was closer to fifteen by the time he arrived. She opened the door to a small dapper man in his fifties with steel-grey hair and a pair of shrewd grey eyes. Mr Emerson followed her up the stairs, accepted her offer of coffee and went with her into the kitchen.

'Thank you,' he said. 'It's much appreciated. Milk and one sugar. That muck they serve at the station is barely drinkable.' He sat down, placing his briefcase at his feet. His shoes were black and highly polished. 'Mr Miller has asked me to pass on a message.'

Jo, holding the coffee pot, glanced over her shoulder. 'For me?'

Emerson nodded. 'He said not to worry about the silver ring he left behind, that you don't need to do anything about it. He'll pick it up when he gets out.'

'Oh,' she said softly, turning her back on him again. Her hands shook a little and some of the coffee spilled across the counter.

'He said you'd understand.'

'Yes,' Jo said. 'That's fine.' So Miller had decided to keep quiet about Silver Delaney. Even if did cost him his liberty. Or was he just waiting to see what happened with the police? She took the two mugs over to the table and pulled out a chair. 'Has he been charged?'

'No, not yet.'

She shuddered at the ominous *not yet.* 'But you think he will be?'

'The interview will resume tomorrow morning. I'm afraid it's not looking good. The evidence against him is purely circumstantial but even so . . .'

'He didn't do it,' Jo said firmly. 'He didn't kill Ritchie Naylor.'

'Well, the onus is on the CPS to prove that he did.' Emerson took a sip from his mug and sighed. 'Unfortunately, Mr Miller is being rather vague about his movements on Sunday evening. It leaves him in a somewhat precarious position.'

Jo remembered what Gabe had told her about how he had spent the weekend driving round the streets of Kellston. She could see how such a story, if he chose to reveal it, could raise as many questions as it answered. How, for example, was he going to explain why he hadn't been prepared to go back to his flat? 'But they have the weapon, don't they? What about fingerprints?'

'To date, the forensic evidence is not especially useful. Either the weapon was wiped clean or the perpetrator wore gloves. They're still waiting on the DNA.' He lifted his shoulders in a small neat shrug. 'Naturally, you can see how it looks from the point of view of the police: Mr Miller returns home, discovers an intruder in his flat, a fight ensues and . . . Well, anyone might panic in such a situation.'

'He didn't kill him,' Jo insisted. 'You do believe that, don't you?'

'All my clients are innocent, Mrs Strong, until proved otherwise.'

'He's not a murderer. Someone else must have done it.'

'Sadly, there are no other suspects under consideration at the moment.'

Emerson peered at her over the rim of his mug. 'Of course, it is possible that Mr Miller has another reason for keeping silent as to his whereabouts on Sunday evening. Perhaps he's trying to protect someone, a lady friend perhaps, who might be – how shall I put it – *compromised* by the disclosure that she was in the company of a man other than her husband.'

Jo stared back at him, a pink flush rising to her cheeks. It was pretty obvious what he was implying. 'Is that what he's told the police?'

'Mr Miller has told the police very little. He has, however, asked me to talk to you. I understand that you met him for the first time on Friday night?'

She gave a tentative nod.

'In the bar at the Hotel Lumière?'

'That's right.'

'And he returned here with you?'

Jo paused before eventually nodding again. She could see where this was going. 'You want to know whether he was still here on Sunday night.'

'Was he?'

Emerson's cool grey eyes were boring into her, making her feel like a guilty witness on the stand. He clearly had her pegged as a scarlet woman, the type of female who cheated on her husband and slept around with strangers. What made it even worse was that she couldn't say a word to clear her name, at least not without raising the taboo subject of Silver. She took a deep breath. 'You're suggesting that I might be his alibi.'

Emerson quickly raised a hand. '*Please*. I'm not suggesting anything at all. That would hardly be appropriate. But perhaps . . . perhaps you could give the subject some thought.'

Jo was already thinking about it. Her mind was racing through the options. She was thinking about what was worse – lying to the police or *not* lying to them. She was thinking about what would happen to Gabe if he was charged with the killing of Ritchie Naylor . . . and what might happen to Silver in the meantime. She was wondering what kind of a sentence she would receive for giving him a false alibi.

'I understand how you may feel reluctant to come forward,' he continued, 'how it might be a little . . . awkward perhaps.'

Jo didn't reply.

Emerson nodded and got to his feet. 'Well, thank you for the coffee and apologies for intruding so late in the evening. Perhaps, in the morning, you could let me know if—'

Jo stood up too. 'Yes, I'll call you.'

He leaned forward and patted her on the arm. 'The police are, occasionally, capable of showing some discretion. Try not to worry too much.'

Jo forced a faint smile to her lips. It was a bit late for that.

Chapter Thirty-six

Marty was cruising the streets, checking out the whores. The filth, urged on by the local council, was forever trying to move the girls on, to shift them over the border and into the next borough. There they would be someone else's problem. He grinned. The irony, of course, was that half their clients were the uptight hypocritical bastards who were so determined to shift them in the first place.

He indicated left and took another turn around the block. He was looking for a particular type but hadn't seen her yet. Still, there was no hurry. The silver Ford he was driving had been stolen a few days before and the number plates changed. There was no way it could be traced back to him.

Leaning over, he slotted in a CD. Petula Clark's 'Downtown' flowed out through the speakers. He joined in, singing loudly. He loved all that 1960s nostalgia stuff: Dusty Springfield, Tony Bennett, Frank Sinatra. He laughed. He was in a good mood and why shouldn't he be? It was all going like a dream.

Marty concentrated on the street again. It had been his job, once upon a time, to keep Delaney's whores in check, to collect all the takings, to protect their territory, but things had changed a lot since then. There were still the pubs and the clubs, still a few in-house girls to keep an eye on, but most of Vic's cash was in bricks and mortar now, in the thoroughly tedious business of property development. Even the drugs were a sideline. Delaney had made so much cash that he didn't need the hassle.

It was the excitement that Marty missed most, the good old days when every penny counted, when the success of a night could be counted on the amount of jaws they'd managed to break and the number of tarts they'd managed to fuck between the hours of twelve and six. He gave a grunt, leaned back and laughed again. These days he spent more time talking to Polish builders than screwing hookers! What kind of a life was that? Delaney had got fat and lazy. He was heading for retirement and Marty knew what that meant for him. Sod all!

He tapped his fingers in time to the music. He could always jump ship and go to work for someone else but why should he? Almost twenty years he'd spent with Vic and he deserved some reward for it all. And he didn't just mean money. That wasn't what this was about. There were the promises that had been made, the glorious future that was rapidly turning into dust. If Delaney keeled over tomorrow, Marty would have nothing but memories to keep him warm at night – and how fair was that?

He stared out through the windscreen. He was looking for a young, slim girl with long fair hair. He was looking for a tart who could pass, at a distance, for Delaney's daughter. It was another ten minutes before he found her. She was standing on a corner, wearing a skimpy red T-shirt, a black leather miniskirt, fishnets and boots.

He took a moment to survey the street, to make sure that none of the old girls were around, no one who might recognise him or who might later tip her off as to who he actually was. After making sure the coast was clear, Marty pulled up beside her.

She bent down and leaned in towards the open window. 'Hello, babe.'

Her small pale breasts, pushed up and enhanced by a red lacy bra, were in his direct line of vision. He reckoned she was in her late teens, eighteen or nineteen, not quite as young as he'd wanted but the right size and shape. Close up, she wasn't as pretty as Silver but she'd have to do. 'What's your name?'

'Destiny.'

He smiled at her. 'Hi, Destiny.' He flashed the cash, a trio of twenties. 'You got a minute?'

She smiled back with that false smile they all had and climbed into the car. She took the money and made it disappear as quickly as only a whore could. As he put the car into gear and set off down the road, she leaned across and laid her hand on his thigh.

He shifted his leg.

'What's the matter, hon?' she said. 'You the shy sort?'

In twenty-four hours she would know the truth. Shyness didn't even register on Marty Gull's repertoire of emotions. Still, there was no point in wasting her presumptions . . . or his sixty quid. He'd keep it friendly, no rough stuff. If he didn't look at her face, he could even imagine that he was screwing Silver. But no, that wasn't a good idea. He'd settle for a blow job instead. He'd overpaid but that was okay. If he played this right she'd just think he was a fool, a clueless moron who didn't know what he was doing.

'Actually, this isn't just . . . only, well . . .' He deliberately stumbled over his words. He looked at her and grinned. 'I mean, it is but I'm also supposed to be organising my mate's stag party. He's . . . you know, last chance and all, the last few hours of freedom. He's . . . we're having it tomorrow night. Would you be interested? Are you free then?'

She shrugged. 'I might be.'

'How much would you, er . . . would a ton be enough?'

Her blue eyes widened. 'Just him?' she said.

Marty nodded. 'Yeah, just him. Just . . . you know.'

'Okay,' she said. 'Why not?'

'So I can pick you up tomorrow, same place, about ten?'

'Sure,' she said.

He pulled up at the side of the road and killed the engine. Despite his best intentions, he couldn't help but think of Silver as she reached over and unzipped his flies. What he wouldn't do to have her here now, to have her head bending down to . . . Well, it was only a matter of time. He closed his eyes, leaned back and groaned. He wound his fingers around the long fair hair. It wouldn't be long now. A few days . . . just a few days. He smiled. Daddy's little girl was about to regret that she'd ever been born.

Chapter Thirty-seven

Jo was sitting in the kitchen drinking strong black coffee. She had slept badly, her dreams of the kind where her legs were made of lead, where she was desperate to escape and where every small step was like wading through mud. She had woken over and over to the same feelings of dread and confusion.

The doorbell rang and she looked up at the clock. It was only ten past seven. She couldn't think of anyone who would call by so early, not even the postman. Her heart skipped a beat. Perhaps Susan was following up last night's threats with something – or rather some*body* – more solid.

The bell went again and she jumped.

Carefully, she approached the window, stood to one side and peered out. There was a blue van parked at the gate with *J.B. Harris, Garage Services* displayed along the side. The name sounded vaguely familiar. And then she remembered where she'd see it before – on the metal disk attached to the set of car keys Gabe had left in the study. She breathed a sigh of relief. Her unexpected visitor must have come to collect the borrowed Mondeo.

Jo went downstairs and opened the door. The man who

was standing on the other side was lean, tallish and in his late forties. She had only a moment to gather these fleeting impressions before her eyes focused on his arms. She gave another tiny jump. They were completely covered in tattoos. And not just any tattoos. A long tangled coil of snakes slithered across his flesh and wound around his elbows and wrists.

'Hello,' he said. 'Are you Jo Strong?'

She forced her startled gaze back up to his face again. 'Are you here to pick up the car?'

'Er . . . not exactly. I'm John Harris, a mate of Gabe's. I'm sorry to call so early but I wanted to catch you before you went to work. I was hoping I could have a word.'

Jo hesitated. She felt wary of the snake man and simultaneously guilty for feeling that way. Never judge a book by its cover, right? But then again, with everything that had happened recently, it was sensible to exercise some caution.

'It is important,' he said. 'I've been talking to Paul Emerson. I understand he came to see you last night.'

'That's right,' she said but still didn't invite him in. On the contrary, she instinctively stretched out her own less decorated arm, leaning her hand against the jamb and effectively blocking his entrance.

John Harris waited patiently. A small understanding smile played around his lips. 'Do you really think Gabe's capable of murder?'

'No, of course not!'

'Well then,' he said gently, 'we're both on the same side.'

Jo slowly lowered her arm and nodded. 'Okay. You'd better come up.'

For a tall man he moved with surprising grace. He glided up the stairs, politely stood aside on the landing and followed her through to the kitchen.

'Take a seat,' she said. 'Would you like a coffee?'

'Thank you. White, one sugar.'

Jo poured the coffee, put the mug on the table and sat down opposite to him. 'So,' she said.

Harris, as if choosing his words carefully, paused for a moment. 'There's no point going round the houses, is there? I know Gabe couldn't have killed that Naylor bloke. I suspect, from what you said, that you believe that too. Trouble is, the cops need someone to hang it on and he's the most likely suspect.'

'Yes,' she said. 'Mr Emerson explained as much last night.'

'Which leaves Gabe, to put it mildly, in something of a hole. They're likely to charge him today if he won't tell them where he was or if no one comes forward to provide an alibi. I'd vouch for him myself but I was out at Heathrow for most of Sunday evening.'

Jo could see what he was angling for. 'So you want to know if I'll do it.'

'Will you?'

Jo leaned back and looked at him. At least he couldn't be accused of being indirect. She tried to keep focused on his face, to not allow her gaze to slide back down to those very distracting arms. He had a somewhat lugubrious face, a pair of sad brown eyes and a soft wide mouth. 'You're asking me to lie.'

Harris gave a shrug as if her interpretation of a lie might

differ slightly from his own. 'I'm asking you to help prevent an innocent man from going to jail.'

'How long do you get for perverting the course of justice these days?'

'Not half as long as you get for murder.'

Jo gave a low groan. She could see why the two of them were friends; they had the same annoying ability to turn an argument on its head and manoeuvre you into the nearest corner. 'All right,' she said, 'I understand that but . . . well, even if I did agree, why should the police believe me?'

'Why shouldn't they?'

This time it was Jo's turn to shrug. 'I could have been paid off. I could be trying to protect him. I could be working for—' She stopped as Harris began to laugh. 'What?'

'Sorry, but you don't exactly strike me as that kind of woman.'

Jo, although aware that there was nothing uncomplimentary about the comment, was less than pleased by his levity. She was the one, after all, who was being put on the line, who was being asked to sacrifice her reputation. God, she could imagine Ruby's response if she ever got to hear about it. 'But I *am* the kind of woman who picks up strangers in hotel bars?'

'Ah,' he said. 'Is that what's bothering you?'

'No,' she said abruptly, suddenly realising how trivial and selfish it sounded in the greater scheme of things. 'It's not just that. It's much more complicated. Look, how much do you actually know about what's been going on?'

'Not much,' he admitted. 'Gabe turned up at the garage on Saturday morning and asked me to help him out. He needed a car. He told me he was in trouble but he didn't tell me why.'

She'd suspected as much. 'Well then.'

'Only that it had something to do with Susan.'

Jo stared at him, surprised. 'He told you about Susan?'

'He didn't need to. Gabe's more serious problems tend to have a habit of revolving around that particular lady.'

'Have they?' The question leapt out before she had time to consider it.

Harris took a sip of his coffee. 'That's the thing about ex-wives. Much as you try, you're never entirely free of them.'

Jo's mouth fell open. *Ex-wives?* She glanced away and quickly clamped shut her jaw. He had been *married* to Susan? She racked her brains, trying to recall what Gabe had told her. They'd been together for a year or so – wasn't that what he'd said? He had certainly never mentioned the M word. So what did that mean? Well, that he'd lied, that was for sure, or had at the very least deliberately avoided telling her the truth.

Harris looked at her, his pale brows arched. 'Are you okay?'

'Yes, yes I'm fine. I'm just trying to think.' Then before he could start realising what she was trying to think about, she rapidly changed the subject. 'Emerson believes that I haven't come forward because I'm worried about my husband finding out. He doesn't know I'm widowed.' She lifted her left hand, showing him the gold ring. 'He made a presumption and I let it pass.'

'That's not a problem. We can put him straight.'

'Won't he think it's odd?'

'It doesn't matter what he thinks. He's a lawyer. He's paid to believe whatever his client asks him to believe.'

'But if I'm not married, what reason would Gabe have for not telling the police about me right from the start? What would he have been protecting me from?'

Harris thought about it. 'We'll figure something out. You could have a boyfriend, perhaps? Or you could have told him that there *was* still a husband on the scene.'

'Why would I do that?'

'Because you were only after a quick . . .' He hesitated, clearly searching for a more acceptable phrase. 'Er . . . you weren't interested in anything serious.'

Jo raised her eyes to the ceiling. 'Oh great, this just gets better and better. And if that was the case, why would I have met up with him again on the Sunday?'

Harris smiled. 'I don't know. Because you were overwhelmed by his boyish charm? Look, the cops won't care why. You just need to make it sound believable.'

'Yes,' she said. 'That's what I'm worried about.'

Jo knew that she had to make a decision one way or the other. She could see how the odds were stacked against Gabe but did she trust him enough – especially after that revelation about Susan – to walk into a police station and lie through her teeth? But then again, this wasn't just about him. There was a teenage girl out there somewhere. *She* was the one Jo needed to be concentrating on. And Silver surely stood a better chance if Gabe Miller wasn't behind bars for the foreseeable future.

Harris, sensing that she was close to making up her mind, didn't interrupt her thoughts. He sat quietly and drank his coffee.

The seconds ticked by.

Jo stared down at the table. Eventually, she lifted her head and said, 'If I do this, how are we going to make our stories tally?'

'It's easy,' Harris said, looking relieved. 'First we get the story straight and then we talk to Emerson. Emerson then gets a little private time with Gabe and repeats what we've told him.'

'Is he allowed to do that?'

'To do what? He's only informing his client that an alibi has come forward.'

'Right,' Jo said dubiously.

'We just need to keep it simple.'

'Simple,' she repeated.

'Don't go into any unnecessary detail.'

'What do you suggest?'

Harris put his mug down on the table. 'Are you absolutely sure you want to do this?'

Jo wasn't. She had never been less sure about anything. She took a deep breath and nodded. 'Just talk me through it. Just tell me what I need to say.'

Chapter Thirty-eight

It was getting on for eleven by the time Jo emerged from the police station. She lifted her face to the sky and drank in the air like a newly released prisoner who'd been languishing in a dungeon for the past twenty years. Her legs were still shaking. What had she done? Well, nothing that could be undone without landing herself in a whole heap of trouble.

John Harris was waiting round the corner in his van. She climbed in, shut the door and leaned back with a sigh.

'Well,' he said. 'How did it go?'

She wasn't sure how to respond. It had been one of the most nerve-racking hours of her life, an hour that had seemed to stretch on for ever as she answered the same questions over and over again.

'To be honest, I don't know. I told them what we'd agreed, that I first met Gabe on Friday night, that he came back to the flat, stayed the night and that we arranged to meet up again on Sunday evening.'

Harris nodded, listening carefully. He put a skinny roll-up in his mouth, lit it and waited for her to go on.

'I told them he arrived at about seven, that we had something to eat and shared a bottle of wine. And then we . . .'

Jo cleared her throat, wondering how she could still feel awkward after having already repeated it so many times. 'And then . . .'

'And then you went to bed.'

'Yes,' she said, 'and stayed there until the morning.'

'Do you think they went for it?'

'I don't know,' she said again. 'They certainly gave me a grilling.' There had been two of them, a male detective sergeant and a female constable. It was the latter who had taken her statement and asked most of the questions.

'They asked me what we ate, what we talked about, if I was absolutely sure that he didn't leave the flat at any time during the evening.'

'And what did you say – I mean, about what you talked about?'

'Just what we agreed. Nothing too specific: my job, his job, life in general. And, of course, the most important point – that I have a steady and rather possessive boyfriend who is currently working abroad.'

Jo had chosen the absent boyfriend scenario in preference to the other option of her simply being in search of a 'quickie'. Out of the two evils, it had seemed marginally less disgusting. However, her shame had felt real enough when she was forced to publicly declare her act of betrayal. It was, perhaps, the only occasion when her tendency to blush had actually worked *for* rather than against her. She had, without much effort, been able to play the part of a woman almost crippled by embarrassment.

'Okay,' Harris said. 'Good. Well, none of that sounds like a problem.'

'So what happens now?'

He switched on the engine and pulled away from the kerb. 'Now it's down to Gabe. So long as he sticks to the story . . .'

'You think they'll release him?'

'It's possible.'

'When?'

'They'll have to check you out first, make sure that you're a credible witness, that you haven't got a criminal record or a habit of providing false alibis.'

Jo frowned, wondering about her credibility. She thought back to the last time she'd stepped inside a police station. It hadn't been here, in north London. It had been at Kellston, eighteen months ago, when she'd been virtually accused of being some crazy woman who wrote letters to herself. But neither of her interrogators, thank God, had raised that particular subject. But then they probably hadn't found out about it yet. Perhaps they never would. She crossed her fingers, closed her eyes and offered up a silent prayer.

'There're still the DNA tests,' he continued. 'There's bound to be some cross-contamination with Naylor's body being found in his flat but it won't be enough for the CPS to prosecute.'

'You must like him to go to all this trouble,' Jo said.

'What trouble?'

'Turning up on my doorstep first thing in the morning, talking me through everything, persuading me to go to the police.'

Harris took a drag on his cigarette and glanced at her. 'You didn't take that much persuading.'

She could imagine what he was thinking. 'It's not like that. It's . . .'

'Complicated?' he said.

Averting her face, Jo looked out through the window. She wished she could talk about it but she couldn't. Whatever Harris was doing, he was doing because he was a mate. Her motives weren't quite so straightforward.

They didn't speak again until he pulled up in Barley Road.

'If it's any consolation,' he said, 'I think you've done the right thing. Gabe's a decent bloke.'

Jo got out of the van and looked back at him. 'I hope so.'

Thirty minutes later, pacing around the flat, she was still hoping. It could be hours, even days, before she learned the outcome of her false testimony. In the meantime, she had no idea of what to do with herself. All she did know was that doing nothing was guaranteed to send her crazy.

She went into the study and started tidying up. First, she stripped the covers off the duvet and the pillows and threw them on the floor. She picked up the clothes Gabe had left on the bed and draped them over the back of a chair. She stared down at the futon. Should she fold it up? If she did, it was like saying that she thought he might not be coming back. If she didn't, she could be tempting providence.

Unable to decide, Jo walked across the room. The keys to the white Mondeo were lying on the desk. She'd forgotten to ask John Harris if he wanted the car back. Still, that was the least of her worries. Opening the top drawer, she dropped the keys inside. She was about to close the drawer when she realised that some of Peter's papers were still lying there. She had looked through them briefly after he'd died and now she casually rifled through them again, looking for . . . for what? It was only when she came to a pile of credit card statements that she stopped and slowly eased them out.

Laying them on the surface of the desk, she ran a finger down the first page, down the list of payees: Tesco, the local petrol station, Amazon, the Italian restaurant on the High Street, more food, more fuel. She flicked through the next few sheets but they were all equally innocuous. Not for the first time that day, she felt ashamed. What was she expecting to find? She wasn't sure. Maybe just some shred of evidence that could connect him to Deborah Hayes. But why should she want to do that? A horrible shiver of guilt ran through her.

Perhaps she'd always been aware that she hadn't been as close to Peter as she'd wanted to be. Although that didn't mean that he'd . . . Shoving the statements to one side, she delved back into the drawer. But there was nothing else to discover, only a few more bills, some magazines and a slim Kodak folder of photographs.

She drew out the folder and slid out the prints. She'd seen them before. There were only three of them. The first was of Peter when he was a child, a wide-eyed, fair-haired infant standing by his parents. It was one of those posed studio portraits where everyone stood upright and gazed into the camera. Ruby, holding a new baby, was smiling but Mitchell wasn't. Peter, as if undecided what to do, had his mouth slightly open and his arms fixed firmly by his sides.

How old was he? Four or five? She stared at it for a moment, the strings pulling at her heart – he looked so young and innocent – before carefully putting it to one side.

The second picture was of Mitchell Strong, standing in front of his shop in Hatton Garden. Perhaps it had been the day it opened. He was a tall, solid man without any of the physical grace of his sons. His shining eyes stared defiantly into the camera. He looked inordinately pleased with himself.

The last photo was of Peter in Thailand. She knew where it was from the writing on the back and knew from the date that he had been thirty-one when it was taken. He was leaning against a wall with a rucksack on his back. He was laughing and she couldn't help but smile too. Happiness seemed to leak out from the picture. It was only as she was staring at it that her smile slowly faded and she thought of the questions she had never thought to ask before: *Who was standing in front of him? Who had taken the picture? Who exactly was he laughing with?*

Jo laid the print back down on the desk. She leaned down and opened the other drawers, even though she knew they were empty. It was the physical lack of history that bemused her, as if Peter had just wiped each period of his life away after it had happened. Hardly any pictures, no letters, no old calendars or diaries.

She sat down on the bed and put her head in her hands. The truth was that she was still angry – angry that he had gone and died on her. And how mad was that? There were, apparently, seven stages of grieving and she still hadn't got past stage three. She'd done the first two, the shock and the denial, but hadn't come to terms with the anger. Did that make her some kind of psychological freak? It wasn't as if he had gone out and got himself run over deliberately.

She thought about the first time they'd met on a busy station platform, a low murmur of dissent emanating from the waiting passengers as the speakers announced yet another delay. In frustration Peter had turned around, accidentally bashed his briefcase into her knee, and apologised. People joked about love at first sight but that was how it had been. She had looked up to see a shock of fair hair, a striking sculpted face, a pair of piercing blue eyes. And then . . .

Jo leapt up. She couldn't do this, she *mustn't.* Soon the tears would start to flow and then she'd be lost. She had to get out of the flat. She had to get some fresh air and clear her head. Grabbing her bag, she ran for the door.

Chapter Thirty-nine

There was a limit to the amount of time anyone could roam aimlessly around Kellston and by two o'clock Jo had reached it. Her feet were starting to ache but her head was still buzzing. Faced with the prospect of returning to an empty flat, she decided to go to Ruby's instead. Emerson had her mobile number. If there was any news, he'd call her.

Jacob gave a sigh as she walked in. 'What are you doing here? You're supposed to be taking time off, to be having a break.'

'What can I say? I'm a workaholic.'

He followed her through to the office. 'Don't you think—'

'I'm all right,' she said, 'really I am. You don't have to worry. And I know you don't need me out front. I noticed the storeroom was in need of a clear-out so now seems as good a time as any.'

'I can get one of the students to do that.'

'What and have them think that the boss never gets her hands dirty?' She gave him a rueful smile. 'To be honest, Jacob, I just want to keep busy. I've got things on my mind. You know what it's like.'

He gave her a long enquiring look but, sensing perhaps that she had no wish to discuss it further, simply reached out and gave her a paternal pat on the arm. 'Don't go lifting anything heavy.'

'I won't.'

For the next couple of hours Jo folded up empty cardboard boxes, jumped up and down to flatten them and piled them up outside for recycling. Over several journeys, she carried reams of paper through to the office and stacked them in a neat pile. She found a new toner cartridge for the printer. She sorted out the numerous gift boxes by size, shape and their suitability as regards weddings, anniversaries, birthdays, christenings etc. After unpacking the latest delivery of little velvet pouches, she separated them into the three different colours, midnight blue, claret and black, and took them through to the shop and placed them under the counter.

It was only when she'd swept the floor, dusted the shelves and given the place a blast of air freshener that she finally stopped. She gazed around the storeroom. It had never been so tidy. But her sense of satisfaction began to leak away. What was she doing? If she wasn't careful, she'd develop one of those obsessive cleaning disorders. Before she knew it, she would be round at Carla's house offering to clear up after the kids and give the kitchen a good scrub.

It was time to concentrate on something more cerebral. She determined to spend the rest of the afternoon mugging up on her knowledge of gemstones. It was a while since she'd got down to any serious study and if she wasn't careful, she'd forget everything she'd ever learned. There were plenty of reference books here and it would give her something else to think about.

Jo made a coffee, took it through to the office and sat down. The CCTV was playing on the screen in the corner. She pulled out a chair, sat down and watched. They didn't normally have too much trouble – all the more valuable items were under reinforced glass – but there was the usual amount of petty theft, of bracelets and chains being surreptitiously slipped into empty pockets. For a Wednesday afternoon, the shop was pretty busy. Trade was on an upward curve, increasing week by week, and soon they would have to employ more permanent staff.

It had been her intention to spend the next ten minutes with her eyes peeled for any signs of foul play, to do her bit for security, but instead of watching the customers she found herself watching Deborah Hayes instead. She followed her progress along an aisle, a young good-looking man in tow, and studied the way she walked and smiled and tilted her head. She saw the way the man's gaze dropped down to Deborah's backside. She saw the way he stared at it. Jo stared at it too. It was small but curvy, its shape accentuated by the clingy jersey dress she was wearing. Was it a better ass than hers? Did it have more sex appeal? Had Peter looked at it and . . .

Jo quickly stood up and turned her back. If she didn't stop this now she would spend the rest of the afternoon stressing over what might or might not have been. She grabbed a couple of books off the shelves and laid them on the desk. It was time to focus on something more useful.

She sat down, opened the first volume at the chapter on

sapphires and attempted to absorb the words – but they just wouldn't sink in. She gazed at the page, rubbed her eyes and drank some more coffee.

She had to concentrate, to try harder. *Sapphires are a member of the same family as rubies.* Jo already knew that, although it was hard, when you looked at them, to make a direct connection between the two. Still, she only had to compare her mother-in-law and Peter to see how two members of a family could be so completely different. Ruby was all hard hot fire, the very personification of red, while Peter had been quite specifically blue. She didn't mean depressed exactly but kind of sad, lost, as if there was a part of him that could never be truly happy.

Jo stared down at the book. Both stones were a combination of aluminium and oxygen. And sapphires weren't necessarily blue – they came in all kinds of different colours, in yellows, pinks and greens. But she knew that too, just like she knew that Liz Taylor had once had a sapphire engagement ring. Although why she was even thinking of that now, how it could be in way important, she couldn't imagine. She flipped back a few pages and tried to start again. The words danced across her pupils – perception, lighting, clarity, transparency, diffusion – and her head began to spin.

Getting up, Jo went over to the safe. Perhaps it would be easier to make sense of it all when she had the stones in front of her. She punched in the code and opened the door. Inside was like a miniature Aladdin's cave. The top shelves were filled with small trays of diamonds, rubies, emeralds and sapphires.

She pulled them out, one by one. Gemstones were Jacob's particular area of expertise. He had lived, breathed and traded them for over fifty years. It was a small but important part of the business. She gazed at the diamonds and picked a couple up. She turned them over in her fingers, held them up to the light and watched them glitter before carefully replacing them again.

On the lower shelves was some of the more expensive gold and silver jewellery, including a number of rings and a few fancy watches. There were several strands of pearls too. She looked at them all but it was the rubies she eventually returned to.

Kneeling down, she picked up one of the finer stones from the tray and rolled it across her palm. She liked the colour, the depth, the intensity but that wasn't why she was so interested. She was still trying to work out why Peter had hated them so much. Was it just to do with his mother?

Burma was renowned for its rubies – that was one thing she'd learned from the textbooks – and they were the best in the world. However, the regime was a corrupt and brutal one. Jacob had always refused to either buy or to sell Burmese rubies. It was a matter of principle, he'd said, and she'd never disagreed with him.

Jo pushed the tray back inside the safe. She was about to close it when she noticed the pile of ledgers sitting at the bottom. She wouldn't normally have touched them, all those columns of numbers were almost guaranteed to send her to sleep, but on a whim she took a couple out and laid them on the desk.

She sipped her coffee as she turned over the pages. They

were about as thrilling as she'd expected: cash in from sales, cash out for wages and purchases. Jacob was responsible for the books and she trusted him implicitly. Once a month they would go through the figures together and the profits were on a reassuringly upward trend.

At the back of the ledger were A4 copies of the April and May payslips. The wage bill varied from month to month, depending on the amount of commission that had been earned and the number of hours the temporary staff had put in. She flicked through them, not paying much attention. It was only as she reached the final page that she almost jumped out of her skin.

Jo blinked hard. What? She stared down at the page, struggling to understand. It must be a mistake, an error, but there it was in black and white: a payment for two hundred pounds made out to Constance Kearns. As if her eyes might be playing tricks, she slowly read it again.

Quickly, she flicked back to the April sheets – and there it was again. Another payment to Constance! Rushing over to the safe, she dragged out the ledgers for the two previous tax years, took them back to the desk and pulled out the sheets at the back. With a trembling hand she ran her finger down the list. It didn't take her long to realise that the payments had been going out once a month, every month, since Peter had died. Well, not quite from that moment but close enough. There was only a six-week gap before the first instalment.

She pushed the sheets aside, dropped her chin on to her hand and bit down on her knuckles. She was starting to feel sick. It was some kind of fraud. It had to be. And Jacob and

Constance must be in it together. But why? Jacob earned a decent salary. Why would he risk his job, his future, for a couple of hundred quid a month? And how the hell had he got involved with Constance Kearns? She thought back to the previous day, to how she'd seen them chatting in the street.

Jo's first instinct was to rush out and confront him but she forced herself not to. This was a conversation that needed to be held in private, with no interruptions and with no one else around to overhear. She looked at her watch. It was half an hour until the shop shut. She had to sit tight and wait.

First, she slipped the sheets to one side and covered them with the textbooks. Then she returned the ledgers to the safe and closed it. She didn't want Jacob walking in and seeing the accounts sitting on the desk.

The next thirty minutes were dreadful ones. She couldn't control the emotions that swept over her: shock, anger, bitterness. She was desperate to learn the truth but dreaded it too. She had laid her trust in him, absolutely and unequivocally. And what had he done? Fraud was too bland a name for it. It was theft, plain and simple. And yet it was impossible to believe. He couldn't. He wouldn't. Not Jacob. Was she jumping to ridiculous conclusions? Could there be another explanation?

Eventually, she heard a couple of the staff pass by on their way to the kitchen. Getting up, she put her head round the door and beckoned Megan Brooks over. Meg was one of the young design students who worked part-time.

Jo smiled – it was an effort – and tried to keep her voice

neutral. 'Hi, could you do me a favour and ask Jacob to pop into the office after he's locked up?'

'Okay,' she said.

'Thanks.'

Jo closed the door and sat back down again. She could have asked him directly but he might have guessed from her face that something was wrong and prepared himself accordingly. What she needed was the element of surprise, to be able to see his expression when she confronted him with the evidence.

For the next ten minutes she listened as the footsteps passed to and fro. It gradually grew quiet. Jo's heart began to beat faster. She tried to regulate her breathing, to keep it steady, to stop herself from going into panic. She hated confrontation at the best of times – and this was more than that. This day, she decided, must be one of the worst of her life. She had spent the morning down the police station and now . . .

When the knock came on the door, she flinched. Jacob didn't need to knock – it was as much his office as hers – but he always did if she was in here on her own. In the past she had put it down to old-fashioned courtesy but now she wondered if it had all been part of a game, a game that involved convincing her that she was in charge, that she was respected, whilst simultaneously ripping her off.

'Come in,' she called out.

There was a short delay before Jacob finally made it through the door. He was carrying two mugs of tea and had a cardboard folder squeezed under his arm. 'I thought you might be in need of a brew.'

'Thank you.'

He pulled out the chair on the opposite side of the desk, sat down and smiled.

She smiled faintly back but found it hard to meet his gaze. What she was about to do, to say, could change everything for ever. Her nervous hands refused to stay still. She quickly shuffled some papers and piled them to one side. 'Has everyone gone?'

Jacob nodded. 'Another day done and dusted. And not bad takings for a Wednesday.' He pushed the folder across the desk. 'That new range has been quite a success. I thought you might like to see the file. Deborah's sure we can get the exclusive rights. It could be worth considering especially as—' He stopped abruptly, his smile disappearing. 'Are you all right?'

She stared at him. Her lower lip was starting to tremble, the fought-back tears gathering on her lashes. Now she was faced with the moment of truth, she could hardly bear to go there, but what choice did she have? He might have been the closest person she'd had to a father for the past two years but she couldn't ignore the evidence, couldn't pretend that it didn't exist. 'We need to talk,' she said stupidly.

'Jo?'

She had thought her anger would see her through but she felt only dismay as she moved the text books aside and slid out the copies of the payroll. 'Constance Kearns,' she said hoarsely. 'Perhaps you'd like to explain?'

Jacob's head jerked forward. His shoulders slumped as he stared down at the pages, the colour draining from his face.

She had hoped he might offer up a simple explanation

but he didn't. He was clearly distraught. She waited but he still didn't speak. His silence was like some terrible admission of guilt.

'Why?' she said softly.

Jacob bowed his head.

'Talk to me,' she pleaded.

But still he refused to reply.

Jo glanced up as the door to the office suddenly swung open. Deborah Hayes was standing there with her coat over her arm.

'No,' Jacob said warningly. He shook his head.

Deborah glared back at him. 'For God's sake, this has gone on long enough. Why don't you just tell her?'

Chapter Forty

There was a prolonged silence as Jo looked from one to the other. Her anger flared again. So Deborah was a part of this too. They had been collaborating, working together to deceive her.

'I thought you'd gone home,' Jo said coldly.

'Well, it's a good thing I haven't.' Deborah advanced into the room and placed her coat on the desk. 'Otherwise you might never have found out the truth. And before you start making any wild accusations, you should be aware that Jacob's only been doing what Peter would have wanted him to do.'

Jo stared at her, astounded. 'Meaning?'

'Meaning exactly that.'

Jo could hardly disguise her resentment. The next question, obviously, was how Deborah could have known what Peter had wanted. But she was feeling too fragile, too anxious, to go down that road. Instead she tried to focus on the more immediate problem. 'So you think he'd have been happy about the two of you . . . the three of you . . . stealing from the business for the past two years?'

'It wasn't like that.'

'So what was it like?' Jo snapped.

Deborah walked over to the shelves at the far side of the room. She ran her fingers along the row of files. 'Give me a minute and I'll show you.'

'No,' Jacob said again, getting up from his seat. 'Leave it!'

'She needs to know,' Deborah said. 'This has gone on too long.'

'So I'll tell her,' he said. 'I'll explain. Please go, just leave, and I'll explain.'

Deborah turned and shook her head, 'No, you won't. I know what you're like. You'll make some excuse, try to take the blame and end up in a prison cell. You've nothing to hide and nothing to be ashamed of. It's time to come clean.'

Jacob sank back down into his seat and buried his face in his hands.

'No one's going to end up in a prison cell,' Jo said. 'Will one of you just tell me what's been going on?'

Deborah took down a file and opened it. She lifted out a pile of papers and dumped them on the desk. 'Here.'

'Stop it!' Jacob said. 'This isn't the way.'

'Bank statements,' Deborah said, ignoring him, 'lots of them, all proving that your husband was making regular payments to Constance Kearns for a long time before he died. Read them! Jacob hasn't been trying to defraud you – he'd never do anything like that. He's just been trying to do what he thought was right.'

Jo's anger was changing into bewilderment. What was *right*? What did that mean? Tentatively, she picked up one of the statements, dating back four years. She scanned the page and quickly found a standing order made payable to

Mrs C. Kearns for five hundred pounds. She scrambled through the sheets and found another and another . . . Deborah was telling the truth. Peter had been making payments from his personal account for years and for larger amounts than the ones that had gone out directly from the business.

Jo raised her head. 'But why, why was he giving her money?' As the question left her lips, she thought of an answer that she didn't want to hear. Perhaps it was not Deborah who'd been having the affair with him but Constance. Why had she never thought of that before? Constance wasn't that old; she was slim and undeniably attractive. And if it was true that the two of them had . . . then who was Leo's father? 'Is . . . was Peter . . .?'

'He was just trying to help,' Deborah said.

'To help,' she repeated weakly. 'Because?'

Deborah looked at Jacob again. He still had his head in his hands. She sighed and continued. 'Her husband, Leonard, used to work for Mitchell Strong. Mitchell spent a lot of time abroad, especially in Burma and Thailand. If you want good gemstones, they're the places to go and Mitchell always wanted the best. It was when they were in Thailand that Leonard met Constance.'

Jo nodded. She swallowed hard, preparing herself for the worst. 'Right,' she said. 'And then?'

'About twelve years ago, on another of those business trips, Leonard got sick. He caught some kind of virus and died. I don't know all the details but Mitchell came back and—'

'Did very little,' Jacob said, slowly raising his head. 'He

gave Constance a thousand pounds and left her to it. No pension, nothing to help with the child. Leonard had worked for him for years but he didn't give a damn about that.'

'Mitchell never gave a damn about anything,' Deborah said. 'He was a complete shit. So long as he was clawing in the profits, that was all he cared about. That's why he and Peter fell out. It's why Peter took off, why he stayed away and why he didn't return until after his father was dead and buried.' She paused, looking at Jo. 'But he didn't know what had happened to Constance. He didn't have a clue. Mitchell had promised he'd take care of her and the kid, and Peter stupidly believed him. It was only when he came back that he realised what a pack of lies it had all been. That's when he tracked her down and tried to make amends. He helped her buy the flat in Barley Road. He got the deposit together and gave her money every month. Constance works hard but she could never have paid the mortgage on her own. You know what London prices are like.'

Jo thought about it. It *was* the kind of thing Peter would have done and all his acts of kindness, either small or big, had always been made with the minimum of fuss. 'But why didn't he tell me?' she murmured.

'I'm sure he meant to,' Deborah said, 'eventually.'

Jo bristled. She knew what was being implied – that because they had only been married for eight months, Peter hadn't trusted her enough to share in the secret. But what she still couldn't comprehend was why it had had to be a secret in the first place.

Jacob must have sensed the growing antagonism between

the two of them because he quickly raised a hand. 'Peter was ashamed of what his father did. He wanted to forget it had ever happened. And Constance Kearns is a proud woman; she only accepted the money for Leo's sake and because Peter convinced her that she was entitled to it. If he chose to keep quiet about what he was doing – and we didn't know ourselves until after he died – it was probably to spare her feelings as much as anything else.'

'You must have wondered when she moved into the flat downstairs,' Jo said.

Jacob shrugged. 'I suspected he was helping her out but I didn't know the details and I didn't ask. That was their business, not mine.'

'And after the accident?'

'She didn't come to me if that's what you're thinking,' Jacob said. 'I was the one who made the approach. I thought she might be having financial problems and I was right. I knew she'd never ask you, she'd see it as begging, and so I told her . . . I told her that Peter had made arrangements for the payments to continue, that it was just a matter of the will going through probate.'

'The will?' Jo said. 'But Peter didn't make a will.'

'She didn't know that and I couldn't think of any other way to get her to accept the money.'

'It was my idea,' Deborah said. 'It seemed the best solution, the only solution. I'm sure it was what Peter would have wanted. He could never have meant for Constance and Leo to be left with nothing.'

Again, Jo flinched. It was the proprietorial tone of her voice that set her on edge, as if Deborah had considered herself privy to all of Peter's thoughts and intentions. 'Of course it wasn't the only solution. You could have come to me and explained. Did you really imagine I'd refuse to help? What kind of a person do you think I am?'

'Well,' Deborah retorted, 'that was the problem. At the time – it *was* two years ago – we barely knew you. If we'd asked and you'd said no, it would've been impossible to take the money from the business. It seemed easier to just—'

'Go behind my back?'

Deborah simply shrugged.

'It was wrong,' Jacob said. '*We* were wrong. I'm sorry.'

Deborah didn't seem quite so willing to apologise. She put a hand on her hip and stared defiantly into Jo's eyes. 'We did what we thought was the right thing at the time.'

'But what about later?' Jo said. 'Were you ever going to tell me or did you intend to keep me in ignorance for ever?'

Jacob ran his hands through his thick white hair. 'I wanted to tell you, we both wanted to, but the longer it went on the harder it became. I suppose we just . . . just . . .'

'And what about the shortfall?' Jo said. 'Peter was giving Constance five hundred, not two.'

'Jacob and I have been making up the difference.'

Jo looked at them both and sighed. 'For heaven's sake.' She thought of all the money she had sitting in her bank account. The insurance had paid off the mortgage on the flat and there had been a life policy as well. Peter had left her more than well provided for. There had been no need for any of this subterfuge. If only he had talked to her, confided in her about Constance before . . .

'So what happens now?' Deborah said.

'Nothing happens.'

Deborah frowned at her. 'Nothing?' She looked a little irked as if she'd been gearing up for a scrap.

'I'm not happy about what you did but I understand your reasons. I'll make sure you're reimbursed for everything you've paid out.'

'There's no need for that.'

'There's every need,' Jo insisted. 'I'll write you both a cheque. And Jacob, you can take Constance off the payroll. I'll be paying her directly from now on.'

'That might, er . . . it could cause some problems with tax and—'

'Well, whatever.' She waved a hand dismissively. 'We'll discuss it tomorrow. We'll sort something out.'

There was a short silence before Jacob slowly got up from his seat. As if all the vigour had been drained from his bones, he suddenly looked old and fragile. He leaned forward and touched her arm.

'I'm sorry, Jo.'

She managed a small wavering smile. 'It's all right. I think it's better if we put all this behind us. There's no point dwelling on it. Just so long as we've got everything out in the open, that there isn't anything else I should know about.'

He didn't reply immediately.

'There isn't,' Deborah said sharply.

Jo glanced back at Jacob. He paused but shook his head. 'No, that's it.'

Seeing his hesitation, she almost asked: *Do you promise? Do you swear?* But even as the words rose to her lips, she swallowed them back down. They sounded too childish, too desperate. He was just shaken up by everything that had happened and she had endured enough humiliation without voluntarily adding to it. 'Goodnight, then,' she said. 'I'll see you tomorrow.'

After they had gone, Jo sat back and groaned. She felt more than weary. She felt exhausted, as if all she wanted to do was curl up and go to sleep. Her anger had washed away and all that was left in its wake was a dull pound of sadness and disappointment. Her head was aching. Although it upset her, she could see the reasons for their initial deception and the subsequent difficulty in owning up to it. Their silence over Constance's plight was just about understandable but Peter's was another matter altogether.

'Why?' she murmured.

Had he suspected, like Jacob and Deborah, that she might not be entirely agreeable to the idea of Constance being helped? But how could he? How could he ever think that? She had never been greedy or grasping. She had never given him any reason to think that she'd object. Stinging tears rose to her eyes. She quickly brushed them away. It was dreadful to imagine that he could have thought so badly of her.

'Why?' she muttered again. 'Why didn't you talk to me?'

Jo gazed around the room, at all the box files lined up along the shelves. There must be over fifty of them. She was reminded of Deborah, only a short while ago, quickly searching for – and finding – that one important file. How had she had known exactly where to look? Jo realised, with a sinking heart, that this was where Peter must have kept all his personal papers. Not at home, not at Barley Road, but right here in the office. It was another piece of evidence to show how little Peter had trusted her.

She was tempted to start looking through the files. What else was hidden here? Perhaps, if she searched hard enough, she could find all kind of stuff relating to Peter's past: papers, letters, photographs.

She jumped to her feet but suddenly stopped. What was she doing? She'd had enough revelations for one day . . . and enough disappointment. She took a deep breath, picked up her bag and headed for the door.

It was time to go home.

Chapter Forty-one

Marty watched as she gazed down at the plans of the building. The crumbling, abandoned factory had been empty for years. She smiled. Finally it was all coming together.

'Delaney's going to freak,' Susan said.

'He's already doing that. You should have seen his face when he got the pictures. I thought he was going to croak right that minute.'

Her eyes widened. 'Christ, I wish I could be there. Are you sure I couldn't—'

'What and leave the kid on her own?' Marty quickly shook his head. It was typical of the bitch to start wanting to change things at the last minute. 'No way. We agreed – we don't take any chances.' He sat back in the chair and put his hands behind his head. 'We're almost there, babe. Let's not screw up now.'

Susan nodded. It was a disappointment but she knew he was right. 'And he's got the cash ready?'

'All you need to do is send the first text through tomorrow night at nine.'

'I tell him to take the money, to go to the club and wait.'

'And then?'

Susan smiled again. 'And then we leave him to sweat for the next three hours. At midnight, I send through the next text with orders to go directly to the factory, to use the side door on Deever Road, to go alone and unarmed.'

'Which he won't,' Marty said. 'He'll take me with him for back-up and he'll have a shooter too.'

'For which blatant disregard of instructions, he'll be made to pay.'

'Naturally. And he won't make the same mistake again. By the weekend, when the *real* exchange takes place, he'll be begging us to take his money.'

'And we will,' she said.

Marty bent down, took a long blonde wig out of a carrier bag and held it up. 'What do you think? It's pretty gloomy in there but there's enough light coming in from the street to be able to find your way about. Plus, I'll make sure we take a torch.'

Susan ran her fingers through the false fair hair. She nodded. 'Yeah, it'll do. Where's the mannequin?'

'Already there. She's looking good but she'll look even better when she's up on the balcony, tied to a chair with her hair and clothes on.'

Susan scowled. 'It's not a *she*, it's just a dummy.'

Marty grinned back at her. 'Hark at you, little Miss Sensitive!' Seeing her face grow darker, he shrugged his shoulders. 'Oh, come on. There's no need to be like that. I'm only trying to get in the mood. Don't forget that *I'm* the one who has to be there. If I can't pretend that I believe it's Silver, how is Vic going to be convinced?'

Slowly, her expression cleared. She didn't like it but she could see his line of reasoning. 'I guess.'

'So have you got the clothes?'

Susan stood up and opened one of the kitchen drawers. She pulled out a new pink T-shirt and a pair of blue jeans. 'These were as close as I could get but I doubt if he'll notice the difference.' She put them on the table and took out the shoes. 'At least these are original. He should remember them. They're Jimmy Choos, pretty new, and they must have cost him a fortune.'

Marty turned the pink satin shoes with their distinctive buckles over in his hand. 'Shit,' he said, tapping the narrow three-inch heels against the table. 'You could kill a man with these.'

'You could,' Susan said. 'But I doubt if any right-thinking woman would want to get blood on them.'

She lowered her head to stare at the plans of the factory again. With her index finger, she traced the route Delaney would take, starting at the door, crossing the floor and stopping halfway up the stairs. 'Are you sure this is going to work?'

Marty groaned. They had been through it all at least ten times already. 'Of course it is. As he reaches that point, he'll be able to see her, although not very clearly. She'll have her head down. He won't think twice. He hasn't got the brains for it. He'll rush forward and then . . .'

Marty saw the look of pleasure that crossed her face. At that moment she reminded him of one of those black widow spiders preparing for lunch. Women, he decided, really were the deadlier species.

Susan took a moment to savour the prospect of Vic Delaney's agony before returning to the practicalities. 'What if someone hears you? What if they report it?'

'Not much chance of that. Anyway, we'll be well gone by the time anyone gets round to checking it out.' Marty stuffed the clothes in the bag and checked his watch. It was almost nine. 'Right, I'm going to split. I need to keep an eye on Vic, make sure he doesn't start having second thoughts.'

'Is he likely to?' Susan said, sounding suddenly anxious. 'I thought . . . what if he decides to pull out, to call the Law instead? What will we do then?'

'He won't,' Marty said impatiently. 'For fuck's sake, don't start stressing. It's only natural that he's going to think about it. He'd be a fool not to. Silver's his only kid, not to mention the fact that there's half a million quid at stake. But he's not going to do anything stupid, at least not when I'm around to remind him of what the consequences could be.'

Susan gave a sigh. 'Yeah, you're right.'

He stood up and laid a hand on her arm reassuringly. 'Don't worry, okay? I've got it covered.'

Susan walked with him to the hall. She opened the door and stood aside. 'Call me.'

'I'll give you a bell tomorrow.'

There was a moment of silence.

'Well,' she said. 'Good luck.'

Marty nodded. 'You too.' Personally, he was of the opinion that luck had nothing to do with it but women were full of superstitions and it never did any harm to pander to their more whimsical notions.

He strolled down the path, got in the car and drove off at

a steady pace. It was a shame that he hadn't had the opportunity to see Silver again but there wasn't much point when Susan was looking over his shoulder. And what the hell, his baby girl wasn't going anywhere in a hurry. There was plenty of time and that was part of the joy of it. What did they call it – delayed gratification? The longer you waited, the better it was.

Marty grinned as he gazed out through the windscreen. The light was gradually failing. The sky, a deep Prussian blue, had only a few pale streaks left in it. He loved the city at night and he especially loved this moment as it began to slide from one world into another. In a few hours' time, the moral commuters would have got on their cattle trains, the upright citizens would have gone home and locked their doors, and the streets would begin to fill with a different population. The city of vice would have raised its head again.

He pulled up in front of a skip, had a quick look round to make sure no one was watching and got out of the car and dumped the carrier bag. He wouldn't be needing the clothes Susan had bought or the wig. They weren't worth the bother. The only items he kept back were the shoes.

As he got back in the car, he thought about Susan again and started to laugh. It always got to him, how bloody stupid women were. And the vengeful ones were the worst. It must be getting on for a year now since he'd first met her, since she'd originally come sniffing round. He'd known she was trouble right from the off. Oh, she was a looker all right, but she'd never quite fitted in with the other girls. And when she'd begun to ask all those questions . . .

It hadn't taken him long to find out what was going on. Susan was digging for information on her sister, a sister who had disappeared about fourteen years ago . . . and the last place Linda Clark had been seen was where she worked – at Vic Delaney's club.

Marty had got in fast. It had started off as damage limitation – he'd intended to warn her off, to get rid of her – but then he'd had a better idea. Why look a gift horse in the mouth? And Lord, it had all been so easy. He had studied the photograph and nodded. Yes, he remembered Linda, of course he did. She'd worked at Honey's. She'd been a nice girl, smart, everyone had liked her. Especially Vic. Hadn't the two of them been going out just before—

Susan's brown eyes, predictably, had grown as wide as saucers. 'What, she'd been going out with *Delaney*?'

And then, naturally, he'd backtracked as quickly as he could. Well, he wasn't absolutely sure. He could be wrong. Maybe his memory was playing tricks. Anyway, it was probably best for her to drop it. Vic was a private guy; he didn't like people delving into his past.

'Why? What's he got to hide?'

'Nothing.' He'd shrugged. 'Well, nothing more than any ex-con with a certain kind of reputation.' And then, as if uneasy that they might be seen talking together, he'd glanced furtively around the room and lowered his voice. 'Look, I've already said too much. Just forget it, okay?'

But of course Susan wasn't going to forget it. Every opportunity she got, she was on his case, urging, begging, pleading with him to tell her more. It was the most fun he'd had in months. Slowly he'd cultivated her suspicions, dropping clues, drip-feeding tiny snippets of information that exploited all her fears about Linda's disappearance . . . and put Delaney firmly in the frame.

Susan's determination, along with her frustration, had grown and grown. But she wasn't completely stupid. 'Why are you telling me all this?'

'Because I liked Linda. I want to know what happened. I want to help.'

He had needed her to believe that he was on side, that he had nothing but contempt for his boss, but Susan was going to take some persuading. She was never going to trust him until he gave her good reason. He had to prove that despite all his years of working with Delaney, they were no longer close. And that had come at a price.

It had cost him a couple of very public beatings. Twice he'd had to wind Vic up, making sure that she was there to witness it. The first time he'd just received a couple of punches. The second time had been more dramatic. It was only when he'd been knocked to the ground, kicked in the ribs and left bleeding on the floor that she'd finally started to believe in him.

Marty flinched at the memory. Three cracked ribs and a bloodied nose – he could still feel the pain. Still, it had been worth it. Susan had finally found an ally, someone who had a reason to hate Delaney as much as she did.

From that point on, it had been plain sailing. Convinced that Delaney was vicious enough to have murdered her sister, Susan was out to get him. It hadn't taken him long to persuade her that the cops wouldn't do anything. If she wanted revenge, she would need to take another road . . . and he'd had plenty of suggestions as to just how twisted that road could be.

Marty pulled the car up at the lights, leaned back and smiled. Kidnapping Silver had been the perfect solution, a means to make Delaney pay for his sins and make some money too. And Susan had jumped at the opportunity. When the time came for goodbyes, he wondered whether she would put up as good a fight as her sister. He had always preferred the feisty ones – and Linda had certainly been that.

Although her features had grown blurry through the years – only that long, thick hair was truly memorable – he could still recall Linda Clark's attitude. She was a girl who wanted to get on. She was also the type who freely displayed the 'goods' on offer but then grew all coy when it came to delivering. A fuckin' tease, that's what she'd been. And nobody messed with Marty Gull that way.

Linda had been happy enough to leave the club with him, to go for a drive and then on to his flat for a late-night drink. The bitch had known exactly what she was doing – all those sultry up-for-it glances, all those flirty remarks – and then, just as things were getting interesting, she'd gone cold on him, said she'd changed her mind, that she wanted to go home. Marty shook his head. Some women had it coming – and that was a fact.

Still, he hadn't expected her to struggle quite so much. Most of them, at least the ones who were smart, gave up after the first slap or two. The stupid cow might still be alive today if she hadn't started blubbing, hitting out and trying to scream like some goddamn bloody virgin. After all, he'd only been after what was rightfully his. It wasn't too much to ask, was it? He'd had to shut her up, shut her up for good, and there was only one way of doing that.

For a while, he lingered on the details of that dreadful and yet somehow wonderful act.

But enough, he eventually thought. It was all very well reminiscing, basking in the pleasures of the past, but he had a job to do. Marty glanced in the rear-view mirror. He spat in his hand and smoothed down his hair. Destiny beckoned and you always had to look your best for the ladies.

Chapter Forty-two

Stevie Hills had asked around. He'd thought he would be able to get a shooter for twenty, thirty quid, but despite all the stories on the news, all the shit about the streets being awash with deadly weapons, none of his contacts had come up with the goods. This was, he concluded, because either the media or his contacts were full of crap but there wasn't much he could do about either of them. It was Thursday already, midday, and time was running out. Tomorrow he was supposed to be meeting the kid on the Green. It would be a shame to see all that easy cash go to waste.

Vinnie would've known what to do but he was still in the Scrubs, doing a five-year stretch for robbery. They weren't due to visit for another week and anyway, it wasn't the kind of thing he could mention in front of their mum. She was pissed enough already at having one son in the slammer. Of course, it wasn't so much the crime that bothered her as the fact he'd been caught and that she now had to make the effort to go and see him every fortnight. This was something she never stopped complaining about from the moment she stepped inside the jail until the moment she left.

Stevie unlocked the door of the flat and went in. 'Mum?'

He waited but there was no reply. Was she on the early shift this week? He couldn't remember. If she was, and she didn't stop off at the boozer, she could be back within the next half-hour. Which didn't leave him long. He had to make up his mind – and quick.

He glanced towards her bedroom. No, it was a bad idea. Definitely a bad idea, except . . . Well, there was no harm taking a look, was there? It didn't commit him to anything. It didn't mean he *had* to take it. Come to that, it might not even be there any more. It was a while since he'd last checked it out.

Stevie went to the kitchen and rooted under the sink for a screwdriver. As he came back into the hall, he thought about putting the chain on the door. He stood there for a while, trying to make up his mind, but decided to leave it. If she came back and found the chain on, she'd know for sure that he was up to something – and it wouldn't take her long to shake it out of him. She was a bruiser, his mum, one strong lady with a mouth to match. It didn't do to cross her. He'd be wiser to just keep his ears pricked for the key turning in the lock.

Her bedroom was tidier than usual, with most of her clothes put away. He hoped it didn't mean she was expecting company. Or, more to the point, that she was expecting John Devlin. He hadn't been around in weeks. It must be more than a month. Stevie hoped they were finished, although he could be wrong. Her lousy boyfriends came and went, and occasionally came back again.

Kneeling down, he pulled the rug aside and stared at the

floorboards. It was impossible to tell just from looking. They were all flush, completely level – there wasn't even a creak if you walked over them – but he knew that the one he wanted was fourth from the left. He knew because he'd been standing behind the door, peering through the crack, when John Devlin had flipped it up and put the plastic bag inside.

Stevie slid the screwdriver into the slim gap. After carefully easing up the board, he sat back and grinned. Result! It was still there. And it would be a shame, now he'd gone to all this trouble, to not do what he'd done on all those other occasions and take a closer look. He picked the bag up with the tips of his fingers and turned it around. Inside was a gun. A real gun or just a replica? He didn't have a clue.

Stevie slipped it out of the plastic bag and held it in his hand. If it was real, was it loaded? He put his finger on the trigger but didn't dare pull. If the thing went off, he could blow one almighty hole in the wall. Not to mention the noise it would make. But he still couldn't resist having some fun with it. Standing up, he took the stance – legs spread, both hands firmly gripping the revolver – and snarled: 'Give it up, punk!'

He laughed, danced around the room and sat down on the floor again. He was about to slip the gun back into the bag when he realised he'd left his prints all over it. The first rule of crime, as Vinnie always insisted, was never to leave any evidence. Sadly, he hadn't followed his own good advice.

Stevie leaned over, pulled an edge of sheet from the bed and carefully wiped the weapon clean. He put the gun in the bag and dropped the bag into its hiding place. It was for the best, wasn't it? John Devlin was a hard nut – he worked for some old gangster – and the smart thing to do was just put it back. But despite his better instincts, another voice was softly nagging in his ear. *Why not take it? Go on. Why not?* Blokes like Devlin probably had lots of guns, hidden all over the place. He hadn't been around for ages. He could have forgotten all about this one.

Slowly, Stevie reached out for it again. The kid had cash and it was just going begging. If he played it smart, he could screw another hundred out of him. He hesitated but only for a second. Grabbing the bag, he slammed the floorboard down and rolled the rug back over.

Chapter Forty-three

Today was the day. Nina Delaney raised her eyes to the heavens. She could hardly believe that Vic was actually going to fork out half a million quid. What a waste! Still, she would have been willing to pay twice as much, had she had it, to keep the little cow permanently locked up. When she'd signed up for this marriage, she'd had no intention of becoming a surrogate mother to the teenager from hell.

In fact, there were a lot of things she hadn't signed up for. Tentatively, Nina touched the bruises on her face. She flinched. Bloody Vic! She couldn't even go out. Make-up would disguise the colour but it couldn't hide the swelling; even with her biggest pair of shades on, the damage was still obvious. And she had no intention of becoming the latest subject of Chigwell gossip.

She was bored. It was only one o'clock and a long afternoon stretched out before her. Perhaps she'd go for a swim. But then she'd ruin her hair and there was no chance of being able to visit her stylist over the next few days; *he* was the biggest scandalmonger of all. No, she was trapped, stuck here in this prison until she was fit to be seen in public again.

She didn't even have Marty to entertain her. He was off

with Vic somewhere, plotting and planning over how they would deal with the exchange. Vic wasn't going to hand over all that cash without a fight – not even to save his precious daughter's skin.

Ever since they had married, Nina had been hoping to fall pregnant – having a child was the only sure way of securing her share of the Delaney fortune – but it had been almost two years now and nothing had happened. She was starting to worry. At this rate, Silver would be up the duff before she was. Maybe Vic was firing blanks. Maybe Silver wasn't even his. She grinned. Now that would be a turn-up for the books.

With nothing else to occupy her, Nina went over to the cabinet, poured a large glass of vodka, added a splash of tonic, and took the glass over to the window. She gazed out across the lawn. One of the gardeners, a tall attractive Polish guy, turned and gave her a smile. She thought about stepping outside and getting to know him better but decided against it. With no idea of when Vic might be back, she couldn't afford to take the risk.

By the time she had downed her third drink, Nina needed a pee but when she went to the bathroom Louisa was there, down on her knees, scrubbing the floor.

'Are you going to be long?' she said impatiently.

Louisa glanced over her shoulder and frowned. 'There is the upstairs, perhaps.'

Nina heard the barely disguised contempt in her voice. It was the kind of tone that she'd never dare use if Vic was around. 'Or you could save me the bother and just step outside for a minute.'

The maid didn't move. She glanced down at the wet floor and back up at her again. 'Mr Delaney, he say he want the place nice for when his girl get back from the holidays.'

'*If* she comes back.'

'She not return today?'

Nina leaned against the door and shrugged. 'Who knows.' *Who cares*, she might have added, but wasn't prepared to waste her breath on the help.

'Oh, but Mr Delaney say—'

'It doesn't matter what Mr Delaney says,' Nina snapped. 'There are some things even *he* can't control.'

'Not control? I no understand. She not come back?'

Nina scowled. Aware that her mouth might have run away with her – those vodkas had been pretty strong – she smartly clapped her hands. 'Well, come on! Are you going to shift or do you want me to pee on the goddamn floor?'

Reluctantly, Louisa got to her feet. She muttered something under her breath as she passed by.

'What was that?'

She didn't repeat it. Even if she had, Nina knew that she wouldn't have been any the wiser; it was just a jumble of incomprehensible words. She went into the bathroom and slammed the door. Why did Vic have to employ all these bloody foreigners? It wasn't as if they were even grateful.

Chapter Forty-four

It was three hours since the last message had come through. The club was packed, the music loud and throbbing. There were two stag parties on the loose and the booze, along with the charlie and all the other shit, was freely flowing. Marty was on the floor, calmly watching the dancers as the punters downed their drinks and slipped their notes into all the smooth and lovely crevices that their wives and girlfriends would never approve of.

He was waiting for Delaney's mobile to go off again. The boss was in the office, stressing, tearing out what remained of his hair. He checked his watch. Three minutes to twelve. Two minutes. One. And then . . .

'Marty!'

Bang on time. Good old Susan! Suppressing a smile, he turned and walked back into the room.

Delaney thrust the phone into his hand. 'Deever Road,' he said. 'The old jam factory.'

Marty stared down at the text. He scrolled through the message as if he was seeing it for the first time. So it was finally happening. 'Right,' he said. 'What are we waiting for?'

Five minutes later they were in the car, heading east. The cash was in a large case sitting on Delaney's lap, half a million quid just there for the taking. As he drove, Marty was aware that he could pull up somewhere quiet, put a bullet through his head, grab the case and . . . But the taking was to do with more than just the money. He hadn't gone to all this effort to see it go to waste.

Despite the endless talking over the past few days, Delaney hadn't come up with much of a plan. But then without knowing where the exchange was going to be, his options had been fairly limited. He could either turn up mob-handed – risky, as the kidnappers were bound to be watching the place – or do as he was told and go alone.

It was Marty who'd persuaded him to opt for the latter. Better to play safe, he'd insisted, to get Silver released before sorting out the bastards who had snatched her. There'd be plenty of time for that later. And anyway, he wouldn't be entirely alone; good old Marty, armed and dangerous, would be right behind him.

Delaney was unusually quiet on the journey, his thick, mottled hands clutching at the case. Occasionally, he let go and picked up the phone, re-reading the instructions as if they might have changed since he'd last looked at them. *As you enter, leave the cash on the table. Then climb the stairs to your left.*

It was the pictures, Marty suspected, that had really done his head in – poor little Silver, wide-eyed and terrified, shackled to a cellar wall. What father wouldn't be upset? Except he couldn't really understand the emotion or, more to the point, couldn't even begin to feel it. It was a form of weakness, this ridiculous attachment people had to their sprogs. It wasn't as if she was even grateful, for ever causing him grief, for ever pissing off at every opportunity. There was only one person in this world who'd been loyal to Vic Delaney and what fucking thanks had he ever got for it?

He glared at the road, his chest tightening. Vic deserved what was coming. *You're like a son to me.* That's what he'd always said. And that was what Marty had always believed until Nina had put him straight. The moment she had told him about the will – which left three-quarters of his estate to Silver, a quarter to her, and fuck-all to the man who had stood by his side for all these years – he'd known he had to do something about it. His rage had been all-consuming. He could have killed him, throttled him with his bare hands, but that would have been too easy. He wanted to make him suffer. And then, like a gift from above, the lovely Susan had come along . . .

He glanced sideways and nodded. 'Okay, we're almost there. Next on the left.'

Delaney turned his head as they slowed. 'You see anything?'

'No.' Marty drove on past, continued for another two hundred yards and pulled in. He switched off the engine. 'You ready, boss?'

He clearly wasn't. His fingers clawed at the case. 'What if she isn't here? Fuck it! This stinks. It's all wrong, fucking wrong! We need some back-up. We should call the boys, get them to come over.'

Marty kept his voice smooth and calm. Vic was beginning to panic and the last thing he needed was a change of plan at the very last minute, especially after all the trouble he'd gone to. It had been no bloody picnic dragging a semi-conscious whore up all those steps. 'It's too late for that. What if Silver *is* here, what if she's waiting for you right now? We can't mess about.'

Delaney grunted. He'd been on the booze for the past five hours, along with a few less legal substances too. He was high as a kite and paranoia was tugging at his nerves.

Marty reached across and opened the glove compartment. He took out the torch. 'Take this,' he said. 'It could be dark in there.'

Delaney still didn't speak or move.

Looking at his watch, Marty gave a sigh and tried again. 'They'll be expecting you, Vic. It's almost half past. They must know how far it is from the club to here. We hang about much longer and they'll start to get jumpy.' He took the revolver out of his pocket and laid it on his thigh. 'Let's go. Come on, I'll be right behind you.'

Delaney's hand automatically rose to his chest, to the place where his own gun was. The action seemed to pacify him. He quickly picked up the case and pushed the torch into his pocket. 'Don't let me down,' he said.

'Have I ever?'

Delaney got out of the car, leaned down and looked at him.

Marty looked back. Suddenly, as their eyes met, he had his one and only moment of doubt. All the years they'd spent together, all the shit they had shared. Was this really it? A few kind words, a single expression of love or gratitude, and he might have been tempted to spare him what was coming.

But Delaney had no kind words and his love, such as it was, was clearly reserved for others. 'Just make sure you watch my fucking back.'

Marty nodded. Watch his back? Oh yes, he was going to do that all right.

Chapter Forty-five

He followed, careful to keep his distance, as Delaney strode along the street and then turned into Deever Road. It was deserted. Of course it was. Marty had chosen the location with care. It was a short dead-end, a purely industrial road with no residential properties. There were people coming and going throughout the day but no one had a reason to be around at night.

He stood on the corner and watched as Delaney approached the entrance. For a second, it looked like he might be about to bottle it but then he tentatively reached out a hand, pushed open the door and stepped inside.

Marty ran to catch up with him. This was what he'd been waiting for and he didn't intend to miss a moment. He arrived, slightly breathless, and slipped in behind. It took a few seconds for his eyes to adjust. It was dark inside but not pitch-black. The lights from the street slid through the cracked and dusty windows and cast a soft orange glow across the factory floor.

Vic had placed the case on the table and was already on his way up the stairs. The torch jumped in his hand, making mad frantic shadows dance across the wall.

There were twenty-four cast-iron steps to the balcony. Marty had counted them. The balcony was where the old offices were situated, where the bosses had been able to stand and gaze down on their minions. A suitable place, he had decided, for Vic to face the consequences of his actions.

Delaney stopped as he came across one of the distinctive pink shoes. He bent down, picked it up and stared at it. 'Silver,' he whispered. He walked up a couple more steps. He shone the torch across the balcony and finally caught a glimpse of her. 'She's here, she's here!'

Marty knew what he was seeing. 'Silver' was tied to a chair, her head lolling forward, her long fair hair tumbling over her face. A shiver of excitement ran through him. He watched as Delaney began to climb again. In his eagerness to reach her, his drunken feet were falling over each other.

Marty counted down the seconds, three, two, one . . .

As Delaney hit the nineteenth step the gun went off with an ear-splitting bang. Marty, although he'd been expecting it, still jumped. He instinctively closed his eyes, then quickly opened them again. He sprinted up the staircase. 'Vic!'

Delaney stood rigid for a moment, unable to comprehend what was happening. Then, as the horror began to dawn – that he had walked straight through a tripwire, setting off a shotgun that had been aimed directly at his daughter – he suddenly lurched forward, freeing his ankles from the string and virtually throwing himself up the last five steps. On reaching the balcony, he dropped both the torch and the pink satin shoe. Through the thin remaining light, he stumbled towards the chair. Arms outstretched, he clutched at the girl's head, pulled aside her hair and then . . . The wail that came from him was almost primeval, a cry that rose up from the deepest pit of human pain. It echoed around the factory and only slowly died away. What he was beholding was beyond his worst nightmares. For a while his hands continued to paw desperately at the lifeless body but then, wide-eyed and stricken, he staggered back. His legs buckled and he collapsed to his knees.

Marty picked up the torch and shone it on him. After all, it was *his* pain he wanted to see, *his* face. And anyway, there wasn't much remaining of hers – the entire left side was just a crushed and bloodied pulp. The light was too dim and Delaney too distraught for him to realise that the wound or the blood weren't fresh.

Vic's mouth was opening and closing but the only sound emerging was a long monotonous groan. Rocking back and forth, a combination of snot and tears was flowing down his cheeks. His fists, tightly clenched, began to bang against the wooden floorboards.

It was curious, Marty thought, what grief did to people. It wasn't as if Vic had paid that much attention to Silver when she was alive. But now he believed that she was dead . . . He stood back and smiled. There was a kind of ecstasy flowing through him, a wave that went beyond joy into a realm that words couldn't even begin to describe. Vic's fat belly was bouncing up and down as his fists continued their relentless, pointless pounding.

How long before he put him out of his agony? Well, not

quite yet perhaps. There was no immediate rush. This was what he had waited for, what he had planned. This was payback – and it should be savoured.

Marty glanced towards the dead girl. A single, half-open eye, stared dully back at him. He tilted his head. Some appreciation, some acknowledgment of what she had done, should surely be given to her.

Thank you, sweetheart.

As if she had understood that her sacrifice was for the greater good, Destiny had barely struggled. She had met her end like all good tarts – with a false smile, a grasping hand and an empty heart. He didn't feel any pity for her. Why should he? She had made her own pathetic choices.

Suddenly, Delaney slumped forward, a faint gurgling noise emerging from his throat. Shit! Marty knelt down beside him. He hoped the stupid bastard wasn't going to have a heart attack.

'Vic? Vic, are you all right?'

But he didn't seem to be listening. Or perhaps he just couldn't hear.

Marty grasped his arms and shook him. This wasn't what he wanted. To make him suffer, yes, but not to fuckin' kill him – that would ruin everything. Death was too easy. He wanted him to remember this moment, every single detail of it, for as long as his miserable existence continued. And this was only the start, the beginning. There was *so* much more to come. 'Vic, listen to me. Listen!'

Delaney raised his head but his eyes were blank.

'It's not her,' Marty said. 'It isn't Silver.'

For a while there was no response. Gradually, as if being

provided with a lifeline he could never have hoped for, Delaney's fleshy hand crept around his. 'What?'

Marty quickly pulled away, stood up and swept aside the girl's hair. 'Look at her!'

But of course Vic couldn't bear to look. All he could see was the smashed up face of his own little girl.

'It's not Silver,' Marty said again. 'I swear. I promise. You think I'd lie to you?'

Eventually, Delaney raised his eyes. 'Oh Jesus!' he said. He got halfway to his feet before collapsing back down again. Doubling over, he gave a moan and threw up. Most of it went over his shirt.

The disgusting stench of vomit permeated the air.

It was left to Marty to try and haul him upright, no mean task when contending with eighteen stone of reluctant blubber. 'Come on. We need to get out of here.'

'I don't . . . I can't . . . Christ, who is she?'

'Fuck knows! It doesn't matter now. We've been shafted. We need to move.'

After a brief struggle, Marty managed to pull him up and together they half-ran, half-fell down the steps. Grabbing the money, he dragged Delaney along the street and bundled him into the motor. He dropped the case on to his lap.

'Wait here. I won't be long.'

Delaney stared up at him. His small piggy eyes still had a glazed uncomprehending quality to them. 'What are you doing?'

'I have to go back.'

'What?'

'You threw up, Vic. Your DNA's all over the place. You want to end up on a fuckin' murder charge?'

That little detail, unsurprisingly, had slipped his mind. 'Shit,' he murmured.

'Don't worry, mate. I'm going to torch the place.'

He was in charge, completely in control. For the first time ever, Vic Delaney was entirely reliant on him and it was a damn good feeling. Perhaps now, even though it was too late, he would finally get the respect he craved. Perhaps now, even though he no longer cared, Vic would finally realise who his *real* family was.

Marty took a can of petrol from the boot, put it in a carrier bag and headed towards the factory. Once he had turned the corner and was out of sight, he took his mobile from his pocket and sent a short message to Susan. 'It's done.' There was no point being selfish; he may as well spread the pleasure around. After all, everyone deserved a bit of good news.

By the time he got back to the car, Delaney's face wasn't quite so white. He had even made a small if ineffectual effort to clean himself up. Marty tried not to gag as he breathed in the stink. 'You okay?'

Vic gave a nod. 'You do it?'

'The whole fuckin' place will be ashes by the morning.'

Marty started the engine, opened the windows wide and put his foot down. With Vic smelling like something in a sewer, it was going to be a delightful journey back to Chigwell. Still, what the hell! It had been worth it. While he drove, he silently congratulated himself. That tripwire had been a stroke of pure inspiration. He had tied the gun to an old factory table, pointed at the hooker's corpse, then had threaded the fine, almost invisible thread down and across the steps, up again to the balcony and around the trigger. So easy and yet so bloody effective. And, just in case the fire didn't do its job, he'd retrieved the shotgun and the thread and stashed them in the boot. He'd also cut the ropes securing Destiny and left her lying on the ground. The cops could make what they could of the charred evidence they would find.

Several minutes passed before the next text message came through. The phone gave an ominous beep and Delaney scrambled for it. His hands were still shaking. It took him a few seconds to press the right button. He read it out loud in a broken, quavering voice: 'You were told to come alone. Be warned! Next time it will be Silver.'

'Bastards!' Marty muttered. He turned his face away and smiled. What a masterstroke, he thought, to take her away, give her back and then take her away for ever.

Chapter Forty-six

Susan flipped her phone shut and laid it on the table. She sat very still, letting the news gradually sink in, then stood up and walked across the kitchen. Opening the fridge, she took out the bottle of champagne. It was almost one o'clock in the morning but this was not an occasion that should pass without celebration. After popping the cork, she poured a glass of fizz and raised her glass.

'Here's to you, Linda!'

It had been a long time coming but her sister was finally getting some justice. A proper trial would have been better – what she wouldn't have given to see Delaney in the dock – but the chances of that had been just about zero. He had covered his tracks too well. Linda's body would probably never be found, never laid to rest, but at least the man who had taken her life was paying for what he'd done. Delaney was suffering and that was all that mattered.

Susan had spent the whole evening imagining how he must be feeling as he waited for instructions, as he entered the factory, as he climbed the steps, as he hurried forward to free his 'daughter' – and then went through the tripwire . . .

She wished she could've been there to witness that

moment of absolute horror. *To think that you had just killed your own child!* There could be nothing more dreadful. How long would it have taken him to realise the mistake? Maybe less than a minute but every second would have been an agony, a pain so keen he would never forget it. It would be seared on to his heart for ever. And it wasn't over yet. Now, slowly, the new fear would come, the fear that Silver would never be released.

Susan stared down at her glass. She'd yearned for this moment for so many years. A thin sigh of satisfaction slid from her lips. It was small revenge for what he had done – and half a million couldn't even begin to compensate for the loss of Linda's life – but it was better than nothing. She was not sure if she would ever be truly happy again but at least she might achieve a modicum of peace.

She took another swig of champagne. She was feeling good, elated, but it wasn't much of a party on her own; she needed some company, someone to share the joy with. Quickly, she stood up, opened the fridge again and took out a can of Coke. She grabbed the bottle and went down into the cellar.

Sliding back the grille, she peered inside. Silver was still awake, sitting on the mattress with her back against the wall. With no natural daylight and no watch, she could only tell what time of day it was by the meals Susan brought her.

'You okay?'

Silver raised her head but didn't speak. Sometimes she was like that, sullen and silent, and sometimes she just wouldn't shut up.

'There's no need to sulk,' Susan said. 'I've got good news. You'll be going home soon.'

It took a few seconds for the words to sink in but then her face lit up. She jumped to her feet. 'Has he paid you? He has, hasn't he? When am I going? Is it now? Am I going now?'

'Hey, calm down, take it easy. I told you – *soon.* Tomorrow, if everything goes smoothly.'

Silver visibly deflated. Her head drooped and her shoulders slouched. For her, another hour, never mind another day, was probably the equivalent of a lifetime.

'I brought you a Coke.' Susan bent down, opened the flap and pushed the can inside. 'Come on, don't worry. It'll pass in no time. You'll be out for your birthday. Think of all the brilliant presents you're going to get, all the money.'

Appealing to Silver's more avaricious instincts proved to be a smart move. She immediately rallied, collected the drink and returned with it to her bed. She opened the can and took a swig. 'How did you know it was my birthday?'

Susan sat down on the floor and raised the bottle to her lips. She took a drink. She was afraid to reply in case her voice betrayed her, in case she lost her nerve and started to cry. She had a lump in her throat that refused to go away. Silver's birthday, 20 June, wasn't a date she had too much difficulty in remembering. *It was the day Linda had disappeared.*

Susan could still recall sitting in that shabby bedroom watching her sister curl her hair, put on her make-up and carefully choose her clothes. She had changed her outfit over and over again, turning around in front of the mirror, taking things off, putting them back on. Even at thirteen, Susan had known there had to be a reason. She had known she must be seeing someone special.

'Who is he?' she'd asked.

'No one,' Linda had laughed. 'I just want to look my best.'

'Yes, but who for?'

But she had simply smiled and turned away. That was the last smile Susan remembered. It was the memory she had carried inside her ever since – that expression of happiness, of sweet anticipation. Whenever she thought of it, her heart flipped over.

Linda, she thought, couldn't have been attracted by Delaney's good looks; he'd have been no oil painting even in his forties. But he had offered her, perhaps, something far more enticing. As an older man, with both money and power, he would have represented an opportunity, a glorious opportunity for her to escape from her dreary, dead-end existence. And who could blame her for chasing a dream?

'Are you still there?'

Susan swallowed hard and looked up. 'Yes.'

'I'll be fifteen,' Silver said.

'Yes,' she said again. She knew that well enough. She had been the one, not Gull, who had chosen Saturday as the date for the final exchange. She had *insisted* on it. This year she was going to make damn sure that Delaney went through hell on the anniversary of Linda's death. He was going to have to spend all day and most of the night wondering if he would ever see his daughter alive again.

However, she was obviously not the only one with the past on her mind.

'My mother left when I was two,' Silver said in a small voice. 'She was called Christine. I don't remember her. At least I don't think I do. Sometimes I think . . . but you can't remember things from that far back, can you?'

'No, I don't suppose so.'

'Do you have a mum?' Silver asked, as though they were a rare exotic species.

Susan took another swig of the champagne. Half of the bottle was already gone but she still felt annoyingly sober. 'Of a kind.'

There was a short silence as if Silver was in two minds how to respond to such a reply. Then she said, tentatively: 'Where does she live?'

Susan frowned, unsure as to whether she was fishing for information or simply making small talk. Whatever the motive, she had no intention of telling her the truth. Thinking of the grey, high-rise block in Kellston, she automatically flinched. 'She lives in Spain.'

'Oh, wicked. I've been there loads of times. Whereabouts?'

Susan's frown grew even deeper. What on earth had possessed her to say Spain? Of course Silver would have been there; a good proportion of Delaney's robbing mates, at least the ones in retirement or on the run, would be living it up on the Costa del Sol. She racked her brains trying to think of somewhere more obscure but the only other place that came to mind was Ibiza. That didn't sound too likely for a fifty-something mother so she settled instead on avoiding the question.

'To be honest, I think it would be better if I didn't tell you.'

'Why not? Why can't you—' Silver stopped and gave a tiny sigh of understanding. 'Ah, I get it. You think I might . . . No, I wouldn't. I swear. I won't tell anyone. You've been cool; you've been good to me.'

But Susan, even if she had been telling it straight, wouldn't have fallen for that old baloney. The kid might believe what she was saying now but she'd soon change her tune when she was safely home. Delaney would prise the smallest of details out of her. 'Best if you've got nothing *to* tell.'

There was another brief silence before Silver, her voice trembling slightly, said: 'Do . . . do you think my mum left because of me?'

Susan raised her eyes to the ceiling. God, this was all she needed – a psychoanalysis session with a neurotic teenager in the middle of a night. As if she didn't have enough problems of her own. 'How would I know?' she said sharply. 'The inner workings of a mother's mind are a mystery to me.' But instantly she regretted not only the words but also the tone of her response. The prospect of Silver turning on her all-too-familiar waterworks was a grim one; she could be stuck here for hours, trying to offer some meagre crumbs of comfort. Quickly, she tried to make amends. 'No, of course it had nothing to do with you, sweetheart. You can't ever think that way. People leave for all kinds of reasons. I guess the most likely one is that your mum and dad just didn't get on.'

'So why didn't she take me with her?'

Because she realised just how bloody irritating you'd turn out to be, Susan was tempted to retort. Instead she shifted her bum on the hard concrete floor, trying to get herself comfortable until she thought of a more diplomatic answer. 'I'm sure whatever she did, it was always with your best interests at heart. Perhaps she wasn't too happy at the time, wasn't coping too well, and thought your dad could offer you a better future.' It was a glib, superficial response but the best she could come up with.

Silver pondered on it for a while. 'Do you reckon? Yeah, you could be right. You know, he once told me that the day I was born was the happiest of his life. He said he got so drunk that night he could barely stand up!'

Susan's hand tightened round the neck of the bottle. Fury swept up from her guts, a hot blind rage that made her want to scream. She knew exactly what he had been doing that night and it went far and beyond the sweet celebration of wetting the baby's head.

Marty Gull had told her how Delaney had been knocking back the booze, how at eleven he had disappeared from Honey's for a couple of hours and come back in a state: 'He was well gone by then, completely off his nut. I didn't think too much about it until the rumours started about Linda. That was a few days later. Vic pulled me aside and told me to say that he'd never left the club. He'd been screwing a tart, or so he claimed, and didn't want Christine to find out. I had my suspicions – I'd seen him with Linda on more than one occasion – but when the cops showed up, I covered for him. I swore he'd been with me all evening. I gave him the alibi he needed.'

Susan closed her eyes and leaned back against the wall. She despised Marty for his lies but it was nothing compared to her loathing for Delaney. What made it worse was that she would probably never find out exactly why he had killed her. Had it been an accident or a premeditated act? Had Linda been threatening to expose their relationship to his wife? Had she struggled, had she tried to shout, had he . . . But these were questions she could ask for ever and the only response she would get was silence.

'Are you still there?' Silver said.

Susan's eyes blinked open again. 'I'm here.'

'So I'll definitely be going home? You promise?'

Susan tipped back the bottle and emptied the last of the champagne down her throat. 'Yes,' she said tightly. 'You'll be back with Daddy soon. Aren't you the lucky one?'

Chapter Forty-seven

Jo sipped her tea and gazed out across the Green. It was early but already the grass was bathed in sunlight. Above, the sky was a clear pale blue. This was the hottest June she could remember in years and today was going to be another scorcher. She watched as the locals made their way towards the station, the men dressed for the most part in shirt-sleeves, the women in light cotton dresses. They all walked more slowly than usual as if drinking up the rays of the sun before they were locked away inside their offices and shops.

She would normally have been preparing for work too but had decided on Wednesday evening that she would have the break she'd intended to take and not go in for a couple of days. A late call to Meg, along with a suitable bribe, had secured her the necessary cover. She was not exactly avoiding Jacob and Deborah but had no immediate desire to see them either. It would be best to give the dust some time to settle.

She had spent all yesterday in the small back garden, mulling things over and waiting for a call from Emerson. It was a call that had never come. She had phoned him twice but only got his answering service. It had seemed pointless to leave a message; if there had been any news he would have let her know.

Surely the point must have been reached by now where the police would have to charge Gabe or release him? The prospect of the former sent a jolt of alarm through her. What if she was forced to stand up in court and repeat her lies? If he was found guilty – and innocent men *did* go to jail – the future wouldn't look too bright for her either. It was a selfish thought, she knew, but one she was unable to avoid.

Jo was still stunned by the act she had committed. If someone had told her a week ago that she would voluntarily lie to the police and provide a false alibi for a suspected murderer, she would have laughed in their face. She had always considered herself a law-abiding citizen; her worst trespasses against society consisted of the occasional speeding fine and a parking ticket or two. And yet she had gone through with it. She hadn't just agreed to provide an alibi but had actually held her nerve and done it.

Suddenly, she found herself harking back to the words Mrs Dark had uttered last Sunday, something about a change having occurred. And Jo felt the stirrings of that change deep inside her. It was only seven days since Silver Delaney had been snatched but in that time she felt as if her life had been significantly altered. It was not just connected to Gabe Miller and the girl but to Peter as well.

The revelation about how he had helped the widow and child of Leonard Kearns seemed to raise as many questions as it answered. It was the secrecy that continued to bemuse her. That Peter wouldn't choose to flaunt the financial arrangement was understandable, but why he should keep her in such complete and utter ignorance of it was a mystery. He had never once mentioned that he'd known Constance's husband, never mind that the man had worked for his father. There was more to this story, she was certain, but how could she uncover it?

Jo finished her tea as she ran through the options. Jacob, she suspected, wouldn't tell her any more than he already had and she couldn't bring herself to ask Deborah. Carla was no good: if she'd known about Leonard Kearns, she'd have had some notion of why Jacob might have been talking to Constance outside the shop. Tony was her best chance – he must have brushed shoulders with most of his father's employees – but she rapidly dismissed that idea too. He would reveal nothing useful without consulting his mother first. He was too dependent on her, too vulnerable to her spite and displeasure. If Jo wanted the truth, she would have to go straight to the top – and it was better if Ruby Strong didn't have any warning about what she wanted to discuss.

Another hour passed before she decided it was a respectable time to ring. By then most of the workers had cleared the Green. Only a few stragglers, a couple of dog walkers and an elderly woman remained. Jo stared at the thin grey-haired woman who was sitting on a bench. She had a disturbing vision of herself in fifty years' time, still here, still looking out of the same window, wondering where her life had gone.

She smartly moved away and picked up the phone. As she punched in the number, however, she was assailed by doubt. She stopped and hung up. Was she getting this out of all proportion? Maybe she was using the Kearns business as some kind of distraction, as a way to temporarily free her mind from the possible fate of poor Silver Delaney. Or maybe that was just cowardice talking. If she wanted to secure an interview with the matriarch from hell, she was going to have to be less than honest over the phone and there were bound to be repercussions when the true reason for her visit emerged.

Jo stood up straight, pushed her shoulders back and frowned. She had been cowed by Peter's mother for long enough. Sod it! She picked up the receiver again. She'd had enough of secrets, of being manipulated. She had a right to the truth and if that meant a little dishonesty along the way, then so be it. If she could blatantly deceive the police, she could tell a few white lies to Ruby Strong.

In the event, she didn't need to – at least not immediately. It was Mrs Dark who answered the call. They exchanged the usual mundane pleasantries before Jo asked to speak to Ruby.

'Just a moment.'

The phone went down with a clink against what she presumed was the glass-topped table in the hall. Jo spent the next few minutes tapping her fingers against her thigh and listening to the silence at the other end of the line.

Eventually there was the sound of life again, a brief clearing of the throat before Mrs Dark spoke: 'I'm afraid Mrs Strong is unavailable at present. Could I take a message?'

Jo raised her eyes to the ceiling. *Unavailable?* The old witch was hardly a captain of industry. She was either having breakfast or just deliberately avoiding her. Having already decided that it wouldn't be wise to mention the name of Leonard Kearns before they were sitting face-to-face, Jo said: 'Yes, er, there's something important I need to discuss about the business. If she's free this morning, about eleven, I'd like to call round. Would that be convenient?'

This time the phone didn't go down. A hand was simply placed across the receiver and muffled words were exchanged. The wait was much shorter. 'Hello? Yes, Mrs Strong will look forward to seeing you at eleven.'

'Thank you,' Jo said. As she hung up, she knew what Ruby must be thinking – that she'd had a change of heart about selling the shop. Well, she was going to be disappointed.

It was getting on for ten-fifteen when Jo shut the front door behind her and climbed into the car. She patted the wheel affectionately. Carla was always going on about 'upgrading', about buying something 'more suitable' but the blue Renault Clio suited her just fine. It might not be the biggest or the flashiest car in the world but it had served her well over the past few years. Anyway, it was easy to park and that was a mighty plus in London. As she reversed out of the drive, she noticed the white Mondeo still sitting on the street and made a mental note to call John Harris later.

The traffic, as always, was heavy but this morning she didn't mind the endless stop-and-starts. She was in no hurry and it gave her time to ponder on what she was going to say. She had the feeling that no matter how sensitively she approached the subject, her enquiries wouldn't be welcomed.

No one liked to be reminded of their sins – or the sins of their nearest and dearest.

She kept her mobile on until she pulled up outside the house in Canonbury but there were no incoming calls or messages. This was fortunate perhaps as any bad news at this particular moment would hardly aid her concentration. She needed to be focused, to have her wits about her, if she wanted to get the better of Ruby Strong.

Jo got out of the car and locked it. She automatically glanced down, checking her clothes for creases and wondering if she was suitably dressed. She despised herself for doing it but the habit, so long engrained, was a hard one to break.

Mrs Dark answered the door with one of her thin enigmatic smiles. 'Good morning. If you'd like to come through, Mrs Strong is in the conservatory.'

'Thank you.' Jo tried not to let her surprise show. She had expected to be received, as was the norm, in the dim and drab reception room. The prospect hadn't been appealing. She found herself relieved that, no matter how badly the interview went, she would be spared those seemingly endless visions of the victims of Waterloo.

Jo followed Mrs Dark to the back of the house, their journey uninterrupted by any further conversation. As soon as they had reached their destination, the older woman turned, gave a brief nod and withdrew.

The conservatory was a grand construction, its interior filled with a lush selection of palms, ferns and exotic orchids. Ruby was standing by the open doors leading to the garden. She was dressed in her trademark black, her only concession to the heat being that the well-tailored suit was made of a fine silky material. Despite her bulk, she moved quickly towards Jo and clasped both her hands.

'How lovely to see you again, dear!'

It was the most effusive welcome Jo had ever received. Well, at least since Peter had died. Back in the early days of her marriage, her mother-in-law had usually made an effort – if not an especially fulsome one – to be pleasant.

Ruby gestured towards the wide bamboo chairs and they both sat down. The chairs with their plump dark green cushions were more comfortable than they looked.

'You'll take tea?'

'Thank you.'

In the confidence that she wouldn't be late, a silver tray had already been placed on the low table. The best china was out, a delicate porcelain with a trailing pattern of ivy. As Ruby poured, Jo watched and tried to find a word for the expression on her face. Gleeful was the one that sprang most readily to mind. She was clearly convinced that victory was near, that her son's upstart widow was finally about to throw in the towel.

Jo added a splash of milk to her tea and raised the cup to her lips. Ruby wouldn't be happy at what she had to say but there was no going back now. And there was no reason for her to be afraid of this bullying, spiteful woman. If she took offence, so be it. There were questions that needed to be answered.

She put down her cup, took a deep breath and looked over at Ruby again. Immediately all her good intentions, along with her courage, began to drain away. Perhaps she was not quite as ready for this challenge as she thought. Confrontation, of any kind, made her feel faintly sick. She had barely recovered from that awful scene with Jacob and now . . . *Coward!* her inner voice taunted as she turned her head and gazed out across the garden.

'What beautiful roses!'

But Ruby was too impatient to indulge in idle chit-chat. As if preparing to gather the glad tidings, she leaned forward and lifted her hands to within a few inches of her ample bosom. 'So, Josephine, you wish to discuss the business.'

'Er, in a way,' she replied cautiously.

Ruby waited, her eyes shining, her lips slightly apart. When Jo didn't continue, she reached across and patted her kindly on the knee. 'Come along,' she urged, 'there's no need to be shy. We're family, aren't we? You can speak freely. Sometimes hard decisions have to be made and there's no reason, no reason at all, why you should continue to be tied to the past. I can understand why you chose to take on such a responsibility – it was admirable, truly it was – but you're entitled to a fresh start, to a life of your own.'

Jo realised that she was mistaking her reticence for embarrassment at having to backtrack on her rather publicly declared statements about Ruby's at Sunday lunch. What did she think had happened in the intervening five days? That she'd undergone a sudden revelation, had a miraculous change of heart, or that Mrs Dark whispering in her ear had persuaded her to take the money and run? It was time to put her right.

'Well, to be honest, it's really more to do with *your* business.'

'Mine? Whatever do you mean?' Ruby's smile wavered for a second but was soon re-established. She was a true pro. Although she sensed there could be trouble looming, she would retain her mask until she was absolutely sure of what she was dealing with.

Jo took another breath and offered up a silent prayer. *Please God, let me hold my nerve.* She had spent too many years pandering to Ruby Strong; she had to start standing up for herself, for what she believed in. And she could find that courage, couldn't she? 'Actually, it's about a man who used to work for you – or rather for your husband. His name was Leonard Kearns.'

Ruby visibly flinched and the smile disappeared for good. 'Kearns?' she repeated, tilting her head and frowning slightly as if trying to place the name. 'I'm not sure if I . . .'

A valiant effort but Jo knew she was faking. She had caught her off-guard and she quickly pressed home the advantage. 'I understand he died rather tragically in Burma, about twelve years ago. He was on a business trip with your husband.' She maintained a pleasant, non-accusatory tone to her voice while she kept her eyes fixed firmly on Ruby's face. It was gratifying to note that it had gone rather pale. There was no glee now, only a harsh, unfriendly wariness. 'At least that's what I was told. Or was I misinformed?'

Ruby gave a casual shrug, unwilling to either confirm or deny it. She was playing for time, still undecided as to how big a problem this was. 'I don't quite see where this is leading.'

The sun was still shining through the glass but there was a definite chill in the air. Jo twisted her hands in her lap, pretending to feel awkward. Incredibly, she didn't feel awkward at all; her misgivings had disappeared at the very same moment as her hostess's smile. Now she was driven by a growing determination. She would get to the bottom of this mystery – whatever it took.

'Ah,' Jo sighed, forcing her mouth to twist down at the corners. 'This is rather difficult.'

'It's all right, dear, you can talk to me.'

'Thank you. You're very kind. It's just . . . well . . . as you must be aware, Peter was providing Constance Kearns with a—' She stopped and sighed again. 'What shall I call it? A regular income, an allowance? And naturally I don't begrudge her that – she has a son to raise and Peter clearly thought that she deserved some compensation – but as Leonard was actually employed by *your* husband rather than mine . . .'

Ruby's eyes narrowed into slits. 'What exactly are you trying to say?'

'Only that I'm . . . I'm a bit confused as to why the payments shouldn't be shared between us.'

There was a short tense silence while Ruby thought about it. It didn't take her long to come up with an answer. She sat back and barked out her reply: 'Oh, I see. So this is what it's all about. Money!'

'No, it's not just—'

'Do you really imagine that Mitchell would have shirked his legal responsibilities to any employee?'

'Of course not,' Jo said. She was tempted to ask about his moral responsibilities but wisely bit down on her tongue. 'I wasn't suggesting that.'

'She was paid what she was due, more than she was due in fact.'

But Jo stood her ground. Something had changed in her recently and she was no longer prepared to accept whatever Ruby told her. Her new-found temerity was faintly unsettling even to herself. Finding the boldness to go up against her mother-in-law was something she had never anticipated but now that she had started, there could be no backing down. 'I'm just a bit confused as to why Peter decided that it wasn't enough.'

Ruby snorted. 'He was always a soft touch; he never could resist a sob story – or a pretty face.' She looked Jo up and down as if she fell into a similar category. 'She came begging and he couldn't say no.'

'So you think I should stop paying her?'

'That's your decision.'

'Right.'

Jo sat back too as if she was genuinely considering it. From the second she had seen that initial reaction, that *flinching*, she had suspected she was on to something. In anyone else she would have put it down to a sense of shame – the treatment of Leonard Kearns' dependents had been truly callous – but Ruby was incapable of such an emotion.

'So I take it we've finished here?' Ruby said, suddenly eager to be rid of her. She lumbered to her feet, glancing at her watch. 'I have a lunch appointment and I don't wish to be late.'

Jo stood up too. With no actual evidence of any legal wrongdoing, she would have to take a gamble or she'd be going home as ignorant as when she arrived. It was now or never. With Ruby convinced that she had got the upper hand, that the subject was closed, there couldn't be a better time to strike.

'I have to say I'm a little surprised by your attitude . . .' Jo paused for effect, deliberately lowering her voice, '. . . after what happened.'

That pulled her mother-in-law up short. Two red spots flared on Ruby's cheeks. For once she was speechless; her mouth opened but then closed again, her tongue nervously snaking out to moisten her thin, dry lips.

'The problem with secrets,' Jo continued, 'is that they usually come out in the end. The past has a habit of catching up.' She was working blind and her only hope of success lay in implying that she knew more than she did.

'I-I have no idea what you're talking about.'

'Do you really think Peter didn't tell me?' Jo made an exasperated sound in the back of her throat. 'I was his *wife*, for God's sake.'

It was a shot in the dark but it hit home. There was a short, stunned silence as panic swept over Ruby. The blood drained from the flesh, bleaching her face white. 'I'd like you to leave,' she hissed.

'What's the matter? The truth too hard to handle? Well, Peter certainly struggled with it.' Something had instinctively clicked into place in Jo's head, a direct connection between what had occurred and his relentless nightmares. She could hardly believe that she was going up against Ruby – but it was too late to backtrack now. Having finally managed to find the strength to confront her, she had to stand her ground. 'Do you have *any* idea of what it did to him?'

Ruby's response was dramatic. For a second her whole body went rigid before a shudder ran through it. She bared her teeth, her eyes ablaze with fear and anger. Lurching forward, she raised a hand, the palm flat as if she was about to slap her.

Jo smartly took a step back.

'Get out of my house!' she shrieked.

Jo didn't need telling twice. She turned on her heel and fled towards the hall. As she slammed shut the door, she was vaguely aware of Mrs Dark's footsteps scurrying towards the conservatory.

Chapter Forty-eight

Jo was over halfway home before her heart rate returned to anything like normal. Her head was still scrambled though and on two separate occasions she almost ploughed into the car in front. After the second near-miss, she gripped the wheel and tried to concentrate. This wasn't easy when all she could see was Ruby's rage-filled face in front of her.

Well, if she had wanted to provoke a reaction, she had certainly succeeded. And it was clear that the woman had something ugly to hide. Unfortunately, Jo was no closer to knowing what that something was. She had a few of the parts – that it was connected to Leonard Kearns, to Mitchell Strong, and that Peter had been involved – but they were just the minor pieces in what she suspected was a complicated jigsaw.

Jo pulled into the drive in Barley Road and killed the engine. For a while she sat, unmoving, and stared up at the house. It was the part about Peter that really bothered her. What had been done that was so terrible he had not felt able to talk about it? She remembered the night he had got drunk and hurled the glass across the room. She thought about the picture of Rangoon.

A cold shiver ran through her.

Perhaps Leonard's death hadn't been as straightforward, as simply tragic as she'd thought. Perhaps . . . but before her imagination could slide into places she was thoroughly unprepared for, Jo quickly got out of the car. What was she doing? She had to keep a sense of proportion about all this. Peter had been a gentle man; he would never, *could* never, have been involved in any act of violence.

She repeated this to herself as she opened the front door. If anything awful had happened, at worst he could only have been a reluctant witness. That much was beyond dispute. Jo nodded as she closed and locked the door behind her. Although she was not sure how much she had achieved by going to see Ruby, she didn't regret it. Even if she was no closer to the truth, at least she had established that there was a truth to discover. And there was one bright side to the whole episode – at least she would never have to sit through one of those dreadful Sunday lunches again.

Jo was at the top of the stairs when the phone started ringing. It could be Emerson with some information at last. She hurried into the living room, dropped her bag on the sofa and snatched up the receiver.

'Hello?'

But the voice on the other end was Carla's. She sounded breathless and her voice, nervously excited, was a pitch higher than usual. 'It's me. My God, I've just had Tony on; he's been getting a right earful. Ruby's having a fit! She is *so* pissed off! What did you say to the old witch?'

Jo couldn't help smiling. News certainly travelled fast

within the Strong family. 'I've no idea. I just asked her about someone and she went off on one.'

'Who?'

'Some bloke who used to work for Mitchell.'

'Who? Why should that bother her? I don't get it.'

'Quite. I don't get it either. What did Tony say?'

'Plenty, but nothing of any use. You know what he's like – he never tells me more than he needs to. He just kept ranting on about how you'd called and arranged to see her this morning, claiming you were going to sell Ruby's and then—'

'I didn't ever claim I was going to sell. I didn't say that at all.'

Carla gave a giggle. 'Whoops! I think that was the impression she got. The old cow must've been mightily disappointed.'

'She was,' Jo agreed, 'but she was even more dismayed when I started asking questions about Leonard Kearns. Did Tony mention that?'

'No, not a word. What's the deal with this Leonard guy?'

'I haven't a clue. I only know that he was in Burma, on a business trip with Mitchell, and he never came back.'

There was a short pause before the penny dropped. 'Oh God, was he the poor sod who died?'

'That's the one. Do you know anything about him?'

Carla sighed down the line. 'God,' she murmured again. 'Not really. I mean, I do remember but it was years ago. I'd forgotten his name. Didn't he catch some kind of dreadful disease or something?'

'Apparently.'

'Yes, it's all coming back now. There was a mighty fuss about what to do, about how or if they could fly the body home. Mitchell was doing his nut, going crazy. There was so much red tape – that country has got serious problems – and it all got incredibly complicated. Anyway, in the end he was buried out there . . . or maybe he was cremated. I'm not sure.'

'Not an easy thing to explain to his wife.'

'I suppose not,' Carla said.

'Constance was his wife – you know, the woman who lives downstairs from me.'

'Really?'

'You never met her?'

Carla sounded puzzled. 'No, why should I? I don't think I ever met Leonard either. Look, what's this all about, Jo? What's going on?'

Jo pressed the phone closer to her ear. She nudged the toe of her shoe against the corner of the rug. 'Was he out there when it happened?'

'Who?'

'Peter,' she said.

'Yes, I think so. Yes, all three of them were there, Mitchell, Tony *and* Peter.'

'And Tony hasn't ever mentioned anything?'

'About what?'

Jo was starting to feel like she was banging her head against a brick wall. Carla was clearly as ignorant as she was. 'About what happened to . . . to Leonard Kearns.'

'He got sick and died. What more *is* there to know? It's very sad but there's no great mystery.' She paused. 'Is there?'

'You're asking the wrong person. But if it's all so straightforward, aren't you curious as to why Ruby is kicking up such a fuss? I mean, it doesn't make any sense.'

Carla gave a thin laugh. 'Yeah, well, working out why Ruby does most things is beyond me. That is one twisted lady. Maybe she thought you were accusing her of something.'

'Like what?'

'Beats me. Look, I'll have a word with Tony and see what I can find out. She was probably just mad because she was hoping to get her grubby little hands on the shop.'

'Perhaps,' Jo said. But she didn't believe it.

They said their goodbyes and Jo put down the receiver. Well, if nothing else she had certainly stirred up a hornets' nest. Now all she could do was cross her fingers and hope that she wasn't the one about to get stung.

Chapter Forty-nine

Jo was in the process of binning the remains of her lunch, a half-eaten tuna sandwich, when the doorbell went. Two short, sharp rings cut through the silence of the flat. Her foot froze, still pressed against the pedal. She wasn't expecting anyone. Her first thought was of Ruby and her heart sank. Please Lord, don't let it be her! She couldn't take another row.

Carefully, as if the slightest sound might travel, she removed her foot and sidled over to the window. Keeping to one side, she glanced along the street. There were plenty of parking spaces but no sign of the old black Bentley. She slowly released her breath and relaxed.

The bell went again, a longer single ring this time. She suddenly realised how pathetic it was, skulking in the kitchen, pretending that she wasn't here. So much for the brave new Jo! One major run-in with the mother-in-law and she was already reverting to her former ways. She ran down the stairs and pulled open the door.

Gabe Miller was standing in front of her.

Her jaw dropped. 'You . . . you're out,' she eventually managed to splutter. 'They let you out.'

He grinned. 'I hope that's an expression of happy surprise rather than horror.'

'Yes. Sorry. I'm just . . .' She *was* glad to see him, very glad. And he didn't look too much the worse for wear. He was freshly shaven and wearing clean clothes. She laughed and stood aside. 'Come on in.'

Gabe didn't move. 'Actually,' he said, 'I've spent rather too long in confined spaces recently. I've got a yearning for fresh air. You don't fancy a walk, do you? Preferably a walk with a pub at the end of it. I could really do with a drink.'

'Just give me a minute and I'll grab my keys.'

Jo jogged back up to the living room, her cheeks glowing. She grabbed her bag off the chair and turned to go back down again. It was only as she caught sight of her reflection in the hall mirror that she stopped to check her face and tidy up her hair. The thought occurred to her: *This was just relief she was feeling, wasn't it?* She pushed a stray strand of hair behind her ear and frowned. Of course it was. What else could it be? If the police had decided to let him go, she was off the hook too. That was more than enough reason to celebrate. And, on a less selfish note, it would have been unbearable to see an innocent man go to prison. So there, that was all there was to it. Whatever else was making her cheeks burn so furiously had absolutely *nothing* to do with his presence. She gave a cursory nod to the mirror and carried on down the stairs.

'There's a decent place off the High Street,' she said, closing the door. 'They've got a courtyard so we can sit outside.'

'Sounds ideal.'

They crossed the road together and strolled on to the

Green. The sun was still high in the sky, still blazing. She assumed from his appearance, from his clean jeans and crisp white shirt, that he must have gone somewhere before coming over to see her. Perhaps John Harris had picked him up from the station. 'So what time did they let you go?'

'About seven,' he said.

'They like to kick people out early then.'

'Ah,' he said. 'It, er . . . it wasn't exactly this morning.'

Whatever warmth Jo may have been feeling towards him instantly dissolved. She stopped dead and put her hands on her hips. 'Last night? You got out *last night*?'

He pulled a face. 'I guess I should have called you.'

'You've been free for over eighteen hours and you couldn't be bothered to pick up the phone?' Her eyes filled with incredulity. 'I've been worried sick. I lied for you. I gave you a goddamn alibi!'

'Yeah, I meant to thank you for that. Look, I'm sorry, okay? I was dead on my feet, completely shattered. You don't get a lot of sleep in those places. I went back to Snakey's place, crashed out and didn't wake up again until this morning. By then, I thought I may as well just come round.'

It took a few more seconds than it should have for her to connect John Harris, with all his snake tattoos, to his nickname. 'Right,' she said sarcastically, 'why not? I mean, what's a few more hours of stress and suffering between friends?'

'Sorry, I fucked up. I wasn't thinking straight.'

'Too true,' she said, unwilling to forgive him quite that easily. She pushed her hands into her pockets and continued walking.

There was a long thirty seconds of silence before he said: 'So is this how it's going to be from now on?'

'What?'

'You giving me the evil eye, the cold shoulder treatment. I'm not saying I don't deserve it but—'

'But you don't think holding a grudge is an attractive trait in a woman?'

'Well, that wasn't what I was going to say but now you mention it . . .' That familiar grin appeared again. 'No, what I was hoping was that maybe you could see your way to cutting me some slack. It's not a great deal of fun being interrogated by Old Bill – especially when they're convinced you're guilty. Another few hours and I'd have started believing it myself.'

Jo shrugged, relenting a little. Perhaps she was being overly harsh.

Gabe continued to wheedle. 'Would it help if I offered to buy *all* the drinks?'

'I presumed you'd be doing that anyway.'

They'd reached the far side of the Green and turned left along the High Street. Jo didn't cross over until after they'd passed Ruby's. She didn't even look at it.

'Still skiving off work?' he said.

'Other things on my mind.' Then, seeing his brows shift up, she added: 'That wasn't a dig. There've just been some . . . some problems recently.' She thought of Leonard Kearns and quickly pushed the thought away. 'You know how it is. Sometimes you need a bit of space.'

Gabe didn't enquire further, for which she was grateful. They walked to the end of the short alley and stepped inside

The Speckled Hen. It was ten past two and although the lunchtime rush was over, there were still plenty of customers. At the bar, after a short wait, Gabe ordered a couple of cold beers and they took them through to the courtyard at the back. They found a shady spot in the corner, next to a large pot of scarlet geraniums, and sat down on opposite sides of the table.

He clinked his bottle against hers. 'Thanks again for what you did.'

'I can't say it was a pleasure but it was certainly an experience. So, is everything sorted now? Are you officially an innocent man?'

'I'm not completely out of the frame – the cops don't like to give up their prime suspects without a fight – but at least I'm not slap bang in the middle of it any more. Fortunately, one of my neighbours came forward, claiming to have spotted a couple of guys going into my flat on Sunday night. One of them was tall and blond, definitely Ritchie, but the other one was a good few inches shorter so that effectively ruled me out. Of course, I could still have come back, caught them in the act of burgling the place and lost my rag but there wasn't any real evidence to support the theory.'

'Oh,' Jo said. She felt a stab of disappointment that her alibi hadn't been the clinching factor in his release. 'So I could have saved myself the bother of a trip down the station.'

'Not at all,' he insisted. 'It was the two things together, your statement *and* the neighbour's, that made all the difference. Even our dim-witted boys in blue could see that the evidence wasn't exactly stacking up in their favour.'

'I suppose that's some consolation.'

Gabe took a pack of cigarettes from his shirt pocket, shook one out, lifted it to his lips and lit it. He leaned back and looked at her. 'It wasn't my idea, you know.'

'What wasn't?'

'The alibi. I would never have asked you to do that. Snakey's a good mate, and his heart's in the right place, but he does have a habit of taking action before thinking through the consequences. I hope he didn't put too much pressure on you.'

'I'm perfectly capable of making up my own mind, thank you.'

'I'm sure you are.' His grey eyes danced with amusement. 'Although I have to admit, I was rather surprised when I heard. Two nights of rampant passion, huh? Who'd have believed it?'

Jo stared back at him. 'As you previously remarked, those detectives *are* pretty dim-witted.'

'Either that or you were mighty convincing.'

She knew he was only teasing, that she shouldn't allow him to get under her skin, but still she bristled. 'What they believed,' she said, 'is that every poor woman can make a mistake now and again, especially when their judgement is seriously impaired by alcohol.'

Gabe glanced at the bottle she was holding and winked. 'Drink up! The afternoon's still young.'

She faked a smile. 'How charming. I can see why you're such a hit with the ladies.'

'Ah, so you've heard about that.'

Jo waved his wisecrack aside. She made a fast study of his

angular face, noting his dark grey eyes, the bump on the bridge of his nose and his smiling mouth. She recalled the cruelty she had thought she had seen on those lips when they'd first met – but she'd been wrong. There was no cruelty in Gabe Miller. 'Anyway, I didn't do it for you. There's still a missing girl out there in case you'd forgotten. She *is* still missing, isn't she?'

'Yeah,' he said, his expression growing instantly serious. 'Snakey got his kid, Gemma – she's about the same age – to call up the house this morning and ask for Silver. Nina answered the phone and said she was on holiday, that she wouldn't be back until next week.'

'So the ransom hasn't been paid.'

'Looks that way.'

'Are you going to try and get in touch with Susan again?'

Gabe shook his head. 'No, I'd rather she didn't know I was out. She's going to feel more confident, too confident hopefully, if she thinks I'm safely behind bars. It's about the only advantage I've got at the moment.'

'She called me on the night you were arrested.'

'You mean the night she set me up.' He took a drag on the cigarette and released the smoke in a long, thin stream. 'And please don't say *I told you so.*'

'No point stating the obvious.'

'That doesn't stop most people.'

Jo took a sip of her beer, wondering how much the betrayal had hurt him. Being turned over to the police by a woman you had once loved couldn't count amongst the best experiences in the world. She searched his face but he wasn't an easy man to read. 'Don't you want to know what she said?'

'Let me guess: keep your mouth shut, don't speak to the cops and consult your conscience before making a decision. Oh yes, and don't trust a word that Gabe Miller tells you, he's got a pretty dubious past.' He gave a light easy laugh. 'Did I miss anything out?'

'No,' Jo said. 'I think that just about covers it.'

Gabe dropped his cigarette, grinding it into one of the paving stones with the heel of his shoe. He sighed, drank his beer and studied the red geraniums.

She decided, if only temporarily, to change the subject. 'Can I ask you something?'

He looked back towards her. 'Ask away.'

'Why do you choose to work for a man like Delaney?'

'I don't work for him, I work for myself.'

Jo frowned. 'Don't dodge the issue. You know what I mean. You do stuff for him – he pays you.'

'And what's wrong with that?'

'He's a thug, a villain.'

He shrugged. 'So what? That's not his daughter's fault. Would you prefer it if he employed some low-life, some chancer *without* my strict moral standards to fetch her back every time she did a flit?'

'No,' she said indignantly, 'of course not. But is that *all* you do for him?'

'Apart from the drug-running,' he said.

Jo raised her eyes to the heavens. 'When people are constantly flippant, it's usually a sign that they're trying to cover up some kind of insecurity.'

'You're right,' Gabe said. 'And in my case it's a chronic case of shyness.'

She smiled but quickly averted her eyes. She looked around the courtyard. 'I used to come here with Susan, back in the good old days. We were here last Thursday.'

'Plotting to overthrow a vicious blackmailer.'

'Something like that. She showed me a photo of you.'

He put his head to one side and lifted his brows. 'And what did you think?'

'That you were a bastard, a complete and utter loser.'

Gabe grinned. 'Wow! You gleaned all that from a photograph?'

'Not all of it. Some of it came from a rather colourful character reference.'

'Yeah, Susan always was my number one fan.'

Jo leaned forward and placed her elbows squarely on the table. Now was probably a good a time as any to ask. 'Really?' she said. 'So is that why you married her?'

Chapter Fifty

If Gabe was taken aback by the question, he didn't show it. He took another leisurely drink, put the bottle down and nodded. 'Ah, I take it the snake man has been opening his big mouth again.'

'Perhaps the snake man didn't know it was supposed to be a secret.'

'It isn't,' he said.

'So you just thought you wouldn't mention it because . . .?'

Gabe shrugged those broad shoulders of his. 'Because it isn't relevant.'

'How can you say that?' Jo protested. Although there was no one sitting close by, she instinctively leaned closer and lowered her voice. 'Of course it's relevant. It's affected your judgement, the way you've dealt with things.'

'And how do you figure that one out?'

'Because you've been as concerned about protecting Susan as getting Silver back. If it hadn't been for her involvement, you could have tipped off the police right at the beginning, made an anonymous call, let *them* sort it out. But you didn't even consider doing that. You thought you knew Susan well enough to be sure that Silver would be safe. And you also thought, and I hate to remind you of this, that she wouldn't double-cross you if you arranged to meet up for a cosy little chat.'

'So I'm a lousy judge of character,' he said. 'So what? You've always known we used to be an item. I never tried to hide it.'

'Yes, an item,' she said, 'but not husband and wife.'

As if he found the expression mildly amusing, Gabe's brows shifted up a fraction. 'It was a brief six-month marriage, a marriage that was over and done with five years ago. The phrase "unmitigated disaster" springs to mind. She dumped me before I got the opportunity to prove what a wonderful husband I could be. Hardly something to be proud of, is it? Not something to go shouting from the rooftops.'

But Jo sensed this went beyond mere dignity or hurt pride. 'So why do I get the feeling that you deliberately misled me, that you didn't want me to find out how involved you'd actually been with her?'

'Paranoia,' he quipped.

Stony-faced, she stared silently back at him. Not for the first time, she wondered why people found it so easy to be evasive with her. She reeled off a list in her head: Peter, Susan, Ruby, Jacob, Deborah – not to mention Gabe Miller himself. Her gullibility, it seemed, knew no bounds. She was the dumb blonde. She was good ol' Jo, the ingenuous wife, friend, daughter-in-law, who'd believe any old rubbish she was told. Her forehead scrunched into a frown. Well, she wasn't going to be that person – not any more. She was gradually changing, becoming someone else. She'd begun that change two days ago when she'd found out that even her husband had been incapable of being honest with her. The only problem – and gradually her frown grew deeper – was that she wasn't sure if the new Jo Strong was a woman she would like.

Gabe must have realised that she wasn't going to back down. Eventually, after thirty seconds or so, he lifted his hands in a gesture of submission. 'Okay, so maybe I did brush over a few minor details.'

'Care to elaborate?'

'What you have to understand is that the situation with Silver is more complicated than you think. I wasn't deliberately keeping you in the dark, but for your own sake I—'

'Let's get one thing straight,' Jo swiftly interrupted. 'Don't even think about giving me any of those glib lines about how ignorance is bliss or you did it for my own good or you were just trying to protect me.'

'Even if they are true?'

Jo shook her head impatiently. 'It doesn't matter if they're true or not. That's not what this is about. We're past that now; I've had enough of secrets and lies. You told me that you didn't know why Susan had taken Silver – well, apart from the money – but that's not the case, is it?'

Gabe looked at her and quickly glanced away. He stared up at the sky, then down at the ground. He picked up his empty bottle and stared at that. 'Let me get a couple more beers,' he said softly, 'and then I'll explain.'

She watched him stroll through the courtyard towards the bar. He had a confident way of walking, almost a swagger but not quite that arrogant. Of the five other tables that were occupied, four of them included females and every woman (with varying degrees of subtlety) turned their heads to look at him. Why? Jo found herself frowning again. What was it about Gabe Miller that always made women look twice? He wasn't ugly but he wasn't God's gift either. She looked down at the table and sighed. Who was she kidding? She had followed his progress with the same look in her eyes as the rest of them.

It was six long minutes before he reappeared. Jo had been tapping her feet and checking her watch. She had been worried that he might not come back, imagining him walking straight through the pub and out on to the High Street. She wouldn't have been surprised. She wouldn't even have blamed him. There were some stories, she suspected, that were just too difficult to tell.

'Okay,' he said, sliding his long legs over the bench and putting the beers down on the table. 'Are you ready for this?'

'As I'll ever be.'

'Good. Then let me take you back five years to when I was a younger, braver man and the world was full of possibilities. It's nine o'clock at night and I'm in Honey's, one of Delaney's very fine establishments. I've just finished a job for him and I'm at the bar, having a drink when—'

'What kind of a job?' she said.

He expelled a short exasperated breath. 'I thought you wanted to know about Susan.'

'Sorry,' she said. 'Carry on.'

'So there I am, winding down after a long, hard day,

minding my own business, when she walks up to the bar. And she's not the kind of woman any man is likely to ignore, at least not any man with blood still running through his veins. She orders a gin and tonic and we get chatting. It all seems to be going well but then she starts asking me how well I know Vic Delaney, how long I've been coming to the club, if I know of any staff who may have been around ten years ago. She says she's looking for information about a girl who used to work there.'

Gabe took a drink and gave a rueful smile. 'Now, I'm just a bloke and I'm easily flattered but by this point even my sad male brain is beginning to clock that it's not my incredible muscles or easy charm she's interested in. She's talking to me because she reckons I'm old enough to have been frequenting the place a decade ago. This, as you can imagine, is something of a blow but as I don't keep my entire ego in my pants, I do my best to get over it.

'I enquire about the girl, what her name was, etcetera, but just as she's about to answer, one of the barmen saunters over and leans against the counter. He's close enough to overhear and Susan suddenly goes all coy on me, says it doesn't really matter, that she was only asking on the off-chance. However, as it clearly *does* matter, that kicks my old curiosity gene into gear and I'm well and truly hooked. I tell her that I'm hungry, that I'm going to get something to eat. I ask her if she'd like to join me.'

As if trying to recall every detail, Gabe half closed his eyes. His face took on a concentrated look. He absently picked up his beer but then, as if surprised to find the bottle in his hand, carefully put it back down again. He gazed at the table. 'There was a small Italian restaurant down the road. That's where I took her and that's where she told me about Linda.'

He fell silent for a while.

'Linda?' Jo eventually repeated, as much to fill the silence as anything else.

Gabe's gaze slowly came back up to her. 'Her sister, Linda Clark. She used to work at Honey's. It was the last place she was seen before she disappeared. She'd been gone ten years by then; it's closer to fifteen now.'

Jo felt a cool chill run the length of her spine. 'When you say disappeared,' she ventured, although she suspected she already knew the answer.

He took a short breath. 'They never found a body. She was last seen about ten-thirty, eleven o'clock, but no one saw her leave the club. No one saw her talking to anyone in particular either. She was just there, and then . . .' He sighed and shook his head. 'What made it worse, if that's possible, was that the cops weren't entirely convinced that there *had* been any foul play. Linda was an attractive but troubled twenty-one-year-old who came from a shitty background – poverty, violence, drugs, an alcohol-dependent mother, an absent father. She'd had a couple of run-ins with the Law before, a caution for possession of cannabis, a suspended sentence for shoplifting. She'd even gone missing several times when she was a teenager. They thought she could've just taken off again.'

'But Susan didn't?'

He nodded. 'There were eight years between them but they were close. Linda was probably more of a mother to her than Pat ever was; she made sure Susan went to school, was decently clothed, got at least one square meal a day and that she wasn't in the firing-line when Mummy's latest boyfriend decided that the only way to prove his masculinity was to give the nearest female a good thrashing.'

Jo flinched, uneasily aware of how little she had known about the woman who'd befriended her. The anger and resentment she had been feeling towards Susan for the past week began to leak away. She thought about her own lonely but comparatively safe childhood. With a spasm of guilt, she thought about how often she had sat in this very same courtyard and talked about herself, about her own loss, and never taken a minute to consider that she might not be alone in the pain she felt. She had been completely oblivious to Susan's private nightmare.

'And before you ask,' he continued, mistaking her silence for some form of scepticism, 'it did cross my mind that she could be wrong. I wasn't so distracted by her big brown eyes that I didn't consider any other possibilities.'

'I wasn't thinking that.' Jo wanted to explain but now wasn't the right time. 'Go on,' she said.

Gabe gave her a long hard look but finally nodded again. 'Linda didn't take any of her clothes or the small pieces of jewellery she'd worked so hard to buy. She didn't take the two hundred quid she had stashed away in her bottom drawer. But most of all, she didn't say goodbye. *That* was why Susan was so sure. If Linda had been planning to leave, she wouldn't have done it lightly. There would have been—' He hesitated, squinting up at the bright blue sky, searching for the right words. 'I don't know, some hint, a clue that even if it hadn't been obvious at the time would have been clear later. But there wasn't. I mean, if that's what you're planning to do, if you know you're not coming back, you don't just walk away with a breezy wave of a hand, do you? Not if you're saying goodbye to someone you love.'

'No,' Jo said, 'you couldn't. Not if you were that close.'

Gabe looked at her almost gratefully. 'Yeah, that's what I figured. Susan was sure she was going to meet someone that night, that it wasn't just work she was getting all dressed up for. Linda was excited, pleased about something – or, more likely, someone.'

Jo felt the first stirrings of understanding; the pieces were beginning to slot into place. 'So Susan thinks the mystery man was Vic Delaney, that *he* was responsible for—'

'No, that's the weird thing. She didn't. Not then. It hadn't even crossed her mind. She was just hoping that he might be able to help, give her some information. It was his club, after all. She only wanted to talk to him, to see if he could remember anything about that night. The problem with guys like Delaney is that they don't care for answering questions, even when they are completely innocent. I could tell she was heading for trouble and so I advised her against it.'

'I bet that went down well.'

He pulled a face. 'Like a lead balloon. She never liked being told what to do. But I could see how easily she'd get his back up. She was too closely involved, too emotional, so I offered to go instead. There was more chance of my finding out something useful. I wasn't exactly mates with Delaney but he had no reason to distrust me.'

'That was very . . . *chivalrous* of you.' Jo had uttered the words without thinking and instantly regretted them. She felt a faint blush of shame blossom on her cheeks. Now was hardly the time for cheap innuendo or unnecessary point-scoring.

But Gabe didn't seem too bothered. The hint of a smile twitched at the corners of his mouth. 'I hope you're not suggesting that I was driven by anything but the purest of motives.'

She smiled, relieved that he hadn't taken offence. 'God forbid.'

'Anyway,' he continued, 'I went to the club a couple of nights later. By then I'd got a cover story worked out. I had a few beers and "accidentally" bumped into Delaney at the bar. I asked him if he knew there'd been a reporter on the snoop, some bloke asking questions about a girl who'd gone missing ten years ago. I watched him pretty carefully. He didn't look too pleased but he wasn't overly jumpy either. I got the impression he was more pissed off than anxious, more concerned about his punters being hassled or the club ending up with a heap of bad publicity.'

'Although psychopaths can be good at that,' Jo said. 'Isn't that their skill – not showing any emotion?'

'Except I wouldn't classify Delaney as a psychopath, at least not in your typical textbook sense. A sadist perhaps; he's a bully, a violent bully, but he doesn't try to hide it. And he doesn't possess any natural charm. What you see is what you get. It isn't nice but it's all right there on the surface.' He gave a slight shake of his head. 'No, even when I mentioned Linda's name he didn't react. In fact, I'm not sure he even remembered it. And he certainly didn't look like a man whose past might be unexpectedly catching up with him.'

'So hardly a number one suspect, then?'

'No, not even on the list. And it didn't strike me that he was covering up for anyone either. I slipped in a few more questions, trying to keep it casual, but then he claimed that he hadn't even been at the club when Linda went missing.'

'Convenient,' Jo said.

'Or simply true. It would account for why he was so vague about the whole incident. I dropped the subject then; I didn't want to look *too* interested. Later that night, I met up with Susan. She was disappointed but she seemed resigned; finding out anything after all that time had always been a long shot. She thanked me for trying, I said I'd keep my ears open and we left it at that.'

Jo waited for him to go on. When he didn't, she said softly, 'Well, not quite. There was the little matter of a wedding ceremony.'

Chapter Fifty-one

Gabe smiled, but when he spoke again there was a hint of bitterness in his voice. 'Oh yeah, how could I forget? The fairytale romance that was Gabe and Susan Miller, the marriage made in heaven.' But as if he instantly regretted the cynicism, he bowed his head. 'It wasn't her fault. Perhaps it wasn't anyone's fault but she was twenty-two and I was forty – which makes me the one who should've known better.'

'Peter was older than me,' Jo said. 'It doesn't mean that it couldn't . . . wouldn't work out.' She had started off the response in good faith but then wondered if it was actually a valid argument. Bearing in mind what she had learned about her husband over the past few days, it seemed increasingly unlikely.

If Gabe noticed her hesitation, he didn't comment on it. She wasn't even sure if he had heard. Having turned over his hands, he was busy examining his palms, scrutinising the lines with an odd bemused expression. After a while he glanced up again. 'Because of what happened to Linda, it was as though she was determined to live every day as if it was her last. She was smart, funny, impulsive . . . and bloody beautiful of course. There were never two days the same when she was around. She had this way of . . .' He stopped suddenly as if his mouth had inadvertently run away with him. 'You've met her. I don't need to explain. I'm sure you understand what I saw in her but what she saw in *me*?' He gave a light shrug of his shoulders. 'I've really no idea.'

Jo instinctively sensed that he wasn't being falsely modest or fishing for compliments. A week ago she couldn't have found anything good to say about him but her opinion, as she had got to know him better, had been gradually improving. 'Maybe someone who was prepared to take her seriously, to listen to her? Maybe someone who could protect her from all the things she was afraid of.'

He gave her a curious look. 'Then I didn't do a very good job.'

'Sometimes no one can save a person from themselves.'

His gaze flickered down towards his hands again.

'Sorry,' Jo said quickly. 'I didn't mean that to sound like some shallow piece of psychobabble. All I meant was—'

'It's okay, I wasn't thinking that. The trouble was . . . *is* . . . that I didn't even try to help. Not properly. I was sympathetic when she talked about Linda's disappearance but it took me a long time, too long, to grasp the true meaning of what she was going through. It was only after we were married that I became aware of how much it haunted her. Over the years, she'd become obsessed with discovering the truth. Susan was only a kid when Linda went missing and the police hadn't listened to a word she'd said. Her mother hadn't exactly kicked up a fuss either; she and Linda had never got on and Pat gave the cops more than enough reasons to believe that her older daughter might have taken off.'

'But *you* believed her, you thought—'

'Did I?' He sat forward, running a hand roughly through his hair. His eyes looked suddenly guilty. 'I might have given that impression but . . . I knew what she *wanted* me to believe – that Linda couldn't have abandoned her, couldn't have just walked away – but I'm not sure if I had any firm convictions one way or another. All I knew was that when I said I believed her, it made Susan happy and when she was happy she became the person I'd fallen in love with.' A thin, sad smile crept on to his lips. 'When it comes down to it, all I really wanted was the good stuff and none of the bad.'

'I'm sure it wasn't that simple.'

'Wasn't it?' Gabe's face contorted as if he was conjuring up a past that had for the last five years been safely locked away. 'It didn't take her long to suss me out. Within a few months we both knew the marriage was a mistake. I wasn't the man she thought I was and she, quite rightly, resented me for it. She was always somewhere else.' He tapped his chest. 'I mean in here, inside. She wanted someone who was prepared to go the distance, to stand by her side and fight for her sister, but all I wanted was *her.* She slowly erected a wall, a barrier; she shut me out. For a brief period of time I'd been her escape but then I gradually became her prison. I didn't understand, couldn't understand, and so I only made things worse.'

Jo, with a sudden jarring of her heart, wondered if it had

been the same for Peter, if he too had dashed headlong into a marriage because he'd been trying to run away from something in his past. Had she been the same disappointment to him as Gabe had apparently been to Susan? It was a thought that made her insides ache. 'And then?'

'One morning I woke up and she was gone. And you know what, the first thing I felt was relief. What kind of a person does that make me?'

'A normal one,' she insisted, perhaps a little too firmly. 'You're being too hard on yourself. It's not always easy living with someone else's pain.'

'I wouldn't know. I didn't really try that hard.'

For a while, lost to their own deliberations, they were both quiet. The sun slipped behind a cloud, throwing the courtyard into shadow. A light breeze trembled through the red geraniums. Jo shivered. She had thought she'd known her husband but she hadn't. You couldn't know someone who wouldn't talk to you. Had that been her fault or his? She stared down at the table, her head full of mess and confusion.

It was only as the sun came out again, as it fell across her arms, that she felt an urgent need to fill the silence. 'So why has Susan suddenly decided that Delaney was responsible? I take it that *is* what all this is about? She's taken Silver for revenge, to get her own back, to punish him.'

'Yes,' he said. 'I think so.'

'So when, *how*, did she decide that he was responsible?'

'Good question,' he said.

He didn't, however, make any further attempt to respond but instead just extended his fingers and began to drum out a soft steady beat against the surface of the table. She left him to it, knowing that he would answer when he was ready. And eventually, after a minute or two, he did. 'We always kept in touch, on and off. Susan never completely forgave me but . . . Well, she never quite let go of me either. We used to talk on the phone, even meet up from time to time. There was always something between us, something that wouldn't quite go away.'

Jo heard the regret in his voice. She felt a pang of compassion but was careful not to express it. Gabe Miller, she suspected, was not a man who would appreciate her sympathy. Accordingly, she kept it short and simple. 'And?'

'About nine months ago she called me. It was late, about three in the morning. She sounded excited, said she knew who'd killed Linda. I was barely awake. All I remember is grunting "What? Who?" but she wouldn't explain. She wouldn't give me a name. She just kept on saying "I know, I know who it was."' He sank his face into his hands and groaned. 'God, I should have listened. I tried to call the next morning but she didn't pick up. She didn't respond to my messages either. I presumed she must have been drinking, that she'd had one of those brilliant revelations that didn't seem quite so brilliant in the cold light of day. It wouldn't have been the first time. To be honest I didn't think that much about it. She'd often ring and then disappear for months on end. And that was the last I heard until . . .'

'Until we were sitting in a black cab and I described her to you.'

'Yes,' he said, raising his head again.

'Which still begs the question of how Vic Delaney ended up as the prime suspect.'

'Yes,' he repeated thoughtfully. 'Either I was wrong about him and she discovered things that I didn't know, or someone with their own personal agenda has been whispering more than sweet nothings in her ear. And whatever the lies are, they must be pretty convincing. Susan might be desperate but she's not stupid; she wouldn't go to these lengths unless she was sure of his guilt.'

Jo weighed up the options. She knew what Gabe thought, and what she privately thought too, but decided to play devil's advocate. 'Maybe Delaney was prepared, ready for the questions you asked him that night. Perhaps he's smarter than you think. You might not have been the first person she'd asked about Linda.'

He considered it for a second but quickly refuted the suggestion. 'No, if she'd been doing the rounds, Delaney would have heard about it. He'd have chucked her out. Innocent or not, he wouldn't have given her free rein to go wandering around asking awkward questions. It might have happened years ago but a missing girl wouldn't do much for his reputation or staff morale.'

'True enough,' Jo agreed. 'So I guess it's more likely to be option number two. And if someone has been feeding her false information, I take it we're presuming it's the same person who murdered Ritchie Naylor and then tried to put you in the frame for it.'

'That would seem likely.'

'So what do we do now?'

Gabe's brows arched up. '*We*?' he said.

Jo looked directly into his dark grey eyes. If someone had given her a get-out clause a week ago she would have grabbed it, but things had changed a lot since then. Now, whatever the consequences, she refused to be pushed aside. 'Oh, sorry, I forgot. For a moment there I thought I was involved in this too. I have this dim, distant memory of having been set up by a so-called friend, of being chased by a pair of oversized goons, of discovering that a girl had been kidnapped, of harbouring a man suspected of murder and then providing an alibi for that very same man.' She folded her arms. 'But clearly I'm not that important in the scheme of things so let me put it another way: what are *you* going to do?'

That familiar grin crept across his mouth again. 'No need to be so touchy, babe. No one's questioning your credentials as a fully paid up member of the victim club, but what I'm going to do, if you don't object, is precisely nothing.'

Jo did object. 'I thought we were beyond all that,' she said sharply. 'Please don't lie to me. Don't pretend that you're going to do zilch because it simply isn't in your nature.'

Gabe leaned forward, folding his own arms in a mirror reflection of hers. 'I'm not pretending. What I meant, what I *mean*, is that I'm not going to do anything today or tonight. I don't need to. It's taken me a while to work it out but I finally understand – I think – where this is going.'

Jo spread her hands out in a questioning gesture.

'It's to do with timing,' he said. 'I should've realised. Tomorrow night is the anniversary, if that's the right word, of Linda's disappearance. That's when Susan's going to want to do the exchange. She's making a point.'

'And so?'

'And so I've got over twenty-four hours to work out what to do.'

'And your first thoughts are?'

He picked up his empty bottle and dangled it by the neck. 'That I could do with another drink.'

'Or a coffee back at the flat,' Jo suggested. He might be coping fine but two strong beers on a stomach containing only half a tuna sandwich were beginning to take their toll on her. She wasn't drunk but could feel the edges of her reason beginning to fade a little.

'Er . . .' Gabe looked longingly towards the bar.

'I've got some bottles in the fridge.'

'Well, if you put it like that.' He nodded as he got to his feet. 'And on the way, you can tell me what's been preying on *your* mind.'

Deliberately avoiding his gaze, Jo looked across the courtyard. 'I've no idea what you're talking about.'

'I never took you for a hypocrite.'

'What?' she said, her startled eyes flicking back to meet his.

Gabe reached out and lightly touched her arm. 'No more secrets, right? Now I've taken the trouble to spew out all the details of my miserable life, you are morally obliged to return the compliment.'

Chapter Fifty-two

Leo stood by the High Street entrance and stared nervously across the Green. He was not sure what he had been hoping for more, that Stevie would be there or that he wouldn't, but the dealer was in his usual place, slightly to the left of the main central path with a black holdall at his feet and a trio of punters huddled around him.

As Leo watched the tattooed hands expertly palming the cash and almost invisibly delivering the tiny packages, his own hands were clutching the handlebars of the bike. He was still in two minds as to whether he was going to go ahead or not. There was still time to do a bunk.

Perhaps the whole gun idea wasn't so smart after all. For starters, where was he going to hide it? The flat wasn't that big and his mother's avid cleaning habits meant that nowhere was completely safe. He frowned. Although there *was* the shed, a place she rarely ventured into; there were too many cobwebs, too many large black spiders, even for her. But that wasn't the point, he reminded himself. Just possessing a gun could get him into all kinds of trouble.

Leo shifted anxiously from one foot to another. He had

to make a decision. If he did a runner now, he'd be throwing away the thirty quid deposit but that was maybe a price worth paying. It was the other price he was more concerned about. There was no saying what Stevie would do if he ever caught up with him. Leo would have to spend the next few months avoiding him and that would mean going the long way home every day, not to mention looking over his shoulder every five minutes in case . . .

But it was too late anyway. While he had been lost in his deliberations, Stevie had finished his deals. He was standing alone now and looking directly over. He raised a hand, not so much in a wave as an acknowledgement of his presence. It was accompanied by the kind of cold blank stare that not only defied Leo to walk away but also reminded him of why he was so scared. Even if he'd wanted to escape, he wouldn't have been able to. His knees had begun to shake and it was not the kind of tremble that was conducive to jumping on a bike and cycling for your life.

No, there was no other choice than to face up to the problem he had created. Slowly, Leo began to wheel his bike across the Green. While he walked, he prayed that Stevie might not have been able to acquire a gun. It was possible, wasn't it? Perhaps he would say that it hadn't been that easy, that it would take a few more days. That would be good. That would mean that he could shrug his shoulders, claim that the deal had been broken and that he was going somewhere else.

But, as he approached, he knew his hopes were about to be shattered.

Stevie's hands moved on to his hips. There was nothing even slightly apologetic about his manner. 'Jesus, man, I've not got all day. What's with the snail pace? You on bleedin' Valium or what?'

'So you've got it?' Leo said.

'Of course I've got it. You got the rest of my cash?'

Leo instinctively reached for his pocket, checking that the notes were still there. 'I want to see it first.' He was still trying to think of ways to avoid the purchase, of any get-out clause that might not involve his head being beaten to a pulp.

'Here,' Stevie said, bending to open his holdall. He looked up at him. 'Don't just stand there. You want the whole fuckin' world to see?'

Leo obediently laid his bike on the grass, knelt down and stared into the bag. What he saw was the last thing he wanted to see: a small dark revolver was nestled in the corner of a plastic carrier. He ran his tongue across his dry lips. 'Where's the ammo?'

'Already loaded,' Stevie said.

Leo didn't have a clue as to whether that was true or not. He had never seen a real gun before and was simultaneously terrified and intrigued by it. Too scared even to touch, his fingers roamed around the edges of the bag.

'It wasn't as easy as I thought,' Stevie said. 'The cops are having a crackdown. It cost a bit more than I thought it would.'

'How much more?'

'Another fifty.'

Leo quickly stood up and shook his head. Stevie had

just handed him the perfect excuse and he was going to make the most of it. 'Sorry,' he said. 'I haven't got that much.'

'We made a deal.'

'For a hundred,' Leo said. 'We agreed on a hundred. I can't afford any more.' He shrugged his skinny shoulders and took a step back. He would have been glad if Stevie had just picked up the holdall and walked away but he didn't. Instead his eyes took on a harder look.

'What are you talking about? I've put my arse on the line for you. Do you have any idea of how hard it is to get hold of one of these?'

'But I can't—'

'You want it or not?' Stevie snarled.

Leo was about to say no, was absolutely determined to say no, when he lifted his eyes towards Barley Road and saw a figure standing in the window of Jo's flat. His stomach took a dive. Jesus, it was *him*! It was the evil bastard she had brought home last Friday. And suddenly Leo was back on the path with his arm twisted up behind his spine and the man's hot breath on his neck.

'I can do an extra t-ten,' Leo spluttered, suddenly determined to have the weapon. He dug into his pocket and thrust the notes towards Stevie. 'Here, eighty quid. That's all I've got. Take it or leave it.'

Stevie hesitated – but not for long. It wasn't as much as he'd hoped for but when all was said and done, it was still clear profit. After grabbing the cash, he bent down, picked up the carrier bag and threw it ungraciously towards Leo. 'This is between you and me, right? You ever tell *anyone* where you got this and I'll fuckin' kill you.'

Leo nodded. He could have mentioned that *he* was now the one holding the loaded gun but knew that he wouldn't appreciate the irony.

Chapter Fifty-three

Susan had never seen him so animated. Marty Gull's cheeks were flushed and his eyes shone with a bright sadistic pleasure as he recounted the events of the night before. She watched him as he paced around the kitchen, his gestures expansive, his voice creepily elated as he relived every vile and lurid detail.

This was what they had planned for, sweated over, for almost ten months. Susan tried to concentrate, to look suitably joyous and impressed. She *was* happy, she knew that, but somehow she just wasn't quite happy enough.

'You should have seen him,' Marty said ecstatically. He threw back his head and laughed. 'You should have seen the look on his fat bloody face.'

'Mmm,' she murmured.

He stopped abruptly, leaned back against the sink and glared at her. 'Are you listening to a word I'm saying?'

'Of course I'm listening,' she lied.

'Well, try not to look so fucking pleased about it all. I thought this was what you wanted.'

Sensing his irritation, a volatile, dangerous emotion that could quite easily flip over into anger, Susan made an effort to placate him. 'I did. I mean, I *do.* I *am* glad – you did a great job . . . but it's not going to bring Linda back, is it?' She buried her face in her hands. 'She's gone for ever. Nothing's going to change that.'

Marty was partly mollified, if not especially sympathetic. 'Yeah, but just don't forget who's doing all the hard work here. I'm the one who has to be with him. All you have to do is sit on your arse and watch the brat.'

Susan resented the implication that she'd got the easier side of the deal – it was no great shakes having to listen to Silver whine all day – but had the sense to keep her opinion to herself. Looking up, she wiped away her tears. 'You're right,' she said softly. And then, because she knew it was what he wanted, promptly added: 'Go on, I want to hear the rest. What happened next?'

He thought about it for a while, pretending not to be that bothered, but ultimately couldn't resist the joy of telling. His chest puffed up with pride. His eyes regained their shine as he continued with the story.

This time, Susan paid closer attention. For the next few minutes she made sure she nodded in all the right places, expressing all the exclamations of amazement and surprise that he was yearning for. Marty Gull was not a modest man – he liked to be praised for his skills and she wisely obliged.

When he arrived at the climax, where Delaney thought he had shot his daughter dead, Susan jumped back in her seat. Even though she'd known what was going to happen, she was still faintly shocked. He was so graphic in his description, so eager to relay every moment of Delaney's agony, that the death of Silver felt almost real.

'Jesus,' she said. 'So he really thought—'

'Chucked up, didn't he?' Marty said gleefully. 'Like a fucking volcano – his guts just exploded; he spewed all over the place.'

'Wonderful,' she said, smiling.

'Which is going to make it so shit easy for tomorrow. He won't fuck us around after this.'

Late tomorrow night, Delaney would be given his new instructions. This time – after what had happened in the factory – he wouldn't dare disobey the order to go alone. It would be Susan's job to pick up the cash and bring it back to the house. Delaney would then be sent on a wild goose-chase to Kent. While that was in progress, Marty could safely slip away from Honey's. The money would be split fifty-fifty before they cleared out the cellar, put a blind-folded Silver in the back of the van and drove her a couple of miles down the road. By the time Delaney was told where to find her, Marty Gull would be back at the club and Susan would be on her way to the airport.

Then it would all be over. Or would it? Susan was starting to wonder. She was starting to wonder about all kinds of things, the most disturbing of which was whether this even qualified as revenge. It was payback of sorts, yes, but the suffering Delaney had endured would soon be coming to an end. Hers would go on for ever.

'What's up?' he said.

'Nothing,' she lied. There was, of course, the other small matter of whether she could actually trust Marty. After what had happened to Ritchie Naylor . . . But it was a bit late to start going down that road. All she could do was to be prepared, to be ready in case he turned against her.

'Don't give me that,' he said. 'Come on, spill!'

Susan stood up, poured herself a glass of water and leaned back against the sink. 'Why do you hate him so much, Marty? I mean, you know my reasons but I've never really understood yours.'

For a second she thought he was going to fly into one of his tempers. His face grew dark but quickly cleared again. He laughed. 'It isn't to do with hate, babe. It's about loyalty and what's owed to me. Almost twenty years I've worked for him. This is my reward, my pension; a little early, granted, but then who knows when the old bugger's going to drop off his perch.'

Susan didn't believe him. This wasn't just about money for either of them. Marty's motives, like her own, were rooted in deeper, darker places. But now wasn't the time to start digging. Instead, she simply nodded and said: 'So we're all set?'

Marty was staring hard at her. 'Tell me you're not getting the last-minute jitters.'

'I don't do jitters,' she said scornfully.

'Nervous anxiety then. Call it what you like.'

Susan sipped at the water before raising her eyes to meet his. '*I* prefer to call it anticipation. Roll on tomorrow; I can't wait.'

Chapter Fifty-four

It was over two hours since Gabe had taken the keys to the white Mondeo and left. Since then, Jo had barely moved from the sofa. She had her bare feet up on the low table and her arms folded across her chest. She didn't exactly regret what she had told him but was not especially comfortable with it either. Informing a man you barely knew that your husband had kept secrets was hardly the ideal way to preserve one's pride. What had possessed her to start telling him the details of her private life? But she already knew the answer to that: four strong beers on an almost empty stomach.

She should have stuck to the coffee when they'd come back to the flat.

That was the trouble with booze: it not only loosened your tongue, stripping away all your finer layers of judgement, but also made the act of spilling confidences feel like the right thing to do. Jo gave a groan. She lifted her right heel and banged it down against the table. Still, there was some small consolation – it wasn't as if Gabe Miller's relationships screamed unadulterated success either. His brief marriage to Susan hadn't been much to brag about. And what did it matter what he thought of her? It didn't. It *absolutely* didn't.

With a sigh, Jo shifted forward. She could feel her T-shirt clinging to her back. She stood up and walked across the room. Looking out of the window, she noticed the greyness of the sky; it had clouded over since the afternoon and the air had taken on a thick, sticky quality. A storm was on its way. She flapped a hand in front of her face but the slight warm breeze did nothing to cool her down.

Tired of stressing out over what she had told Gabe, she turned her mind to what he had told her instead. His plans for tomorrow weren't exactly sound. They consisted of little more than hanging around outside Honey's on the off-chance that Delaney might take off at some point in the evening.

'And then?' she had said.

'I'll follow him.'

'Won't he be watching out for that?'

'He might. Which is why I'll be careful. I'll keep my distance.' Gabe had dropped his elbows on to his knees and his chin on to his hands. 'I'm not going to do anything stupid. If the exchange goes ahead, well and good – I won't interfere or put Silver's life in danger – but I just want to be there in case anything goes wrong.'

'And if it does go wrong?'

'I'll deal with that if and when it happens.'

The emphasis, she suspected, should have been placed more firmly on the 'when' rather than the 'if' but she hadn't said anything. Apart from the usual goodbyes, these were the last words they had exchanged. Jo thought about them while she stretched out her arms. She felt restless and frustrated. As if the approaching storm was seeping into her bones, she couldn't stay still. She paced from one side of the room to the other, trying to get her thoughts in order. The only thing she ended up knowing for sure was that she could no longer bear to be inside the flat.

As Jo slammed the door behind her, she still didn't know where she was going. But it didn't take her long to figure it out. She had spent too many years with her head buried in the sand – it was time to start searching for the truth.

She half-walked, half-jogged across the Green. It was Friday, seven-fifteen, and with the grey sky threatening rain, the High Street was quieter than usual. Ruby's, as it should be, was securely closed and shuttered. She took a moment to look at the window display, to gaze bleakly at Deborah's artistic display of sapphires, before going in. She locked the door behind her, turned off the alarm, went through to the office and flicked on the light.

For a moment, as the room was illuminated, she stood very still, held her breath and listened. There was no sound other than the gentle hum of the traffic. Slowly, she relaxed. What was she doing? This was *her* office and she had every right to be here. She had no need to feel like an intruder, like a burglar who had furtively crept in and was intent on taking what didn't belong to her. And yet the analogy wasn't completely off the mark. She was here to search for valuable goods, for whatever her husband might have chosen to hide.

But where to start? Jo glanced around. Immediately, she dismissed the safe – if there was anything in there, she would have come across it by now. She disregarded the two tall filing cabinets as well; these only contained papers relating to the day-to-day running of the business and she was always in and out of them. No, the most logical place to begin was with the three long shelves of box files.

First, she took down the file that Deborah had shown her on Wednesday and laid it on the desk. She quickly flicked through the bank statements but found nothing, apart from a few old bills, lying underneath. She looked at the statements again; there could be all kinds of clues in the payments Peter had made but that kind of scrutiny would take time and patience. It was a job, she decided, that was better done at home. Going through to the shop, she grabbed a large carrier from under the counter and went back to the office and dropped the whole file into the bag.

Next, she searched the boxes that had been sitting either side of the space she had created but drew a blank. She scanned the shelves, checking out the scribbled labels but nothing obvious jumped out at her. She tried picking out several files at random but that proved equally unproductive. There was, she knew, only one logical way of doing this: she would have to start from the beginning and work her way methodically through to the end.

The task was daunting – there must be over fifty files – but she wasn't going to leave until she'd checked out every single one of them. The irony that she was hunting for information that might only cause her hurt and distress was not lost on her. Was she mad, stupid? Perhaps she was, but she had come too far to stop now.

'Okay,' she said. Her voice sounded odd in the quietness

of the room, unnaturally loud and somehow not quite her own. She cleared her throat and tried again. 'Okay, let's get on with it.'

By the time she had spent over an hour ploughing through endless reams of advertising material, promotional fliers, journals, old business forecasts and accounts, Jo had come to two important conclusions: one was that the office needed a damn good clear-out and the other was that if anything important *had* been here, it had probably already been removed.

She immediately thought of Jacob. Reaching for the phone, she punched in the first few digits of his number but then recoiled from the idea of talking to him. She quickly slammed down the receiver. There was something intrinsically embarrassing, even shameful, about having to admit what she was doing.

With a sigh, she stared back at the shelves. She wasn't finished yet. There were still ten more boxes to go. The next file she pulled out was old, black and tattered and didn't look any more promising than the others. She opened it to find yet another pile of catalogues relating to auctions that had long since come and gone. God, why wasn't anything ever thrown out in this place? But as she carelessly pushed them aside, her heart gave a tiny leap. Underneath was a bundle of letters. There were about thirty of them, secured by an elastic band, and a quick look through established that the thin blue airmail envelopes were all addressed to Peter Strong.

Jo backed across the room and sat down. She dumped the catalogues on the floor. Then she tentatively removed the bundle and laid it on the desk. For a while she sat and stared at it. Her heart was beating faster now. She didn't even have to open the letters to know who they were from – the elegant slope of Deborah's handwriting was already familiar to her.

So, she had been right all along! There *had* been something between them. The only question remaining now was when the relationship had ended. She flicked through the envelopes again, noting the various addresses of Thailand, India, even China. They had all been sent to Peter while he was abroad which suggested, surely, that these were simply the sentimental reminders of an old affair. It would be easy to slip the top one free of the elastic band, to ease it out and read the contents of the letter inside. And yet somehow Jo couldn't bring herself to do it, not here, not right now. She would need a large drink in her hand before she could face that particular ordeal.

Returning to the box, she picked out a slim Kodak wallet. This time she didn't hesitate before opening it and spreading out the six photographs. Five of them were of Deborah standing alone, a younger-looking version of the woman she knew, with her striking red hair worn loose and almost reaching her waist. But the sixth, and the one her eyes were constantly drawn back to, had Peter in it too. He was standing behind Deborah, his arms wrapped tightly around her waist, and there was something about the intimacy of the pose, about the expression on both of their faces, which made her flinch. What she saw – or believed she saw – was a couple who were passionately in love.

Jo took a few deep breaths while she continued to gaze

down at the picture. What she mustn't do, she told herself, was overreact. People fell in love – and then out of it again. It happened. She had to keep things in perspective. This was all ancient history. Peter was dead and it was crazy to be jealous over some old girlfriend. So what if Deborah had once been important to him? It was her, Jo, he had chosen to marry. By then Peter had been thirty-eight and it was inevitable that he'd have had a past.

But somehow that line of argument didn't have quite the effect she'd hoped for. Jo didn't feel any better and she instinctively knew why: *if it had been anyone but Deborah Hayes . . .*

She shifted in her chair, crossing her legs and uncrossing them again. There was something fundamentally wrong about the fact he hadn't even mentioned the relationship. This was a woman he worked with every day, whose love letters – and she had no doubt that they *were* love letters – he hadn't just carefully preserved but also gone to the trouble of hiding. She had never enquired about his exes and so, technically, Peter hadn't actually lied to her but there was, perhaps, an even more invidious form of deceit and that was the sin of omission; by choosing not to tell he had created a barrier that would always be between them.

Unable to bear looking at the photos any more, Jo shoved them back in the wallet. There was now only one item remaining in the file, a plain brown A4 envelope. Its bland exterior gave no indication of its contents. She picked it up, unpeeled the still slightly sticky edge of the flap and drew out the stapled sheets.

Laying it down on the desk, she scanned the first few

lines. It was clearly some kind of legal document but she screwed up her eyes, confused, as she realised that it was a tenancy agreement. The lease, which Peter had signed and dated three years ago, was for a one-bedroom flat in Fairlea Avenue. But that didn't make any sense. Three years ago they had both been living in Barley Road. It took a few seconds before the awful truth dawned on her.

Jo felt her body take on a peculiar and unnerving stillness. She didn't seem able to move. In the back of her mind, she was faintly aware of the room having grown darker, of a smattering of rain against the window. Her hands were clenched so tightly that her nails were beginning to pierce the soft skin of her palms. She felt clammy, sick. Leaning forward, a low pained moan escaped from her lips. Oh God, what she would do to turn the clock back a few minutes, to have not picked up the envelope, to have *never* looked inside!

Bur it was too late for that. What was done could never be undone. The date on the contract danced in front of her eyes. Her husband had rented a flat, a flat she had known nothing about, barely a month after they were married.

Chapter Fifty-five

The skies had opened and the rain was coming down hard as she stumbled back across the Green. Thunder rumbled in the distance. Jo was wet through by the time she reached Barley Road. Clutching the dripping carrier bag to her chest and with her head bowed low, she didn't notice the bright red Toyota parked outside the house.

The door of the car opened and Carla got out. 'Hey,' she said, 'I was about to give up on you.'

Jo turned and stared at her. She didn't smile. She didn't even say hello.

'God, you're drenched,' Carla said. 'Where have you been? I tried to call but your phone's been turned off so I thought I'd just drive over and . . .' Her explanation petered out as she realised something was wrong. 'Are you okay? What's the matter?'

'Why didn't you tell me?'

Carla shrugged her shoulders and frowned. 'Tell you what?'

'About *her*.'

Again Carla shrugged. 'I don't—'

Jo's voice was small, strained and bitter. 'Please don't

pretend you didn't know. You must have. I mean, it was going on for long enough. Were you all having a good laugh at my expense?' When Carla still didn't show any sign of understanding, she sighed and spelled it out for her. 'Peter and that woman, Peter and Deborah bloody Hayes.'

'Ah,' Carla said, comprehension finally springing into her eyes. She seemed relieved as if there was no great crisis at hand. 'For heaven's sake, that was all over years ago.'

'Was it?'

'Of course it was. It's ancient history. You can't seriously be bothered about *her*. She's just an old girlfriend. She wasn't—' Carla, catching the look on Jo's face, abruptly stopped. Her brows shot up. 'Are you kidding?'

Jo held the bag closer to her chest. She wasn't sure if she was still crying or if it was just the rain trickling down her cheeks.

'Oh, love,' Carla said. 'I'm so sorry. I didn't know, I swear I didn't.' She put an arm around Jo's shoulder and led her towards the front door. 'Come on, let's get out of this rain before we both catch pneumonia.'

Inside, Jo was gently pushed into the bedroom and ordered to change. A towel was collected from the bathroom and put into her hand. She went though the motions, slowly drying herself before getting changed. When she came back out to the kitchen, dressed in an old pair of joggers and a black T-shirt, her sister-in-law was busy rooting through the cupboards.

'Do you have any brandy?'

Jo shook her head. 'There's some wine in the fridge.'

'That'll do.' She took out the bottle and poured a generous

glass for Jo and a smaller one for herself. 'Here,' she said, putting the two glasses and bottle down on the table.

As they sat down, Jo was reminded of all those times after Peter had died when the two of them had sat here together. The memory made her want to cry again. It was Carla who had helped her through all those dreadful days, who had listened to her endless ramblings, tried to comfort her, forced her to eat and . . . well, just about dragged her back into the daylight again. She felt a blush of shame at how she'd spoken to her earlier. 'I'm really sorry about before. I didn't mean to accuse you of anything.'

'Forget it. You were upset and rightly so. But are you absolutely sure about this? I mean, do you have any actual evidence?'

Jo glanced towards the carrier bag leaning up against the washing machine. 'Tell me what you know about the two of them first.'

Carla puffed out her cheeks while she thought about it. 'It's not much.'

'It doesn't matter. Just tell me anything, anything you know.'

'Okay.' Carla took a sip of wine, put the glass down and dropped her chin on to her hands. 'I think they met about fifteen years ago, when Peter was in his mid-twenties. I'm not sure where or how but they were still together when I started going out with Tony a couple of years later. I met her a few times but only in passing. Peter, as you know, wasn't the most sociable man in the world. They were together for a while and then . . . well, he was always travelling, always on the go. I think Deborah wanted him to settle down, to make some kind of commitment, but he wasn't prepared to do that. Eventually they split up, she met someone else, got married and . . .'

'And now they're living happily ever after,' Jo said.

Carla looked at her. 'Perhaps they are. She's got a couple of kids, hasn't she?'

That's never stopped Tony, Jo almost said, but quickly bit her lip. 'She still came back to work for Peter.'

'So they worked together. So what? That's business. It doesn't mean she was cheating on her husband.'

'She used to work at Asprey's. How much do you think she earned there? It must have been a damn sight more than Peter could have afforded to pay her.'

'That still doesn't mean there was anything going on.'

Jo knocked back her glass of wine. She picked up the bottle and poured herself another. She wasn't sure how many drinks it would take for her to stop feeling so lost and angry but it was certainly more than one. Standing up, she walked over to the carrier bag, snatched out the brown envelope, took out the lease and laid it down in front of Carla. 'Look at this.'

Carla stared down at the tenancy agreement. She was quiet as she read it through. 'Fairlea Avenue. Wasn't that where—'

'Where Peter was run over? Yes. And this proves that he was secretly renting out another flat. And why would he do that unless he was seeing someone else?'

'There could be all kinds of reasons. Peter was always a bit of a loner. Some men need to have their space. Perhaps he was just—'

'What, so desperate to get away from me that he needed a bolthole half a mile down the road? It was only a month, a *month* after we'd got married.' Saying it out loud seemed to bring the full force of the betrayal home to her. Jo gulped down a sob. 'How could he do that? *Why?*'

'You can't go jumping to conclusions. What if he . . . I don't know . . . perhaps he . . .'

'Exactly!' Jo said. 'There's no other explanation than the stark horrible truth and the sooner I come to terms with it, the better.'

Carla shook her head. 'But he loved you, Jo, I know he did. Being with you, it changed him. I hadn't seen him so happy in years. And he wasn't like Tony; he didn't play around. He was a one-woman man. It wasn't in his nature.'

Jo snorted. 'Maybe they were more alike than you think – Peter just hid it better.'

'I can't believe that.'

Jumping to her feet, Jo said: 'This is no good. I have to go and see Deborah, ask her straight out.'

'No,' Carla insisted, grabbing her wrist. 'You're not going anywhere. For one, you've been drinking and for two you can't go around making wild accusations. For God's sake, think about it. Even if you're right, she's going to have no choice but to deny it if you confront her in front of her husband. What are you going to achieve? It's not as though you have any real evidence.'

'I'll have that when I see the look in her eyes.'

'And what about her husband, not to mention her kids? What do you think this will do to them?'

'Why should I care?'

Carla's fingers tightened round her wrist. 'Because none of this is their fault, even if it's true. Can you imagine how they'll feel if you turn up on the doorstep, ranting and raving and shouting the odds? I've never thought of you as the type of person to deliberately hurt someone else.'

Jo slowly sank back down. For a moment she just hadn't cared, hadn't given a damn and that frightened her. 'I only . . .'

'I know,' Carla said, slowly releasing her hold. 'And I know what it means to feel like you do, to want to lash out. I've been there often enough. All that I'm asking is that you take some time to think about it, to not do anything too rash. You don't have any proof. You don't even know that he was still seeing Deborah.'

'I think he was.'

'You can't be sure.'

'Yes, I can,' Jo said, placing a hand against her stomach. She gave Carla a thin faint smile. 'Call it gut instinct, call it whatever you like, but I *am* sure. I always knew that something wasn't quite right between us. There was always this . . . this kind of distance. I used to think it was to do with the family, with the problems he had with Ruby and Mitchell. One minute we'd be really close and the next, it was like he deliberately brought the shutters down. I tried to pretend that it was nothing to do with me but I was only kidding myself. I should have listened to that little nagging voice but I didn't.'

'You were in love,' Carla said softly. 'No one ever listens to that voice when they're in love.'

Jo looked at her. In the past, she had only paid lip-service to Carla's suffering, to the pain she had endured through

Tony's endless lies and infidelities. Now she was beginning to understand just how agonising that pain could feel. Anger bubbled up in her again. 'Maybe that bitch ran him over!'

'Why would she do that?'

Jo swiped at her cheeks with the back of her hand. The tears were running down her face again. 'Because he was a two-timing, double-crossing, lousy piece of shit?'

Carla leaned forward and folded her into her arms. 'Well, if that's the truth, sweetheart, then the two of them had a lot in common.'

Jo tried to answer but she couldn't. She couldn't speak. She bent her face into Carla's shoulder and wept.

Chapter Fifty-six

The clock said nine-twenty-five. Jo wondered where the time had gone. Her eyes felt red and sore. It was a while since she had stopped crying but there was still a lump in her throat. 'It's getting late. Won't Tony be worried?'

'That would be a first,' Carla said. 'Anyway, I don't want to leave you on your own.'

'I'll be fine. I'm not going to do anything stupid – well, nothing more stupid than opening another bottle of wine and spending the rest of the night feeling thoroughly sorry for myself. And look, you haven't even told me why you came round.'

'Oh, it'll keep,' Carla said, flapping a hand.

'Come on, it must have been important to drag you out on a night like this.' As if to prove her point, a flash of lightning lit up the sky. It was followed by a loud clap of thunder and the rain thrashing even harder against the windows. 'I presume it's to do with Ruby, with the row we had this morning.'

Carla nodded. 'Yeah, I had a talk with Tony and . . .' She hesitated, screwing up her face as if reluctant to go on. 'You know, we really don't need to do this now. Why don't I give you a call over the weekend and—'

'No,' Jo insisted. '*Please.* Whatever it is, it can't be any worse than what I've already learned tonight.' But she saw Carla's eyes nervously flick to one side and a shiver of apprehension ran through her. 'Can it?' she said. 'Is it to do with Leonard Kearns, with how he died?' Abruptly, all her earlier fears rose to the surface. Before Carla had a chance to reply, she said: 'It is, isn't it? Oh God, was he . . . was he murdered?'

'What?' Carla said, jumping back in surprise. 'Jesus! What? No, of course not. Whatever gave you *that* idea?' As she recovered herself, she lifted her fingers to her lips and laughed. 'Blimey, I know Mitchell was a bastard but I think even he drew the line at killing his own employees.'

As soon as she'd said it, Jo had realised how ridiculous it sounded. It had been one of those festering suspicions that had lost its power the second it was expressed. 'I didn't mean Mitchell,' she said, although that wasn't entirely true. 'It was just that Ruby's reaction, as soon as I mentioned Kearns, was so extreme that I wondered what she was trying to hide.'

Carla was still grinning. 'And so you presumed the poor guy must have been bumped off?'

'No. Yes. I mean, I didn't know what to think. I just felt there was something peculiar about it all. There's this man who dies in Burma and Ruby throws a fit the second his name is mentioned. What's with that? If everything is above board, why is she freaking out? It just did my head in. I guess with all this stuff about Peter, I've not been thinking straight.'

'I can understand that,' Carla said sympathetically, 'and,

if it helps, you weren't completely wrong: Ruby *was* trying to cover up. Not anything as dramatic as a murder, I'm afraid, but there is something that she's desperate to hide. It took me hours to squeeze it out of Tony.'

Jo waited expectantly.

Carla pulled another of her faces. 'If he knew I was telling you this, he wouldn't be too happy.' She stared down at the table before slowly lifting her gaze again. 'Look, I can't make you swear to keep quiet, that wouldn't be fair before you've heard what I've got to say, but will you at least promise that you won't do anything before talking it through with me first?'

'Now I'm starting to get worried again,' Jo said.

'Just promise.'

'Okay, I promise.'

Carla put her hands on the table and took an audible breath. 'You never met Mitchell, did you? You were lucky. He was only interested in two things – one of them, the most important, was money and the other was . . . well, you wouldn't have wanted to get on the wrong side of his roaming hands. If Ruby wasn't such a cow, I might almost feel sorry for her.' She briefly raised her eyes to the ceiling before continuing. 'Anyway, to get back to the business side of things, he was always after the best deal, the cheapest deal. He travelled all over the world but Burma was where he went for his rubies. There were government auctions twice a year and he always bought from them but he used to buy from other sources too. There was a huge black market behind the scenes and Mitchell had his contacts.'

'So he was buying gems illegally,' Jo said.

'Got it in one,' Carla said, 'and then smuggling them back into Britain. He'd pay the duty on the cheaper legal stones and make a killing on the rest. He had plenty of customers who weren't too fussed about the paperwork. Burmese rubies, especially those at the top end of the scale, are always in demand.'

'And so Leonard Kearns was . . .?'

'Yeah, up to his ears in it, which is why Ruby threw a wobbler when you mentioned his name. It's not how the poor guy died that she's stressing about, it's the prospect of Customs and Excise finding out what Mitchell was up to. She thinks you're threatening to grass her up to the taxman and once that ball starts rolling there won't be any stopping it.'

'My God,' Jo murmured as a smile crept on to her lips. A small shiver of satisfaction ran through her. *Shadenfreude* – wasn't that what they called it? Taking pleasure in other people's misfortune. She recognised that it wasn't a nice response but in the case of Ruby Strong it was hard to resist; that woman deserved some kind of payback for all the misery she had inflicted over the years. Not that she was actually planning on picking up the phone and dropping her in it – she would never go that far – but there wasn't any harm in making her sweat. 'So I guess she's getting pretty worried?'

Carla, however, didn't seem quite so happy at the prospect. Her hands twisted anxiously on the table. 'If this comes out, it could ruin her,' she said.

And Jo instantly knew what she meant: that it could ruin Tony too. One little whisper of Mitchell's dodgy dealings and the whole business would start to crumble. 'So why are you telling me all this?'

'Because I know what you're like,' Carla sighed. 'The more you get stonewalled, the more suspicious you're going to get. I'm just the same. And if you dig deep enough, ask enough questions, you'll eventually discover some of the truth. I thought it was better that you heard the whole story from me.'

Jo had an uncomfortable thought. 'It's not still going on, is it?'

'Of course not! All that ended years ago. Can you really imagine Tony as an international gem smuggler? He may be a lying, deceitful sod but he'd never have the nerve to do anything like that.'

'But Mitchell did.'

Carla nodded. 'It was how he made his money, how he moved into the big time. How else could he have dragged himself out of the gutters of Kellston and into a fancy shop in Hatton Garden? At the beginning he had nothing to lose and later . . . well, I guess the cash, the profit, was just too much to resist. Tony swears that he and Peter had no idea what he was up to and I think, for once, he's being straight with me. Neither of them had a clue until that trip to Burma twelve years ago.'

'When Peter had the big bust-up with his father,' Jo said.

Carla nodded again. 'That was the last time they ever spoke to each other. When Leonard Kearns got sick and died, Mitchell went into panic. He had some top-grade gems in his possession but no mule to carry them home. That was when it all came out about the dealing, the smuggling, the way he'd actually built up his oh-so-respectable business. But it was his attitude towards Leonard that really shocked Peter. Mitchell didn't give a damn about the poor sod; all he was concerned about was his rubies. Peter had always looked up to him, admired him, but he finally saw his father for what he really was.'

'And Tony?' Jo said. 'How did he feel about all this?'

'He wasn't overjoyed but he never had quite the same moral standards as Peter. He didn't have his intelligence either. Cutting the family ties and going it alone was never an option for him.'

'Moral standards?' Jo said, her hand instinctively closing around the contract again.

She gave a thin brittle laugh. Somehow, those two words and Peter didn't seem to sit that comfortably together any more.

Carla leaned forward and gently eased the lease from between her fingers. She folded it in two and put it to one side. 'I don't know what this means – perhaps neither of us ever will – but I do know that he loved you. I don't have any doubts about that. So please don't write him off, Jo. Don't dismiss everything the two of you had just because of a few stupid sheets of paper.' She slowly rose to her feet. 'You've got a lot to think about. I'd better leave you to it.'

Jo stood up too. She had already made one decision. 'You don't have to worry. I won't say anything about what you've told me tonight.'

Carla's eyes widened with relief. 'Do you really mean that?'

'I only wanted to understand what happened out there

and now I do. It's finished, done with. None of it was your fault and I don't see why you or the kids should suffer for what Mitchell did in the past. So you can tell the old witch that her secret is safe; no one is going to be stirring it up or calling the taxman.'

'Thank you,' Carla said, hugging her close. She stood back and grinned. 'Although, if you don't mind, I might not tell her the good news straight away.'

The two of them, understanding each other, exchanged a small complicit nod. If Ruby was forced to endure a few sleepless nights, it was nothing more than she deserved.

It was another hour before Jo picked up her glass of wine and wandered through to the living room. She stared at the wall, at the picture of Rangoon. Now she'd had some time to think about it, she wondered if Carla had told her the whole truth. There was still something missing from the story, she thought, a piece that still needed slotting into place. But did it really matter? She wasn't sure if she cared any more.

Her anger had long since subsided, replaced by a dull, painful ache. It was as if her very heart had contracted, shrivelling into something small and insignificant. She walked over to the photograph of Peter, ran a finger over the contours of his face and gently placed the back of her hand against his cheek. She still wanted to believe that some part of their love had been real and true but that hope was fading by the minute.

Chapter Fifty-seven

It was seven long days since Susan had been outside. Feeling hemmed in and restless, she roamed aimlessly around, going up and down the narrow flight of stairs, wandering through the rooms in search of distraction. Not that there was anything left to discover; she knew every nook and cranny of the bland terraced house, every crack in the plaster, every chip in the yellowing paintwork, but still she persisted, her bare feet padding softly over the worn beige carpet.

In the front bedroom she paused to look out of the window, to gaze along the dark and empty street. It was from here that she had seen Gabe dragged out of the pub. Quickly, she turned away, not wanting to think about it. He would be all right, she told herself; Gabe Miller was one of life's survivors.

The only furniture in the room was a double bed, a flimsy white wardrobe and a matching set of drawers. The mattress on the bed was bare. Since arriving, Susan hadn't slept in either of the bedrooms, choosing instead to spend her nights on the narrow uncomfortable sofa downstairs. From there, if she kept the kitchen door to the basement open, she could hear if Silver cried out. It had been a constant dread that something might happen, that she might accidentally choke or get herself entangled in the chain. The girl was stupid enough to do either of these things and a lot more besides.

Bending down, Susan pulled the small suitcase from the bottom of the wardrobe and laid it on the bed. There wasn't much to pack but she may as well do it now as later. If nothing else it would help pass the time. She cleared the hangers and emptied the only drawer that she had used. She was travelling light, intending to buy new clothes wherever she finally found herself. Where that would be, she had no idea. Making detailed plans was too much like tempting providence; she would only decide when she had the cold hard cash in her hands.

When she was finished with the packing, she left the case on the bed and went downstairs. First she checked on the girl. She had closed the door while the storm was going on and Silver, safely cocooned in the old brick cellar, had thankfully slept through it. She was still sleeping now, curled up beneath the blanket with her face up close to the wall.

Susan went back to the kitchen and switched on the kettle. She knew that she should try to get some rest but still felt too restive, too anxious. These last twenty-four hours were going to be the toughest. By this time tomorrow it would be over but that point still seemed a distant dot on the horizon, the long, empty hours stretching on for ever. There wasn't even a TV in the house but she did have a radio. She turned it on as she made a cup of tea, keeping the volume low in case it woke Silver.

It was eleven o'clock when the news came on, first the national headlines with their usual gloomy content, then the more local stuff. She was only half listening as a report began about a fire that had taken place at a factory in Shoreditch. It took a moment for the penny to drop, for her to realise it was the same place Marty had taken Vic Delaney to play out their gruesome little game. She frowned. Marty hadn't mentioned anything about a fire. And just as she was trying to get her head around that, there came the revelation that the body of a woman had been found in the building. Couldn't these idiots tell the difference between a mannequin in a blonde wig and a real body, Susan thought, when the reporter went on to say that the murdered girl had now been identified as a local prostitute called Kelly Browning. Also known as Destiny, the eighteen-year-old hadn't been seen since Thursday evening.

Susan sat frozen as the bombshell gradually registered. For a while only the single word 'murdered' continued to revolve in her mind. Then suddenly, all the blind denials, the crazy explanations, came crashing and tumbling into her brain. She leapt up and started pacing from one side of the kitchen to the other. No, that couldn't be right! It must be a mistake. No one had been killed, no body retrieved. Or if they had, it had been nothing to do with Marty Gull. At worst, he had simply left the door to the factory open and the girl had wandered in later, looking for somewhere to sleep or somewhere private to take a punter. Yes, that's what must have happened. Maybe she had started the fire herself, a careless cigarette thrown on to the ground. Susan stopped and took a few deep breaths. Or hell, maybe Marty *had* lit the fire, wanting to destroy the evidence, to make sure there was no trail for Delaney to try and follow later. It had just been a horrible accident. There was no way he would have . . .

But a deepening sense of panic was gathering inside her. She remembered the casual way Marty had dropped the jeans and the T-shirt into the carrier bag. It was only the pretty pink shoes, the Jimmy Choo specials, he had been really interested in; she could still recall the way he had touched them, the way his fingers had gently caressed the long spiky heels. She remembered his brown eyes, fiercely determined and greedy with anticipation. And later, when it was all over, what had been in his eyes then?

But still she refused to believe the worst. She couldn't accept that he had deliberately used and killed Kelly Browning – the very idea that she had been the girl strapped to the chair, the girl Delaney had thought was his daughter, went beyond her worst nightmares. She tried again to fight against the obvious, making her last big push and final argument: Marty couldn't have done this, couldn't be a murderer, because he would have known that the moment it was discovered, the moment she found out about it, she'd be out of here. And when she walked out, the whole deal was over. And if the whole deal was over, everything fell apart – and the money was gone too.

Except, as Susan quickly realised, there was one major flaw to this line of reasoning: it was purely by chance that she *had* even heard about it. Locked away in the house with no television, no newspapers and no visitors, she was completely adrift from the outside world. This was, perhaps, what Marty had been relying on. He wasn't even aware of the tiny transistor radio she had nestling behind the kettle.

Suddenly, as if the blinkers had fallen from her eyes, she saw it all clearly. She had been played right from the start. She had been taken for a fool. Marty Gull had skilfully laid his trap and she had walked straight into it. The game that was being played out was not theirs but *his*.

Susan sat down at the table and dropped her face into her hands. Now she understood, it all seemed so blatantly obvious. 'No,' she murmured, 'Christ, no.'

But she couldn't escape the facts. Ritchie Naylor, after he had served his purpose, had been conveniently disposed of – she had never really believed that Gabe had been responsible. Now there was yet another victim. Who was next on the list? It didn't take a genius to work it out. From the moment she picked up the ransom, she would be at his mercy. And God alone knew what plans he had for Silver; she had already seen the pleasure he took in terrifying her.

How, why, had she ever put her trust in him? But she already knew the answer to that: because she had *wanted* to. Her desperate need for retribution had blinded her to the truth. She had willingly believed everything he had told her, all the rumours and the lies. The defining moment had come with Delaney's alibi for the night Linda disappeared, an alibi she now realised that hadn't just saved Delaney from any further investigation by the cops but had put Marty Gull firmly out of the frame too. And that in turn begged the question of what exactly *he* had been doing that night.

Susan jumped up, her heart pumping. She had to get

away. Although there was no need to rush – surely Marty would be sticking like glue to Delaney for the next twenty-four hours – she couldn't bear to spend a minute longer than she had to in the house. She was about to dash upstairs, to grab her case and flee, when she suddenly had second thoughts. Doing a runner was all very well but what about the girl?

She stood, undecided, in the middle of the kitchen. She was tempted to just leave her. Why not? Tomorrow evening, when she was far enough away, she could call Delaney and tell him where to find his daughter. But somehow that option didn't sit too comfortably: the chances of Marty Gull turning up in the meantime were slim but it was still a risk she was unprepared to take. The man was crazy, unpredictable. What if he took it into his head to make one last visit before the exchange? He would not only discover that she was gone but that Silver was still here. The poor kid wouldn't stand a chance. It would be like handing her to him, trussed and bound, to do with as he liked.

Susan drew her lips tightly together. No, even her meagre conscience couldn't cope with that. She started pacing, walking from the sink to the door, from the door to the sink. Well, she could always shove her in a cab and send her home but that wouldn't be such a smart move either. The minute she got there Marty would know about it – and would also know he'd been betrayed. How long before he came looking for his treacherous partner in crime? Not long, she suspected, and certainly not long enough for her to be able to put an adequate distance between them. And, unless she could find a way of tipping off Delaney, Silver would be in serious danger too – she'd be walking straight back into Marty's welcoming arms.

She tried to concentrate, muttering softly to herself. 'Come on, come on. You have to make a decision.'

While she was still pacing, the little matter of the ransom suddenly raised its head again. At this late stage, it seemed a crying shame to let all that cash slip so easily through her fingers. Running away was all very good but just how far could she run with no money in the bank? If she wanted to come out of this alive *and* solvent, she was going to have to think of something more useful than a speedy getaway. She needed a plan. She needed to think things through. But not here and certainly not now. It wasn't sensible to hang around. She needed somewhere safe to hide.

But where?

Her mother's flat was out of the question. Turning up with a kidnapped teenager would be too much even for her addled brain. And then it suddenly came to her. Susan smiled. There was somewhere she could go and somewhere not so far from here. Perhaps now was as good a time as any to think about renewing an old friendship.

Chapter Fifty-eight

For a moment, as she awoke, Silver seemed perfectly calm but then suddenly sat bolt upright, kicked out her legs and scrabbled back against the wall. 'What . . .?'

Susan quickly clamped her hand across her mouth. 'Shush,' she ordered. 'Don't make a noise.'

A pair of wide scared eyes stared back at her.

'It's me,' Susan said. 'You know me, don't you? You know my voice. You don't need to be afraid. I'm not going to hurt you.'

Very gradually, Silver relaxed.

Susan kept her hand pressed hard against her lips until she was sure that the girl wasn't going to scream. Then she smiled and sat back. 'It's time to go.'

'I'm . . . I'm going home?'

'Yeah, you're going home, sweetheart, but not right this minute. We're going somewhere else first, just for a little while. You have to listen carefully to me, okay? This is important. Are you properly awake? Are you listening?' She waited until Silver gave a tiny nod before continuing. 'This is what's going to happen: I'll take off the chain and then we'll go upstairs together. My friend's waiting outside the house and when we leave he's going to follow us. Please don't think about doing anything stupid. If you run or scream or draw any kind of attention to yourself, I won't be able to protect you. Do you understand what I'm saying?'

A flash of fear crossed Silver's face and she instantly nodded again.

'Good.' Susan took the key out of her pocket and held it up. 'If you do as you're told, you'll be perfectly safe. Now, give me your wrist.'

Silver held out her hand.

As she turned the key, Susan automatically braced herself for any sudden movements. But nothing happened. As the chain fell away, all Silver did was to look down and rub at the chafed skin on her wrist.

'Okay,' Susan said, taking hold of her elbow and helping her to her feet. 'It's time to go.' She pushed her gently towards the door. 'You first. And don't touch anything.'

Silver went up the steps cautiously, constantly glancing over her shoulder, frowning as if she feared this might be some kind of trick. When she reached the kitchen she immediately stopped dead, temporarily dazzled by the brightness of the light.

Susan pushed her forward again. 'Straight ahead. Go on, quickly, we haven't got all night.' Silver's anxiety was starting to infect her; she could feel the panic returning, a horror that Gull might suddenly turn up on the doorstep.

In the hall, she unzipped the suitcase and took out a pair of high-heeled shoes. 'Here, put these on.' If Silver's placid obedience was all an act, the moment she got outside she might try and make a run for it. The heels would at least slow her down a bit. She picked out a dark hooded top as well. 'And this. Keep the hood up over your face.'

Susan hesitated before she unlocked the front door. This could all go horribly wrong but what choice did she have? Leaving the kid here just wasn't an option. Of course there were always the handcuffs they had been intending to use for the move tomorrow night, but if she cuffed the girl's wrist to her own, she wouldn't be able to drive and if she cuffed the girl's hands together someone might notice. No, she would have to rely on good old-fashioned threats.

Squeezing Silver's arm hard enough to let her know she meant business, Susan stared into her eyes and said: 'Don't forget, he's waiting out there. He's watching your every move. You understand?'

Silver's head bobbed up and down again. Her mouth opened and closed but she didn't say a word. Her throat made a jerky swallowing motion.

'Right,' Susan said. 'This is what you're going to do. The car is parked directly outside, a pale blue Fiesta. It will take you six or seven steps to reach it and while you're walking you're not going to look around, you're not going to speak, you're not going to do anything other than get in the back of the goddamn car and lie down. Got it?'

Silver gave her by now familiar nod.

Susan squeezed her arm a little harder. 'Are you sure?'

'Y-yeah,' Silver said, her voice thin and shaky. 'I get straight in the car and lie down.'

'Okay,' Susan said, slowly releasing her hold. She picked up the suitcase, flung her handbag over her shoulder and turned the key in the mortice lock. 'Let's go.'

As she stepped outside, pulling the door shut behind them, it occurred to her that it would have been smart to do a recce first. She should have checked that the coast was clear. For all she knew, Marty could be parked up in the street watching the house. She shivered. It was the kind of weird creepy thing he would do.

Following closely behind Silver, her eyes darted rapidly to the left and right. *Please God, don't let him be here.* She had only the light from the streetlamps to rely on but the vehicles lining both sides of the short street all appeared to be empty. She heaved a sigh of relief. Now all she had to worry about was whether the girl would behave.

The beep as she opened the car doors sounded unnaturally loud in the silence of the night. Other than the pub (which had thrown out the last of its customers over half an hour ago), this was a predominantly residential area and most of its inhabitants were already tucked up in bed. She held her breath as Silver climbed inside the car. Then, before she had any more time to question the wisdom of what she was doing, she quickly jumped in too.

A few seconds later they were on their way.

In the confines of the small Fiesta, Susan became overly aware of Silver's musky scent. She wasn't sure how much of it was fear and how much was sweat and dirt. The girl probably hadn't washed for a week. She glanced over her shoulder before opening the window an inch.

Silver was lying very still, curled up with her knees almost touching her chin.

The traffic, even though it was a Friday night, was light. The earlier storm had cleared most of the streets and the pavements too. Susan had to curb her desire to put her foot down. Instead she made a point of keeping well within the speed limit.

For the next twenty minutes she circled the centre of Kellston, taking random left and right turns in case Silver was trying to memorise the route. The less she knew about the location of where she'd been imprisoned, the better. When Susan finally pulled into the station car park, her nerves were jangling. The forecourt was deserted; the last train had long since come and gone. This was as good a place as any to dump the car. Even if Marty Gull did a thorough search of the area, even if he eventually found the Fiesta, it wouldn't tell him anything more than that they might have caught a train somewhere.

'Are we there?' Silver whispered, her blue eyes looking wide and scared.

'From here we walk. It's not far.'

It was still raining lightly and an occasional rumble of thunder echoed in the distance. Susan, holding the suitcase in her left hand, linked her right arm through Silver's and kept her close. When they reached the High Street, where the late-night café was still open, she tightened her hold.

'Keep your head down,' she instructed.

This was another of those dangerous times when the kid might suddenly decide to take her chances. But if she had any such notions she didn't act on them and shortly after they passed through the entrance to the Green.

Susan deliberately looked over her shoulder.

Silver glanced back too.

'What did I tell you?' Susan hissed.

Silver smartly bowed her head again, her shoulders hunching. If she had noticed the lack of any obvious shadow, she wasn't responding to it.

The Green was empty and the air smelled of wet grass. Susan stayed on the central path. She tried to step up the pace but Silver, tottering in a pair of shoes two sizes too big for her, struggled to keep up.

The short march seemed to take for ever.

But Susan was finally rewarded for her troubles. As they reached the far side, her eyes quickly scanned the houses in Barley Road. She saw, with relief, that there was still a light on in the upper flat of number twelve.

Chapter Fifty-nine

Had she been paying a little less attention to her wine glass and a little more to the time – it was well after midnight – Jo would have thought twice about answering the door before first establishing who her late-night visitor was. As it was, she trotted down the stairs with some vaguely muddled notion of how Carla might have forgotten something or how Gabe Miller could have found himself in need of shelter again.

It was only as she saw the two hooded figures standing on the step that her stupidity hit home. This was London, for God's sake, the capital of crime. What was she thinking? Instinctively, she drew back. Quickly gripping the edge of the door she prepared to slam it shut. Then the taller of the two pulled back her hood and smiled.

'Hello, Jo.'

Jo's mouth dropped open. 'Laura!' she said, automatically reverting to the name she had originally known her by.

'Hey, it's nice to see you too.' Susan turned to her smaller skinnier sidekick and shoved her forward. 'Get in,' she said. 'Go straight up and don't touch anything.'

'What are you doing?' Jo protested. 'You can't—'

'It's an emergency,' Susan said, barging past. 'I've got a problem. It's best if we talk inside.'

Jo, although the shock had sobered her up, was still too slow to prevent the double invasion. By the time it had registered properly, her two uninvited guests were already halfway up the stairs. She slammed shut the door, locked it and scurried up behind them.

'For Christ's sake, you can't just . . .' Jo's objection faded as she walked into the living room. Susan's companion had dropped her hood to reveal a small heart-shaped face with big blue eyes. A swathe of long, rather greasy blonde hair hung down to her waist. Jo, although she had never seen her before, didn't have any difficulty in recognising who she was. 'Oh shit,' she murmured.

Susan calmly placed her suitcase beside the sofa. 'First things first. You don't mind if the kid has a bath, do you?' She looked at the girl and wrinkled her nose. 'No offence, love, but you do whiff a bit.'

Silver Delaney stood with her arms hanging limply by her sides. She seemed curiously impassive, disinterested or perhaps just disconnected from everything that was going on around her.

'No!' Jo said. She couldn't believe what was happening. It was unreal, like something in a dream. Susan had brought the kidnapped girl here – *here* to her flat. Fear and confusion battled for precedence in her still slightly fuddled mind. 'Nobody is doing anything until you tell me what the hell's going on.'

'Oh, don't go into one,' Susan said peevishly. 'I've had a bad enough day as it is. Believe me, I wouldn't have come near this place if I'd had any other choice. And I *will* explain, of course I will. For once I'm trying to do the right thing but . . .' She tilted her head towards Silver. 'You can spare a bit of hot water, can't you?'

'It's not a bloody hotel,' Jo snapped. What she really meant, although her dry lips seemed incapable of forming the words, was: *What are you thinking of? What are you doing here? How dare you drag me into all this – again!*

Susan strode over to the window, gazed out for a moment and smartly pulled the curtains across. She turned back to Jo. 'I'll take that as a yes.'

'No,' Jo said. 'You will not take it as a yes.' And then, guiltily aware that she hadn't even asked Silver how she was, she turned and gently touched her on the arm. 'Are you okay? Are you all right?'

The girl, recoiling from her touch, shrank back.

'What have you done to her?' Jo said, glaring at Susan.

Susan gave an impatient sigh. 'She's fine.' She frowned at Silver. 'You're fine, aren't you, sweetheart? Tell her that no one's hurt you.'

Silver gave a quick short nod.

Jo thought the girl looked abnormally pale but then she didn't know what she normally looked like.

'And you'd like a bath, wouldn't you?' Susan said.

The girl obediently nodded again. Her voice was soft and compliant. 'Yes, please.'

Jo wasn't sure what to do next. Had she been completely sober her responses might have been different – faster, smarter – but her brain, battling to overcome the disadvantage of too much alcohol, was still struggling to make sense of it all.

'Well then,' Susan said. She waltzed off into the bathroom, turned the radio on loud and started running the water. She beckoned Silver in. 'Come on, love. There are clean towels in the cupboard and I'm sure we can find you something to sleep in.'

'Sleep in?' Jo echoed.

Susan frowned at her. She waited until Silver was in the bathroom, until the sound of the radio and the running water drowned out any conversation, before closing the door and replying: 'It's almost half-twelve. Are you really going to throw us out at this time of night? Would you rather we slept on the streets?'

'I'd rather the poor girl slept in her own bed,' Jo huffed back. 'What is she doing here? What are *you* doing here?' Having Susan in the flat was bad enough but harbouring the kidnapped daughter of a violent gangster was verging on the crazy. She was beginning to get scared, very scared.

'I don't like it either,' Susan said, 'but there's not much I can do about it.'

Jo stared at her, incredulous. 'What do you mean there's—'

'Don't look at me like that,' Susan said, sitting down on the sofa and curling her legs under her.

'Like what?'

'Like you're about to call the filth.'

'And why shouldn't I?' Jo could feel her temper rising. She had to take control of this situation but wasn't sure how. 'She's been missing for a week. No, she's been *imprisoned* for a week. How exactly do you expect me to react?'

'With a little calmness,' Susan said. 'Look, I'm trying to

help the kid, not harm her. If you'd sit down and listen for a second you'd realise that. You call the cops and they'll take her back to Daddy and then she'll be in a hundred times more danger than she is now.' She gave a disappointed shrug. 'Unfortunately, it turns out that my partner wasn't quite the man I thought he was. I can't go into detail but let's just say that home isn't the safest place for her at the moment.'

Jo perched on the edge of a chair. 'You mean it's someone in the family?'

'Someone connected to the family.'

'So you tell the police, you warn them about him.'

'I don't think so, sweetie. Anyway, I'm sure you don't want to rot in jail for the next ten years any more than I do.'

Jo felt a tightening in her chest. 'What do you mean?'

'Well, they're hardly going to shake my hand and say thank you very much for bringing her in, are they?' Susan smiled slyly. 'If you grass me up to the cops, I'll tell them that you were involved too.'

Jo jumped up off the chair. 'No way! Don't be ridiculous! They won't believe that.'

'Really? As you may have noticed, I can be quite convincing when I want to be. In fact, I might even say that it was all your idea. If they check the hotel CCTV for when Silver was taken, they'll find some pretty compelling evidence. I mean, you were at the hotel that night, weren't you? You did keep Gabe Miller occupied in the bar.'

'I-I'll tell them about the laptop, about how you persuaded me to help.'

Susan snorted. 'And you think anyone's going to fall

for that pathetic story?' She left a short pause before administering the killer blow. 'And then, of course, there's that other little matter: you did rent out a house in Kellston, a house where the girl has been kept for the last seven days.'

'But I didn't—'

'Oh, I think you'll find you did. You signed the lease and paid three months' cash in advance.' This time her smile was more triumphant. 'Yeah, it took me a while to master that signature but, as you know, I'm very resourceful.'

Jo felt like a noose had been put around her neck. She swallowed hard. These weren't just idle threats. If Susan went down, she was going to make damn sure that she didn't go alone.

'What's the matter?' Susan said brightly. 'Having second thoughts?'

Jo, unable to contain her rage any longer, almost screamed at her. 'What did I ever do to you? I thought we were friends but . . . but you don't even know the meaning of the word. Why the hell do you hate me so much?'

'I don't hate you,' Susan said. 'Don't be so dramatic. It isn't anything personal. I simply had to protect myself. You can understand that, can't you?'

Jo couldn't. She didn't understand anything about this woman whom she had once shared so many thoughts with. She made one last attempt to bring the nightmare to an end. 'You can still take her home. We can drive her there right now, leave her at the gate. Or I can take her on my own. You can call her father anonymously and tell him what's been going on.'

Susan shook her head. 'It's not that easy. I can't let her go, not until I've made some arrangements.'

'What sort of arrangements?'

But Susan didn't answer directly. 'I saved that kid's ass tonight. If it wasn't for me, she'd have ended up on a slab. I'm sure of it. At least give me some credit for getting her out of there.'

Jo glared at her. 'If it wasn't for you, she wouldn't have been there in the first place.'

'Has anyone ever told you how bloody self-righteous you are?'

But there was something defensive in her tone that Jo immediately picked up on. She had a sudden flash of insight. 'Saved *her* ass or saved your own?' She saw a flicker of annoyance pass over Susan's face and knew that she was right. 'Yeah, that's it, isn't it? It's not the girl you're worried about – it's yourself!'

'Believe what you like,' Susan replied, her voice cold and insolent. 'It doesn't make any difference to me.'

Jo had heard enough. Something inside her snapped and she angrily rushed towards her. It was an instinctive reaction, fuelled by bitter resentment, and she had no clear idea of what she was intending to do. Whatever it was, it was almost instantly curtailed as she caught a foot on the corner of the rug, stumbled and fell forward. She put out her hands to break the impact but somehow they didn't end up where she wanted them to be and the next thing she felt was a sharp crack to her forehead as it made contact with the edge of the coffee table.

There was a peculiar silence. And then the pain kicked

in. Jo groaned as she lifted her fingertips to a spot just above her left eyebrow and saw the blood. Groggily, she tried to clamber to her knees.

'Don't move,' Susan said, disappearing into the kitchen. There was the sound of a couple of drawers being opened, of running water and then she was back. 'Here, let me take a look.'

Jo slapped her away. 'Leave me alone.'

'Well at least put this on it,' Susan said, pushing a clean wet J-cloth into her hand. 'Press it hard against the cut. It'll stop the bleeding.'

'What do you care?' Jo said, but still did as she was told. She winced as the cloth came into contact with the open wound. Then, when she had got her breath back, she bared her teeth and snarled: 'This is all your fault.'

Susan knelt down on the floor beside her. 'You'll survive. I think it looks worse than it is. You feel sick or anything?'

'No.' The pain was starting to dissolve into a dull throbbing ache. 'Yes,' she corrected herself, darting a venomous glance in the direction of her erstwhile friend. 'I feel sick that I ever met you, that I ever trusted you.'

Susan sat back and sighed. 'It wasn't all a lie, you know.'

'What wasn't?'

'You and me.'

'Yeah, right,' Jo said. 'That's why you decided to stitch me up, to threaten me and generally make my life a living hell. Which part of our glorious friendship, exactly, *wasn't* one big fat lie?'

Susan's eyes widened a fraction. 'I liked you. I still do.'

'Huh?' Jo said.

'What I mean,' Susan said, almost wistfully, 'is that if it hadn't been for . . . for certain circumstances, I wouldn't have had to do the things I did. I wish I hadn't involved you, I honestly do. If I could go back and change it I would, but . . .'

'But it's too late.'

Susan lifted her shoulders and then slowly, perhaps even sadly, dropped them down again. 'It's complicated.'

Just for a second, Jo thought she caught a fleeting glimpse of the Laura James she had once known. She remembered what Gabe had revealed at the pub, about how her sister had disappeared, had in all probability been murdered. That was enough to send anyone over the edge. It wouldn't do any harm, she decided, to try and make a connection with her. 'So why don't you tell me about it?' she said softly.

Susan opened her mouth but hesitated. Suddenly her eyes grew dark and suspicious. 'I don't think so,' she said, getting to her feet.

'I wasn't—' Jo began.

But just at that moment the door to the bathroom opened and Silver Delaney came out. She stood there, docile as a lamb, staring at them both. She had one towel wrapped around her head and another round her skinny body. If she was surprised to see Jo sitting on the floor with blood running down her face she didn't show it. Perhaps it simply confirmed all her worst fears about Susan.

Chapter Sixty

The light that came through the window was gloomy and grey. Jo lay on the futon, squinting up at the sky. She had a throbbing headache, although how much of that was from the blow to her brow and how much from the bottle of wine was impossible to distinguish. She twisted up her wrist and looked at her watch. Ten to eight. Gradually, the events of the evening before began to filter back. A low moan shivered from her lips.

Tentatively, she swung her legs over the side and sat upright. She didn't feel great but at least she wasn't nauseous. Her bare foot made contact with an almost empty glass of water, spilling the last remaining drops across the carpet.

She rescued the glass and very slowly stood up. Her legs felt a little shaky but she was otherwise okay. She stretched out her arms, rolled her shoulders and flexed her hands. Yes, she was still in the land of the living. She slipped on a T-shirt and went through to the living room.

Susan was sitting on the sofa with a mug of coffee in her hand. 'Morning,' she said. 'How are you?'

Jo ignored her and walked straight to the bathroom. She

shut the door and locked it. Then, preparing herself for the worst, she went over to the mirror. The sight that met her eyes was not a pretty one. The inch-long gash was narrow and not too deep but the swollen flesh it nestled in was a vicious, ugly shade of purple.

'Oh, great,' she murmured. She looked like the victim of an angry man's fist.

With a sigh, she stripped off the T-shirt and climbed into the shower. While she washed and shampooed her hair, she tried to figure out a plan of action. After ten soapy minutes she had the basic foundations. It was not, she had to admit, the greatest plan in the world but it was the best she could come up with at short notice: *When in doubt, call for reinforcements.*

Susan glanced up again as she came out of the bathroom.

Jo, continuing to ignore her, went back to the study. She had let Silver Delaney sleep in her room last night – the girl, after everything she'd been through, deserved the meagre consolation of a comfortable bed. Susan hadn't objected, volunteering to sleep on the sofa. This, Jo suspected, was more down to her desire to make sure that no one tried to creep out of the flat than any more altruistic motives.

Jo towelled herself dry and got dressed in a pair of cream cotton trousers and a crisp white shirt. That she had had the presence of mind to grab some fresh underwear and a change of clothes before relinquishing her bedroom amazed her. It was surprising what you still remembered to do when you were less than sober, shocked to the core and suffering from mild concussion. What she hadn't remembered, however, was the hairdryer. She sighed and ran her fingers through her short fair hair.

She looked at her watch again. It was eight-twenty. The minutes were ticking by; it was time to set the plan in motion.

As she walked from the study to the kitchen, Susan got up and followed her. 'So I'm getting the silent treatment now?'

Jo shrugged as she opened a jar, spooned a hefty amount of instant coffee into a mug and poured hot water over it. 'What do you want me to say: It's lovely to have you here? Hope your stay is a happy one? Please make yourself at home?'

Susan folded her arms and leaned against the counter. 'There's no need to take that attitude. Have you put some antiseptic on that eye? It looks a bit—'

'I really haven't got time for this. I have to get to work.'

'I don't think so,' Susan said, staring at her. 'You're not going anywhere.'

Jo, although she'd been expecting it, pretended to be surprised. 'Are you kidding? I *have* to be there. I've got one of the most important designers in the city turning up at ten o'clock.'

'Someone else can deal with it.'

'Like who?'

'Like . . . I don't know . . . whatshername, that bitch you were always going on about. Isn't that her job?'

'She's on holiday,' Jo lied. She didn't even have to fake a frown. Thinking of Deborah, of the letters, of Peter, made her even more determined to get out of the flat as quickly as she could. 'I'm not going to throw away the greatest opportunity

Ruby's might ever get just because you've decided to bring all your goddamn problems to my door.'

'Forget it,' Susan said. 'You're not throwing away anything. Just ring and reschedule and then call the shop and tell them that you're sick.'

Jo gave the coffee a stir, picked it up and took a gulp. She sighed as the caffeine kicked in. 'And how have I got so incredibly sick since yesterday?'

'Okay then, say you've got a family emergency, that you have to go away for a few days.'

Jo raised her brows, a gesture she immediately regretted. A thin shooting pain ran sharply through her temples. 'What, the kind of family emergency where I just have to nip over to Australia? My parents are the only family I've got and Jacob knows it.'

'You'll think of something.'

'No, I won't think of something because I don't need to. For God's sake, Susan, I'm not going to go to the police. You've made it pretty clear what the outcome would be if I did. You think I want to spend the next ten years in jail?' She walked into the living room and glanced towards the door behind which Silver was sleeping. She lowered her voice. 'All I want to do is go to work, keep my business running smoothly and try to forget about this nightmare for a few hours.'

Susan hesitated but shook her head. 'No, it's better if you stay put.'

Jo stood her ground. 'Well, unless you're going to wrestle me to the floor, tie me up and keep me prisoner, it really isn't going to happen.'

A tight look came into Susan's eyes as if she was seriously considering the idea but faced with the prospect of having to keep two people captive, she eventually relented. 'All right, but if you tell anyone, if you breathe a word . . .'

'Who the hell am I going to tell?' Jo retorted. 'I'm not stupid!' The one trump card she had at the moment was that Susan didn't know that Gabe Miller was free. And he was the one person who might actually be able to sort this mess out.

Before Susan could change her mind again, Jo went into the kitchen, dumped her mug beside the sink and grabbed the plastic carrier with the letters and the lease inside. She thought about asking for her mobile back – Susan had picked it up last night and put it in her bag – but decided not. There was no point pushing her luck. She would just have to cross her fingers and hope that Gabe didn't decide to give her a call in the brief period of time it would take to cross the Green and get to Ruby's.

Chapter Sixty-one

Leo was standing by the side of the house, waiting for Jo to appear. He had been waiting for over an hour. It wasn't cold but a light drizzle was falling on his head and shoulders. He swiped a hand through his hair, shaking out the raindrops. Usually, on a Saturday, she left at about eight but it was already a quarter to nine and there was still no sign of her. He twisted his fingers round the handlebars of the bike. He was starting to get worried.

Last night he had heard the bell to the upstairs flat, two short muffled rings that had woken him from the light sleep he had only just fallen into. He hadn't been sure of the exact time but it had definitely been after midnight. Had it been *him*? Leo wasn't sure but who else would call so late? He had got up to look out of the window but whoever it was had already passed out of sight. There had been the faint murmur of voices, footsteps on the stairs, and it had all gone quiet. But only for a while. The bang, when it had come about twenty minutes later, had shaken the ceiling. It had sounded like something heavy being dropped or someone crashing to the floor . . .

Leo's heart began to drum in his chest. He should have

reacted. He should have done something. The man was sick, violent, the lowest of the low. What if Jo was lying dead up there, beaten to a pulp? What if he could have saved her and instead had done nothing? He shifted from one foot to another, feeling guiltily afraid, and tried to decide what to do next. Perhaps he should go and ring the bell but if he did, and she answered, what would he say? He needed a good excuse but his brain was too messed up to think of one. And what if *he* answered? Leo shuddered. He still had the bruises from their last encounter. Was he really brave enough to face him again?

Fortunately, before he had to make that decision, he heard the front door open and a second later Jo came out. She was still in the process of shrugging on her jacket. A pair of large sunglasses covered her eyes.

'Hi,' he said, wheeling his bike on to the drive.

Jo visibly jumped. She raised a hand to her chest. 'Leo! God, hi, you gave me a fright.'

'Sorry,' he said. However, he was so relieved to see her that he couldn't stop grinning. Quickly, he tried to take control of his renegade lips. 'Are you going to work?'

She nodded.

'I'm heading for the High Street too. I'll walk with you.' He was surprised by his own boldness. In the old days, when Peter had been alive, he had chatted quite comfortably with her but over recent months he had grown strangely shy.

Jo gave a faint worried smile before glancing up at the first-floor window.

Leo automatically looked up too. He thought he might

have seen a movement but couldn't swear to it. It could've been his imagination. It was only as he lowered his gaze, as he looked at her again, that he noticed the cruel purple swelling on her brow. It was almost hidden by the shades but not quite. He sucked in his breath. 'What happened to your eye?'

A pink flush suffused her cheeks. Jo raised a hand, self-consciously, to her forehead.

'Oh, this,' she said. 'It's nothing. I just tripped and bashed into the door.' She laughed. 'I'm such an idiot sometimes.'

Leo smiled too, although he knew she was lying. It was the kind of excuse women always made when they were covering up for someone. He had seen it on TV, seen the way certain men lashed out and how the women pretended it had never happened. He had a good idea of who had really caused the damage. A wave of anger washed over him. He looked up at the window again but it was still empty. 'Are you sure you're all right?'

'Of course I am.' Jo strode briskly down the drive, glanced left and right and crossed over Barley Road.

Leo, still wheeling his bike, had to run a few steps to catch up. 'Only it looks kind of painful.'

'It's fine,' she said firmly. 'I'm absolutely fine.'

And that was something else women always said, either because they were too scared or too ashamed to reveal the truth. Leo sensed it would be unwise to pursue the subject. For a while, he walked quietly beside her. He didn't mind the silence. It was good just to be near her. There was something about how she made him feel when she was close enough to touch. He told himself that the feeling was purely one of protectiveness – who else would take care of her now that Peter was gone? – but that didn't entirely account for the palpitations of his heart or the hot prickling of his skin. He tried not to stare too intently at her chest. Through the thin white cotton of her blouse he could clearly see the outline of her bra.

When they were almost halfway across the Green, she suddenly turned and said: 'Do you remember anything about your dad, Leo?'

Surprised, he shook his head and frowned. 'Not really. I don't think so. I was only two when he died.'

She nodded.

Leo waited but she said nothing more. He was too curious to let it go. 'Why? Did you know him?'

'No, no, we never met. He used to work for Mitchell Strong, didn't he?'

'Yeah, but Mum didn't like him. Mitchell Strong, I mean. She says he was a . . .' Leo stopped abruptly, mortified at the thought that he was in the process of insulting Peter's father. His cheeks went bright red and began to burn. 'Er . . . I didn't . . . she didn't . . .'

'It's okay,' Jo said, picking up on his embarrassment. 'There's nothing she could have said that hasn't been said a thousand times before – and worse. By all accounts, he was a complete and utter shit.' She paused and pulled a face. 'Although it might be better, all things considered, if you didn't quote me on that.'

Leo grinned back at her, outrageously pleased that she had told him something she didn't wish to have repeated.

That was almost the same as a secret. 'Mum really liked Peter though,' he said, wanting to give her a gift in return. 'We both did.'

She gave another small nod. 'It must have been tough on her, being widowed when you were so young.'

'I guess,' Leo said. That was what made Jo different from most girls, the way she thought about the feelings of others. But perhaps she was *too* soft-hearted. There would always be people, especially men, who would be more than willing to take advantage. He glanced at the cut above her eye again and scowled. The idea that anyone could even think about hurting her filled him with an all-consuming rage.

'Well,' Jo said as they passed through the gate to the High Street.

Leo got on his bike, pretending he had somewhere to go. He would do a spin round the block and then head home. 'See you later,' he said.

'See you later.'

When he had cycled a short way, he pulled in and looked back over his shoulder. She had crossed over and was standing at the door to Ruby's. 'Jo!' he yelled.

She turned, scanning the street. It took her a moment to find him.

He raised an arm and waved. 'Have a good day!'

'You too,' she said.

Leo couldn't actually hear the words above the sound of the traffic but, watching her mouth, was able to read her lips. He gave another quick wave and cycled off.

Chapter Sixty-two

John Devlin had been none too pleased when he'd prised up the floorboards and discovered that the shooter was gone. Since then he'd been searching for Stevie, on and off, for the past twenty-four hours. When he finally found the scrote, he was going to turn him upside down and shake him until his stupid thieving brains fell out.

Standing by the gate, he lit a fag and softly swore. 'Fuckin' bastard.' No one stole from him. *No one.* He leaned back against the black wrought-iron railings. From here he could see both the Green and the all-night caff. They were two of Stevie's regular haunts. The kid was usually around early Saturday and Sunday eager to provide any returning party-goers with their uppers and downers or whatever other crap they needed.

So where was he? Hiding out probably. Perhaps his mother had tipped him off. Devlin had already given her a good slap. The bitch had sworn she knew nothing about it but that hadn't stopped him. She was his bleedin' mother, wasn't she? It didn't matter what she did or didn't know. What was the point in having sprogs if you couldn't control the little bastards?

Devlin took a long drag on his fag. Just to add insult to injury, it was raining. He turned up the collar of his jacket; if he stayed here much longer, he'd get soaked to the skin. It was yet another aggravation to add to his growing list of resentments. He'd give it five more minutes, then grab some breakfast in the caff.

A slim blonde and a teenage kid with a bike were walking across the Green. As they came closer, Devlin made a quick practised survey of her body. Not bad, although he preferred his tarts with a bit more up top. Still, he wouldn't throw her out of bed. They came out of the gate, turned left and strolled right past. He had a leer ready and waiting but the blonde didn't even glance at him. At least he didn't think she did. It was hard to tell with those big shades she was wearing.

They were ten yards down the street before it occurred to him. Didn't he know her? He was pretty sure he'd seen her somewhere before. He screwed up his eyes while he considered it. He was good on faces – you had to be if you worked the doors – but he couldn't quite place her.

Pushing away from the railings, Devlin followed at a discreet distance. He may as well stretch his legs. She crossed the road and the kid pissed off on his bike. Then the boy stopped and yelled at her. 'Jo!'

It was only as she turned that it suddenly clicked. She was the tart he'd seen last Friday down by Euston Station. Yeah, he was sure of it. She had stood on the pavement and stared directly at him. He'd been certain she wasn't going to move – she'd looked rooted to the spot – but then, as if someone had put a cattle prod up her arse, she'd leapt into the street and straight into a cab with that bastard Miller.

Devlin watched as she went into Ruby's. He hung back a moment, then crossed over and strolled casually past the shop. A closed sign was still on the door. He peered through the glass but she'd already disappeared. Never mind. He knew where she worked now. He knew where to find her.

Chapter Sixty-three

Jo, preparing herself for the next cross-examination, gritted her teeth as she stepped into Ruby's. Sweet as Leo was, she could have done without his company this morning. She had been hoping to have a few quiet minutes to herself, a chance to try and get her head together. Still, that hadn't been his fault and at least his questions hadn't been too hard to deflect.

She gave a breezy wave of her hand as she passed through the shop and went straight into the office.

Jacob, predictably, hurried in behind. 'It's good to see you again,' he said, closing the door behind them. 'I wasn't sure if you'd be in or not so I arranged for cover. I can always send one of them home if you don't think they're needed. Except it is Saturday and we could be quite busy later so if you're not planning on staying then . . .'

Jo knew he was talking too much to cover up his discomfort. She was feeling awkward too. Although they had had one brief conversation on the phone, it was a couple of days since they had actually seen one another. As she turned and took off her glasses, she saw his dark eyes fill with horror.

'My God, what happened to you, Jo?' He rushed forward, grasping both her hands.

His voice was so emotional, his face so full of worry, that a lump came to her throat. If she had ever had doubts about Jacob's affection for her, they were instantly extinguished. 'I'm fine,' she said, her reply a little more high-pitched than it should have been. She would have liked to have sunk into his fatherly arms, to tell him everything, but she couldn't. She couldn't afford to come clean; Susan was still at the flat and Silver's future still hung in the balance. 'Hey, it's nothing. I'm good. It was just an accident. I had one too many drinks, tripped over and banged by head against the door. Pretty stupid, right, but we're all entitled to hit the bottle once in a while.'

'Have you been to the hospital?'

'It doesn't need stitches. It's only a cut.'

'You just fell?'

'I just fell,' she repeated, smiling. Gently, she slipped her hands out of his. Did he believe her? Probably not, she thought, although her story wasn't actually that far from the truth. No one had hit her. No one had deliberately hurt her. 'Look, is there any chance you could get me a coffee? I just need five minutes. I have to make one quick call, then we can sit down and have a chat.'

Jacob gave her a long interrogative look and nodded.

Before he was even out of the door, Jo was lifting her wallet from her bag. She flipped out Gabe Miller's card, laid it on the desk and quickly dialled the number. It rang and rang but he didn't pick up. Eventually it went into answer mode. 'Damn,' she muttered, slapping her palm against the desk. Where was he? Should she leave a message? She couldn't decide. What if the police had pulled him in again? What if someone else had his phone? She hung up.

Leaning back, she grabbed a copy of the Yellow Pages off the shelf and looked up *Garage Services.* Her finger ran down the entries. There it was: *J. B. Harris* in Dalston. She dialled the number and said a short prayer. Please God, let someone answer. Eventually, after about ten rings, somebody did.

'Yeah?' a male voice snapped impatiently down the line.

She couldn't tell from the single word whether it was Snakey or not. 'Er . . . is that Mr Harris?'

There was a pause, then the voice grew instantly friendlier. 'Yeah. Hi, is that you, Jo? How are you doing?'

'Fine,' she said for what felt like the tenth time that morning. 'Look, I'm trying to get hold of Gabe. Do you know where he is? I've tried his phone but he's not picking up.'

'He's upstairs in the flat. Could be in the shower. You want me to go get him?'

She heaved a sigh of relief but aware that Jacob could be back at any moment, said, 'No, I can't wait but could you give him a message? I need to see him. It's urgent, *very* urgent. I'm not at home; I'm at Ruby's. And could you tell him not to call me on my mobile. If he can't make it, he can ring the shop. Oh, hang on, I'd better give you the number. Do you have a pen?'

'Don't worry. He'll be there.'

'Thanks,' she said gratefully, 'and you won't forget about the mobile? He *mustn't* ring me on it.'

He gave a low chuckle. 'Give me some credit, love. Even my short-term memory isn't that bad.'

'Sorry,' she said. 'I didn't mean . . .'

'It's okay. I'll go and tell him now. Take care, yeah?'

'You too,' she said again before hanging up. It was only at that point that she realised Snakey hadn't even asked what was going on. Was that down to diplomacy or simply a self-preserving wish to not get dragged any further into this mess? Probably the former, she decided, recalling his earlier inability to leave well alone.

She had only just replaced the receiver when there was a light knock on the door and Jacob came back in. He placed a mug of coffee on the desk.

'You're an angel,' she said, lifting the mug to her lips and taking a couple of much-needed gulps. Whether the caffeine would actually do much for her headache was debatable, but at least it would get the blood running through her arteries again. 'Grab a seat,' she said, gesturing towards the chair in front of her.

Jacob sat down. 'I'm glad you came in, Jo. I . . . I wanted a chance to clear the air, to explain to you why we—'

'There's no need for that,' she interrupted, aghast at the thought of having to go through it all again. 'I told you it was finished, done with, and I meant it. I'm not holding any grudges. I promise. I understand why you did what you did. I was upset at the time but that was just the shock.' She took another sip of her coffee. 'That's not why I wanted to talk to you.'

Jacob pursed his lips, uneasy perhaps as to what was coming next.

'But first,' Jo said, 'I want you to have these.' She took a couple of cheques from her bag and slid them across the desk.

'You don't have to—'

'Yes, I *do*,' she insisted, 'and I'll be insulted if you don't take them. There's one for you and one for Deborah. I hope it covers everything you've paid out.'

Jacob stared at them for a moment. Several emotions seemed to pass across his face – pain, sorrow, regret – but he slowly reached out his hand, folded the cheques and put them in his pocket.

'Thank you,' Jo said. What she had to ask next she wasn't looking forward to. Having just claimed that the past was in the past, she was about to resurrect a part of it. 'If you don't mind me asking, Jacob, how well did you actually know Leonard Kearns?'

'A little,' he replied cautiously.

She took a deep breath before she continued. 'Enough to know that he was acting as a mule for Mitchell Strong?'

He stiffened, his face turning pale. 'Who told you that?'

'Does it matter?'

He leaned forward and placed his elbows on the desk. 'Whatever you might have heard, Leonard was a decent man.'

'So tell me about him,' she said softly. She didn't really know why she was digging it all up again. What she should be concentrating on was that Susan was currently holed up in her flat with the kidnapped daughter of a violent gangster. She was hardly prioritising her problems but she didn't give a damn. Silver Delaney was currently safe, Gabe was on his way, and there were still things about the past, about Peter, that she needed to make sense of.

Jacob briefly closed his dark, tired eyes. When he opened them again he didn't meet her gaze. Instead he stared down at the surface of the desk. 'Leonard was a local boy. Like lots of kids, he got in trouble when he was young. He had a record, including a conviction for theft, but he'd been straight for years. Mitchell found out about it a few months after taking him on. He could have sacked him but he didn't.' His eyes flicked up to meet Jo's again. 'It would have been better if he had.'

She understood what he was saying. 'Mitchell used it to his own advantage.'

'Leonard still had a choice,' Jacob said, 'although not much of one. Mitchell Strong was always good at timing and for a long while he didn't say anything. He took him under his wing, paid him well, took him abroad on buying trips. He waited until Leo was born before applying the thumbscrews. By that point Leonard needed the job too much.'

'So he did whatever Mitchell asked.'

'He couldn't afford to lose his position. If he'd left, it would have been without a reference. And word soon gets around; Mitchell would've made sure that no one else in the trade took him on.'

'Delightful,' Jo said. 'Did Constance know?'

Jacob shook his head. 'She never liked Mitchell, never trusted him but she had no idea what he was forcing Leonard to do.'

'But you did?'

'Not the details. I had my suspicions; nobody gets that rich that quick in this business by keeping it strictly legal. I tried to talk to Leonard but . . .' His shoulders lifted and fell in a gesture of resignation. 'He was too afraid of Mitchell. It wasn't until years later, until Peter came back to England, that I found out what had really been going on. He got the whole story from his father before the two of them parted company.'

'You stopped working for Mitchell too,' Jo said.

'Yes. He was a man who would trample over anything and anyone to get what he wanted but after what happened with Leonard . . . well, I'd had enough. I didn't want to be around him any more. I was close to retirement so decided to call it a day.'

'And then Peter inherited Ruby's, came home and persuaded you to help get it up and running again.'

'A labour of love,' Jacob said quietly. He glanced around the office. 'They were good times.'

Jo left a respectful pause before continuing. 'Why did you decide to keep all this from Constance?'

'You think it would have been a kindness to tell her? That her husband was a criminal, a smuggler of gems, that he was not the person she imagined him to be?' He gave a weary sigh. 'You think it would have been a *good* thing to take away all her good memories and replace them with . . . with what exactly – the soul-destroying clarity of the truth?'

'Except the truth might have enabled her to get a decent pension out of Ruby.'

'Only through blackmail,' he said. 'You clearly don't know Constance very well. She's a proud woman, decent and hard-working. She would have been ashamed of what her husband had done. If she'd had even an inkling of what he'd been involved in, she wouldn't have accepted a penny off Peter.'

Jo sat back, taking a minute to absorb it all. She could understand his thinking, his desire to protect Constance, but wasn't sure if he was telling her everything. Again, she had that feeling – the same feeling she had experienced after talking to Carla – that there was something *more.* It niggled away at her, refusing to let go.

'Okay,' she said eventually, 'so long as you remember that not all people need protecting. Some of us can't move on until we know the truth – no matter how difficult it is to face.'

The words hung between them for a moment. Jacob's eyes met hers but she couldn't say for certain what she saw in them. It could have been indecision or perhaps it was simply concern. Either way, he did not respond to the challenge.

Chapter Sixty-four

It was a further twenty minutes before the internal phone rang. Jo had been impatiently pacing up and down the room. She snatched up the receiver. 'Yes?'

'There's a Mr Miller here to see you,' Meg said.

'Thanks. Send him through, would you.'

Jo stopped her pacing, sat down and stood up again. She waited by the window with her arms crossed. It was another twenty seconds before the knock came on the door. 'Come in.'

Gabe strolled into the office wearing a pair of faded blue jeans and a navy shirt. 'Hey, sweetheart, where's the fire?'

Jo couldn't recall the last time she'd been so pleased to see anyone – especially a muscled six feet plus of anyone – but, unwilling to give him the satisfaction, made every effort to disguise it. 'You took your time,' she said brusquely.

'Did no one ever tell you that damsels in distress are so supposed to show a little gratitude when their knights in shining armour show up?'

'Did no one ever tell *you* that it's the twenty-first century?'

It was only as she turned to fully face him that he noticed the cut above her eye. 'What the—'

'Don't even ask,' she said. 'It's fine, I'm fine. It was just an accident.'

'Okay,' he said, lifting a cynical eyebrow. 'So everything's fine. I guess that's why you wanted to see me so urgently – to pass on the good news.'

Jo embarked on a glare but quickly abandoned it. The defiance slipped from her eyes and she glanced down at the floor. What was she doing? Her pride was getting in the way of what was really important. She needed this man's help and she needed it desperately. This was no time to be standing on her dignity. The tightness in her shoulders loosened. She sighed and slumped down into her chair. 'Look, you'd better grab a seat.'

Sensing the sudden change in mood, Gabe's face grew serious. Without so much as a minor wisecrack, he pulled out the chair opposite to hers.

She paused, forming the words in her head before speaking them aloud. Her hands did a small dance on the desk. 'That fire you mentioned – well, it's at number twelve Barley Road. Susan turned up last night with Silver Delaney in tow.'

Gabe jerked forward and the breath whistled out between his lips. He jumped up and sat down again. 'You're kidding me? *Shit!* Is she all right – the kid, I mean?'

Jo nodded. 'A bit quiet but I don't think she's physically hurt.'

'So what the hell's going on?'

'I wish I knew,' Jo said. 'I couldn't get much out of Susan other than that she's had a falling out with the guy she's been working with.' She proceeded to tell him the tale from the moment of their arrival until her own departure from the flat an hour ago. It wasn't a long story and took less than five minutes to complete.

Gabe sat frowning as it all tumbled out. He leaned back and scratched at his chin. He hadn't shaved that morning, probably as a consequence of her early morning call. It was a while before he responded. 'And she didn't mention the name of this guy?'

Jo shook her head. 'Only that it's someone close to the family.'

'That might not be true.' He stared up at the ceiling and thought about it. 'Then again . . .' His dark eyes dropped to meet hers. 'To be honest, I'm surprised she let you out of her sight. That was a risk.'

'Not much of one. I was hardly going to go running to the police after what she'd told me. With my name attached to that lease, I'm as much in the frame for this kidnapping as she is. And who else was I going to go blabbing to? So far as Susan's aware, *you're* still locked up and safely out of the way.'

'Did she say that?'

'No, she didn't mention you.'

Gabe's face, as if it had just been slapped, twisted slightly but abruptly to one side.

Jo wished she hadn't said it or at least hadn't said it in quite so brutal a fashion. She had made it sound as if Susan didn't give a damn about getting him arrested or that he might be looking at a life sentence for murder. In truth she didn't know whether Susan cared or not but he clearly did. 'What I meant,' she added hurriedly, 'is that the subject didn't come up. There was so much else going on; I was all over the place. It was a shock to see her again. I'm only presuming that's what she—'

'You don't have to apologise for her,' he said.

'I wasn't.'

'Susan gave up on me a long time ago. I don't suppose my future – or lack of it – would provide her with too many sleepless nights.'

Jo opened her mouth but swiftly closed it again. From the corner of her eye, she could see the carrier bag containing all of Deborah's letters and the contract to the property on Fairlea Road. She knew, perhaps almost as painfully as him, how it felt to be betrayed.

They were both quiet. He was the first to break the silence. 'So that cut on your head . . .?'

'I've already told you.' Jo's fingers automatically fluttered up to touch the edges of the wound. 'It was an accident. I tripped and fell.'

That mobile brow of his shot up again.

'No!' she exclaimed sharply. She knew what he was thinking and instantly railed against it. 'You're wrong. She didn't touch me. You think I couldn't defend myself against the likes of Susan Clark?'

'Well, you are kind of—'

'What?' she snapped. 'Puny, weak, pathetic?'

Gabe grinned. 'What I was actually going to say was – kind of jumpy.'

Jo realised that she had overreacted yet again. For the first time since he had turned up at the office, she managed a smile. 'Well, you'd be bloody jumpy if you had Vic Delaney's daughter hidden in your flat.'

Although their smiles soon faded, the exchange seemed to break the tension between them. 'So,' he said, 'do you have any idea what she's planning on doing next?'

Jo shook her head. Pulling out the top drawer, she removed a set of keys and slid them across the desk. 'I was hoping you might like to ask her.'

Chapter Sixty-five

The palm-fringed terrace was more suited to a Mediterranean villa than a mock-Tudor house in Essex. With his left hand, Marty slapped away the long wet fronds that brushed against his arms and face while with his right he flipped shut the phone and put it in his pocket. Devlin's call had come a week too late. The blonde piece wasn't of interest to him any more. He already knew where Miller was.

Marty sat down by the pool and stretched out his legs. Under the protection of a large striped umbrella, he watched the rain pock the surface of the turquoise water. He had heard on the grapevine that Miller had been picked up by the filth over Ritchie Naylor's murder. The news had surprised him. The guy was supposed to be a pro; he should have had it on his toes the minute he knew about the killing, the minute he realised he'd been stitched up. Instead the idiot had managed to get himself arrested.

But Marty wasn't worried. On the contrary, he was pretty sure Miller would keep quiet about the kidnapping of Silver Delaney. He didn't have anything to gain by shouting his mouth off and in fact had a lot to lose. For one thing the kid could end up dead – he wouldn't want that on his conscience – and for another, he could end up being implicated himself. No, at the moment he'd be concentrating on more pressing matters, like how to explain away the presence in his flat of a young man with his head caved in.

The corners of Marty's lips twitched into a smile. He wouldn't mention the arrest to Vic. With Miller out of the picture, he might just start wondering who *had* been responsible for Thursday's little drama. The aftershocks of that particular incident were still reverberating through the household. On their return from the factory, Vic had taken to his bed for twelve hours, then hit the bottle, raved, cried, shouted some more and taken to his bed again. So far as Marty was aware, he was still there now, safely tucked up with his drunken nightmares.

A soft flip-flop sound alerted him to Nina's approach. He looked over his shoulder to see her coming towards him, carrying a tray. Despite having never taken a minute's exercise in her life – apart from sexual activities – she was dressed in a pair of white jazz pants and a skinny white cut-off Nike vest. Her flat, tanned midriff sported a diamond piercing, the rock almost as large as the one she had on her finger.

She dumped the tray on the table and sat down. 'You gonna tell me then?'

Marty assumed his innocent expression. 'Tell you what?'

'You know what.' As she lit a cigarette, her sly cat's eyes narrowed into two thin slits. 'You've been avoiding me. What's going on? What happened on Thursday night?'

'Nothing.'

'Yeah, right,' Nina sneered, exhaling a long thin stream of smoke. 'So why's Vic been acting like he's seen a bloody ghost?'

'Because he's worried,' Marty said. 'We turned up with the ransom and they didn't show with Silver. I don't know what you're complaining about. You should be pleased.'

'Pleased?' she retorted, glancing down at her arms. There were fresh dark bruises there, evidence of Vic's latest outburst of rage and frustration. 'And how exactly do you work that one out?'

'Because there's half a million quid still sitting in the safe, half a million quid he hasn't spent yet.'

'*Yet*,' she repeated sulkily. 'He's still going to pay up, isn't he?'

Marty shrugged. 'What choice does he have?'

'For fuck's sake, it's all a con. Why can't he see that? The little cow is just taking him for a ride.'

'I doubt it,' Marty said. 'Her boyfriend's dead, remember? I don't think she's capable of running this show on her own.'

Nina gave him a long, cool stare. She sucked on her cigarette and exhaled into the damp morning air. 'Whatever.'

Marty leaned forward, took the lid off the pot and peered inside. In the periphery of his vision he could see the skinny foreign maid scuttling around the conservatory. Had she made the brew? If she had, she'd probably spat in it. The first thing he'd do when *he* was in control of this house was to send the bitch packing.

'You gonna pour it then or just stare at it?' Nina said.

And the second thing he'd do was get rid of the leech. Vic

Delaney didn't need a wife and especially one who was such a drain on his resources. But of course Vic would see that himself once he got beyond the shock of Silver's brutal death. He'd remember how unsupportive she'd been, how unwilling to part with the cash – and if he didn't, Marty would be sure to remind him.

He poured the tea and passed her the first cup just in case there had been anything undesirable floating on the surface. 'We need to keep Vic off the booze. He got another message yesterday. The exchange is supposed to take place tonight. He's going to have to drive so he'd better be sober.'

'And what if no one turns up again?'

'I reckon they will. It's her birthday after all. They must have chosen the date deliberately. Thursday was just a warning, a shot across the bows to remind him of who's really in charge.'

Nina shifted forward and gave him another interrogative glare. 'What kind of shot across the bows?'

There she went again, Marty thought, desperately trying to dig the dirt. Well, he wasn't going to enlighten her and he doubted if Vic intended to either. Nina had one of the biggest gobs in existence and the last thing Delaney needed was for her to go spreading the news of that fiasco. Being taken for a gut-spewing fool wouldn't do much for his reputation. That she'd managed to keep quiet about the kidnapping of Silver was a bloody miracle . . . although maybe not. He checked out the bruises on her arm. Vic, in his inimitable style, had probably made his feelings clear on that score.

'All I meant,' Marty said, 'was that it was pretty cruel to raise his hopes like that.'

'No, there's more,' she insisted. Knowledge was power and she resented being out of the loop. 'What's the big secret, Marty? What is it you're not telling me?'

'There's no big secret.'

'Like fuck,' she muttered, rolling her eyes towards the heavens. When she lowered them again they were filled with hostility and suspicion. 'And here was me thinking I could trust you.'

Aware that now was not the time to have Nina in the mood from hell – he needed her on side for the rest of the day – Marty raised his hands, palms out. 'Okay, okay.' He glanced over his shoulder as if to check that no one was within earshot, then leaned towards her and lowered his voice. 'Look babe, Vic would kill me if he thought I'd—'

'It's not as though I'm going to tell him.'

Marty pulled a face before pretending to give in. His breath of sham submission rolled gently into a sigh. 'To be honest, it was kind of embarrassing. Vic just lost the plot, got a bit upset, but then, shit, who wouldn't? This is a kid we're talking about, his only kid.'

A small gleaming light came into her eyes. 'What do you mean by *upset*?'

Marty looked back over his shoulder again. By a stroke of good fortune, the foreign bitch had come out on the terrace. He tilted his head in her direction. 'Let's drop it for now, yeah? I'll fill you in on the details later.'

'She won't understand. The silly cow doesn't speak more than ten words of English.'

'Ten words too many,' Marty said.

He sat back and relaxed. At five o'clock the first text

would arrive from Susan, ordering Delaney to be at the club by eight. At ten he would receive the next one, providing instructions of where to drop off the ransom. It was all cool. They were heading towards countdown. There were only twelve more hours to go – twelve long, frustrating but purely *delicious* hours. It was all in the waiting, in the sweet and glorious expectation.

Chapter Sixty-six

Jo sat in the office and pondered on whether her decision not to accompany Gabe Miller was down to good sense or plain old-fashioned cowardice. She had persuaded herself that he stood a better chance of sorting things out if he went to the flat alone. Now she couldn't help questioning whether that really was the case.

Gabe and Susan had, to put it mildly, a somewhat chequered history. What if the encounter had gone horribly wrong and turned into a full-blown fight or worse. Anything could have happened. What if Susan was armed? What if she had a gun or a knife? There had been no evidence of a weapon last night but then, with the booze and the shock, she had hardly posed much of a threat. In fact, if Susan had been intending to use any force she had effectively been saved the trouble by Jo's self-inflicted bump to the head.

But then she had another worrying idea. Perhaps it wasn't just Susan's reaction she should be concerned about. Gabe Miller had more than enough reason to want revenge on the ex-wife who had set him up with the police. How well did she actually know the man? Well enough, she thought, to believe him incapable of violence towards a woman – but since when had her judgement been worth a jot? She remembered the expression on his face when she had mentioned that Susan hadn't even asked after him.

Suddenly Jo found all sorts of unwanted scenarios sliding into her mind, most of them involving screams, twisted bodies and the wide, frightened eyes of a teenage girl. No, she should never have let him go there alone! She leapt up, reached for her jacket but stopped mid-flight. For a moment, like a participant in the children's game of musical statues, she stood completely still, one arm outstretched, one leg slightly bent at the knee.

What was she doing?

Gradually the panic left her and she sank back into her chair. Over three hours had passed since he'd left Ruby's and gone to the flat. If they were going to kill each other, they'd have done it by now and if they weren't . . . well, what good could she do by barging in. She had to trust him because if she couldn't, there was no one left *to* trust and if that was the case . . .

Jo shook her head, unwilling to peer under that particular stone. She took a few deep breaths and tried to get her thoughts in order. If there was one thing she was sure of, it was that Gabe would not endanger the life of Silver Delaney. He could've done a runner, taken off after she'd been kidnapped, but he hadn't. He'd stuck around and got himself arrested for his trouble. And Susan wasn't in any kind of a position to start kicking up a fuss; she was separated from her partner in crime, up to her neck in it and desperate for a way out.

Jo decided that she was better off leaving them alone. Or was this just the latest excuse for her to avoid yet another confrontation? Before she could start going over old ground, she leaned down and lifted the carrier bag off the floor. If she was going to stay put, she needed a distraction and this one was guaranteed. Turning the bag upside down, she watched as its contents spilled out on to the desk.

She put the lease to one side and stared down at the bundle of letters. She had read some but not all of them last night, picking them out at random and scanning through the contents.

It had been an act of pure masochism. Part of what she'd felt, despite her drunkenness, was shame and embarrassment; the sometimes stumbling expressions of love, of shared passion and desire, of memories of time spent together, had never been intended for her eyes. She was like an eavesdropper listening in to someone's private conversation and hearing exactly what she didn't want to hear. But what she had felt most of all was anger and despair. All of Deborah's letters had been written in response to Peter's and the intensity of her words was like an echo of his own equally deep feelings.

The knowledge that he had loved her so much made Jo's heart turn over. She had known when they'd first met that he must have had serious relationships but he'd never talked about Deborah, never even mentioned her. And that wasn't right, was it? Especially when the two of them were working together every day. Especially when . . .

Jo glanced across the desk at the folded sheets of the lease. She might have been able to cope with his past, to have put aside her suspicions, if it wasn't for those few terrible pages.

She pulled the top letter free of the elastic band. It was the last, chronologically, in the set and had been posted to Thailand eight years ago when Deborah had written to inform Peter of her engagement to Tom Hayes. It was one of those 'This is your last chance, if you really love me you'll come back and make a commitment' sort of letter. She didn't specifically say that she would leave Tom but the meaning was pretty clear.

There was some consolation, perhaps, in the fact that Peter hadn't come back. It had been another three years before he'd stepped foot on British soil again. But he hadn't been slow in getting in touch with her. And why would Deborah have agreed to work with him, giving up her lucrative job at Aspreys, if there hadn't still been something simmering between them?

Poor Tom, Jo thought, understanding how he would feel if he ever read the letter. It wasn't easy being second-best. Folding up the sheets, she shoved them back in the envelope and slid the envelope under the elastic band and on to the top of the pile.

There was, she knew, no real evidence of betrayal sitting in front of her. Most of it was just ancient history, a chronicle of an old love affair. Even the lease didn't put Deborah in the frame. It was only Jo's instincts that placed her there.

She might have let sleeping dogs lie, put the letters back into the bag and taken them home with her again, if Deborah hadn't chosen that moment to come into the office. Without bothering to knock, she swanned in with a couple of cardboard files under her arm. She was wearing an elegant designer suit, sheer tights and high heels. Her distinctive fine red hair was twisted up in a complicated top-knot. Seeing the state of Jo's face, she wrinkled her nose but didn't ask what had happened.

Instead, after dropping the files into their rightful place in the cabinet, Deborah turned and said: 'You're not intending to work out front like that, are you?'

'No,' Jo replied, bristling at her supercilious tone. 'I wouldn't want to scare the customers.'

'Quite.'

It was that thin, clipped *Quite* that really got under Jo's skin and propelled her into a decision she might not otherwise have made. 'Oh, before you go, there's something I wanted to ask you.' Having covered the letters with her hands she now, very slowly, withdrew her fingers to reveal what was hidden underneath. 'I was wondering if you wanted these back?'

It took a moment for Deborah to realise what she was looking at. She took a step forward before her eyes widened with surprise and alarm. 'W-where did you get those?'

Guessing that she must have made a search of the office after Peter died, Jo replied: 'They were here all the time. You just didn't look hard enough.'

For a moment Deborah was speechless. The tip of her tongue skimmed anxiously across her drying lips. But she quickly rallied. Putting one hand defiantly on her hip, she tilted up her chin and declared: 'It's not what you think. Peter and me – that was all over years ago.'

'Really,' Jo said.

'If you've read them, and I'm sure you have, you'll be

aware that we split up before he even met you. I married Tom and . . .' She gave a light shrug of her shoulders and moved a little closer. 'And yes, if you don't mind, I would like them back.'

'Perhaps you'd like this too,' Jo said angrily, snatching up the contract, unfolding the pages and thrusting them in front of her. 'The lease to Fairlea Avenue. It may help bring back some happy memories.'

Deborah flinched and went pale.

If Jo had retained any residue of doubt, it instantly disappeared. Some part of her, deep down, had still been hoping that it wasn't true but that guilty response told her otherwise. With her heart hammering, she pressed home her advantage. 'Did you think it was your precious little secret, that I didn't have a clue about the two of you?' If there was nothing else she could salvage, there was still what remained of her pride. She gave a thin bitter laugh. 'Peter always was a lousy liar.'

Deborah stammered: 'It wasn't . . . we didn't . . . He just needed someone to talk to.'

'Oh, *talking*. Is that what they're calling it these days?'

The woman at least had the decency to blush. She opened her mouth as if about to offer up another excuse for why they might have been meeting in private but clearly had second thoughts. There was no point. The game was up. Her eyes closed briefly before fluttering open again. 'I'm sorry. We never meant to hurt anyone.'

'How could you imagine that I wouldn't be hurt?' Jo snapped, full of rage and indignation. 'Or Tom for that matter. I presume he doesn't know anything about this.'

A visible shudder passed through Deborah's body. Her voice went very quiet. 'Are you going to tell him?'

'Why shouldn't I? He has the right to know, doesn't he, the right to know that his wife was cheating on him for years.'

'But he's my husband,' she said almost pleadingly.

'And Peter was *my* bloody husband.'

'Only for eight months,' Deborah retorted, almost sneeringly. Perhaps thinking she had nothing left to lose, that Tom was bound to be informed, she was suddenly on the offensive again. 'And the only reason he married you was . . .'

'Why? Because he couldn't have *you*?'

Deborah glared at her for a second but then glanced away. Her eyes roamed around the room and the tightness in her face gradually dissolved. She looked back at Jo, shook her head and sighed. 'No, I didn't mean that.'

'So what did you mean?'

'Just that Peter was always trying to run away from his problems.'

'Problems,' Jo repeated under her breath. A lump had come into her throat. Was that what she had been to him, some kind of temporary escape from his *problems*? And then, perhaps, she had become the biggest one herself. 'Lucky that you were there then – to pick up the pieces when it all went wrong.'

'You don't understand.'

'No,' Jo said. 'I don't. How could I if the only talking he was doing was to you?'

'That was only because he didn't want to spoil things between the two of you.'

'Oh, right,' Jo snorted. 'So he decided to sleep with his old girlfriend instead.'

There wasn't much Deborah could say to that and so she didn't even try.

Jo was aware that there were certain protocols to be observed on occasions such as these. She had read enough books, seen enough films, to be sure of what she *ought* to be doing. At the very least she should be rising to her feet, taking those few necessary steps forward and delivering a well-aimed stinging slap to her adversary's cheek but somehow she couldn't summon up the required energy. Her anger was ebbing, leaving only a dreadful emptiness in its wake.

'What I'm trying to explain,' Deborah eventually continued, 'is that he wanted to put the past behind him. There were things that had happened, awful things he couldn't deal with. He wanted to wipe the slate clean, to make a fresh start – to make a fresh start with *you.* He felt he couldn't do that if you knew—'

'Knew what?' Jo interrupted. The only dark secret she was aware of was what Carla had told her. 'Is this to do with Leonard Kearns?'

Deborah gave a tiny jump. She stared at her, frowning. 'What do you know about that?'

'A little more than you and Jacob originally chose to tell me,' Jo said, hoping to sound confident enough to prise more information from her. That Mitchell Strong had been trading illegally, that Kearns had been his unwilling mule and had died abroad, were reasons enough for Peter to be unhappy but they hardly accounted for the kind of trauma that Deborah was hinting at.

She was about to pursue it when there was a knock on the door and Jacob poked his head in. Sensing the chilly atmosphere, he glanced from one to the other with a growing look of concern.

'Is everything all right?'

'Five minutes,' Deborah said sharply, splaying out her palm.

Jacob looked at Jo.

She nodded. 'We're almost done.'

He hesitated but then, with the wisdom of a man who knew better than to get caught in the crossfire, smartly withdrew. 'Five minutes,' he repeated as he closed the door behind him. 'We're getting busy out here.'

'So,' Jo said, her gaze immediately fixing on Deborah again, 'seeing as we're all pushed for time, perhaps you'd like to enlighten me as to what was really troubling Peter.'

'I can't do that.'

'Can't or won't?'

Deborah shook her head. 'I promised.'

'Peter's dead. There's nothing you can say or do that can hurt him now.' But Jo could see from Deborah's fixed expression that she wasn't going to budge. Quickly, she made a decision. There was nothing else for it; she would have to resort to more underhand tactics. She gently pushed the letters and the lease across the desk. 'Tell me everything and you can have these back. I won't even mention the affair to Tom.'

Deborah's eyes filled with hope and then suspicion. 'How do I know I can trust you?'

'You don't,' Jo said. 'You'll just have to take my word for

it.' What she was doing was part bribery, part blackmail – neither of which cast her own character in the greatest of lights – but she was past caring about what was right or wrong. She would play as dirty as she needed to in order to find out the truth.

Deborah's loyalty to Peter clearly had its limits. Offered the possibility of saving her own marriage, it didn't take her long to come to a decision. 'You're not leaving me much choice.'

'There's always a choice,' Jo replied coldly.

Chapter Sixty-seven

Deborah sat down, placed her hands neatly in her lap and took a moment to collect her thoughts. She stared at the floor before slowly lifting her eyes. She looked in need of a very stiff drink. 'What do you know?'

Jo took a moment of her own before replying. She had to be careful about what she said next. Either too much or too little could be a mistake. She didn't want Deborah spinning her some yarn. Keeping it simple but factual seemed the best way forward. 'That Leonard Kearns smuggled gemstones for Mitchell, that he died out in Burma.'

'Anything else?'

'That Peter and Tony were there when it happened.'

Deborah nodded. She waited but when Jo said nothing more, she took a deep breath and began to speak again. 'Leonard got ill shortly after they arrived. Mitchell should have called a doctor but he didn't. He wasn't what you'd call the most sympathetic of men. He viewed illness as a weakness, something to be ignored and overcome. They were only there for three days and Leonard spent most of them in bed in his hotel room.'

'Why didn't Peter call a doctor?'

'Because he didn't realise how sick he was. They were out all day and in the evenings Mitchell insisted that they shouldn't disturb him. He said Leonard had a mild dose of flu, that he'd be fine if he got some rest.' She stopped suddenly, her right hand leaving her lap and hanging briefly in the air before slowly dropping down again. 'Peter never forgave himself for that. He always thought that if he'd just gone to see Leonard it might never have happened.'

Jo turned her face away. She didn't want to see the pain or emotion in Deborah's eyes. This, she suspected, was only the beginning of Peter's regrets. There was worse to come. 'And?'

Deborah lifted her head, exposing the long, slender curve of her very pale throat. She swallowed hard. 'On the day they were due to leave, Leonard was up and about in the morning. He didn't look too good but claimed he was feeling okay. He even drank some coffee with them in the hotel dining room. They were due to fly home early that afternoon but in the meantime Mitchell had a couple of last-minute deals to do. They left Leonard at the hotel and when they got back . . .'

'He was dead,' Jo said softly.

'And that's when Mitchell lost it. He went completely crazy.'

Jo, recalling what Jacob had told her, had been pretty well keeping up with events to this point. 'I guess he wasn't too happy about losing his mule.'

'Oh, that didn't bother him much; men like Mitchell can always find some other sucker to do their dirty work. It was only his precious rubies he was bothered about.'

'How to get them back into Britain,' Jo said.

'How to get them *out*,' Deborah said.

'That's what I just said.'

Deborah's face twisted with frustration. 'You still don't get it, do you? How do you think Leonard usually smuggled the rubies out of the country – put them in his suitcase, crossed his fingers and hoped for the best?'

Jo shrugged. She hadn't really thought about it. 'I don't know.'

'He had to *swallow* them,' Deborah almost shouted. She clamped her hand across her mouth and her voice slipped into a whisper. 'The poor guy thought he was going home. He had them in his stomach already.'

Jo stared at her. 'What?'

But Deborah wasn't listening. She was lost to another place, another time. 'Once he was dead there was only one way for Mitchell to retrieve them. Peter would have stopped him, I know he would, but by the time he got to the room it was too late. Mitchell had already lost the plot. He'd cut him open, sliced through his guts and . . .'

'No,' Jo murmured. She felt her own stomach shift.

'And you can imagine the result,' Deborah said. 'It wasn't as if he even knew what he was doing. He'd cut through the skin with a Stanley knife, dug through his flesh, his intestines and . . .' Her eyes blazed into anger. 'It was vile, disgusting. What Peter saw that day he couldn't ever forget: Leonard's butchered body, his father's hands covered in blood, the stench, the bloody awful horror.' She leaned forward over her knees and made a small retching sound. When she looked up again her face was grey.

Jo gazed at her, speechless.

Deborah wiped her mouth with the back of her hand. 'And then there was all the tidying up to do – and I don't just mean the remains of the poor sod lying on the bed. Mitchell had intended to grab the rubies and run but Peter knew, even if they did manage to make it home, they wouldn't get away with it. They might even be looking at a murder charge if the cause of Leonard's death proved inconclusive. The only way out was to start flashing the cash, to try and buy a cover-up.'

'And so that's what Peter did,' Jo said.

Deborah nodded. 'Tony, as usual, was fuck-all use; he went to pieces, got hysterical and started crying like a baby. If it hadn't been for Peter, they would have all gone down. It took some risky calls and a lot of hefty bribes to get the body out of the hotel room and safely disposed of.'

Jo understood now why Ruby had been so uptight. She also understood the source of Peter's nightmares. If only he had told her, if only he had shared the horror, everything might have been different between them. Instead, he had turned to Deborah Hayes for comfort.

'And Constance?' Jo said softly. 'What was she told?'

'Only the bare minimum. That he'd taken ill suddenly and died of a fever. Peter had managed to acquire a forged death certificate and Mitchell spun her some line about how the authorities, not knowing the cause of the fever, had demanded a quick cremation. Constance didn't know any better. She was in a foreign country and her English at the time wasn't that good. She had no one to turn to, no close friends to go to for advice.' Deborah paused and her mouth slid into a grimace. 'Mitchell even presented her with some ashes a couple of weeks later, claiming he'd had them flown over from Burma. Constance had them interred in Kellston Cemetery.' She gave a small hysterical laugh. 'God knows who or *what* they were, probably the remains of someone's Golden Labrador.'

Jo found that she was taking deep breaths, almost gulping for air. All she could see was Leonard Kearns lying prostrate on a hotel bed with his guts hanging out and . . . She squeezed shut her eyes, trying to block out the image that was already scorching itself on to her brain.

There was a silence in the room while the full force of the disclosure settled around them.

'And so that's it,' Deborah said eventually. 'The whole sordid story.' Her fingers crept across the desk.

Jo's eyes snapped open and she quickly slammed down her hand on top of the letters.

'We're not finished yet.'

'But I've told you everything!'

'Not quite. I want to know if any of this is connected to Peter's death.'

Jo had expected a look of incredulity, an instant denial, but what Deborah provided instead was a small uncertain shrug.

'I don't know.'

'So what are you saying, that you think . . .?'

Deborah's forehead scrunched into a frown. Her fingers nervously rose up to her mouth again. Her eyes scanned the room and returned to the pile of letters. She stared at them with the greedy expression of a junkie desperate for a fix.

They seemed to focus her mind. 'All I know is that it was deliberate.'

'What do you mean?'

'I mean the car went straight for him. He didn't stand a chance.'

It took Jo a moment to absorb what she was saying before her heart started pumping again. She felt the hairs stand up on the back of her neck. 'You were there, weren't you? You were there when it happened!'

'Not with him,' Deborah said. She couldn't quite meet Jo's gaze. 'I was in the flat. I was watching from the window.'

'Before or after?'

'I'm sorry?'

'You know what I mean,' Jo said.

'What does it matter?'

'It matters to me.'

'After,' Deborah reluctantly admitted. 'He was standing on the corner outside the flats.' She bit down on her knuckle. 'He was just about to cross the road. I only saw the car out of the corner of my eye. I couldn't even tell you what colour it was – something dark, I think, green or blue. But it went straight for him. It seemed to slow, then it suddenly accelerated and went right up on the pavement.'

'You . . . you were *there*,' Jo repeated, her voice so strangulated she could hardly get the words out. 'You witnessed the whole bloody thing and you didn't go to the police!'

'There was nothing I could have told them. I couldn't see who was driving. It all happened so fast. I didn't even notice what type of car it was.'

'But you were there, you were a witness. You could have—'

Deborah quickly shook her head. 'Done what? I couldn't have told them any more than I'm telling you now. And what would that have achieved? And before you say it, yes, I was protecting myself, protecting Tom and the kids, but maybe just a little bit of me was protecting you too. I didn't want you to find out about us that way, to—'

Jo thumped her fist down on the desk. 'Don't you even *dare* pretend that you were thinking of me! The only reason you kept quiet was to hide your own filthy little secret.'

Deborah drew back. 'I know how angry you must feel but I have tried to tell you, over and over, that his death wasn't an accident.'

'Huh?' Jo said confused. 'And when exactly did you . . .' She stopped mid-sentence as the answer suddenly occurred to her. 'Oh God, *you're* the one who's been sending all those notes!' She glanced down at the pile of letters in front of her and groaned. 'I should have guessed.'

'I just wanted you to keep asking questions, to do what I couldn't do.'

'No,' Jo spat back, 'to do what you were too cowardly to do. You didn't mind lying on your back for him but you weren't prepared to stand up and be counted when it really mattered.'

'That's not fair. I was just . . .'

'Just what?' Jo snarled.

Deborah bowed her head and wrapped her arms around her chest. 'I'm sorry.'

Jo couldn't bear to look at her any more. She couldn't even bear to be in the same room.

She pushed the letters and the lease across the desk. 'Here, take them. Take them and leave me alone.'

'What are you—'

'Just take them before I change my bloody mind!'

Deborah snatched up the pile and headed for the door. She opened it and looked back over her shoulder. 'I'm not sure if you're going to believe this but you really should – it was *you* Peter wanted the future with, not me. It was you he married. I was just . . . just someone to share the pain with.'

Jo stared at her, her dry lips sliding into a thin empty smile. 'And I'm sure you had a damn good time sharing it.'

Chapter Sixty-eight

Jo had no memory of actually putting on her jacket, sliding on her sunglasses or of leaving the shop. She had a vague notion of having mumbled something to Jacob but couldn't recall exactly what. It was only when she was halfway across the Green that she began to come to her senses. Immediately, thinking that she might be being watched, she looked up at the windows of the flat. They were blank and empty. Was that good or bad, she wondered? Then it occurred to her that she didn't really care. There was only so much grief, so much bewilderment, that anyone could take and she had already reached her limit. Whatever was going on in there was between Gabe and Susan. She had never asked to be involved. They could sort it out between them.

As Jo reached the end of the Green, she glanced up at the windows again before crossing the road, walking up the drive, getting into the car and quietly closing the door behind her. She put the key in the ignition, wincing as the engine leapt into life. It was only as she was reversing out that she realised, with a tiny pang of conscience, that she had even stopped worrying about Silver Delaney.

Did that make her a bad person? The question hung in

her mind as she accelerated too quickly along Barley Road. She passed a woman holding a toddler by his hand, a couple of teenagers and a big man tugging on a cigarette. They registered on the very edge of her consciousness, were seen and dismissed. On reaching Kellston High Street, she wound her way aggressively through the traffic. She dodged and swerved and honked her horn. Usually she was the most polite of drivers but today she had no time for the normal courtesies.

Where was she going? She didn't know. What was she doing? She wasn't sure about that either. She was just driving, determinedly pushing forward. Her head was starting to spin. She was thinking about Leonard Kearns again, about Peter, about all the lousy mess in her life. She was thinking about why it had all happened, about what had been done and not done, and why *she* had been left with the impossible task of dealing with it all. Maybe she was in one of those dodgy stages that Buddhists believed in, one of those reincarnations where people who had done wrong were now paying for their sins. She certainly felt like she was being punished. The trouble was that if you didn't know how you'd sinned, how were you supposed to correct it? And weren't you supposed to come back as a lower form of life?

Then it occurred to her, as she took a sharp left, that perhaps humanity *was* the lowest form of life. There was no denying its cruelty, its ability to inflict deliberate pain. No species did unnecessary nastiness quite as effectively as the human race. Maybe the trick was not to work your way up from the scuttling insect life but to work your way *down.* Maybe the highest form of life was an ant or a bee or a butterfly.

Twenty minutes later, with her head still a jumble, Jo cruised into Canonbury. The first thing she noticed as she approached Ruby's house was Carla's distinctive Toyota parked out in the street. Jo pulled up behind it and killed the engine.

She frowned at the red car in front of her. What was Carla doing here? Passing on the good news possibly, about how Jo had agreed to keep her mouth shut about Mitchell's illegal dealings. She wondered how much Carla really knew about Leonard Kearns and what had happened to him. Was her sister-in-law part of the cover-up too? Jo sighed and shook her head. No, she was just being paranoid. Carla was the one person she *could* trust in the Strong family.

Before she could think too much about what she was going to say, Jo got out of the car, locked it, and strode up the short path to the house. She rang the bell and waited. She was still waiting a minute later. If it hadn't been for the presence of Carla's car, she might have given up. Instead she pressed her finger against the button again, two sharp rings followed by a longer one.

There was another delay before she finally heard a faint scuffling behind the door. It was opened, although not widely, by Mrs Dark. She peered out through the gap.

'Oh, Mrs Strong,' she said without enthusiasm.

'Hi,' Jo said. 'I'm here to see Ruby.'

'Er, I'm afraid she's not in. Perhaps you could . . .'

Whatever she'd been intending to say was cut short by the sound of raised voices in the background. The tone, if not the words, travelled down the hallway. Two people, two women, were having a row and it didn't take a genius to work out who they were.

Jo pushed against the door and rudely forced her way in. 'Sorry, but I'm afraid this can't wait.' As she strode quickly through the chill gloomy hall, she was aware of Mrs Dark scuttling behind. Turning, she looked her straight in the eye and said firmly: 'I can find my own way, thank you.'

'But . . .' Mrs Dark hesitated, her eyes uneasy, but she gave a small brisk nod and disappeared in the direction of the kitchen.

Jo followed the sound of the voices, the angry words gradually becoming more distinct as she approached the rear of the house. She was almost through the dining room, only a few feet from the conservatory, when she heard Carla say: 'You know that's not true!'

Ruby gave one of her familiar snorts. 'I didn't know it two years ago and I still don't know it now. Just because you say it's not true doesn't mean I have to believe you.'

Carla had her back to Jo, standing directly in front of Ruby. Jo was invisible to the two sparring women. She hadn't made any attempt to disguise her arrival but her footsteps on the deep pile carpet had been soft and quiet. She was about to make a subtle noise, a small cough or a clearing of the throat to announce her presence when some sixth sense kicked in. Instead she stood still and did nothing.

'How many times!' Carla almost screeched. '*It was an accident!* How was I to know that he wouldn't move? He saw me coming, he had plenty of time; he could easily have got out of the way.'

'But he didn't,' Ruby snarled back viciously. 'And as a result I had to bury my son – and that's something no mother should have to do.'

Jo had the sensation of being thumped in the chest. She couldn't breathe properly. She couldn't breathe at all. *Bury my son, bury my son.* And then, as the air eventually heaved its way out of her lungs, she stumbled forward a few steps.

Carla must have moved slightly too because Ruby suddenly came into Jo's line of vision. She saw the old matriarch's eyes widen with shock. It was a moment before Carla realised what was happening. She seemed to turn very slowly, as if in slow motion. On seeing who was there, her face filled with horror.

'Oh God,' Carla groaned lifting her hands to her mouth. 'Oh God, oh no.'

Jo's legs, although they were shaking, propelled her forward between the open doors and into the humid space of the conservatory. The words seemed to slice themselves out from the very depths of her throat. They were as fine as a razor blade and as sharply accusatory.

'You . . . killed . . . Peter.'

'No,' Carla said, staring at her pleadingly. She started to shake her head. 'It's not what you think. It wasn't like that. I didn't . . . I didn't mean . . .'

It's not what you think. Wasn't that what Deborah had said too? Jo began to shiver, an icy tremor that started with the chattering of her teeth and rapidly worked its way down to her toes. She could feel her whole body trembling. She wasn't sure how much longer her legs would keep her upright.

Carla clutched wildly at her arm. 'Oh Christ, Jo, listen to me. Listen to me. I didn't . . . All I wanted to do was talk to him. I swear. I didn't mean to . . .'

'Get away from me!' Jo said, roughly pushing the hand away. She couldn't bear to be touched by her.

Carla staggered back. She slumped down on one of the bamboo chairs and buried her face in her hands. She started to cry, her broad shoulders lifting and falling, her heavy sobs echoing around the hot glass room.

'You killed Peter,' Jo said again. Her voice sounded weird, distorted, like somebody else's.

Carla abruptly stopped crying and looked up. 'It's not . . . I never meant . . . it was an accident. You have to listen to me,' she begged.

'Like I listened to you after Peter died? Like I listened to all your sympathy, all your pity, all your kind words of encouragement?' Jo stared down at Carla's red, tear-stained cheeks. Her horror was rapidly transforming itself into the kind of anger she had never felt before. It was the one and only time in her life that she had actually felt capable of killing someone. Another quick breath burned its way out of her lungs. 'You lied to me! You lied to me then and you've been lying ever since!'

'That's not true,' Carla whimpered, shrinking back. For a moment she seemed completely submissive, almost pathetic, but then, like a cornered rat with nowhere left to go, she suddenly sat forward and bared her teeth. 'No more than Peter did. *He* was the one screwing the slag, having it away while he preached right and wrong to everyone else. Mr Oh-so-righteous, Mr Morality.'

'Carla!' Ruby said warningly.

But it was too late. She was on the kind of roll that no one could stop. She glared at Jo. 'Yeah, you were right. He *was* screwing the lovely Deborah, had been for years and you were the only one stupid enough not to realise it. All I wanted to do was to talk to him, to try and make him see sense. I mean, who did he think he was, telling us what we should or shouldn't do with our money? As if we didn't have enough bills to pay without supporting that Chinky bitch and her half-breed sprog. We didn't owe her anything.'

Jo stood and stared at her.

Carla's lips curled into a sly, cruel smile. 'Peter wouldn't stop going on about how we should all take responsibility for what had happened to her "poor" husband, how we should try to make amends. It was ten years and he was still banging on about it. As if we needed all that shit being raked up again! So I went to the shop. Then I followed him to Fairlea Avenue. You should have seen them, him and Deborah, all over each other before they even got inside. Your husband was a dirty little cheat, Jo.'

Jo already knew it. This was one revelation that wasn't going to knock her off her feet. 'Which was a good enough reason to kill him?'

Carla seemed to suddenly deflate, the bravado leaking out of her. 'It was an accident. I only . . . I only meant to scare him.'

Jo leaned down and hissed into her face. Their noses were only inches away. 'Tell it to the judge.'

Carla's eyes darkened into fear. 'You can't . . .'

As Jo straightened up again, she saw Ruby staring at her.

She wasn't sure what she saw in her face; it was twisted and angry but maybe there was pain there too. Suddenly, afraid of her own growing rage, Jo knew she had to get out of the house. She turned and ran. She ran back through the living room, along the long hall and out through the front door.

She was vaguely aware of someone following her, someone hot on her heels, but she didn't stop to look. It was only as she jumped into the car that she glanced over and saw Mrs Dark climbing into the passenger seat.

'Get out,' Jo demanded.

Mrs Dark, ignoring her, pulled the seatbelt across her narrow chest. 'We need to talk.'

Jo slammed her hands down on the wheel. 'Did you hear me? Get out of my car! Now!'

'Do you want to know the truth,' she said softly, 'or do you just want to keep on running from it?'

As it happened, running still seemed a pretty inviting prospect. Jo didn't want the weird woman anywhere near her but other than physically pushing her out couldn't see what choice she had in the matter. Quickly, she turned the key in the ignition. Unwelcome passenger or not, she had to get away from the house. She took a right, drove too fast around the square, and then pulled into a side street. She kept the engine idling. 'You can walk home from here.'

'Are you going to the police?' Mrs Dark said, not moving.

Jo, her hands still on the wheel, slowly turned her head. 'What do you think? Carla's just admitted to killing my husband. Tell me you'd do something different.'

'I think it might be worth thinking it through.'

Jo gave a hollow laugh. She leaned against the wheel and

stared out of the window for several seconds. 'Okay, I've thought about it. Now will you get the hell out of my car and leave me alone.'

Mrs Dark looked down and carefully stroked out the creases in her skirt. 'You're still in shock. If you go to the police there will be consequences.'

'Too true,' Jo said. 'The kind where Carla ends up where she belongs – behind bars.'

'And the children?' Mrs Dark said. 'What about Mitch and Lily? It won't be easy for them, finding out what their mother did, spending the next God-knows-how-many years without her.'

'She should have thought about that before she ran Peter over.' In truth, Jo had no immediate intention of going to the cops. How could she with a teenage kidnap victim still stashed away in her flat? Drawing unnecessary attention to herself would hardly be the smartest move in the world. But Mrs Dark didn't know that – and Jo was more than happy to keep her in ignorance.

'And then, of course, there's the other little problem.'

Jo shook her head in frustration. How was she going to get rid of the damn woman? All she wanted was to be alone. She thought about jumping out of the car and walking away but that was ridiculous. Where would she go and what if Mrs Dark was still here when she got back? No, the easiest solution was to just sit and hear her out. 'And what would that be?'

'If Carla gets arrested, she won't – if you'll excuse the cliché – go quietly. She'll make sure the whole world knows exactly what happened to Leonard Kearns and why. And *that* will be the end, socially and financially, of the Strongs.'

Jo glanced at her, surprised. 'Do you know *all* the dirty secrets of that family?'

'People tend to let things slip when communing with the spirits.'

'Ah, the blessed spirits.' If Mrs Dark heard the sarcasm in her voice she didn't respond to it. 'Why should I care?' Jo continued. 'Why should I care what happens to any of them?'

'I understand that you don't think very highly of Ruby – granted, she is not an easy woman to like – but she did lose her son and if you believe that hasn't hurt her, then you're sorely mistaken.'

'She still chose to keep quiet to protect her murdering daughter-in-law.'

'No,' Mrs Dark corrected, 'what she chose to do was to protect her remaining child. Had Ruby pursued the matter of Peter's death, had she handed Carla over to the authorities, she would have also been condemning Tony to jail. She would have lost both her sons and probably her fortune too. She made a pragmatic decision. Perhaps not one you approve of but nevertheless . . .'

Jo watched her narrow shoulders rise and fall in the smallest of shrugs. 'Well, thanks very much for sharing all this with me. It's been . . . illuminating.'

But Mrs Dark, either not getting the hint or deliberately ignoring it, said: 'You have to ask yourself if you want justice, revenge, whatever you wish to call it, at *any* price. I mean, will it change anything? Will it, and pardon me for speaking so brutally, but will it bring your unfaithful husband back to life?'

Jo wasn't even sure the charges would stick if she did go to the police. Carla would deny it. And Deborah was hardly likely to come bounding forward as an enthusiastic witness. It would only be her word against Carla's, and Jo's word would amount to little more than the neurotic ravings of a grief-stricken widow. 'So you expect me to do nothing.'

'On the contrary. There's plenty you can do. You must realise that the information you possess puts you in a very powerful position.'

'What are you suggesting?' Jo said incredulously. 'Blackmail?'

Mrs Dark shuddered. 'Such an ugly word, dear. I prefer to call it negotiation.'

Jo shook her head. She stared at the thin red lips of the woman sitting beside her. 'Oh you're good, very good. I hope Ruby's paying you well. What is the going rate these days for helping to cover up the disposal of a mutilated body, illegal trading *and* a fatal so-called accident?'

'Ruby did not ask me to follow you or to talk to you. At present you may desire nothing more than to see the family torn to pieces but there could be a more positive outcome from this . . . this tragic situation.' Mrs Dark paused, gathering her thoughts together. 'You may wish, for example, to consider Leonard's widow and his son. I'm sure that Ruby, with the right incentive, could be persuaded to make a more suitable settlement – something perhaps of a size that would secure both their futures. A more useful result, wouldn't you say, than the rather messy alternative of digging up the past and all its horrors?'

'Perhaps they would prefer to know the truth,' Jo said,

although she didn't really believe it. The truth, as she had learned to her cost, didn't always bring closure or peace of mind.

Mrs Dark ploughed on regardless. 'And then there will be the tricky problem of what happens to poor Mitch and Lily. If both parents go to jail, who will take care of them? The responsibility, I suppose, will fall to Ruby but she is . . . well, a lady of a certain age and possibly lacking the patience or the necessary sensibility to deal with young children. The likely financial crisis wouldn't ease the situation either.'

Jo thought of the kids forced to live with a bitter, broken grandmother. It was not a fate she would wish on them. She turned her face away. She wanted to put her hands over her ears, to shout 'lah lah lah' at the top of her voice, to refuse to listen. She wanted to hold on to blind anger, to that Old Testament-type of retribution: an eye for an eye, a tooth for a tooth. People should be made to pay for their sins. Everything simple, black and white. None of these awful conscience-shaking shades of grey. She turned back and snapped: 'For someone who claims an aversion to blackmail, you're remarkably free and easy in its use. Of the emotional variety at least.'

'I am simply pointing out the inevitable consequences of the . . . the perhaps somewhat impulsive, if understandable, action you may be intending to take.'

'Yeah, right,' Jo said. 'So what's in it for you?'

Mrs Dark made no attempt to deny her self-interest. 'Naturally, I have concerns for my own future. I'm getting older – and more than a little tired. I currently have a good position, a roof over my head, and my responsibilities are not too onerous but if things were to change . . .'

'You could be out on your ear.'

'Indeed.'

'So why should I take any notice of what you tell me?'

Mrs Dark's only response was another slight shift of those thin narrow shoulders.

Jo closed her eyes. She already knew that she'd been out-manoeuvred, forced into a corner she couldn't escape from. How would she ever sleep at night if the kids were separated from their mother, if their lives were ruined by some notion of revenge that *she* had chosen to pursue? None of this was their fault but they were the ones who would ultimately suffer. A few seconds of silence lapsed into a minute. She wondered what Peter would want, then wondered why she should even give a damn. What exactly did she owe to the memory of a man who had betrayed her so badly? A small moan whispered from her mouth as her eyes blinked open again. 'Do *you* think it was an accident?'

Mrs Dark gave due consideration to the question. The answer, when given, landed firmly on the fence. 'I don't know. Maybe she doesn't even know that herself.'

Jo tried to imagine Carla outside the flats on Fairlea Avenue waiting for Peter to come out. What had been going on inside her head? A slow, festering resentment, perhaps at how the Strong men treated their women with such blatant disrespect. Years of humiliation had built up inside her. How long had she waited? An hour, maybe two, plenty of time for her to painfully relive all those unexplained absences of her own husband, all those late nights, all those lies, all those cheap excuses. Was it even Peter she had seen as he stepped out on to the pavement? There was a part of Jo that could almost understand that awful rage, that single moment of absolute madness.

'But if I keep quiet, accident or not, she gets off scot-free.'

'I wouldn't say that. It's unlikely that Tony will ever agree to a divorce; she knows too much about his past. And Carla won't push it – he knows too much about her too. They're bound together by secrets, by fear and suspicion. He will never forgive her for killing Peter; she will never forgive him for the years of misery he's inflicted on her. They will spend the rest of their lives thinking of ways to hurt each other. And in the middle of it all will be Ruby, still holding the purse strings, still making them both dance to whatever tune she chooses to play.'

Jo had heard enough. One more word on the subject and she thought she might scream. 'If I promise to think about it, will you promise to do something for me?'

A flicker of a smile touched Mrs Dark's lips. 'Anything.'

'Then will you *please* get out of my car right now.'

Chapter Sixty-nine

Marty had wandered casually back outside, checked that the coast was clear and made his call to Susan. Now, ten minutes later, he was still standing beside the striped umbrella, gazing down at the water. The rain had stopped and the surface of the pool, apart from an occasional ripple, was calm and glassy.

Marty squeezed the phone between his fingers. He couldn't say for certain what had alerted him. A peculiar tightness in her voice perhaps? But then she had every reason to be anxious – in fact, half a million quid's worth of reasons. Or maybe it was because she hadn't asked any of the expected questions: Are you sure he'll come? Are you sure he'll come *alone*? Are you sure he doesn't suspect anything? No, there'd been none of that. All she had said was that everything was fine, everything was ready.

He gave a sniff. Something was wrong. It was just a gut instinct but his guts were usually reliable. A low growl came from the back of his throat. He replayed the conversation in his head but this time wasn't so sure. Maybe it was only nerves that had made her sound so suspicious. He could be reading too much into it.

Turning, he retraced his steps along the terrace, pushed open the wide French windows and went back into the house.

Delaney was sitting on the sofa. Although he had risen from his bed several hours ago, he hadn't yet bothered to shower or shave. A thick stench emanated from his body, and his clothes – the same as he'd been wearing yesterday – were stained and crumpled.

Marty tried not to breathe too deeply. A moment ago he hadn't been sure what he was going to do but now, faced with the prospect of spending what remained of the afternoon in this stinking stifling room, the decision was an easy one. 'Bit of a problem,' he said, lifting his phone. 'I need to go out for a while.'

Vic raised his head and glared at him. 'Problem?'

Once that glare would have made his bowels turn to water but Marty wasn't scared of him any more. All that was left of the man he had once admired was an excess of blubber and bluster. Delaney was a spent force, a has-been, an old fat man. 'Over at the Wapping site. Those fuckin' Polaks are kicking off again.'

'So send Parry.'

'Are you kidding? He's more likely to cause a bleedin' strike than prevent one. Nah, I need to sort it myself.' Marty glanced at his watch. 'I won't be long. I'll be back well before—' He stopped, careful not to refer directly to the kidnapping or ransom. Yesterday he had mentioned the K word and Vic had flipped, completely done his nut. *Walls have ears, you stupid fuckin' bastard!* And this despite the fact they'd been alone. Yeah, Vic had really lost the plot. And that was fine, but what Marty really didn't need was for him to fly into a temper again. If he did, he might never get out of here. 'Look,' he said calmly, 'nothing's going to happen before tonight, is it? They're gonna wait until it gets dark.'

Vic lumbered to his feet.

For one awful moment Marty thought he was going to suggest coming with him. How the hell was he going to wriggle out of this one? But then Vic shuffled slowly over to the cabinet and started rooting through the bottles. Which was almost as bad. If he was too pissed to drive tonight, then . . .'

'What are you doing?'

For a while, as if he hadn't heard, Vic kept moving the bottles around. But then he looked over his shoulder and said, 'You got any shit? I'm sure there was some here.'

Marty suppressed a grin. He took a couple of wraps from his pocket and passed them over. The white stuff was preferable to the booze – and it might pep him up a bit. 'That's all I've got,' he lied.

As Delaney shuffled back towards the sofa, Marty edged out of the door. 'See you later, then.' If the traffic was light he could be there and back in an hour. It was probably an unnecessary journey but it would help put his mind at rest.

Chapter Seventy

As Jo unlocked the door and stepped tentatively inside, she heard the murmur of voices coming from upstairs. Her body tensed in disappointment. She had been hoping that the flat would be empty, that by some miracle Gabe Miller might have ghosted his ex-wife and all her associated problems out of the building. But no such luck.

She glanced down at her wrist. Her watch, surprisingly, said half past four. Where had all the time gone? She couldn't remember much of what she'd been doing for the afternoon. Just driving around and thinking. Or maybe not even thinking that much.

'It's me,' Jo shouted up in case her arrival was mistaken for someone less welcome. She had no desire for another black eye.

Walking into the living room, she expected to see two people drained by the effort of a long and emotional discussion. Instead she was presented with a picture bordering on domestic harmony. Gabe and Susan, their shoulders touching, were sitting side by side on the sofa. They looked calm and comfortable, *too* comfortable. Their faces were without anxiety and their hands, at least now, were innocently clasped around their matching coffee cups. She looked from one to the other, feeling a spurt of resentment: So she'd been worrying all morning for nothing! But that wasn't the only thing that bothered her. She felt, although she hated to admit it, a hint of jealousy too. Gabe's attention seemed completely focused on his ex. From behind the closed door of the bedroom came the sounds of a pop music channel playing on the TV.

'So?' Jo said, a little more aggressively than she'd intended. She addressed the question directly to him.

'It's sorted,' he replied coolly. 'You don't have to worry. Susan's leaving tonight. There's a ten-thirty flight to Palma; I've booked a ticket.'

'And?'

'And what?'

Jo scowled at him. 'Well I presume she's not taking Silver in her hand luggage. What happens after she's gone?'

'I'll call Delaney and arrange to take the kid home.'

Her hands flew out in a gesture of frustration. 'And tell him what?'

'I'll figure out something.'

'And would that be the kind of something where you end up face down in a ditch with a bullet in your brain?'

Susan flicked back her long auburn hair and sighed. Her knee nudged against Gabe's. 'What did I tell you? Jo doesn't do simple. She has to make a crisis out of every drama.'

'I am not making a—'

Gabe quickly raised his hands. 'Pull in the claws, girls. We have more important things to worry about.' He got to his feet and looked at Jo. 'You got any cleaning stuff here?'

'What?' The question threw her off balance. For one mad moment Jo thought he was planning on cleaning the flat. Huh? She looked around, wondering just how much dirt had gathered over the past seven days.

'I need to clear out the house where Silver has been kept,' he explained. He gave her a long hard look. 'That's the deal.'

It didn't sound like much of a deal to Jo. She threw an angry glance towards Susan. 'Why should you clear up after *her*? Let her do her own dirty work.'

'Sure,' Gabe said. He shrugged. 'I won't bother if that's what you want. Only as it's *your* name on the lease, I thought you might . . .'

'Under the sink,' Jo said.

A few minutes later they were on Barley Road. Jo, faced with the choice of staying with Susan or clearing up the mess her erstwhile friend had left behind, had gone for the lesser of two evils. After the kind of day she'd had, she didn't trust herself to be alone with yet another person who had used and betrayed her. She didn't have much faith in the ability of any man to do a decent cleaning job either. If her future was dependent on some random fingerprints she'd rather scrub away the evidence herself.

Gabe strolled past the white Mondeo and walked another ten yards up the street. He got into a battered blue van.

Jo, with a carrier bag full of bin-bags, bleach and J-cloths, climbed in beside him.

She guessed that this was one of Snakey's vehicles. She slammed the door shut. 'What's to stop her from just taking off with Silver?'

'She won't.'

'And you know that because . . .?'

'Because she wants *out.* She's had enough. Why do you think she turned up at your place last night? Before long she'll be on her way to Spain.'

'And?'

'What makes you think there's always an "and"?'

Jo tugged at the seatbelt and pulled it across her chest. 'Experience,' she said. 'So who's this guy she's been working with?'

Gabe started the engine and set off down the street. 'That's part of the deal. She'll call me from the airport tonight and tell me his name.' He sighed. 'Look, I know what you're thinking, that I'm just letting her off the hook, but to be honest if we want that guy's name, what other choice is there?'

'We could threaten to tell the cops, we could beat the name out of her.'

He smiled. 'Are you offering?'

'The mood I'm in . . .' she said drily. She guessed that Gabe had struggled with his conscience. Choosing to let Susan go free after everything she'd done, not just to him, but to Silver Delaney too, couldn't have been easy. How much of his decision had been made from the point of view of practicality and how much from sentiment was impossible for her to judge.

'I'll call Delaney as soon as the plane's taken off and . . .'

There was that *and* again, strung up in the air, suspended. Jo groaned. Susan was as proficient at manipulation as the enigmatic Mrs Dark. 'So did you find out what's been going on?'

'Guy's got a psychotic streak apparently. It just took her a while to figure it out. Hurting Silver was never on the agenda – not for her at least – but she thinks he has other ideas.'

'Do you trust her?'

He briefly turned his face. 'She's run out of options. What's not to trust?'

Jo could have offered to write a list but knew it was a waste of time. He'd already made up his mind and there was nothing she could do or say to change it. She may as well keep her mouth shut.

But he shifted in his seat and glanced at her again. 'I have to do this, Jo. It doesn't mean there's . . . I mean, there's nothing between us any more, me and Susan, but I can't just walk away. It's all too complicated. I have to think of Silver too. Do you understand?'

She wasn't exactly sure what he was trying to say but sensed that he was trying to make amends for the lack of support he had shown her at the flat. 'It's not a problem.'

His face twisted a little. 'Isn't it? Only you've been good to me and I wouldn't want you to think that . . .'

'I don't,' Jo said quickly.

He left a short pause. 'You're important to me too. You do know that?'

She was tempted to laugh it off, to make some kind of wisecrack, but something stopped her. The expression on his face was serious. Instead, she simply nodded.

Clover Road was only a five-minute drive away. They spent the last four minutes in silence. It was similar to most of the other roads in the area, two neat rows of terraces with their wheelie bins standing sentry in the tiny front yards. Number forty-five was on the right, about three-quarters of the way down. There was no space directly outside the house and Gabe had to pull in across the road.

For a while they sat and stared at the windows. Then, leaning down, he picked up a heavy-looking holdall from the floor. The bag made a chinking, metal against metal sound. 'Right. Let's get on with it.'

They got out of the car, crossed over and walked up the short pathway. Jo, although it was an effort, didn't look around. To any prying eyes she hoped they would appear innocent enough, just a couple returning from a shopping trip, her with the Tesco bag and him with the holdall. Just the latest tenants to rent out the property. This was London, after all – no one took *that* much notice of their neighbours. Gabe took the key from his pocket and slid it into the mortice lock. It twisted easily enough and seconds later they were inside.

The door opened straight into the living room. It was a long bright oblong, bisected by an arch. A beige-coloured carpet covered the floor and the sofa and chairs were a darker shade of brown. There was a mirror on the wall but no pictures. They both stopped, ears pricked, listening for any other signs of life. But there were none. A simultaneous sigh slipped from their lips.

The kitchen was at the rear of the house, part original building, part extension. A window overlooked the concreted back yard and was covered with a net curtain. Gabe put the holdall on the table and unzipped it. He took out a box of latex gloves, the thin disposable type that dentists use, pulled on a pair and pushed the box towards her.

Jo's eyes widened a fraction. 'You make a habit of this?'

'Nothing wrong with being careful.'

To their right was an open pine door that led to the basement. Gabe picked up the bag again, flicked a switch on the kitchen wall and started down the flight of old stone steps. Jo followed close on his heels. A couple of dim light bulbs, one at the top and another at the bottom, cast dancing shadows across the walls. She glanced nervously over her shoulder. Some kind of alarm was going off in her head, a primitive warning about being trapped, about dangerous predators and dark enclosed spaces.

At the base of the steps were two rooms leading off a narrow corridor. The first, without a door, was about twenty foot square. It had a neon strip running along the centre of the ceiling. When Gabe turned it on, it buzzed and flickered, then suddenly leapt into life. They both peered inside. The room was empty. The walls had once been whitewashed but were now stained and peeling, small heaps of flaking paint and crumbling plaster accumulating on the floor. She sniffed; that weird musty smell, the odour of all cellars, was assailing her nostrils.

The second room did have a door. It was ajar and they both paused to stare at it. At the top was a roughly constructed grille with a sliding panel and at its base what looked like a large cat flap. He slowly pushed the door open to reveal the prison cell beyond. The light, a naked bulb of no more than 20 watts, was still on.

'Very cosy,' he murmured.

Jo frowned as she looked around. This room was much smaller. There was a toilet and sink in the left-hand corner and a single mattress on the right. On top of the mattress were a pillow and a thin grey blanket. Beside these was a low bedside table with a lamp, several glossy magazines and a bottle of water. But what really focused her attention was the long heavy chain attached to the wall; it was like something that would be used to restrain a vicious dog. So this was where Silver had been imprisoned. The odour in this room was slightly different, as if the mustiness was underlain with stale breath, sweat and a sharper more disturbing smell that may have been a residue of fear. Jo shivered. Poor kid – she must have been terrified.

'Let's get on with it,' Gabe said. 'I need to get this door off its hinges. You need to clean down anything Silver may have touched. We don't want any record of her ever having been here.'

Jo nodded. Where to start? She decided on the worst job first – the loo. As Gabe got out his screwdriver, she dived into the carrier bag and pulled out a pack of sponge scourers and a bottle of Cif. For a while they worked almost in silence, the only sounds being his muttered complaints as he tried to remove the screws – *what kind of bleeding idiot put this up* – and her manic scrubbings of the pad against the old stained porcelain. She covered the whole area, paying most attention to the seat, the handle of the flush and the cistern but leaving none of it untouched. It was surprising, she thought, how quickly you could work when your liberty might depend on it. By the time she had finished, he was almost done too.

'Okay,' he said, dropping the final screw into his pocket. 'Can you give me a hand to get this upstairs?'

Within twenty minutes, they had the stashed the door, the mattress and the blanket in the back of the van. Jo had cleaned the sink. Gabe had snapped through the chain with a pair of bolt-cutters. While he was still attempting to remove the large iron ring that had been cemented into the wall, she carried the small table and the lamp (after a thorough wiping) upstairs. After putting them back where they probably belonged, in the front bedroom, she glanced out of the window and along the street. Seeing The George on the corner, she remembered how Gabe had been set up. Had Susan stood here and watched her ex-husband's arrest? Jo wouldn't put it past her.

After checking out the bathroom, and removing an abandoned bottle of shampoo and a bar of soap, she headed back downstairs. Next, she cleared out the kitchen, emptying the contents of the freezer, the fridge and the cupboards into a black bin bag. The food was of the purely basic variety. Still, if nothing else she'd have plenty of pizza, bread and baked beans for the next few weeks. There were four litres of milk and an almost full bottle of brandy too.

Jo gave the kitchen sink a quick once-over, not to erase any fingerprints – according to Gabe (who had heard it from Susan), the girl hadn't touched anything outside the cellar – but just to leave things clean and tidy. She knew from past experience how fussy landlords could be; it was best if she gave them nothing to whine about.

After dumping all the bags in the back of the van, including the holdall and the rubbish from the kitchen bin, Jo returned to the cellar. She wondered, as she walked past the brightly lit larger room, whether this had all once been a children's play area or a teenage den. It would account for the plumbing. A good place for the kids to get away from the parents – and vice versa.

Gabe was carefully wiping down the walls. It looked very different now to when they had first arrived. Emptied of all the obvious signs of imprisonment it seemed benign, normal, like any other neglected basement room. She saw that the iron ring had been wrenched from the wall and gave a sigh of relief.

'All done?' he said.

Jo nodded.

They stood and surveyed their work. It was impossible to tell that anyone had been there, and especially anyone held against their will. There was only the lingering whiff of disinfectant but that would soon fade.

'Time to go,' he said.

They were in the kitchen when the bell rang, a short sharp ring that cut through the air. Jo jumped and shrank back against the wall. Gabe put a finger to his lips. They both stood very still. It was about fifteen seconds before it went again: two longer more determined rings.

Jo's heart was starting to thump. It could easily be a salesman, she told herself, or a Jehovah's Witness eager to spread the word. There was no reason to think that . . .

But the bell went again and the letterbox clattered. A voice floated clearly through the living room. 'Susan? Susan, you there?'

'Fuck,' Gabe murmured.

The letterbox rattled again. There were three more rings, a long pause and the sound of retreating footsteps.

'He's gone,' Jo whispered with relief.

Gabe shook his head. 'Don't kid yourself. He won't give up that easily. He's probably gone back to the car for a crowbar.'

'But it's broad daylight. He can't just . . .'

'You want to hang around and find out?'

Jo didn't.

'We've got two choices,' he said. 'Either we head upstairs, wait for him to break in and go to the cellar, then try to leg it through the front door – or we go out the back.'

Jo didn't fancy being trapped upstairs. It would only take him seconds to realise that the cellar was empty. What if he heard them coming down? What if he was armed? She glanced out of the kitchen window. That idea didn't seem so great either. The back door led to an enclosed yard with tall fences either side of it. A couple of rotting outhouses leaned against an even higher wall running along the rear. How the hell were they going to get out? 'I don't know,' she said. 'You choose.'

Gabe didn't hesitate. 'Out the back.'

Chapter Seventy-one

Even as Gabe was closing the door and locking it behind them, they heard the soft splintery sound of breaking wood. This guy didn't mess around. They sprinted down to the end of the yard.

'What now?' Jo spun round to face him.

'Up there,' he said gesturing towards the crumbling roof of one of the outhouses. From the ground to the lowest level of the roof was about ten feet. From there it sloped up to within reaching distance of the top of the wall. He dropped the bag, bent his body at the knees and linked his hands together. 'Come on!'

Jo could see how with his help *she* might get up there but how was he going to follow her? 'But—'

'For God's sake,' he said. 'Just shift it, will you?'

Jo, after one frantic glance back at the house, did as she was told. Standing to his full height, Gabe swiftly hoisted her up. For a moment she seemed to be sailing through the air but, stretching out her arms and hands and with him pushing hard on the soles of her shoes, eventually managed to scramble on to the roof. Instantly a couple of tiles dislodged from under her. They slid down and smashed on to the ground.

'Keep going,' he urged.

Flat on her stomach, Jo slowly inched forward. Every time she moved, another wet, slippery tile dislodged, temporarily removing her foothold. She kept looking behind her. Her breath was coming in short, fast gasps. Her stomach was clenched tight, her heart pounding. Gabe dashed back across the yard. Jo stared at him. What was he doing? Even with a run-up there was no way he was going to make it.

Suddenly, the back door broke open with a sickening crash.

The man who came hurtling out was not especially tall or big but he *was* fast and very, very angry. It was odd, Jo thought, how much you could absorb in a matter of seconds. She noticed his blue shirt, his black slicked-back hair and how his dark eyes flashed with rage. But what she noticed most of all was the long slim bar of iron extending from his hand.

'Where is she, Miller?' the guy screeched as he ran towards them.

The next few seconds exploded into terror. All Jo was aware of was the man, the iron bar and of Gabe's futile attempt to escape. He wasn't going to make it. Oh God! He didn't stand a chance! Then she realised that he wasn't heading directly for the roof. He had another route in mind. Veering abruptly to the left, he launched himself towards the top of the adjacent fence, managed to haul himself up on to the narrow ledge and then, with one leg still hanging down, grabbed for the edge of the roof. Jo shuffled back and reached out for his hand.

But she was too late. The psycho was there before her, snarling and cursing. He swung the bar towards Gabe's leg.

'Watch out!' Jo yelled.

Gabe managed to twist his leg away in time and the bar, with a terrible crunch, went straight through the fence. He kicked out but was too precariously balanced to get any force behind it. Jo watched him struggling and knew that if she didn't do something soon he'd end up on the ground. Wildly, she looked around her. The only ammunition to hand was the broken tiles on the roof. They were better than nothing.

Her first piece hit their pursuer on the shoulder, but not hard enough to make a difference. Her second shot missed completely but the third and fourth landed squarely on the top of his head.

He staggered back with a grunt, his hands automatically rising to protect his face. Jo kept throwing while Gabe steadied himself and managed to clamber up beside her.

'Over the wall,' he said, grabbing her wrist and hauling her up the last few feet.

Beneath them, the madman swung wildly at the edge of the roof with the crowbar – but they were both already out of reach.

'I'll kill you! I'll fuckin' kill you!'

Jo peered over the rim of the wall. The drop was lower on the other side, only about eight feet, but it still seemed pretty daunting. Gabe was already halfway over. 'Come on!' he urged.

She hesitated, but as she did so, the iron bar came

whistling through the air, only missing her by inches. It clattered noisily into the alley below. Now was not the time, she decided, to be worrying about anything as trivial as a broken leg or two.

Chapter Seventy-two

Marty Gull bent down and retrieved the crowbar. The alley, as he'd expected, was empty. They were well gone. In the time it had taken him to dash back through the house, run down to the bottom of the road and around the corner, they had made their escape. Was it worth driving around to see if he could spot them? He decided not. Best to let them think they'd got clean away.

Quickly, he made his way back to the car. He pulled the door shut and slammed his fist against the wheel. *The bitch had screwed him over!* He'd find a way to make her pay. But why had she done it? He shook his head and sighed. That question wasn't hard to answer. Half a million quid instead of a quarter. Even if she was giving Miller a hundred grand for his trouble, she'd still come out on top. So much for all that shite about vengeance for her sister! All Susan Clark was interested in was cold hard cash.

Marty's face screwed up with anger and frustration. He hadn't known that Miller was out of the nick. And it hadn't even crossed his mind that the two of them were in cahoots. Not to mention the little blonde tart. He rubbed at the sore points on his scalp where the broken tiles had rained down on him. He'd bloody well sort her too.

No one made Marty Gull look like a fool! No one!

He banged his fist against the steering wheel again. He sat back and took a few deep breaths. He had to stay calm, stay focused. All was not lost. It wasn't over yet. He thanked God for the fact Devlin had been hanging around Kellston Green this morning, evidence, had it been needed, that Marty had the blessing of a higher authority. Perhaps this was simply another test, a way of making him prove his worth. Throw a spanner in the works at the last minute and see how Marty Gull responds to it.

A thin smile crept on to his lips. Yeah, that's what this was all about. Well, Marty Gull could deal with it just fine. He hadn't come this far and worked this hard to let it all slip through his fingers. He raised his gaze to the heavens and let the anger slowly seep out of his bones until his mind was cool, clean and pure.

Would they proceed with the ransom demand tonight or had they changed the plan entirely? No, they'd go ahead. He was sure of it. It was too risky to make Delaney wait any longer. After Thursday's little incident, Susan would know that he was already on the edge, on the verge of cracking up. They would change the location and maybe even the time but they'd still wait until dark before going ahead. All of which gave Marty a good few hours to work out what to do.

The address of the blonde was scrawled on a scrap of paper in his back pocket. He pulled it out and looked at it. Barley Road. It was about five minutes' drive away. The address was for a first-floor flat. Was that where Silver was being held?

Yeah, it made sense. It was close enough to the other house to make moving her relatively simple. He was tempted to pay them a visit but there was no point charging round like a bull in a china shop – and especially a bull armed only with an iron bar. No, there were smarter ways of doing things.

Suddenly his phone started ringing. Marty checked out the caller. Delaney. He gave a grunt and flicked the phone open. 'Vic?'

A roar came down the line. 'Where the fuck are you?'

'I told you. I've been sorting out—'

'Get down the club,' Delaney demanded. 'I've heard from them.'

'Another text?' Marty said.

'Nah, a fuckin' bunch of roses. What do you think?'

'I'm on my way,' Marty said. He threw the phone down on the passenger seat and nodded. So he'd been right; it *was* going ahead. What now? He had to figure out how Susan was going to play it. He also had to work out how he could be in two places at the same time. While he was babysitting Delaney, who was going to keep an eye on Barley Road? He snatched up the phone again.

By the time he had finished the brief conversation, John Devlin was on his way over to Kellston – along with strict instructions to call if anyone entered or left the flat.

Marty put the car in gear and set off for Honey's.

He glanced in the mirror. His face was taut and white. The rage was beginning to simmer inside him again. No one had the right to snatch his little girl away from him. Silver was *his* and, whatever it took, whatever it cost, he was going to get her back.

Chapter Seventy-three

They had zig-zagged through the side streets, keeping away from the main roads, constantly looking over their shoulders. For the entire journey, Jo's heart hadn't stopped thumping. She had seen the rage in the crazy guy's eyes and couldn't forget it. His name, according to Gabe, was Marty Gull.

'Delaney's pet rottweiler.'

'Pet?' she said.

'Yeah, so much for man's best friend.'

A wave of relief flowed through her as they finally turned into Barley Road. Rushing up the path to number twelve, she unlocked the door and called up. 'Susan?' There was no reply but the faint sound of the television, still tuned to the music channel, floated down to her.

Jo quickly climbed the stairs. The living room was empty. She glanced towards the bathroom; that was empty too. The bedroom door was ajar. Susan must be in there with the girl. She called out again but there was no reply. Then, spotting a note lying on the coffee table, she snatched it up and read it: *Sorry but I'd rather wait at the airport. Call you later. S.* No apology for any inconvenience caused. No thanks for the hospitality. Not even a goodbye. Typical Susan.

She thrust the note towards Gabe. 'She's cleared off. She's gone.'

'What?' Without even reading it, he hurried towards the bedroom. Jo followed him, her eyes widening as the door swung open to reveal Silver lying on her side on the bed, her wrists cuffed behind her. She had one of Jo's silk scarves wrapped around her mouth and another tied around her ankles.

'See if you can find the key,' Gabe said as he bent down to free her.

Jo dashed back into the living room. It took her a minute to find the tiny silver-coloured key lying on the floor under the coffee table. She must have knocked it off when she'd picked up the note. Running back, she pushed it into his hand.

By now Gabe had untied the other restraints. He muttered softly to Silver as he took off the cuffs. 'Sorry, love. I'm really sorry. I had no idea. I didn't know she was going to do this.'

She slowly sat up, wiping her mouth with the back of her hand.

'Are you okay?' Jo said.

Silver gave her a long hard glare and turned her face away.

Jo wasn't surprised. The girl barely knew her from Adam and she must be completely shell-shocked. For the past week she'd been shackled in a cellar, then she'd been brought to this flat in the middle of the night, and then –

just as she must have thought the nightmare was over – she'd been trussed up like a turkey and abandoned. By now she wouldn't have a clue as to who could be trusted and who couldn't.

Silver rubbed at her wrists. After a while she looked up at Gabe, her eyes red-rimmed and full of tears. 'You're going to take me home, right?'

'Yes,' he said.

'Now? Right now?'

'Soon,' he said. 'I promise. A few hours, that's all.'

As if she had heard it all before, Silver groaned and lay back down. She curled into a ball and pulled the duvet around her.

'Hey, sweetheart,' he said, touching her gently on the shoulder. 'You're safe now. It won't be long. I swear.'

She shifted away from him. 'Leave me alone.'

Gabe hovered for a moment, glanced at Jo and shrugged.

'Why not now?' Jo said as they walked back into the living room. 'She's been through enough. Why wait?'

He shook his head. 'You know why.'

'But Susan's gone. No one's going to have a clue which airport she's at or even if she's at an airport at all. And you already have the name you need. There's nothing to stop you calling Delaney.'

'I gave her my word.'

Jo sucked in her breath. 'And your word's more important than reuniting that poor girl with her dad?'

'We wait,' Gabe said stubbornly. 'A few hours. What difference is that going to make?'

Chapter Seventy-four

Marty was sitting in the office with his feet up on the desk. The club was gradually filling up, the music growing louder. He could hear the dance beat reverberating through the walls. He would have preferred to be at Barley Road but couldn't leave Delaney again – at least not without arousing suspicion. Disappearing once today was bad enough; he couldn't get away with it twice. Anyway, he'd be free soon enough. When Vic left to deliver the ransom, Marty's time would be his own.

He had already worked out what he *thought* was going to happen. Susan, after sending new instructions through to Delaney, would take Miller along to pick up the cash – safety in numbers and all that – while the blonde bit was left to take care of Silver.

Once Susan and Miller were on their way, he would have the perfect opportunity to strike at Barley Road. He would get rid of Devlin, break into the flat and then . . . Marty sat back in his chair and grinned. He patted the pocket of his jacket where the gun was concealed. They would come back eventually and he'd be ready and waiting.

Reaching up his hand, he touched the sore tender spots

on his head where the blonde had pelted him with tiles. He was going to make her pay for every single cut and bruise. With a little encouragement, she was sure to tell him everything. And after he'd finished with her, after he'd finished with everyone who'd betrayed him, Silver – and the money – would be his.

Susan checked her watch. It was ten to ten. She had a grumbling, slightly sick sensation in the pit of her stomach, part hunger, part fear and adrenaline. She watched as the minute hand slid slowly round the face.

Once the text was sent, it shouldn't take Delaney more than twenty minutes to get here. His instructions were to stop outside the gates of the primary school, deposit the case in the small bin attached to the lamppost and then drive straight off. The street was long and straight, with clear views in both directions. If he stopped again or if anyone was following, she'd be able to see. But of course no one would be following. Marty Gull would make sure of that.

He had called her in the afternoon but she had kept her cool. Marty didn't suspect anything – she was sure of it. He had been stuck in Chigwell all day, too preoccupied with keeping the fat bastard off the booze to suspect *her* of any foul play. Anyway, he was too arrogant to consider that a mere woman might have the nerve to try and screw him over.

Gabe had been ringing too, seven times to date, but she hadn't picked up. She hadn't listened to the voicemail he had left her either. There wasn't any point. He'd only be having a go about how she'd cleared off and left Silver on her own. She had more important things to worry about. But she would still stick to her side of the bargain. As soon as she had the cash, as soon as she was safely out of here, she'd call and give him the name he needed.

The clock on the dashboard read five minutes to ten. This was going to be the longest wait of her life. She was sitting, hunched down low in the car she had managed to retrieve from Kellston Station. That the Fiesta had still been there, albeit with a ticket slapped across the windscreen, had come as a pleasant surprise. Now it was parked diagonally opposite to the school. She was facing the direction Delaney would be coming from. Once he'd dropped off the ransom and driven away, she'd be safe to move. After manoeuvring across the street, it would take her only seconds to jump out and grab the case.

At weekends, when the school was closed, this was a relatively quiet area. It was one of the reasons Marty had chosen it. Quiet but not *too* quiet. There was a small but steady flow of traffic. Even though she knew it couldn't be Delaney yet, Susan jumped as every car passed by. Still watching the clock, she tried to focus on something else.

She thought about Gabe. It had been a shock, him turning up at the flat like that, but it hadn't taken her long to turn him around. A suitable amount of weeping, an outpouring of remorse – *she had done a terrible thing, she hadn't been thinking straight* – and she had soon had him on side again. He wasn't stupid but he was sentimental. Although history should have taught him otherwise, he was still prepared to believe whatever she told him.

It had occurred to her, while she was crying on his shoulder, exactly what she *could* do next. Why back out now after all her hard work? Vic Delaney might not have killed Linda but the cash was still up for grabs – and she deserved something for her trouble. What if she went ahead with the ransom demand? Marty Gull didn't know she'd done a bunk – and there was no reason, until he arrived at the house tonight, why he should find out. By the time he was ringing on the bell, she could have picked up the ransom and be heading towards the motorway. When he discovered she was gone, that everything was gone, it would all be too late.

Susan smiled. She had sat in Jo's living room, sniffling and nodding and agreeing to every suggestion Gabe made. *Could he really get her on a flight to Spain? Yes, that was what she wanted, what she wanted more than anything. She couldn't say how grateful she was. She just wanted to put this nightmare behind her, to get free of the past and start again.*

While he was on the phone, she had put the final touches to her plan. With half a million quid to transport, she had no intention of going near an airport: too many possible hitches, too many security checks. There was no way she could take the cash through as hand luggage and she wasn't prepared to take the chance of some sleepy baggage handler inadvertently diverting her suitcase to Dubai. No, she'd drive south instead, dump the car at Dover, find a hotel to stay in overnight and get the first ferry out in the morning. Once she was in France, she could hire another motor and drive across country.

Susan stared at the clock. Two minutes to go. She tapped

her fingers impatiently against the wheel. Suddenly, the phone started ringing. Her heart leapt but then she saw that it was Gabe again and immediately relaxed. Raising a hand to her chest, she took a few deep breaths. Stay calm, she told herself – hold your nerve, girl, and nothing can go wrong.

She concentrated on the clock. Only a minute to go, forty seconds, thirty, twenty, ten, five . . . At precisely ten o'clock she pressed down the button on her phone and sent the text.

Delaney came crashing through the door, his face deathly pale. 'Connor Street in Kellston,' he said. 'Outside the school.'

Marty stared at him, astounded. 'Let me see.' He frowned as he scrolled through the text. It was exactly as they'd arranged – same time, same place, same bloody everything. He didn't get it. Susan must know by now that he'd found out what she'd done. He didn't get it at all. Unless . . . shit, was it possible that she *didn't* know? But why wouldn't Miller have warned her? It was hours since they'd had the run-in at the house.

Delaney opened the safe and pulled out the case.

Marty was rapidly reviewing the situation. If Miller hadn't managed to make contact with Susan, perhaps it was because she was in the process of double-crossing him too. Perhaps the bitch had left him to clear up the mess at Clover Road, to deal with the problem of returning Silver, while she picked up (and then cleared off with) all the cash. And if Susan *was* sticking to the original arrangements it would still be possible to intercept her. He knew the area of the drop like the back of his hand; he was, after all, the one who had chosen it.

He passed the phone back. 'Sure you don't want me to come with you?'

Delaney snarled at him. 'After last time – what do you fuckin' think?'

'Okay, but take it easy,' Marty warned. 'You've got plenty of time. Don't drive too fast. The last thing you need is to be stopped by the filth.'

Marty gave him a twenty-second start before putting the Saab in gear and accelerating out of the car park. If he really put his foot down, and Delaney was sticking to the speed limit, he should be able to whip through the side streets and get in front of the Jag. He still couldn't believe that Susan was going ahead with it. He laughed out loud but quickly stifled the sound. Apprehension was creeping over him. No, it couldn't be this easy. A worried breath hissed out through his lips. What if there was a more complicated game going on, a double-bluff, some trap that he was walking into?

Proceed with caution, Mr Gull.

He couldn't afford to get careless. He had to keep his wits about him, to keep his eyes and ears open. To lose it all now, to lose Silver, would be a tragedy.

The Saturday night traffic wasn't too busy and a quarter of an hour later, as he approached his destination, he was pretty sure he had gained at least three or four minutes on Delaney. Marty took a right and then a left until he was parallel with Connor Street. Directly opposite the school was a kiddie's playground and it was on the far side of this long, grassy oblong that he pulled up the black Saab.

He got out of the car and under the cover of darkness crept past the ghostly hanging ropes, the swings and roundabouts. The ground, softened by the rain, squelched softly under his feet. Crouching down behind the bushes that lined the iron railings, he made his way towards the two wide concrete pillars that flanked the entrance. From here he could clearly see Susan's Fiesta. He couldn't see her though. She was keeping well down.

Marty pulled back into the shadows. He felt for the gun in his pocket. He would only have a few seconds, a brief window of opportunity as she got out and snatched the case. But that, he acknowledged with a smile, would be more than enough.

Susan heard the powerful engine slow as the Jaguar approached. She sank even lower into the seat and her heart began to race. It was *him*, it had to be. Fighting against the impulse to look, she stayed completely hidden as the car drew to a halt. She didn't move, not even an inch, as she listened first to the sound of the door opening and then the heavy tread of footsteps. The engine was still running. Delaney didn't hang about; a few seconds later, the door slammed shut again and the car accelerated away.

Susan waited, her ears alert to any other sound. Before making a move, she had to be sure that she was safe. But she couldn't wait too long. She had to grab that cash as soon as she could. But, if she wanted to keep Delaney at bay, she would need to keep him occupied for the next few hours.

Stabbing at the phone, she sent through the next set of instructions, the orders that would send him on a fruitless journey through Kent. It was only then, cautiously, that she raised her head. The street was empty, the pavements too. She quickly started the car and swerved across the road. Jumping out, she snatched the case from the bin, turned around and . . .

Marty Gull had a gun aimed right at her.

Clutching the case to her chest, she stifled a scream.

'Hello, Susie,' he said. 'I think you and me need to talk.'

Chapter Seventy-five

The hours had dragged by with infinite slowness. Silver had spent all of them lying on the bed, silent and listless, staring blankly at the TV. Gabe had spent most of them pacing the living room floor until Jo had pleaded with him to stop. He'd slumped down, lit a cigarette, puffed on it impatiently, smoked it right to the butt but then leapt up again. He had made a call to Snakey asking if he could find someone to fix the doors at Clover Road. He had lit another cigarette. At regular intervals he had tried to call Susan but the result was always the same – straight to voicemail.

At ten-thirty Jo looked at her watch. 'It's time.'

Gabe was standing by the window. He shook his head. 'Ten more minutes.'

'What for? Come on, she isn't going to ring now.'

'The plane could have been delayed.'

'Yes, it *could* have but . . .'

Gabe's face was strained and white. 'She promised me. She swore. No, something's wrong. It has to be. Something must have happened.'

Jo knew exactly what had happened: Susan had spun him one of her fairy tales where the handsome prince saved the beautiful princess and everyone lived happily ever after. When would he wake up to the truth? She wondered if he would ever see his ex for what she really was – a damaged, single-minded woman who would stop at nothing to get what she wanted. Susan had never had any intention of calling him; all she had wanted was a free plane ticket and enough time to get clear.

But seeing the desperate look of concern on his face, Jo felt a rush of guilt. God, who was she to be criticising who he did or didn't believe in? When it came to love and marriage, she was hardly in the premier league herself.

'You think I'm a fool,' he said.

She saw the pain in his eyes and squeezed out a smile. 'No more than the rest of us.' Earlier, with so much time on their hands, she had ended up telling him about what she had learned this morning, about Peter and Deborah and what Carla had admitted to. He hadn't judged her then and she had no right to judge him now. If anyone was a fool it was her. She had been so blind, so naïve.

Gabe slapped his fist softly against his thigh. 'I know she's messed up but she still brought Silver here. She didn't want the kid to be hurt. That says something about her, doesn't it?'

Jo nodded. She suspected that Susan was only taking care of number one but that wasn't the answer he wanted to hear. 'Maybe she's scared of Gull coming after her.'

'But there's no chance of that if he doesn't know where she is.'

'Maybe she's just making sure.' In the wider scheme of things it didn't really matter whether she rang or not – they already had the name they needed – but for Gabe it was a matter of principle. No, it was more than that. It was a matter of *trust.* He had put his faith in Susan and she had let him down again.

Jo got to her feet and went to stand beside him. Pulling aside a corner of the curtain, she gazed out across the Green. It was dark and deserted. The rain had started up again, an angry shower beating hard against the glass. She thought she sensed a movement beneath her but when she glanced down towards the drive there was no one there. She frowned. It was nothing, just her nerves playing tricks.

A week, just a week and a day and so much had changed. She had gone from being a grieving widow to . . . to what? She wasn't sure who she was any more. A big part of her wished that today had never happened. The truth was not always something to be welcomed. Deborah's confession had confirmed her very worst fears and then Carla had . . . God, what Carla had revealed could never be forgotten.

As Jo dropped the curtain and turned back towards the room the first thing she noticed was the framed picture of Rangoon on the wall. She suddenly understood why Peter had put it there. It hadn't just been a dramatic panorama, a glorious view to fill an empty space – no, for him it had been a constant and guilty reminder of what his father had done and of what *he* had done to cover it up. She stared at it with growing horror in her eyes.

'Jo?' Gabe said.

She couldn't speak. She couldn't even look at him. Running to the bathroom, she slammed the door shut and leaned over the basin. She had thought she was going to be sick but only a vile, dry retching came from her throat. Leaning her forehead against the cool tiles, she felt the tears running down her cheeks. She lifted her head and stared into the mirror. Her face was pale and bloodless, her eyes as helpless as a child's. She had loved Peter, loved him so much, but their marriage had been a sham. He had lied and cheated. He'd deceived her – and so had all his family. 'Jo Strong,' she murmured. Even her name was a joke.

Quickly, she wiped the tears from her eyes. Now was not the time to be falling apart. The regrets, the sorrow and even the self-pity would have to wait. After throwing some cold water on her face, she patted it dry with a towel. She was not the only one whose life had been turned upside down recently. There was a frightened teenage girl in the bedroom, a girl who needed to be reunited with her father.

As she walked back into the living room, Gabe was in the process of putting away his phone. He looked as pale as she did. She didn't need to ask. She knew that he'd tried to call Susan again and that she still wasn't answering. It was almost eleven and the time for any reasonable doubt was over.

Leo's mother had left at eight for a nightshift at the hospital. He had gone out at the same time, pretending he was on his way to Jimmy Talbot's. Although Leo was well past his fourteenth birthday, she still refused to let him stay alone overnight in the flat. There was no point arguing with her; once she had made up her mind she was immoveable. Normally, he wouldn't have minded that much – Jimmy was a mate and they always had a laugh together – but tonight he had good reason for wanting to stay home.

At around six o'clock he had seen Jo come back from work. It hadn't been accidental; he'd been sitting by the bedroom window waiting for a glimpse of her. She had looked odd, kind of scared and had scurried up the drive to unlock the front door. The big guy, the bruiser, had been on her heels and had followed her inside. Leo hadn't liked it, not one little bit.

After watching his mother get on the bus, he had jogged back to the flat and let himself in. After what had occurred last night, he wasn't prepared to leave Jo alone. Someone had to protect her. He had seen the expression on that brute's face and it wasn't one of love and affection.

For the rest of the evening, Leo had been listening out for any sounds that came from upstairs but what he had heard hadn't made much sense. Just footsteps mainly, heavy footsteps, going back and forth. Like someone pacing, then pausing, then pacing again. The ceiling would creak for a while and then go silent.

Every half-hour he had slipped outside and stared up at the windows. A couple of lamps had gone on but the curtains were drawn tight. Occasionally, he pressed his ear to the door but the wood was too solid; all he could hear was the steady splash of the rain against the drive.

Sitting right on the edge of the sofa he examined the gun he'd bought off Stevie Hills. It was a dark, snub-nosed revolver, so small and light that it was hard to imagine it doing much damage. But then again, appearances could be deceptive. Was it loaded? He had no idea. He was scared of messing with it, scared of the damn thing going off and blowing a hole in his leg . . . or worse. He turned it over very carefully in his hands. He looked at it from every angle. If there was a safety catch, he couldn't find it.

Leo was about to embark on his next patrol when he heard a soft knock at the door. He thought about ignoring it but changed his mind. What if it was one of his mother's nosy friends who had seen the light on and knew she was at work? The last thing he needed was some busybody ringing her at the hospital. He put the gun down on the sofa but then picked it up again and slipped it into his pocket. Best not to leave it lying around.

Forgetting how late it was, Leo opened the door without bothering to attach the chain first. A black-haired guy in a leather jacket was standing in the shadows outside.

'DS Hale,' the man said, briefly flashing a badge in front of his face. 'I need to talk to you. Do you mind if I come in?'

Leo's first thought was of the gun. His stomach lurched. Oh Jesus, no! His heart began a pounding so extreme that he was sure it must be audible. Stevie must have grassed him up. He was probably down the cop shop this very minute, pulled in on some drug-dealing charge and already confessing to all his other illegal activities. 'W-what?' he croaked.

'It's about your neighbour, the young lady living upstairs.'

It took a few seconds for the words to filter through to Leo's terrified brain. When they finally did he stood aside in relief. 'You mean Jo?'

The cop nodded as he stepped into the hallway. He pulled the door ajar and kept his voice low. 'We think she may be in trouble.'

'Is this to do with that guy, the one who's with her now?'
'You know him?'

Leo wiped his sweaty palms on his jeans. He was still overly aware of the revolver nestling in his pocket but his fear was gradually diminishing. This wasn't about him or the gun. 'Yeah, course I do. He's a real nasty bastard, off his head, a nutter. He had a go at me last week.' He rubbed resentfully at the fading bruises on his arm. 'I've been looking out for her, you know, making sure that he doesn't . . .'

'We've noticed,' the DS said wryly. 'We've been across the road, watching the house for most of the evening.'

A light flush rose to Leo's cheeks. He hoped the cop didn't think he was some kind of stalker.

DS Hale peered towards the living room. 'Are you here on your own, son?'

'Mum's on the nightshift.' Then, worried that she might get in trouble for leaving him alone, he quickly added: 'But I'm sixteen. I can take care of myself.'

Fortunately, Hale didn't seem too interested in the issue of parental care. 'Okay, let me explain what's going on here. We have a warrant for Mr Miller's arrest but, as they say, he's unlikely to come quietly. Obviously, what we don't want is a hostage situation where the young lady may get hurt. We need to get her out of the house before we go in.' His forehead crunched into a frown as if he was in two minds whether to continue. He sighed and ran his fingers through his hair. 'Look, we don't normally like to get members of the public involved but if Jo trusts you, if she'll answer the door to you at this time of night . . .'

'She will,' Leo said eagerly. He could see what Hale was

planning now. If the police started banging on the door, the crazy guy was likely to panic, to do something stupid, but if it was just the skinny kid from the flat below . . . And once he had lured her downstairs she'd be out of the bastard's grasp for ever. She'd be safe, free of danger. And Leo Kearns would have been the one to save her!

'Good lad,' Hale said, patting him on the arm. 'Shall we get on with it?'

It was only then, as the cop turned to go back outside, that Leo noticed the deep red scratch marks running down the left side of his neck. He looked like he'd been in a fight with a cat.

Gabe was getting ready to leave. He had the car keys in his hand and was waiting for Silver to come out of the bathroom. Jo, who had spent the last hour urging him to take the girl home, was now starting to have second thoughts. Delaney still wasn't answering his mobile. He wasn't at the club or his home either. His wife, Nina, would only say that he was 'out'. She had sounded (according to Gabe) as if she already had half a bottle of vodka inside her and when pressed for further information had simply slammed down the phone.

'Maybe you should wait and talk to him first, make sure he realises that you had nothing directly to do with all this.'

Gabe shrugged. 'It's not going to be too hard for him to work out. If he's still got his cash *and* he's got his daughter back, then I'm hardly in the frame as her abductor. Anyway, Silver knows I didn't have anything to do with the kidnapping.'

'Does she? I doubt if she's too clear about anything at the moment. Don't you think it would be better if you—'

Suddenly two thin sharp rings of the bell cut her question dead.

She stared at Gabe.

He walked to the top of the staircase and looked down.

Jo, reminded of what had happened at Clover Road, remained frozen to the spot. But the voice that floated up was reassuringly familiar.

'Jo? Jo, are you there? It's only me. It's Leo.'

'Leave it,' Gabe said softly, moving back into the living room.

'I can't,' she whispered. 'He knows I'm here. He can see the lights.'

'He'll go away.'

A few seconds passed.

'Jo, are you there?'

Now there was a more plaintive note in his voice. She couldn't close her ears to it. Leo was her neighbour, her friend. If something was wrong – and why else would he be ringing the bell at this time of the night – she couldn't ignore it. Quickly brushing past Gabe, she glanced over her shoulder as she headed down the stairs. 'Just give me a minute, okay?'

As she opened the door she was aware of Leo taking a few steps back. He was dressed in blue jeans and a black hoodie although the hood wasn't up. He silently beckoned her forward. His hair was wet, slicked flat against his skull and on his face was an expression of . . . She was still trying to work out exactly *what* it was when she heard a swift movement beside her and felt the cold press of steel against her head.

'Don't scream, sweetie. Don't even move.' A voice was whispering into her neck. It was hard and vicious and not entirely unfamiliar.

Chapter Seventy-six

Jo couldn't clearly remember the climb back up the stairs. She retained only a series of fleeting impressions: the horror in Leo's eyes, the strong musky smell of Marty Gull's body, the painful pressure of the gun barrel just above her right ear. In the living room, Marty had forced her down into one of the armchairs and was now positioned behind and slightly to the left of her, barking out his orders.

Gabe and Leo, standing by the sofa, obediently placed their hands on their heads. Gabe looked like thunder. Leo looked like he was going to cry. Jo found herself thinking with a lucid and peculiar calm: *Is this it?* There could be, she realised, only one logical outcome to the scene that was unfolding.

'Where is she?' Marty said. Then he raised his voice. 'Silver?'

The door to the bathroom opened and the girl walked out. She stared first at Marty Gull, then at everyone else. Her face registered only the mildest surprise at this sudden shift in power.

Marty gave her a thin smile and gestured with the gun. 'On the other chair, kid.'

Silver, saying nothing, walked across the room, sat down and folded her hands neatly in her lap. She had an odd, disturbing blankness about her as if she was still watching television, as if this was just the latest episode in a rather dull on-screen drama. Jo wondered what kind of psychological damage the last week had done. Then with a start of horror, she realised that it was nothing compared to what Marty intended to inflict on the poor girl next.

She saw Gabe frown as he glanced down. Following his line of view, she inwardly groaned. The handcuffs were lying on the coffee table. Why the hell had she put them back there? And that hadn't been her only mistake. Why, oh why, had she answered the door? What had she done! Jesus, this was all her fault.

'Pick 'em up,' Marty said to Leo. He was pointing the gun at Jo's head.

Leo slowly bent down and lifted them with trembling fingers.

'Hands behind your back,' Marty said to Gabe.

Jo saw him hesitate, but only for a second. He had no choice, at least not one that left her skull intact. Reluctantly, he put his wrists together and Leo snapped on the cuffs. She flinched as she heard the metal links click securely into place.

'Now sit down – both of you!'

They slumped down together on the sofa.

'Well, this is cosy, eh?' Marty said. 'All of us together like this. Quite a reunion.'

Gabe glared at him. 'You're wasting your time. You know it's over. Susan's gone; she's bailed on you. And yeah, sure, you can shoot each and every one of us but that isn't going to stop her from calling Delaney.'

'We'll be well gone by then,' Marty said softly.

Jo glanced anxiously at Silver but, as if oblivious to the inherent menace of that word 'we', she remained completely indifferent. Her wide blue eyes were looking at Marty Gull but they displayed no emotion.

'Maybe she's already called,' Gabe said. 'Maybe he's on his way here right now.'

Marty grinned back. 'Oh, I dunno. Last time I heard, Vic was heading for Kent.'

His tongue snaked out and ran slickly along his thin upper lip. 'And when Susan and I had our little chat tonight, after she passed over the cash, she didn't seem too arsed about making any calls.'

There was a second of absolute stillness in the room.

Jo fixed her gaze on Gabe. She could see the blood draining from his face. And suddenly she knew, just as he did, that Susan hadn't gone to the airport. She hadn't gone to Palma. She had done what she had always planned to do on the anniversary of Linda's disappearance: *she had gone ahead with the ransom demand.* Jo felt a hot rush of breath burn out of her lungs. Oh God, if only Susan had answered her phone, if only she had talked to Gabe . . .

'What have you done to her, you fucker?' Gabe said. His voice was low and full of rage.

Marty shrugged his shoulders. 'Done to her? Nothin' mate. Why should I? I think you'll find that *you're* the one she's done the dirty on. Nice of you to clean up after us though. Very thoughtful.'

Jo could see Gabe's chest rising and falling but he was helpless to do anything.

Leo, his face still stricken, was staring at Marty. His fingers were splayed across his thighs and a thin chattering noise came from his mouth.

'You know,' Marty said, 'we really should have some music. I mean, it's not much of a party without a few sounds, is it?' He looked over at Silver. 'Switch on the radio, kid.'

She got to her feet and went over to the music system. She studied the controls for a moment, then pressed a button.

As the sound of 'Toxic' floated out across the airwaves, Jo had one of those hysterical thoughts: not only was she going to die but she was going to die to the dulcet tones of Britney Spears. Could it get any worse?

'Louder,' Marty said.

Silver turned up the volume.

'Good girl. Now go and wait in the bedroom. I need to have a private talk with my friends here.'

For the first time, Silver showed some signs of animation. Perhaps she was finally starting to realise what was going on. She bit down on her lip and her eyes slowly narrowed. She looked at Marty and then, as if seeking reassurance, gazed over at Gabe.

Gabe forced a smile and nodded. 'Go on. It's okay.'

When the door had closed behind her, Marty gave a small hollow laugh. 'She's so young. Be a shame for her to witness anythin' . . . unpleasant.'

'Delaney's going to find out,' Gabe said. 'And when he does—'

'Sure he's gonna find out,' Marty interrupted. 'He's gonna find out that you stole his precious little girl. And I'm going to explain exactly what happened. I had a tip-off, see, got straight over here but sadly it was too late.' He paused, smirking. 'Too late for his daughter, at least, and these other two poor souls. And faced with the horror of what you'd done – well, what decent man wouldn't take matters into his own hands? Vic's going to understand that. In fact, he's going to go down on his knees and bloody thank me for it.'

'And the cops?' Gabe said. 'How much thanking will they be doing?'

'Oh, I'll have the perfect story ready for when they arrive. And I'm sure they'll see it from my point of view. I mean, it's going to be your prints, not mine, all over this gun. You were the only one left alive when I got here. It was a shock what I saw, too much to bear. And yeah, I went for you, I won't be denying it. We fought, we struggled, the shooter went off and . . .'

'Very good,' Gabe said. 'But what about the ransom? How are you going to account for why *that* is still missing? There has to be someone else involved in this, someone who was picking up the cash whilst I was taking care of Silver.'

Jo knew that he was playing for time. There wasn't anything else *to* do. And psychos like Marty Gull always needed to show off, always needed to prove how smart they were. But he wouldn't play along for much longer. She thought about the phone sitting in the bedroom and wondered if Silver would have the wits to pick it up and dial 999.

'Gone,' Marty said. 'Done a runner.'

'And when they find Susan?'

Jo heard the desperate note of hope in his voice. He was still praying, against all the odds, that she was still alive.

'What, that useless tart?' Marty snorted. 'There's no reason why they should connect *her* body to any of this.'

'You fucking bastard!' Gabe lurched forward, his eyes blazing.

Marty pushed the gun hard against Jo's head. 'Don't even think about it.'

As Gabe fell back down, she gulped in a breath. Wasn't it your entire life that was supposed to flash by just before you died? In her case it was only the last eight days, every vivid awful second from the moment she had stepped inside the Lumière, through every painful discovery about Peter and the Strongs, to these final few terrifying moments. 'Any last requests?' Marty said. Then he leaned down into her neck and murmured, 'Bye bye, sweetie.'

Jo squeezed shut her eyes and prayed.

A loud bang echoed around the room.

It was a second before her eyes flew open again. Had she been shot? She must have been. He couldn't have missed from that range. Tears were flowing from her eyes but she couldn't feel anything. Maybe her body had gone into the kind of shock where the pain had been cut off. But then she was suddenly aware of Marty falling to his knees beside her. The gun slid out from his hands. Cursing, he clutched at his left thigh. Between his fingers flowered a widening stain of red.

Stunned, Jo looked around.

Leo was sitting on the very edge of the sofa. In his hand

was a small revolver. Where had that come from? As if he was thinking exactly the same thing, his gaze dropped to the gun and his mouth fell open.

At the sound of the shot, Silver had come flying out of the bedroom. She had stopped dead, her face as confused as Jo's.

'The gun!' Gabe yelled, struggling to his feet.

Jo came to her senses, bent down and picked up Marty's revolver. She jumped out of the chair and sprinted across the room. Even though he was no longer armed, even though he was curled over on the floor, she wanted to put as much space between them as she possibly could. Her heart was still pumping as she grabbed hold of Gabe and leaned in against his shoulder. Her legs were shaking so much she could barely stand. Her chest was heaving, her breath escaping in short fast pants of relief. It was over! She could hardly believe it. They were safe!

As Jo was still recovering, Silver walked across the room, smiled and gently took the gun from Leo's shaking hand. 'It's all right,' she murmured. But then she did something that couldn't have been anticipated. Turning quickly, she pointed the gun straight at Jo's head. 'Drop it!' she demanded.

'What the fuck are you doing?' Gabe said.

'Get back on the sofa,' Silver yelped, 'unless you want me to blow her bloody brains out!' Both her hands were wrapped around the little gun, her index finger on the trigger. She waited until Gabe had sat down and said again: 'Drop it!'

Jo, with her brains barely recovered from her last close

encounter, carefully laid the revolver down on the coffee table. Was this really happening? It couldn't be. It just couldn't. This was insane, crazy, like one of those dreadful nightmares you couldn't wake up from. What was wrong with the damn girl?

Silver quickly snatched up the gun and retreated. 'You okay, Marty?' Her eyes grew wide and fearful as she saw the blood. 'Oh God, you're hurt. It's bleeding.'

'Just give it to me,' he snapped impatiently, reaching out. 'And get a towel to put round this.'

She passed over the revolver, laid Leo's gun by his feet and rushed into the bathroom.

Marty, keeping the weapon aimed at Jo, hauled himself clumsily into the chair and winced a little. He glanced at Leo and his voice was filled with menace. 'You really shouldn't have done that.'

Leo shrank silently back against the cushions.

'And keep your fuckin' hands where I can see them!'

Jo saw with regret that the bullet had merely winged him. The wound, although bloody, was only superficial.

'And you,' Marty said, turning his attention back to her. 'Sit down in the middle.'

Jo did as she was told, squeezing in between Gabe and Leo. She gulped down her fear. She could feel the clamminess of her hands, the dread leaking down her spine. There they were, three in a row, perfect targets for whenever he was ready.

Silver, returning with the towel, went down on her knees. 'Does it hurt, does it hurt much?' She wrapped the towel carefully around his leg. 'Is that okay?'

'Good girl.'

She smiled up at him triumphantly. 'I *was* good, wasn't I, Marty? No one ever suspected.'

'Yeah, you were great, babe. The best.'

'They never had a clue. No one did. We fooled them all.'

'Are you mad?' Gabe said. 'Don't you realise what he is?'

Still crouched on the floor, she turned and glared at him. 'Marty loves me. This is the only way we can be together.'

'For fuck's sake,' Gabe said. 'If he loves you so much, how come he got some low-life to drug you. How come he kept you chained up like a dog?'

But she had an answer for that too. 'We planned it together. I *wanted* to do it. It had to look right. Susan had to think it was for real; we needed her to pick up the ransom.'

Gabe shook his head. 'You've got this all wrong. Whatever he may have told you, he was never intending for you to leave that cellar. Susan realised that. It's why she brought you here.'

Marty started laughing, a vile mocking sound that made Jo's blood run cold. 'You think she's stupid?' He put his hand on Silver's shoulder and lightly squeezed. 'He thinks you're stupid, babe. The only reason Susan brought you here was because she wanted to grab all the cash for herself. She tried to cheat us but she just weren't smart enough.'

'Is that why you killed her?' Gabe said.

'Shut up!' Silver hissed. 'Marty ain't killed no one. He *couldn't.*'

'Why would I?' Marty said quickly. 'Once she knew she'd been sussed, she couldn't wait to get on that plane.'

'You see?' Silver said. There was something wild and blazing in her eyes: madness, obsession, need? Perhaps a combination of all three. 'It doesn't matter what anyone says. We're in love, ain't we, Marty?'

'Yeah, babe. It's just you and me from now on.'

She gazed at him longingly. 'And we're going to be together for always. You'll take care of me, Marty, won't you? You'll look out for me, like you always have. You won't ever leave.'

Jo felt sick just listening to her. The kid was clearly besotted. She was also blind – in the way damaged teenagers often were – to her twisted lover's true nature.

Marty tightened his grip on Silver's shoulder. 'What have I always said? No one's ever gonna treat you bad when I'm around. You know that. You're my girl now and no one messes with my girl.'

Silver's head jerked up and down in a rapid series of nods. 'And I'm never going home again.'

'You and me, hun, we're for life. No one's ever gonna separate us.'

'You see?' Silver said, glancing over at Gabe.

'So what about your other boyfriend?' Gabe said. 'What about poor dead Ritchie Naylor?'

'Ritchie ain't dead either,' she snorted, 'and he never was my boyfriend. He was doing a job, that's all . . . you know, *pretending*, so that everyone would think we'd run away together. You think I could ever be interested in that pathetic junkie?'

Gabe, determined to make some kind of connection, tried again. 'I thought we were mates, Silver. I thought you trusted me. We used to talk, remember? When we were in Blackpool—'

'You never really cared,' she said petulantly. 'You only came to find me because Daddy paid you to. And that was all part of the plan. We knew he'd send someone eventually and when he did . . .'

'They'd be the perfect scapegoat.'

As if she was still capable of finer feelings, a light flush rose to her cheeks. 'I never wanted you to get hurt or nothin'.'

'Bit late for that.'

Jo knew that it was getting a bit late for everything. The end of the line was rapidly approaching. As soon as Marty Gull had sufficiently recovered, he'd be finishing what he'd begun. Her heart was thumping in her chest. It was time to start praying again.

Silver got to her feet. Twisting a strand of long fair hair between her fingers, she moved restlessly from one foot to another. 'Can we go now, Marty?' she whined. 'Can you walk? I don't like it here. I'm tired. I want to go.'

'Sure, baby,' he said. 'Whatever you want.'

What happened next would be engraved on Jo's memory for ever. It would slide into her head at any time of day and she would dream about it in her sleep. The Kaiser Chiefs were pounding out from the radio – loud enough to cover the sound of any footsteps – when two guys suddenly marched into the room. Jo wondered if she was hallucinating. She knew them, not their faces perhaps but . . . She had a flashback to standing on the Euston Road trying to choose between the menace of their approaching figures and a frantic-looking Gabe beckoning to her from a black cab.

It seemed like no one else had noticed until Silver released a gasp.

As Marty spun round in the chair, he found himself staring down the barrel of a sawn-off shotgun. There was that second where he had the choice, where his hand made the tiniest of movements, but then he weighed up the odds and slowly released the gun he was holding.

The third man who came in was big too but in a far more rounded kind of way. He was older with a grey, jowly face. A massive stomach drooped over the low belt of his trousers.

'Daddy,' Silver whispered.

As he stared at his daughter, Jo saw the conflicting waves of emotion pass across his eyes: relief and anger, love and hate.

'Jesus, Vic!' Marty said. 'There's no need for the shooter. I was just about to call. Look, I found her, I—'

'Don't,' Delaney snarled softly. 'Don't make it even worse.'

Silver ran forward and grabbed hold of his arm. 'No, you've got it all wrong. Marty saved me! He wasn't . . . he didn't . . . They were going to kill me. They kept me locked up and—'

Delaney looked down at her. It was a fearsome look, a terrible mixture of sadness and contempt. A tiny breath slipped from her lips and she instantly let go.

'Someone turn that fuckin' racket off!' he said.

The guy who wasn't holding the sawn-off crossed the room and switched off the music. There was one of those strange silences while their ears adjusted to the change. Delaney was the first to speak again.

'Parry, take Silver down to the car and stay with her.'

'No, you can't.' She grabbed hold of his arm again. '*Please,* Daddy. You don't understand.'

Delaney gently shook her free. 'Don't argue with me, sweetheart. Don't say another word.'

Silver's mouth opened in protest but swiftly closed again. It was over and she knew it. As Parry led her away, she began to cry, a thin, plaintive sobbing that might have been for Marty but could just as easily have been for herself.

Chapter Seventy-seven

Grim-faced, Delaney bent down and picked up Leo's gun. He put it in his pocket and walked over to the window, pulled aside the curtain and stared down into the street. His right hand, clenched tightly in a fist, banged rhythmically and ominously against his thigh. Eventually, there was the distant sound of a car door slamming. He released the curtain and turned to look at Marty Gull.

Marty smiled at him. 'You forgot to wish her a happy birthday, Vic.'

With a speed belying his weight, Delaney stormed back across the room. Marty instinctively raised both his hands to protect himself but he was too late. The blow caught him squarely on the jaw. There was the splintering sound of bone as his head jerked back. Delaney was going in for the kill when Jo leapt to her feet.

'Stop it!'

Delaney, with his fist still raised, turned to stare at her. In fact, *everyone* turned to stare at her. Jo found herself the centre of attention and her heart began to pound. When Delaney had first arrived she had been relieved beyond belief but now she could see they were in as much danger as before. Being witnesses to Marty Gull's murder would mean that they could never leave this room alive. Well, she couldn't just wait for the inevitable to happen. It was time to start fighting back. Her mouth was dry but she forced herself to speak.

'This is your . . . your argument, not ours, Mr Delaney. I'm really sorry about what happened to your daughter but it wasn't down to us. We don't need to be here. Why can't you just let us go?'

Delaney's small cruel eyes bored into her. 'What are you saying, love? That this is none of your business?'

'Y-yes,' she stammered.

He gave a soft laugh. 'Except it *is* your business, ain't it? Mr Miller was kind enough to give me a call tonight. He left a message, telling me all about our mutual friend's . . . activities.'

Jo, surprised, looked over her shoulder.

'I told you that your daughter was safe, that I wanted to get her back to you,' Gabe said. 'I didn't tell you where we were.'

'No, you didn't.' Delaney glanced at the shotgun man. 'It was Devlin here who told me how Marty had developed a sudden interest in the place.' He moved behind the chair and placed a thick-fingered hand on Marty Gull's neck. 'That was careless of you.'

Marty flinched at his touch.

Gabe shifted on the sofa. 'Look, I didn't know they'd gone ahead with the ransom. I had no idea. If I had been directly involved in any of this, I'd never have called you. I'm not that bloody stupid.'

'Possibly,' Delaney said bitterly. 'But you still kept me in the dark. You had information right from the start which you chose to keep to yourself.'

'Yeah, well, that might be true but I got the impression that you weren't much in the mood for listening. And I could have just left you to it but I didn't. I've spent the last week, at least the part where I wasn't down the cop shop, busting a gut to find Silver.'

Marty abruptly lurched forward. As though he'd decided that if he was going down he was going to take the rest of them with him too, he said: 'Don't listen to him, Vic. They were in this too, all of them. Even the kid.'

Leo, terrified, curled up in the corner of the sofa.

'That is such a lie!' Jo cried out.

'The boy doesn't know anything,' Gabe insisted. 'It's complete chance that he's even here tonight.' He glanced up at Jo. 'And she's got nothing to do with this either. Let them go. They won't say anything.'

Jo was about to object – she had no intention of leaving him here alone – when Marty began spreading his poison again.

'He's lying. They're all in it, up to their necks. They tried to grab the ransom for themselves. She's as bad as him, and that little bastard had a gun.' He glared at Leo. 'He shot me, for Christ's sake.'

Delaney's eyes darted from one to the other before finally settling on the man who had betrayed him. He walked back around the chair to face him. 'Why'd you do it, Marty?'

Marty, still nursing his broken jaw, smiled up at him.

There was a thin glistening film of sweat on his forehead. 'Why do you think?'

'I treated you like a bloody son.'

'More like a bloody servant! Just look at the state of you,' Marty sneered. 'Fat and useless. Even your own daughter hates your guts. You're an old, sad man and you don't even know it. All those years . . . all those years when . . .' He paused to wipe the blood and saliva from his mouth. 'All those useless, empty promises.'

Delaney shook his head. He leaned down close and stared into his eyes. 'Nah, don't give me that shit, Marty. You only did it because you *could*. You did it because you're fuckin' evil!'

'And if I am . . . well, who made me like that?'

A hush descended on the room.

Slowly, Delaney stood up straight. He took a few deep breaths and when he spoke again his voice was hard and cold, stripped of all emotion. 'Poor Marty,' he said. 'Poor little Marty.'

Jo, wincing at his tone, began to wonder if they would ever see tomorrow. Were they really going to die, here in this flat? No, she refused to just give in. She'd go down on her knees and beg if she had to. She made one last-ditch attempt to win him round. '*Please*. Gabe did everything he could to try and find Silver, to try and *save* her. He's always been on your side.' It would be truer to say that he had always been on Susan's side but now was not the time for too much candour. 'If it hadn't been for his call, you wouldn't have found out where your daughter was. In fact, you probably wouldn't ever have seen her alive again. He's not to blame for any of this. You should be thanking him, not—'

Delaney gave her a long hard look.

Jo instantly shut up. Had she gone too far?

'Get out,' he suddenly said. 'All of you. Get out now!'

They didn't need telling twice. As Gabe struggled to his feet, Jo grabbed the key off the table and with fumbling fingers eventually managed to get the cuffs unlocked. Leo, who could hardly stand up, had to be helped. Jo put her arm around him. His face was a sickly shade of white.

Gabe flexed his fingers, getting the circulation back in his hands and wrists. He threw a furious glance towards Marty Gull. 'Where's Susan? What the fuck have you done to her?'

'You've got thirty seconds,' Delaney growled.

'Come on, Vic. I need to know where she is.'

Delaney shook his head. 'None of my business, son.'

Gabe took a step towards Marty but Devlin immediately aimed the sawn-off at him.

'Ten seconds,' Delaney said. 'Make up your mind. Staying or going?'

Jo could feel it all starting to go wrong again. 'Please,' she urged, tugging at Gabe's sleeve. She knew what it meant to him but Susan was already dead. It was the living he had to think about now.

Gabe, after what seemed like an interminable pause, eventually nodded at Delaney.

He gave the slightest of nods back. 'Close the door on your way out.'

Marty immediately started his goading again. 'You just gonna let them walk, Vic? Christ, you really have lost your bottle. They'll be straight down the cop shop. You'll be hearing the sirens before—'

'Shut up!' Delaney yelled.

Suddenly all of Marty Gull's bravado seemed to drain out of him. Panic invaded his face. He shuddered and gazed up at the three of them. 'You can't leave me here. You can't. You *know* what he's going to do!'

Jo hesitated but Gabe pushed her forward. She didn't look at Marty again as they fled from the room. She knew there was pleading in his eyes and she couldn't bear to see it.

Epilogue

Jo laid the white roses on the grave and stepped back. She shivered in the chill December air. It was now six months since Susan had been laid to rest. Her twisted body had been found lying between the swings and roundabouts of a kiddie's playground. She'd been strangled, although not before she had put up a fight. The police were in no doubt as to the identity of her killer – forensics had scraped slivers of Marty Gull's skin from beneath her fingernails – but as to who had despatched Gull with a single shot to the back of his head, and then dumped him by the side of a busy road, remained a mystery to them.

The funeral had been a sad, spare affair. With only five of them present to pay their respects – Susan's mother and her partner, Snakey Harris, Gabe Miller and herself – their collective Amens had barely raised a ripple in the large draughty church. It had been July by then but a brisk wet wind had whipped around the building and rattled the old windows.

After the service, Pat Clark had taken Jo's hands in her own. 'Thank you so much for coming. I know what great friends you were.' She had leaned forward and kissed her on the cheek. Her breath had smelled of booze. The boyfriend, a thin surly man in need of a shave, had stood to one side, impatient to be going and making no attempt to hide it.

Jo gazed down at the grave and sighed. Six months. Sometimes it still seemed like yesterday.

Gabe slipped his arm through hers. 'You want to walk?'

She nodded. That Gabe Miller had been unfortunate enough to be connected to two murder victims in quick succession, Ritchie Naylor *and* his ex-wife, had raised more than a few eyebrows at the police station. But whatever their suspicions, they hadn't been able to charge him with anything. He remained a free man or at least as free as his regrets allowed him to be.

Jo was still not sure if she was recovering from what had happened. Perhaps she never would. Perhaps it was more a matter of finding a way to deal with it. Her first attempt, involving a journey out to Sydney to see her parents, had proved singularly unsuccessful. If she'd been looking for a shoulder to cry on, she'd been searching in the wrong place; neither Anne nor Andrew Grey, although both moderately pleased to see her, had encouraged the sharing of any confidences. Jo had told them nothing of her nightmare and after two weeks of sightseeing had flown back home again.

Her next steps had been more practical. She had put the Barley Road property and the shop on the market. To her relief the flat had sold quickly and she was now living in a small rented maisonette in Highgate. Whether she wanted to stay in London or move on to somewhere else was still up for debate.

Gabe paused as they came to a divide in the path. With his spare hand he took his cigarettes from his pocket, eased one from the pack and lit it. 'I still don't understand why you've decided to flog Ruby's to that woman.'

That woman was Deborah Hayes. 'Why not?' Jo said. 'She has a wealthy husband ready to stump up the cash and she did help establish the shop in the first place.'

'She was also shagging your old man.'

Jo looked at him.

He pulled a face. 'Sorry.'

'Don't be. It's the truth.' She dragged a heel across the icy path, scuffing up a narrow ridge of snow and dirt. 'When she first put in the offer, I had the very same reaction. But the more I thought about it, the more advantages I could see. For one, she's willing to keep Jacob on for as long as he wants to work, and for two . . . well, it's better than selling to Ruby. I could hold out for another buyer but that might take months.'

'So you hate Ruby more than Deborah?'

'I don't hate either of them.' She saw his sceptical expression and shrugged. 'Okay, so that's not entirely true but I *am* trying. Let's just call it a work in progress.' She scuffed at the ground some more. 'I'm done with living in the past. If Deborah wants the place that much, she's welcome to it.'

Gabe took a long drag on his cigarette. He stared thoughtfully up at the sky before slowly lowering his dark grey eyes. 'You get a good price?'

She grinned. 'Mind your own business.'

Stevie Hills stood in the middle of the Green and drank in the cold winter air. Even after six months, he still couldn't believe that he had got away with it. Well, not clean away –

he could clearly recall that stinging black eye – but it was nothing compared to what Devlin might have done. The man was built like a brick shithouse and nicking his gun hadn't been the smartest move in the world.

Mum had given him a mouthful of course, the usual bollocks about not taking stuff that wasn't his – pretty rich considering her record – but she had still stood up for him. After Devlin had thrown his first punch, she had cursed and yelled and dragged him off. The big guy had stood back and laughed. He had said they should both be bloody grateful that the only thing he was planning on cracking open that night was the champagne.

Stevie didn't know the ins and outs but it seemed Devlin had got himself some kind of promotion. The old gangster he worked for had unexpectedly found himself short of a right-hand man. 'Stepping into dead men's shoes,' his mum called it, but that didn't stop her from sharing her bed with him *or* spending his cash.

She claimed that his new boss was loaded. Devlin had told her a tale about how, after a late meeting one night, the geezer had left a case full of readies in his living room and gone upstairs to get some kip. In the morning he'd come down to find it gone. Some foreign maid, allegedly, had pissed off with half a million!

Stevie reckoned it was just one of Devlin's tall stories. The guy was full of bullshit. He scratched absent-mindedly at his balls while he waited for a punter to appear. He wondered what had happened to the kid he had sold the gun to; he hadn't seen him around for a while.

*

Together Jo and Gabe walked past the poignant rows of war graves, each one marked by a small white stone, and into the older, much wilder part of the cemetery. Jo found herself surprised by the stillness of the place. The main road wasn't that far off but the relentless flow of traffic could no longer be heard. There were no sounds here apart from the birds, the occasional rustle of a squirrel and their own light footsteps.

Some of the tombs had survived intact but most were broken or cracked, the stones listing to one side and tangled up in weeds. She gazed at the dates, at the endless roll call of births and deaths, the terrible toll of children lost, of husbands and wives separated, of parents reluctantly consigned to the earth. A grey stone angel, hands clasped in prayer, raised its eyes to the heavens. Jo sighed, her breath a steamy white cloud in the cold December air.

Gabe's voice cut across her thoughts. 'You heard from Leo?'

She nodded. Ruby, sticking to her side of the bargain, had managed to unearth some 'misplaced' shares in the Strong chain of stores that should have been allocated to Leonard Kearns. Constance was now a relatively rich woman. She had sold the flat and moved down to the coast. Leo had sent a few postcards telling Jo about his new school and the friends he had made. 'He sounds happy enough but . . . I don't know, do you think he'll ever be able to get over it?'

'If he's old enough to buy a gun, he's old enough to deal with the consequences.'

'You don't mean that. He's only a kid.'

Gabe threw his cigarette down and ground it under his heel. 'A kid who wanted to shoot me dead.'

'*Scare* you, I think,' Jo said, 'rather than actually kill you. And I don't suppose he ever wants to see another gun for the rest of his life.'

They left the path and wound their way between the graves. The snow was deeper here, nudging at their ankles. They were both, she knew, thinking about the same thing. That night would continue to haunt them for a long time yet. They could not forget what had happened in the flat or how close Marty Gull had come to wiping out all three of them. No, all *four* of them: he would, without doubt, have murdered Silver too.

Jo stopped, slid her arm out of his and stared into the distance. At the far end of the cemetery she could see flashes of green and red – Christmas wreaths that had been laid on the graves. 'I prayed that night,' she said.

Gabe looked at her. 'Me too.'

But Jo knew that they had asked for different things. She had prayed to stay alive. He had prayed that *Susan* was still alive. And only one of them had been lucky enough to have their prayers answered.

They had grown closer over the past few months but it was still too soon to think about any lasting commitment. There was something between them, a bond, but she had no idea how lasting it might be. Shared trauma was hardly the basis for an enduring relationship. What did it say in the magazines? Never fall in love on the rebound. They were both still coming to terms with their own individual losses.

Gabe was the first to break the silence. 'Any regrets about not reporting Carla?'

'About making a deal with the devil, you mean? Yes, plenty, but the alternative was even worse. Mrs Dark, although I hate to admit it, was talking sense. I think I made the right decision. If nothing else, I have the consolation of knowing that Carla and Ruby will be at each other's throats for the next twenty years.'

'That family has a lot to answer for.'

'Strong women,' Jo said softly. 'You have to watch out for them.'

Gabe Miller smiled as he slipped his hand into hers. 'You could have a point.'